P9-CFM-617

Raves for *Reserved for the Cat*:

"The fifth in the series involving the mysterious Elemental Masters, this story of a resourceful young dancer also delivers a new version of a classic fairy tale. Richly detailed historic backgrounds add flavor and richness to an already strong series that belongs in most fantasy collections. Highly recommended." —*Library Journal*

"The Paris of Degas, turn-of-the-century Blackpool, and the desperation of young girls without family or other protection come to life in a story that should interest a broad readership." —*Booklist*

"This most recent entry in Lackey's series is a nicely paced, pleasant read. Nina is a sympathetic protagonist readers will root for, and the story holds together well." —*Romantic Times*

"A fantastic cat-and-mouse game among a shape-changing troll, Elemental Masters and a gifted dancer in Victorian England makes Lackey's latest Elemental Masters installment a charmer. This is Lackey at her best, mixing whimsy and magic with a fast-paced plot." —*Publishers Weekly*

RESERVED
FOR THE
CAT

RESERVED
FOR THE
CAT

The Elemental Masters, **Book Five**

MERCEDES LACKEY

DAW BOOKS, INC.
DONALD A. WOLLHEIM, FOUNDER
375 Hudson Street, New York, NY 10014

**ELIZABETH R. WOLLHEIM
SHEILA E. GILBERT
PUBLISHERS**

http://www.dawbooks.com

Copyright 2007 by Mercedes R. Lackey.
All rights reserved.

Cover art by Jody A. Lee.

DAW Books Collectors No. 1417.

DAW Books are distributed by Penguin Group (USA).

All characters and events in this book are fictitious.
All resemblance to persons living or dead is coincidental.

The scanning, uploading and distribution of this book via the Internet or any
other means without the permission of the publisher is illegal, and punishable
by law. Please purchase only authorized electronic editions, and do not partici-
pate in or encourage the electronic piracy of copyrighted materials. Your support of the author's rights is appreciated.

First Paperback Printing, October 2008

3   4   5   6   7   8   9

DAW TRADEMARK REGISTERED
U.S. PAT. AND TM. OFF. AND FOREIGN COUNTRIES
—MARCA REGISTRADA
HECHO EN U.S.A.

PRINTED IN THE U.S.A.

To the volunteers of the Emergency Animal
Rescue Service (EARS)
who are selflesslty going into disaster areas to
save our best friends.
http://www.uan.org

1

NINETTE Dupond lined the toes of her pointe shoes with lambswool carefully, making sure there were no little bits of grit or near-invisible lumps that would make themselves known in the middle of the performance. Then she took surgical tape and bound her toes, so that if the inevitable blisters *did* break and bleed, the blood wouldn't seep through and stain the pink silk of the shoes. It did not do for a pretty little sylph to have bleeding feet. It spoiled the illusion.

She had already spent half an hour pounding on the toes of her shoes with a hammer to break up the glue just so. *Old shoes for practice, new shoes for performance.* It was a mantra, like so many other mantras of a ballet dancer. Ninette was only a *sujet,* a soloist, and a new-made one at that—one step up from the *coryphées,* and two from the *quadrilles* of the chorus, but not yet to the exalted status of the *premier danseurs* and as far from the *etoiles* as she was from the stars in the sky. *Coryphées* did not often have new shoes; one could see them backstage at rehearsal covering their old shoes with new silk, reblocking and reglueing the toes. A soloist, yes, as a soloist she got a pair of new shoes for every new production.

Ninette did not get the sort of pampering that the *etoiles* got. But as a soloist, she could, at last, do what she was here to do in the first place.

Not to become a star performer, oh no. Her goal was more oblique. To catch the eye of a rich old gentleman.

Her mother Marie Dupond had made no bones about it when she had enrolled her daughter in the ballet school of the Paris Opera. There were not many options open to a pretty little girl like Ninette, alone with her mother in Montmartre. She could become a washer-woman and starve, and possibly marry some poor working-man who would overlook the fact that she had no father, and bear a dozen children, bury most of them, and die young. She could work for the painters, as her mother did, and also starve. With them she would have no reputation, and go to bed with them because at least they *had* beds and food most of the time, and were al-ways generous if improvident. She could simply become a whore, because no respectable man of any means would marry a girl with no father. Never mind that her mother had a marriage license and all; such things could be faked and when there was no live father and no grave—

And even if one accepted the license, well, the man had deserted the woman. Likely he had a dozen wives or more, which would make Ninette a bastard. Not many respectable men with good positions would take the chance on marrying a pretty girl whose back-ground—or relatives—might come back to haunt him.

So Ninette could marry a poor man, who would not have such concerns. Or she could put herself where rich men would see her and become something better than a mere whore. She could become a courtesan.

One of the places to be seen by men with money was on the stage, preferably the opera or ballet, though the *Folies* were marginally acceptable. And it was clear to Marie Dupond, when she saw her flower-like child dancing almost before she could walk, that the place for her was the Paris Opera Ballet. Many rich old men in large fur coats took mistresses from among the little ballerinas. And if the girls were clever, they kept their rich old men very happy and were given a tidy little something as a parting gift when another little ballerina took their place. By then they were known at Maxim's and on the boulevards and another rich old man would quickly take the place of the former one.

If they were not clever, of course, they ended up drinking absinthe to excess and showing their legs at the *Moulin Rouge* or even less desirable places, and ended up as washerwomen and starved. But along with ballet lessons, little Ninette received lessons in being clever from a very young age.

And the very first one, repeated so often that Ninette thought if one were to take off her skull it would be engraved on her brain, was this:

Never fall in love.

Maman had fallen in love. She had fallen in love with an Englishman, and they had even married—she truly did have the license to prove it—and set up housekeeping in a little garret apartment and, Ninette supposed, had been very happy. Then one day shortly after Ninette was born, when she was wailing away in her cradle and Maman had been at her wits' end to soothe her, Papa had gone out.

And he had never come back again.

And that was all Ninette knew of her Papa. There had, most certainly, been no trace of him whatsoever. No bodies had turned up, no one even remembered seeing him in their street. He was just—gone. And there was Maman, with no money and a tiny baby and no idea how to keep them from starving except to take in washing and take off her clothes for the artists in their quarter. So she did both. And Ninette grew up in an atmosphere where the smell of harsh soap and paint drying meant comfort. Meager comfort, but nevertheless, comfort, for soap and paint meant cabbage, beans, bread, and cheese, and perhaps even sausages sometimes.

The artists were kinder than the people who sent them laundry to clean. The artists bounced her on their knees when she was quiet to make her laugh, sang out-of-tune songs with questionable lyrics to soothe her to sleep, and sometimes had musician friends who played music that made her dance. The artists were more generous too, which was strange considering that the people who sent them laundry had far more money than the artists did.

Learning to dance was hard work. Dancing was even harder. Ninette had liked making up her own dances and not having to do them teetering on her burning toes, with her calves and arches aching. Ballet hurt. She ended every performance—and she had been performing since she was twelve—with cramped and blistered feet, with aching ankles and knees. She ended every rehearsal wishing she could have been anywhere else. She was not one of those few for whom the stage was a fairy-tale place where nothing bad could ever touch them. The stage for her was one thing: a show window, where she would somehow manage to catch the eye of someone with a great deal of money while, at the same time, keeping the *etoiles* and the *premier danseurs* from noticing that she had done so.

As she wedged her feet carefully into her pink satin shoes and bound the pink ribbons just so around her ankles, the scent of the ballet filled her nostrils—rosin and sweat, chalk-dust and flowers, perfume and gaslights, the heavy makeup they all wore, the pomade on their hair to hold it in place. All the sylph-girls wore their hair in stiff little buns with wreaths of white artificial flowers around them; the Scottish girls all had the same stiff little buns but wore Scottish bonnets over them, so they didn't need as much pomade.

The orchestra was tuning up on the other side of the red velvet curtain, and the house was filling. She could hear the murmur of voices out there, a kind of dull rumble in which individual voices were submerged into an oddly slumberous whole.

Ninette, of course, was a Sylph. This was a very long ballet, and it often seemed to Ninette that it got longer every year, with more and more solos, duets, trios, *pas de quatres* and Variations added to satisfy—

Who?

Presumably the rich old men in fur coats in the boxes, who delighted in seeing their kept darlings flitting across the stage. Each of them watched with proprietary pride, knowing—or at least thinking—that their pretty little thing was being ogled by all, but like the white doe in the legend was not to be touched by any save the one whose collar they wore so prettily.

Well, Ninette was going to *be* one of those kept darlings, and when she was, she was going to *stop* dancing. Or at least, she was going to dance only what and as she wanted to. Perhaps . . . she thought longingly . . . perhaps in the style of *La Belle Isadora,* Isadora Duncan, with her bare feet and little Greek tunics, bare arms and freedom . . . perhaps like Loie Fuller, who had only to swirl enormous draperies around in colored lights.

But that day was not yet, and this day was another skirmish in the war to win what her mother never had.

She missed her mother; every night going home to the now-empty apartment, every Sunday visiting the unmarked pauper's grave, she missed Maman dreadfully. That might seem strange to someone who only saw the Maria Dupond who lectured and scolded her daughter, always pushing, pushing her. But Ninette knew the desperation that had been behind the scolding, and felt that same desperation watching the pleasant spring and languid summer march towards fall, towards winter, when the little garret would have little or no heat and the wind would whistle through the cracks till the water would freeze solid in the pitcher and washbasin. It had been hard enough to sustain life with both Marie's income and hers. With the meager salary of a soloist . . .

Ninette rose to her feet and began her warming up exercises. She never put these off. She had seen far too many girls hurt because they scanted their warm-ups—and an injured dancer is not a dancer at all, and there were plenty more waiting to take her place if she faltered and fell.

Stretches first; toe-touches, *plies* in all five positions, back and leg stretches along the backstage *barre* followed by similar exercises *en pointe*, and limbering exercises for the arches—

This was only a matinee, and the audience would mostly be children and their governesses, old people who could not afford the evening prices—but some of those rich old men still liked to fill the box stalls even at a matinee. For some, the reason was because the matinee was where the fresh, young talent was trotted out and seasoned, like young horses running local races before attempting the *Grand Prix.* For others, it was because their constitutions no longer permitted the late hours of a long production. And who knew? There might even be some ballet lovers among them, as opposed to lovers of little ballerinas.

Since it was only a matinee, Ninette had not even thought much about the fact that the Sylphide herself,

Mademoiselle Jeanmarie Augustine, was nowhere to be seen. The *etoile* was possessed by one of those rich old men, performed her warm-ups in the privacy of her own little ballet studio in her luxurious flat, and was rushed to the theater in her paramour's own motorcar. But an uncharacteristic stir backstage caught her attention, as did the sound of raised voices signaling something was wrong, and she looked up from her stretching among all the other little sylphs to see the ballet master, the wardrobe mistress, and the company manager hurrying towards her own little knot of girls carrying, respectively, a wreath of artificial orange blossoms of the sort that winter brides wore, the slightly larger and more elaborate wings of *La Sylphide* herself, and a sheaf of papers. . . .

And they were looking straight at her.

A thrill of excitement together with a chill of anxiety sent blood rushing to her cheeks and gooseflesh to crawl on her arms. Something must have happened to La Augustine. But surely they weren't—

They were.

The other girls scampered awkwardly out of the way as the three approached, the portly, be-suited manager, with his little fringe of hair combed hopelessly over his bald pate, looking particularly red-faced and out-of-sorts. When they reached hearing distance, they all started talking at once.

"Of all the wretched inconveniences—"

"Ma belle, we haven't time to change—"

"Petite, I know you can—"

"*Enough!*" roared the company manager, getting complete silence. "Look here, girl—" he scanned the papers in his hand. "Ninette. La Augustine managed to trip on the curb and sprained her ankle. Her understudy didn't come in." The look on his face told what he thought was the reason—a man, too much wine, and

a big head after. "The second understudy is already in
the harness—"

The harness. Of course, the harness that attached to
the ropes that would make the Sylphide fly through the
air to tease James. There were really two Sylphides, a
dancing one and a flying one. The harness was built into
a costume that was impossible to actually dance in. The
dancing Sylphide would flit offstage and the flying one
would be pulled by three strong men out of the wings
and through the air, only to have the dancing one take
her place again to flit with James in pursuit. It was one
of the tricks that made this ballet so popular.

"That leaves you. Pierre says you can dance it—"

The ancient ballet master, gray-haired, tall, and leo-
nine, smiled encouragingly. She wrapped her arms
around herself, suddenly elated and terrified all at once.
"Mais oui, I have studied the part, rehearsed it, but—"

"I have seen you in rehearsal after rehearsal, cherie,
and you will be admirable." The ballet master patted her
shoulder. "Do not think. Just dance."

"It's only a matinee," the company manager growled.
"The balletomanes are always after us to put new young
dancers on the stage—"

"Ah, but you know why we have the *etoiles* dance
even the matinees," the ballet-master interjected. "The
balletomanes are few, and the public many, and the
Parisian audience is loyal to a fault. They wish to see
their *etoiles*, and barring accident—"

"Yes, yes, yes, I know," the manager growled. "Well,
there *was* an accident. Get those wings on her!" he
barked at the inoffensive wardrobe mistress. Unflap-
pable as ever, the competent old woman in her eternal,
rusty-black dress was already taking the smaller wings
of a soloist off the small of Ninette's back. "Thank all
the Saints the costumes are so alike; we'd never have
time for you to change." The ballet master plucked the

smaller, scanter wreath from Ninette's head and pinned the Sylphide's wreath in its place.

The stage manager, evidently already apprised of the situation, was mustering the chorus. Anton Deauville, the rather aging *etoile* in the part of James, was arranging himself in the armchair onstage. The orchestra had finished tuning and was falling silent. So was the babble of sound from the other side of the curtain. The company manager gave Ninette a despairing look and stalked off to stage center front, to part the curtains and walk through.

"Ladies and gentlemen." She heard his voice, muffled first by the heavy velvet, then the fire curtains. "Due to an accident, the part of La Sylphide will be danced this afternoon by Mademoiselle Ninette Dupond. Thank you."

She went cold. She had been in the theater so many times when it was someone else's name announced in place of the *etoile*. There had been restlessness, murmurs of discontent—after all one had paid to see the *etoile*, and one should get what one had paid for! Sometimes there were whistles and catcalls, more often cross murmurs as the members of the audience searched in their playbills for the unfamiliar name. Once in a great while, people walked out.

Were they walking out right now?

"Places!" called the stage-manager, as the wardrobe mistress got the wings securely in place.

And Ninette had a moment of panic. *Do I enter stage left, or stage right?*

She froze. But the ballet master had been anticipating this reaction. He steered her to her mark.

And then it was too late to panic. The curtain was rising. She heard her cue, lurched up onto pointe, and blindly made her entrance into the glare of the stage lights.

The performance was a blur, punctuated by moments of brilliant clarity. Anton, his face made into an almost immovable mask with stage makeup, looking encouragement at her with his expressive eyes. A moment of fleeting ecstasy as a lift went so flawlessly it felt as if she were in the harness and flying. Another of joy as she finished a piece of excruciating footwork so beautifully that the audience broke into spontaneous applause. Feeling sweat run down her back, having to keep it all look magical, effortless.

And through it all, Maman's orders. *Pick one side or the other, left or right, it doesn't matter, so long as you keep looking to that same side during the whole performance. Look to the boxes. In a moment of rest, smile there, pretend you can see past the footlights. I know you can't and you know you can't, but those rich old men up there don't know that, and every one of them will be certain you are smiling at him.*

Finally, James cast the poisoned scarf around her, and her wings fell off, and she "died." The other sylphs came and took her up, and carried her offstage, and onstage, the flying sylphs rose into the "sky" with a life-sized sylph doll in their arms. Her part was, at last, done. She was "done" before that, though; this was the one section where, as in Giselle's mad scene, there was a lot of room for interpretation. La Augustine made a long process of the dying, often forcing the conductor to signal the orchestra to repeat bars of music as she staggered about the stage. Ninette was too drained. The moment that her wings came off, she came down off-pointe, stared at James blankly, made a feeble motion of entreaty, and dropped like a shot bird. It was her fellow sylphs that followed the music then, gathering around her, carrying her off.

Exhaustion struck her like a blow, and once they put her down offstage, she just sat there, breathing hard.

Onstage, James wept, watched as the wedding procession of his betrothed Effie and her former suitor Gurn went by, railed at the witch Madge, tried to kill her, and was killed in his turn. Madge did a little pantomime of triumph and the curtain came down. Offstage, Ninette finally got to her feet.

Applause. There was applause at least. So she had not driven anyone out. There were no hoots or whistles. She must have done well enough.

First the Scots *coryphées* and *quadrilles* took their curtain calls, then the sylphs. Then the *sujets*. Then—first Madge, then Effie's mother, then Effie and Gurn, and then—

Then Anton was taking her hand and drawing her onto the stage, and the applause rose, and there were shouts of approval; she made the bow she had practiced ever since she was a tiny tot, deep and appreciative, and smiled at the box seats on both sides of the stage.

And there were flowers, bouquets brought on stage by the little pages. She remembered to take a rose from hers and give it prettily to Anton. Then the continuing applause reminded her to make another bow; and wave graciously to the rest of the company and bow to them, then they all came forward and bowed, and the curtain came down, then rose again—

This went on two more times before the applause finally died down. And she went back to the dressing room in a daze, and sat in her little seat in the crowded room shared by all the *sujets* and stared at herself in the mirror and didn't know if she was glad or disappointed that the evening's performance was not La Sylphide, but Giselle, and La Augustine's understudy for *that* was certainly pounding on the toes of her new shoes at that very moment in a fever of excitement.

A thin, rangy, tabby-striped tomcat surveyed the departing audience from his perch on the overhead scaffolding with satisfaction. *That went well.*

The little brownie that kept the *sujets'* dressing-room reasonably clean raised a skeptical eyebrow. *You really are an evil creature. Tripping a ballerina! La Augustine is furious.*

La Augustine's patron will buy her an emerald bracelet and take her to Maxim's. Everyone there will make much of her and she'll have enough champagne sent to her table to bathe in it. She won't do badly out of this, and if she is wise enough to do all of the exercises she can, she won't lose anything. Just a few performances. The tabby cat's tail twitched. *She might even end up with a new patron.*

The brownie smirked. *And so might Ninette. Get a patron in the first place, that is, not get a new one.*

The only betrayal of the tomcat's sudden anger was the increased twitching of his tail. *She won't need a patron after this.*

The brownie snorted. *She'll get one. Like it or not, she'll get one. She certainly wants one, and this performance should net her one. And as for her not needing one, don't count your chickens before the eggs have hatched. She's not an* etoile *yet.*

She will be. The tomcat said it with passion. *She will be.*

The next morning at class, as always, everyone from the *coryphées* to the *etoiles* had their noses in the papers, looking for a mention in the reviews. The instructor had not yet arrived and girls were doing their warm-ups over spread-out newsprint, chattering like a flock of sparrows. The papers went from hand to hand, Ninette was certainly not immune, and discovered that in most of them, the matinee reports were mostly full of La Augustine's injury, and her performance rated only "*Sujet* Ninette Dupond was called upon to replace the *etoile* and managed a creditable, if sometimes naïve, interpretation."

"You are damned with faint praise, Ninette," laughed Jeanne LaCroix, another of the *sujets.* It was not a nice laugh, but Jeanne was not a very nice person. "By hook or by crook" seemed to be her motto for getting ahead. One expected a certain amount of that backstage, but Jeanne seemed to take delight in it. She never let an opportunity pass to make another feel small if she could help it.

"Oh!" cried Madeline Clenceau from the other side of the room. "Listen to *this!* It's the reviewer for *Le Figaro!*" Now everyone took notice, for *Le Figaro* was universally thought to be the newspaper for artists and thinkers. *"The matinee performance of La Sylphide was notable for the substitution of the* sujet *Ninette Dupond for a suddenly injured La Augustine, and one can only applaud the stroke of fate. Mademoiselle Dupond is far lighter on her feet than La Augustine, and brought to the part the proper air of fragility and otherworldliness that La Augustine lacks. Her Sylphide is innocent and unworldly as a butterfly, she entreats the earth-bound James to come play on the wind with her; La Augustine's Sylphide seems about to invite him to a Montmarte bistro for wine and sausages. Of particular note is the death scene. La Augustine is well known for drawing this out until one is tempted to rise from the audience and give the Sylphide a mercy stroke to put her out of her misery. Mademoiselle Dupond, however, made the scene heartbreakingly brief. One moment, she is borne on the wings of the zephyr; the next, the cursed scarf has worked its sinister magic, her wings fall away, and she is stricken, and drops lifeless to the ground before we, or James, have quite realized that anything is wrong. The pathos then is*

*all the clearer; like a naughty boy with his first bow and
arrow, James has shot at a bird and brought it cold and
dead to the earth, destroying with his clumsy touch what
he had only wanted to cherish. This is not to say that La
Augustine is a poor dancer, but let her be confined to the
parts where sensuality is an asset—La Fille Mal Gardee,
for instance, or Corsair. And let us hope that this will not
be the last time Mademoiselle Dupond graces the stage as
the tragic Sylph."*

The chatter in the rehearsal room had stopped dead.
Ninette bit her lip. The first thing that struck her was
how very wrong the critic had been—he had mistaken
her own exhaustion for deliberate art!

But the second thing was this. La Augustine was probably reading the review at this very moment.

And she was not going to be pleased about it.

2

LA Augustine was furious.

Ninette was in hiding; one of the sympathetic teachers, Isabella Rota, a former *premier danseur* herself, had hidden Ninette in a tiny closet when La Augustine came storming through the ballet school, limping heavily and in the sort of rage where she would snatch objects up and throw them—not actually at anyone, or at least not yet, but certainly doing some damage to walls and the objects themselves.

La Augustine was very popular with the audience. The critic at *Le Figaro* undoubtedly knew this. He also knew his review would provoke angry letters, and angry letters sell newspapers. The ballet company of the Paris Opera was an established organization, and *Le Figaro* took the position that anything that had been established for more than a handful of years deserved skewering on a regular basis. The critics of *Le Figaro*, considered themselves far more intelligent than the general run of an audience, and, being mostly poor, were openly contemptuous of the balletomanes, the rich old men in the private boxes.

But the critic in *Le Figaro* would probably never have to face the wrath of La Augustine himself. He probably submitted his work under a *nom de plume,* and thus was secure from retribution by means of the blanket of anonymity. The only one who was going to suffer in this instance was Ninette, and she had known from the moment when La Augustine began her rampage through the studios and classrooms that if a head had to go beneath the guillotine, that head would not belong to the managers or the ballet master.

As she huddled in the small, stuffy black closet among old rehearsal costumes, brooms, a mop and a bucket, she tried to plan how she should deal with the managers. Should she weep? That might be good. After all, she had done nothing wrong and none of this was her fault! She expected to be demoted to the *coryphées* again. And that would be hard. She did not know how she could keep the little garret apartment on the salary of a *coryphée* without augmenting it somehow. She might have to call upon her mother's artist friends and model for them. And somehow manage to stay out of their beds. If she could keep her head, perhaps she could somehow fit in dancing elsewhere. Perhaps—perhaps she should find another place to live; a smaller room, a cellar instead of a garret, although the idea of the mice and rats and black beetles gave her horrors. Maybe she should . . .

But all these plans came crashing down when Madame Rota came for her. Ninette emerged, blinking in the light, from the closet. The old woman's face told her that it was worse than she had dreamed. But even she could not have guessed *what* she had done—until Madame Rota told her.

"Oh, *petite,* you have done the unthinkable," Madame Rota said sadly, patting her hand. "La Augustine's patron was in the boxes, for he was entertaining friends and, once his paramour was safely bestowed on her maids, saw no reason why he should not continue to do so." She shook her white head in its little black lace cap. "You smiled at him, *cherie*. And worse, he was taken with you. And worse still—he said as much to La Augustine." Madame Rota let go of her hand and sighed. "I am sorry, little one," was all she said. "In the managers' eyes, the good review would balance La Augustine's anger at the insults to her in that same review. After all, you scarcely put the critic up to it, and not even she could claim that. But when her patron expresses his admiration—that is never to be forgiven, and not even the director of the company can save you."

Numb now, Ninette followed the old woman to the office of the director of the company. It was the first time she had entered those august precincts; the office was a jewel box of red velvet and gilt, much like the expensive private boxes in the theater itself. It was as well that she was numb, for the blow was a cruel one, and a final one.

She was fired. Turned out. Ordered to collect her belongings and go.

Not *quite* thrown out on her ear . . . but the whispers followed her as she changed out of her rehearsal dress and into her street clothes, and the looks followed her too, some pitying, some smug. And at three o'clock in the afternoon she found herself outside the building, as the music from the rehearsal rooms rang out over the street, a mishmash of five or six pianos all playing different pieces at once.

And she hadn't the least idea of what to do.

Despair gave way to tears; she hung her head to hide them and slowly made her way through the narrow streets to her building, then up the three flights of stairs to her little apartment. Very soon not to be hers at all,

for the rent was due and she had no salary to pay it with.
Three days was all she had, three days in which to find
work. If she could.

A good review of a ballet matinee performance, it
seemed, meant nothing whatsoever to the managers of
the *Folies Bergere,* the *Moulin Rouge,* the *Comedie
Francais.* Patiently or impatiently, the company managers gave her the cold facts; she learned that such a
thing could have been a fluke, her one good performance of a lifetime. Or it could merely have been spite on
the part of the critic, who used her as a vehicle to lam-
baste La Augustine. Oh, she could audition—but there
were no openings. Not for a mere chorus dancer. And at
any rate, this was not ballet, it was a very different style
of dance. Had she danced in such performances before?
No? Thank you, mademoiselle, but your services will
not be required.

The artists were sympathetic, but penniless. No one
was buying paintings. The Philistines were on the ascen-
dant. They could not pay her to sit.

At the end of the third day of fruitlessly hunting for a
position, she returned to the garret knowing there was
only one course left to her . . .

She would go back to the *Folies.* She had just enough
time to alter her one good dress; tighten the bodice,
drop the neckline. She would go, not to the stage, but to
the bar, and she would linger and flirt, sidle up to anyone who did not already have a *grisette* and hope . . .

She dropped her face into her hands and cried. What
a ghastly thing to hope for! That some ordinary, uncul-
tured man would hand her enough money to pay the
rent for another few days so he could take her into his
bed! And then she would have to do it all again the next

night, and the next—possibly even more than once in the same night!

It had been one thing to hope for a rich old man, well mannered, dignified, who would take care of her. That would not have been so bad, it might not have been bad at all. It would certainly have been no worse than an arranged marriage. She had seen some of the patrons and they seemed kind, they often gave the little girls sweets and nosegays of violets. There was some dignity to the idea, courtesans were established, they had a kind of respect—and if the arrangement was not forever, or the man was careless or cruel, well, that was not so bad as being tied in a lifelong loveless bond of drudgery to some old man for whom one was unpaid cook, nurse, housekeeper. A poor man, a legal spouse, could be just as cruel and abusive as a rich one. More, actually; the only people a poor man could take his frustrations and anger out on were his wife and children. A courtesan at least had a gilded cage, servants, luxuries. Good food, a soft bed and fine wine, beautiful clothes and jewels would make up for a very great deal indeed.

But this! This was—sordid. And once she started on this path—how could she ever hope to rise higher? Many were the tales of courtesans who fell to the streets but few of those who managed the journey in reverse.

But what choice did she have? Tomorrow she would be *in* the street, and even more vulnerable, unless she got money tonight.

Ninette—Ninette, please do not cry!

A voice—

Startled, she choked off her sobs and looked wildly about the little room. The golden light of the descending sun, filtered through the Parisian smoke, filled the garret. And there was no one there. No one and nothing, except for the rangy tomcat, a brown tabby, who sat on the win-

dowsill. He was no one's cat, but he had been around and
about for as long as Ninette could remember—him, or at
least, one just like him. In good times he got their scraps,
and in bad, at least he was a warm companion in bed.
Maria would never have allowed that, but the cat had
always insinuated himself inside somehow, and out
again before the morning fires were lit. And as he never
had fleas, Ninette had been happy to share her blankets.

So now she was hearing things . . .

You are not hearing things. You are hearing me, the
voice said.

Again, she looked wildly about. "Who is there?" she
demanded, her despair fueling her anger at this un-
asked for invasion. "Show yourself!"

You are looking at me, Ninette. The tomcat jumped
down off the sill and strolled up to her. *It is the cat. Call
me Thomas if you like.*

Her mouth dropped open as the cat jumped up onto
the little table and sat down again, curling his tail neatly
about his feet. She shook her head a little wildly. "No,
no, this is impossible—"

*Clearly not, since you can hear me speaking to you. So
do not cry, Ninette. I will make things right for you. I
should have spoken to you when Maria died, but I was
afraid you would never believe—I have watched over
you all your life.*

She stared into the cat's unblinking eyes. "Oh? And
so fine a job you have made of it!"

*Did you ever starve? Was there always money to pay
the rent?* the cat retorted. *Do you remember the
sausages, the cheese, the fish that were left on the table
that you thought were from your artist friends? The little purses Maria just "found" in the street when the rent
came due? Maria would never have believed in any of
the other things I could have done. I had to confine myself to what she would believe in.*

Ninette bit her lip, her mind a whirl. She felt as if her entire existence had been turned upside down. Talking cats! Talking cats that claimed to have been taking care of them! And yet . . .

And yet there had been those mysterious gifts of food when they needed them the most. Maria was incredibly lucky when it came to finding windfalls on the street. Even the artists had remarked on it, saying that she must have a good fairy looking out for her.

A good fairy. . . .

Not exactly, the cat said wryly. *But close enough. Ninette, will you trust me? Will you put yourself in my hands?*

"Paws," she corrected absently, still feeling her mind reeling. If this was madness then—so be it. She might as well be mad. What did she have to lose? If she was truly mad, then none of this was happening, and someone would find her wandering about and take her to an asylum where she would continue to live in her fancy. Or she would fall into the Seine and drown, and all her problems would be solved in that way.

All right then. You have to say it out loud. That's the way these things work. It's like a contract. The end of the cat's tail twitched, restlessly.

"I trust you. So go and do whatever you want. I won't go to the *Folies* just yet, I will give you your chance—"

Stay right here, the cat said, fiercely. *Pack a small bag with anything you do not want to leave behind. Change into your good gown. I will be right back.*

Abruptly, he stood up and whisked out of the window so quickly he might have been enchanted. She was left staring at the spot on the table where he had been sitting.

Pack a bag. With anything she did not want to leave behind.

She bit her lip and stared out at the evening sky. What in the name of God could this all mean?

As sunset turned to *l'heure bleu* and became dusk, then dark, she waited. Through her open window she could hear the sounds of the street—artists arguing at the little café, someone with a guitar, children, released from whatever job they did during the day, finding a little energy to play. Through the window came cooking smells; cabbage, the eternal cabbage, the staple of the poor. Sausages frying. Her stomach growled, and she finally got up, lit a stub of a candle, and rummaged the last of her bread from beneath the bowl where she had put it to keep it safe from mice, chopped up the last of her cabbage and made a thin cabbage soup, and ate it, slowly, dipping the hard bread into the broth. There was nothing more in the flat. Which did not matter, because if she had been imagining the talking cat, she would be in the street tomorrow anyway, and if she hadn't she would—

Where would she be? Why would a cat tell her to pack a bag?

The last of the soup a memory, the last crumb of bread gone, she finally got up from the table, and did pack that bag, an ancient carpetbag, worn to the weft. She put it on the bed and when she was done it was scarcely half full. There was not much to put in it. A few bits of clothing, Maman's marriage license, a little jewelry not even the pawnshop would take. Everything they had ever had of value had long since been pawned, except for the furniture, and she could not, in any event, strap a bed to her back and carry it off. She packed her ballet shoes, her rehearsal costume. She put on her good dress, as instructed, tied her shawl about her waist, and sat down to wait. The candle slowly burned down to a small puddle of wax, until it was just a bit of wick sporting a tiny flame.

Finally, as she began to doze at the table, there was a *thump* at the window, and a second as the cat leapt from the floor to the top of the table.

He had a square piece of pasteboard in his mouth.

Take it, he said insistently, and dumbfounded, she did. *I will be right back,* he said before she could ask any questions, and leapt away, and out the window, like the Spirit of the Rose in the ballet sketch.

She held it sideways to the light to see what it was. To her astonishment, it was a railway ticket, Paris to Calais, common carriage.

The boat-train. What on—

There was another *thump* and the cat returned, this time with a purse in his mouth, which he dropped at her feet. *Put that in your pocket,* he said. *Then get your bag. We haven't much time to get to the train.* He wandered over to the old, worn carpetbag and swatted at it with a paw. *Ah good, there will be room in there for me. That will make things easier.*

She picked up the purse. It was an ordinary little thing of leather, and she felt and heard coins in it. She opened the mouth and poured the money out into her hand. It held twenty-three francs, a 50-centime piece, four 20-centime pieces, seven 10-centime pieces, three fives, and nine single centimes, which was nineteen francs more than she had seen of late, and much more than her mother had ever had at one time. There was nothing to identify the owner.

She looked up to see the cat insinuating himself into the bag. "You stole this!" she said, aghast. "The purse, the ticket—"

And what if I did? It was from no one who would be terribly harmed by the loss. Now hurry up! You can buy

*dinner on the train or at a station. You will have to catch
the Metro and then the train!*

"But why are we going to Calais?" she asked. There
was no answer.

The cat's tail disappeared into the bag. With a feeling
that things had spun completely out of control, Ninette
picked up the bag, now made heavier by the addition of
the cat, and hesitated again.

She looked around, with the odd feeling that this
would be the last time she ever saw this apartment. This
was where she had mostly grown up; she had scarcely
known any other home.

Yet when she left, no one would really miss her. The
rest of the dancers had probably forgotten her already.
As kind-hearted as the artists were, they were very
much of the sort to put everything but their painting
right out of their minds. If she had been sitting for any
of them—if she vanished, whoever she was sitting for
would have been angry of course. But as she wasn't,
well, she was just another forgettable little dancer and
model who went away somewhere, and they would not
trouble themselves too much over where that was, so
long as none of them were called to identify a sad little
corpse at the morgue.

The place was clean, but threadbare and rather
dreary. Despite having so many artists in and out, the
only pictures on the wall were those cut out from discarded magazines and framed with little bits of wood
from old crates. Even those tended to go for kindling in
the winter. The bed didn't even have proper blankets,
just rag-blankets made of skirts too stained, worn, or
torn to ever be worn again by anyone. There was nothing in this room that had not been used and discarded
by someone else.

Even me . . .

The Metro, girl!

The candle guttered out. She took that as a sign. She stole down the dark stairs and into the night, leaving nothing of herself behind.

The Metro was crowded, but not so overcrowded that she had to stand. She had to run to catch the boat-train however, and by that time the bread and cabbage had worn very thin. She was, in fact, desperate for some food. The bag was heavy, she was tired, and her mind was in a dazed state where all she could think about was her growling stomach and the ticket in her hands.

She took a seat, the bag at her feet, and as the train pulled out of the station, and the conductor began his journey through the car, collecting tickets, she had a moment of panic. What if he knew the ticket was stolen? What if it wasn't a real ticket at all? What if—

But he looked at it, collected it, and moved on without a second glance. She sighed, and when a vendor came along the aisle selling sweets and cones of nuts, she fumbled in the stolen purse for coins and bought some. Then she tucked back into the shadows of her seat and ate, slowly, savoring each bite. She had not had sweets *or* nuts since one of the patrons had brought some for all the girls. And here she had a cone of nuts and a whole bar of chocolate to herself.

The cat in the bag at her feet was quiet, but warm; her shoes were so thin she could feel his warmth and the vibration of his purr. She had never been on a train in her life; the carriage seemed very grand, with its scarlet upholstery and its brass fittings. There were lovely lamps at intervals all along the car, fitted in between the windows. The windows were tightly closed, but there was a smell of soot in the air; some smoke from the engine escaped into the car.

She peered through the windows, hoping to see something. She had never been outside of Paris either. But it was too dark to see; the best she got were glimpses of an occasional, dim light in the distance from some farm or other, the vague shapes of the towns the train passed through, and the lit platforms they occasionally stopped at.

Despite the clattering, soot-scented, noisy reality of this journey, Ninette could not believe in it. It had an air of unreality for her, as surreal as any of the wildest canvases of the artists of Montmartre. She, Ninette Dupond, could not be doing this, sitting in a boat-train on the way to Calais. This must be a dream, a curiously vivid dream....

When the train pulled into the station, she picked up the bag and the cat and drifted out onto the platform still wrapped in that unreality.

The cat slipped out of the bag and stood beside her on the platform, looking about alertly. *Go and sit over there,* he directed, with a nod of his head. *Don't move. I'll be back.*

She looked down at him askance, but got no further word from him. The fact of his talking, however, only reinforced her feeling that this was all a dream, that in a moment she would waken in her bed back in Paris, and try to think of some prospect she had not yet considered as the means of paying the rent.

But, because it seemed the right thing to do in a dream, she went and sat as directed, and watched people stream by on their way to and from the ferries. And thought about food. The chocolate and nuts were long gone. Dared she see if there was a café somewhere near here?

Just as she was thinking about looking for one, she felt a nudge at her ankle.

It was the cat, with a thick pasteboard rectangle held daintily in his teeth. She knew, without even looking at it, what it must be.

A ferry ticket.

She could not even manage to protest that she didn't want to go to England, because by this time, aside from her hunger, this was all too absurd to be real. And in a way her hunger only enforced the absurdity; if she were lying somewhere, mad or delirious, and dreaming all this, well she *would* be hungry, wouldn't she?

So she just reached down and took the ticket, wordlessly. The cat climbed into the bag again, and she joined the stream of passengers heading towards the boat.

Finally, once aboard, she found real food; inside the ferry, someone was selling sandwiches wrapped in paper, and hot tea from a window. She bought both, carried them away to the warmest bench she could find, and sat there eating in tiny bites. She heard some complaints around her about the bread being stale, the cheese inferior, but she thought she had not tasted anything so good in a long time.

With a lurch, the ferry pulled away from the dock and began the nearly three-hour trip to Dover.

Ninette got another sandwich.

The crossing was smooth; preternaturally smooth, according to the comments. As late as it was, there was not much to see. Ninette amused herself by observing the passengers and trying to guess which of them was smuggling liquor into England to avoid the duties. The man with the tall hat? He could easily fit a bottle of brandy in there.

And that made her think suddenly that there would be a Customs man examining her bag in Dover. The cat! He would discover the cat, and surely one was not allowed to bring a cat into England!

But then in the next moment, she laughed at herself for being so absurd. She had by now convinced herself that this was all an illusion, a dream built of hunger and maybe fever or madness. It wouldn't matter. There wouldn't be a Customs man, or the cat would turn himself into a hairbrush or something. . . .

In fact, when the ferry docked and she joined the long crocodile of people leaving, she realized that her bag was much lighter. The cat had vanished. And when she reached the examining counters, the Customs man poked through her meager belongings with utter indifference before waving her on.

And then she found herself staring at the trains waiting to take on passengers without the slightest idea of what to do next. Where was she to go? Was she supposed to catch another train? Find some place to stay in Dover? She only had French money; where was she to get English money?

She felt herself on the verge of crying, when there was a warm brush against her ankles and she looked down to see the cat—once again with a pasteboard rectangle in his teeth—poking his head from under her skirt. She reached down and took it; he got into the bag as she placed it on the ground. Clearly her next act would be to get on the train. So, lacking anything better to do, she followed his directions, still somehow coming into her mind, to the one he wanted her to get on. It looked very different from the French train: less stylish, more purposeful. She got on and took a seat in the farthest, darkest corner of the compartment.

At this point, she was moving in a fog of exhaustion, and as the sun came up and pierced the windows of her railway car, she stopped thinking altogether. They arrived at an enormous train station, full of noise and smoke and bustle, full of the sound of foreign words in foreign voices. She got off and followed the cat when he jumped down out of the bag. She sat on a bench at his command, until he returned with first a new purse containing strange-looking money, and then another railway ticket. She followed him to the new train, let him get into the bag, and boarded.

It had all the characteristics of a dream. She got off the train in a new city, one that, she quickly realized from the scent of the ocean and the chill, damp wind, was a seaside city. The cat eeled out of the bag and looked up at her. *It's not far now,* she heard him say. *Just stay with me. Trust me.*

Well, why not? She had trusted him this far. She followed the cat into a shabby-genteel neighborhood of small shops and tiny boarding houses. The cat led her to one that displayed a French flag in the window.

The woman here is from Lyon. She is a widow and takes in holiday guests. Tell her you are here to visit your sister who married an Englishman, the cat said, brusquely. *Give her one of the small gold coins. She will take you to a room, and there you can sleep. I will tell you what to do when you awaken.*

Numbly, she did as the cat said. At this point, the dream had gone far beyond madness into something else. The woman who answered her knock was thin, worn, tired-looking, but at least she spoke tolerable French. She asked few questions when Ninette timidly handed her the coin. Instead, she merely led Ninette up a set of very narrow stairs to an equally narrow—but clean—room.

"I serve breakfast at six, which you are too late for," the woman said, "Luncheon is served at noon, and from the look of you, you will probably sleep through that. So I will make an exception for you, and serve you a good tea, which I normally do not serve—unless you also sleep through tea-time, in which case you may join us for supper at seven."

Ninette nodded, and set her bag down. The woman took this as the signal to leave, and did.

Ninette managed to get her dress off and climb under

the blankets. For a moment she was very cold, and thought that this surely was a sign that she was about to wake up.

But then a warm, soft body slipped into the bed with her, sliding his way up to nestle against her stomach where he began purring. A moment later she was warm.

I cannot be falling asleep if I am already asleep. Or does this mean when I fall asleep I am going to wake up? Or am I never going to wake up, and that is why I am dreaming of falling asleep . . . The questions circled around and around until she couldn't sort them out anymore. A moment after that, she truly was asleep.

NINETTE woke to the sounds of voices and footsteps running up the stairs. Normally that would not have woken her, but somewhere in the back of her dreams, she realized that they were speaking a foreign tongue—

Except, somehow, she could understand them. Imperfectly, but . . . she could understand them.

She came a little more awake, clutched the bedclothes with her eyes still closed, and listened to the young women trudge up the stairs to their rooms and chatter about their shop-jobs, the horrid customers. By the voices, there were five, two of whom had French accents, and who seemed to be working for a perfumer and a milliner. *How can I understand them?* she thought, baffled.

And then she *truly* woke up. She was in a strange room, in a strange bed—a room and a bed much, much nicer than any she had ever had before. The smells were all wrong; pleasant, but wrong. There was the faint scent of lavender, the fainter scent of the sea, and just a hint of baking bread. The sounds were all wrong also; the staircase was solid, not creaky, the voices in the street outside were nothing like as loud as in Montmartre, and were neither raised in argument nor song. And it was raining. This was not France.

It had not been a fever dream. She was, truly was, in England. And how was it she could understand those young women?

Because I gave you the language.

The warm place at the small of her back moved, and the cat insinuated himself out from under the bed-clothes and sat on the pillow, looking down at her.

"How?" she whispered haltingly.

I put it into your head by magic.

But she didn't believe in—

You are speaking to a cat. If you do not believe this is magic, what do you think it is?

She blinked. And blinked again. She was awake, in England, possessed of two purses of money, and speaking to a cat. There really was no explanation other than madness, and if she was mad . . . then she wasn't here at all, and it all certainly felt real.

But the whole situation was so . . . impossible. . . .

If you get up and get dressed, you will be able to get supper with the rest. Trust me. I know what I am doing. I will help you make your fortune.

Her stomach growled, and that decided for her. This might be madness, this might be impossible, but there was food down there, and she had missed too many meals already in her life. At the moment, she did not care about fortunes, she cared about a good dinner.

She spent a good long time brushing out her skirt and jacket, then washing up in the basin on the dresser and combing out her hair. Unlike some of the other ballet girls, her hair was not down to her waist; it was only just long enough to be put up into the proper, stiff little bun. She pinned it up tidily, donned her clothing, and when she heard a bell ring and the sounds of footsteps and voices in the hall and on the stairs, she joined the others.

The other young women glanced at her curiously, but all were clearly hungry and in a great hurry to get to the table. Nor did she blame them. The savory aromas nearly made her faint.

She followed the others to a dining room; in the manner of the rest of the house it was very clean, very neat, but nothing in it was new. A huge, plain table with a white tablecloth could easily seat ten. There were eight plain, ladder-backed chairs around it now. A little maidservant was bringing in the last of a set of platters, this one holding a loaf of bread already sliced. Gaslights illuminated the table in the growing dusk.

It was all she could do to remember her manners, remember that she was *not* supposed to be a starving little dancer, nor a Montmartre refugee, but a respectable girl visiting her married sister. She waited until the others were seated, then took the only vacant chair. She bowed her head over her clasped hands while Madame spoke a brief blessing. She looked up as Madame finished; despite longing to reach for the nearest plate, she kept her hands in her lap.

"This is Miss Ninette Dupond," Madame said gravely. "She will be staying with us for a few days while she visits her sister, before returning to the Continent. I trust you will make her welcome."

Madame had a very strong accent, but so far as Ninette could tell, her English was quite correct. The others murmured welcomes, and then the passing of dishes from hand to hand began.

The main course was a cassoulet of white beans, with pork and mutton and a bit of bacon. There was of course, far less pork and mutton than there were beans, but this was several steps above what Ninette had been eating of late, and there was plenty to go around. With this were plenty of boiled potatoes and cabbage, and that wonderful, big, crusty loaf of bread. Ninette ruled herself at that meal with a will of iron. She did not grab, she did not fill her dish to overflowing. She did not take the last of anything. She ate slowly, with small bites. She did not pour half the sugar in the bowl into her tea.

She knew, as she ate, that she could not possibly be mad. Not even in madness could she have imagined eating enough at a meal that she was actually full. Madame was not stingy with her guests, though it was very clear that she made the most economical meals possible. But she also made them well, and filling.

Mostly the other girls were involved in chatter about each other. Quiet, well-mannered chatter, but nonetheless, it was simple gossip. Madame did not join in, but neither did she make any gestures of disapproval. Now and again, one of the girls remembered her manners and thought to ask Ninette something about the supposed sister. The questions were infrequent enough that Ninette was able to concoct a plausible sounding story by the end of the meal. Her sister had met the man who was to be her husband when he traveled to Paris as a salesman of steel cutlery; she had been working in a shop at the time. They were married in Paris. On becoming a husband and father-to-be he had taken another job with his firm as a clerk, so that he did not have to travel. This was their first child. It had gone well, but Maria needed her sister's company. The flat was too small for a visitor to stay in.

This was all accepted without anything other than a nod or two. Madame enquired as to whether she would be taking luncheon at the house. Ninette told her "yes." "I do not want to be a burden on them," she said, in her new, broken English. "They must watch their pennies."

Madame nodded with approval and attention moved on to the new playbill at the Alhambra music hall, which seemed, from what Ninette could gather, to be pretty much like the old playbill. The comedian was said to be a little funnier, the magician not so good as the last. There were ragtime singers from America in place of *Rose and Violet* and *Three Young Men*. There were jugglers instead of acrobats, and dogs instead of the sketch comic. The young ladies voiced their discontent.

Ninette concentrated on her dinner. But it occurred to her at that moment that she might, just might, be able to leverage her cachet as a French dancer into a position at one of these music halls. Respectable shop girls and respectable boarding house owners went to these performances; while not the Paris Opera in terms of artistic quality, these places were at least attracting something other than the bohemians, the *grisettes,* the whores and *apaches*. They *might* even have their own versions of the old men in fur coats, who liked to make the lives of little ballet girls more comfortable.

She could not continue to live here, of course. She was rather sure that the salary of a dancer would not extend to a place like this, and even if it would, she doubted that Madame would permit someone like a dancer to live among her shop girls. But perhaps the cat could find her a place that catered to entertainers.

Not an impossible idea. . . .

Dinner ended with something that Madame called "treacle pudding," which Ninette regarded with a dubious expression, and which was rather more sticky sweet than she was used to. Still, it was a luxury. The last day had been full of luxuries. She had actually had enough to eat for the first time in . . . well, certainly since Maman had died. She had sat in a railway carriage and then in a ferry, she had slept in a bed between sheets that were not tearing apart with age and gray with washings, beneath warm, whole blankets. It was like a miracle.

But it was not, thank le bon Dieu, perfection. She

would have suspected perfection immediately. Perfection would have meant that she was lying delirious in a ditch somewhere, or mad, or even dead or at least dying. But no, this was reality. The cassoulet was just a bit scorched on the bottom, the mutton and pork in it were thrifty re-use of leftovers, for she tasted a memory of mint on the mutton and of rosemary on the pork. The treacle pudding was something she had never tasted or even heard of before, and surely she could not have invented anything like it in her own mind.

So once again this was brought home to her: she was in England, and a talking cat had brought her here. She had paid for lodgings for a week. So, for a week at least, she would live like a decently paid shop girl.

At the moment, that was more than enough.

The other girls began to push away from the table, thanking Madame, as the little maidservant came to clear away the last of the plates. Some went into the drawing room; pleading the long journey, Ninette excused herself and went back up to her room. When she entered the room, it was empty. When she turned back from closing the door behind herself, the cat was on her bed.

Turn out the purse, he said, imperiously. *The English one, not the French one.*

Obediently, she did so. The cat delicately separated the coins into neat little piles.

This is a sovereign, he said, pointing to the pile of the largest of the coins. *These are worth the most. They are also called pounds. You had two, you gave Madam one, and she returned you the change. These are shillings. Twenty of these make a pound. You have seven now. These are pennies, or pence. There are twelve of them in a shilling and you have fifteen. These two here are three penny pieces, and you have two, they are also called thruppence. These four are six penny pieces, called six-*

pence. You have eleven of these half-penny pieces, called ha'pence, and eighteen of these little fellows, each worth one fourth of a penny, called farthings. Your rent and meals, with the maid to do your laundry, for one week, came to fifteen shillings. So, I am going to drill you in this money, and then I am going to drill you in how much is reasonable to pay for something.

"But why—" she began.

Because you need a few more items of clothing right now, and because I am going to make it possible for you to live here and live well, and I should be very much obliged if you didn't allow yourself to be cheated. Now. What is this? An imperious paw tapped one of the piles of coins.

It was a very good thing that she had gotten that sleep, because her eyes were weary and sore by the time the cat allowed her to scoop the coins back into the purse, change into her threadbare little spare shift, blow out her candle, and go back to sleep. By this time, she was well aware that she was possessed of more money than she'd ever had in her life. She knew exactly how much she should expect to pay for the pieces of clothing the cat insisted she get tomorrow. But one of the expected purchases very much puzzled her. She understood going to a second-hand shop for most of it. . . .

But why would she be going to a ragman for a dress?

She went out early the next day, ostensibly to visit her mythical sister. It was still wet—not raining, but a kind of heavy mist. She headed purposefully down the street, her shawl about her shoulders, her hat pinned firmly on her head and her hair in the same tight little bun she wore when performing. She looked as if she knew exactly where she was going. In fact, she was following the cat.

Tall, narrow houses mixed with shops along a street heavy with traffic. Horse cabs, omnibuses, wagons, the occasional motor truck or motor car moved along slowly but steadily; this was nothing like her street in Montmartre. There, little cafes put their tables out on the sidewalk, produce shops racked their wares in front to entice buyers, street peddlers bawled out encouragement to buy from their carts, and everywhere there were the bohemians, sitting on steps, on balconies, hanging out of the windows. Dancing to a street organ, making music of their own. Arguing, brawling, making love in public. Here, there was none of that, only the stiff rows of houses and shops, and the stiff people moving purposefully to their destinations.

It will change with the holiday season. Then, you will see. This is the off-season, when it is hard to let rooms and hard to fill theater seats.

The cat turned down a side street. Then another. And another. They grew progressively narrower with less traffic, until at last, at long last, she found herself in a neighborhood that *did* remind her of home.

Not that there were artists and musicians thronging the place. But this was not a place where those good little shop girls would come to buy. Safe enough now, it was not a place where she would care to be after dark. There were no houses here, only buildings full of cheap flats that must have been home to enormous families. There was another accent in these streets; not being a native speaker, she couldn't place it, but there was a veritable horde of red-haired children running about. And though there may not have been artists and musicians, there was music, of drum and fiddle and tin whistle, coming from a public house that was already open.

But the cat paused at a doorway and twitched his tail at her. She pulled the door open to the ringing of a little bell, and the cat slipped inside, under her skirt.

It was a used clothing shop. But the clothing here was more than a mere cut above the neighborhood; it was remarkably good. Some of the gowns she sorted through were several social strata above the shop girls at the boarding house.

She confined herself at first, however, to the merely "good" clothing, buying a skirt and jacket that were identical in color and style to her own but of much better materials and repair, and three shirtwaists. But then, at the cat's urging, she bought beautiful under-things of the sort she had only seen on the kept *etoiles.* She asked for, and got, permission to change into these things in a stall at the back of the shop, discarding her old clothing. She scarcely felt like herself in the soft, delicate bloomers, the finely crafted corset, the dainty corset-cover and petticoat, the silk stockings that were tea-stained, but not where anyone would see them. And the new outer clothing . . . it was strange, very strange, because it looked the same but—it was unmended and only a little worn. It felt more substantial.

And, at the cat's prodding, she bought a sturdy umbrella. *You will need it,* he told her laconically. *There are only two sorts of weather in Blackpool. Raining and about to rain.*

Finally, as a girl came in with a bundle while she was looking at cloaks, it dawned on her what this was. Often part of a maidservant's wages was the cast-off clothing of her mistress. This was where the superior maidservants came to sell their windfalls.

So it was with a little surprise, as she waited for the shopkeeper to bundle up the items she wasn't wearing, that she heard the cat say from under her skirt, *Ask about the cut-up dress!*

Too surprised, in fact, to do anything other than stammer, "And would you have a ruined day gown, velvet perhaps, or silk twill, that has been cut up badly?"

The shopkeeper looked at her in astonishment, pausing for a moment, before answering, "Why . . . as a matter of fact . . . I do. But why do you need such a thing?"

Fancywork, hissed the cat. *Shoes. You are covering shoes.*

"I am re-covering dancing slippers," she said, and the man nodded with understanding, and pulled a basket from beneath the counter.

There were three gowns in there, but the cat was only interested in the blue velvet one. They were all in rags; it looked as if someone had taken a knife to them and slashed them up.

"The girl works for the most mean-spirited woman I have ever heard of," the shopkeeper said, shaking his head over the ruins of what had once been a magnificent gown. "Rather than let her maids have her old clothes, because she can't bear the idea of someone of lower rank than she wearing what she once wore, she slashes the things to rags before throwing them out. The girl brings them here anyway; I generally sell them to the rag and bone man—"

"My great fortune then, that you had not yet," smiled Ninette as he added that to her purchases. He did them all up in a brown paper parcel, which she carried out, wearing her new clothing and new cloak. The cat led her onwards, back to better neighborhoods, where he directed her purchases of other small items, and then it was time to return to the boarding house for luncheon.

She slipped carefully up the stairs, keeping her parcel hidden as best she could in her cloak. It wouldn't do for Madame to suspect she had been doing anything other than dutifully visiting the supposed sister. She quickly unwrapped her new things and put them away in her bag, putting the brown paper into the fireplace where it burned nicely. She made very certain that the ruined dress was hidden under the rest of her clothing, and sat for a moment in quiet contemplation of her new "wealth." Not since she was a little girl had she had a nightdress; she and her mother had simply gone to sleep in their underthings in summer, or fully clothed in the winter when you needed everything to keep warm. She touched the soft linen, the bit of lace, with wondering fingers. And as for the dress and jacket she was wearing, perhaps they were plain by the standards of the woman who had discarded them, but . . . they were scarcely worn. The skirt had never been turned. The hems had not been taken up or let down. There were no patches, no darns, no mended seams. For the very first time in her life, she had an almost-new gown. To be sure, she was very glad it had been gaslit night when she went down to dinner; those girls would have known her for an imposter if they had clearly seen her clothing.

Finally, she closed the bag and left the window open for the cat to come in. Then she went down to the much-diminished group for luncheon.

When she arrived at the table, there were only three other girls here. One of them was a dark-haired, studious-looking girl with very short hair and gold-rimmed spectacles. Madame was not in evidence, but luncheon was. Tea, bread and butter, currant jam, cucumber sandwiches. Clearly there was only one sandwich apiece, but as much bread and butter as a girl would want. The two who were sitting together, still wearing shop-girls' aprons, gave Ninette a friendly nod, but did not stop their gossip, which was entirely in French. They must have known she could understand them, but since it was inconsequential stuff about other girls in the shop, she ignored them. The dark-haired one was engrossed in a book that did not look at all like a novel; that left Ninette alone with her meal. This, she did not at all mind. Plain as it might be, she savored it, at the same time trying not to let on she was very nearly in transports of joy over the fact that she was eating real butter and a piece of fresh bread she had herself just cut from the loaf, and not salted lard or the grease carefully saved from cooking scraped thin over the top of old, stale bread sold cheap at the corner bakery.

The two girls together—Marie and Jeanne—ate quickly and were as quickly gone; likely their time for luncheon was very short, and allowed only because the English tended to scant luncheon and eat a large tea, which meant they would be there to serve customers at an hour when the other girls would be gone. The book-ish girl ate slowly, absently, and methodically, as if she were a steam engine and food was only fuel. Ninette was done before she was, took her plates to the serving hatch as the others had, and left them there.

Then, because she was supposed to be going back to this nonexistent sister, she went out again. The cat went with her, of course. She felt far less conspicuous in her "new" clothing; she no longer looked like the scullery maid, but as if she belonged on this street. Frankly, she had to wonder if Madame would have turned her away if she had spoken English instead of French.

But perhaps the gold sovereign had done the speaking for her.

For some time, she just followed where the cat led. Finally he turned around and looked at her over his shoulder. *Where do you want to go?* he asked, sounding a bit baffled.

She thought about that. It wasn't raining, so there was no reason to seek shelter inside a shop or some public building. Finally, after making sure there was no one near enough to hear her talking to a cat, she replied. "Actually, just somewhere we can talk. I want to know just what you plan. I know you are planning *something,* but I can't keep living at that house, pretending to visit a sister that does not exist. And are you going to keep stealing purses?"

She stopped then, because someone opened the shop door just behind her. The cat flicked his tail and moved off.

Follow me, was all he said, and so she did.

He led her to a pretty little park, where there were young mothers with toddlers and babies in prams. That is, she assumed that the women were the children's actual mothers. This neighborhood did not look as if the people living here could afford nursemaids for their children. Like Madame, they probably had a cook and a maid-of-all-work, but looked after their children themselves.

The *grisettes* of Bohemia and the Left Bank, of Montmartre and garret or basement flats did not have servants at all, and were unburdened with children. Or if they had children, they were left at the door of an orphanage, or the *grisette* abandoned her Bohemian life to find some way to keep them.

Little ballet girls did not have children either. But that was because, illegal as it was, there were still ways to be rid of a child before it interfered with one's dancing.

Perhaps that was why the artists had all made a pet of her. She was a rare thing in their lives. They would probably have made even more of a pet of her if she had ever been able to sit still long enough for them to paint her.

The cat found her a relatively secluded bench. There he sat down at her feet—on her feet, actually, and regarded the pigeons with a meditative expression.

I intend to make you an etoile, he said. *Here. In the music halls. It will not be like the ballet; they are more like the Follies.*

"I should not mind that at all," she said instantly. "But I don't see how you are to do that. If they have a steady chorus of dancers, I might rise to be the soloist, but I would never be an *etoile*. In a place like that, one must have an act, costumes, even scenery sometimes. I have one pair of shoes and one rehearsal costume. And no act."

Or, he replied, *one must have a Name. A Reputation.*

She rolled her eyes. "Which I also do not have. As I was told many times, one good review in *La Figaro* does not a reputation make."

I did not say we would use your *name.*

She stared down at him, but he did not meet her eyes. His were fixed on the pigeons. "Whose name, precisely, did you intend to use? And how do you expect me to get away with this impersonation?"

How far from their companies do most dancers ever travel? He countered with a question. *Ballet dancers, I mean, and not the sort that have no company, like Isadora and Loie Fuller. You do not want that sort of life. You will need a setting; a theater where you are the resident* etoile. *Not your own theater, having one's own theater is foolishness and a waste of money. You need an impresario who will set productions around you, so that you are the* etoile *of that company. And—more than just ordinary dancers, how many* etoiles *ever travel?*

"None at all, really," she replied after a moment. "Unless the company goes on tour. But that is very expensive to mount, and unless the Company has a sensational reputation, like Ballet Russe, it is really folly to go on tour. And the *etoiles* are almost never allowed to dance for other companies."

So, we will borrow the name of someone unlikely to ever hear about your impersonation, the cat said calmly.

"So I am to walk up to an impresario, and without any way of proving it, nor worldly goods to back my claim, tell him I am a great *etoile* from some far away place and expect him to believe me!" She laughed. "You are a very clever cat, but you have a woeful understanding of humans."

I have a rather better idea than that, the cat replied. *But for now, I should like you to go to the Imperial and see what it is you are going to be joining.*

Once again, the cat led the way. It was not a long walk, as Ninette was used to. The Imperial Music Hall was right on the seaside, and it offered a "continuous" show of the sort where one could purchase a ticket, walk in at any point, and leave when the act you had first seen came on again. The cat hid himself under her skirt, Ninette purchased the cheapest possible ticket, and both of them ascended to the fourth balcony.

The place was . . . rather fantastic. She was used to the grandness of the theater, but the Paris Opera, though grand, was old, and showing its age a bit. This was new, and opulent. Even the least expensive balcony was lush with velvet and gilding. At this hour, it was mostly empty and she had her choice of seats. Not at all averse to heights—after all she had spent a good many hours of her young life suspended by wires above the stage of the Paris Opera—she took a seat near the middle of the first row and leaned over the railing.

The act at the moment was a *tableaux vivants,* which at the Follies would have consisted of several young ladies clothed in not very much at all posing as a classical painting. Botticelli's Venus was always a favorite. In this case, however, the *tableaux* consisted of a herd of wretched little children in costume posing as a classical painting. The ones at the back fidgeted. The ones at the front seemed frozen with boredom rather than discipline. The orchestra played, the audience was supposed to note how perfect the imitation was, and then the lights came down, only to come up again on another *tableaux.* Needless to say, none of these were Botticelli's Venus.

Three of these, and the way was cleared for the next act, performing dogs, with one poor monkey in a jockey uniform.

After that, a young lady in a man's suit sang a song. The audience seemed to know most of the words and sang along; Ninette got the impression it was called "Champagne Charlie." She sang two more, then made way for the "ballet."

This at least was interesting for Ninette, although even the soloist would have been relegated to the front of the *coryphées* at the Paris Opera Ballet. It was definitely true that she could out-dance these girls. The question was if she would be allowed to prove it. And how was she to become an *etoile* in such a place as this? There was no underlying story to these performances, no unifying whole. There was no single principal performer who was brought out again and again to show some new variation on her skill. This was something like the *Moulin Rouge* or the Follies; a variety performance. And yes, Loie Fuller performed at such places and only needed to do her "act" once at each performance, but that was not the sort of thing that Ninette was good at. La Loie had novelty and effect; Ninette had skill and grace and two feet. Nor, did she think, something like the can-can would make an *etoile* of her.

Still, the cat had said to study the acts and the theater, so study them she did.

She spent the rest of the afternoon there in the balcony, watching, studying. This was where she supposed she aspired to be, this stage or one like it.

The only question was, how was she to get there?

You must listen to me and do exactly as I say, with no questions, the cat said from his place under her skirt, curled warmly around her ankles. *Have I not brought you this far? It will be hard, it will take all your wits, and the beginning of it, at least, will be very uncomfortable for you. Can you do that?*

"I don't see that I have a choice," she whispered under cover of the orchestra playing.

You could go and be a shop-girl.

"I don't know how to be a shop-girl. And someone would find out that I don't belong here." She thought a moment, and firmed her chin, stubbornly. "And besides, I want to be an *etoile*. I want to be made much of. I want my own dressing room, and flowers and champagne and chocolates in it. I want young men to send me flowers and old men to send me jewelry. I want a dresser and an apartment and a maid. I want to find a wealthy man who will—"

Then listen to me and you will have all those things, the cat said, interrupting her. *Now, study this place. A hall like this will soon be the place of your triumph; study it, study the acts, and above all, study the audience. It is, after all, they you must win.*

4

FOR the next four days, Ninette and the cat went out in the morning and returned in the evening. Every moment of those days she spent studying the music hall; on the whole she was rather glad that she was doing that, for the cat was correct, it seemed to rain at least part of the day, every day. First, she watched the acts and as much of the action behind scenes as she could see from the front of the house, and then, by cunningly pretending to have been sent to deliver things, or otherwise slipping in back-stage, she studied the acts, and the way that things were run, from backstage. It wasn't hard; she knew where to go and how not to be noticed backstage in almost any the-ater. She would bustle about, head down, carrying a bun-dle of cloth from one place to another. Everyone assumed she was someone else's dresser. She would sit in a corner and pretend to sew; everyone assumed she was someone else's costume girl. The one thing that would have made even these pretenses difficult at the Ballet, where everyone knew everyone else and what their busi-ness was, made it easy here. No one really knew anything much about any of the other acts. They rotated among the houses, making the music hall circuit, never spending more than a week at any one place. Half the people here were going on together, into London to make the rounds of several music halls called one "Empire" or another, which were all owned by the same man. But the rest were scattering to the four winds, every direction but East. All but the girl who sang "Champagne Charlie"; she was going on to something called the "Panto" as a "Principal Boy," whatever that was.

Things were run in a very different fashion in this place, where the acts never remained for more than two weeks. The orchestra had to learn new music with each new act; the acts had to rehearse on a new stage with new stagehands every time they migrated to a new booking. It was, Ninette thought, distinctly inferior to what she was used to—a setting where the performances changed, but the players, the supporting members, and the orchestra remained the same. It was even distinctly different from the music halls of Paris, where there was a resident company of dancers who performed pieces that framed the performances of artists who would remain for long bookings, six weeks to even a year or more. The orchestra had no feeling of loyalty to the performers; after all, they would be gone in a week. As a consequence, they also had no particular interest in supporting them past the absolute minimum required. The first morning rehearsals, known as "band calls," could be terrible things, taking far longer than they needed to. Performers supplied their own sheet music, and this was often a cause for acrimony, as the performers were not inclined to buy new music until they absolutely had to, which meant musicians were often forced to deal with music that was just barely readable. And when the performer was not in their favor, well. . . .

Morning rehearsals could end up in shouting matches, with both sides appealing to the stage manager, and often threatening to escalate to the theater owner.

The only time this did not happen was in the case of the very popular performers, the equivalent of the *etoiles*. They might supply music fully as old as the most down-at-heels and outdated comic, the most woefully inadequate singer, but the most the musicians dared to do was grumble, and send up the orchestra leader to the performer—or more likely the performer's assistant—to urge that this time, really, he *should* buy some new music.

For these very prominent performers did not attend the morning walk-throughs themselves, oh no. They had assistants to do this for them. And they might not put in more than a cursory appearance at the rehearsals just after lunch, unless they were practicing a new "turn." This baffled Ninette; no matter how lofty the *etoile,* he or she was *there* at every rehearsal. Warm-ups might be done in the luxury of one's little studio in one's grand flat, but rehearsals? Rehearsals were sacred. You did not go all out in them, of course; that would be absurd, you would exhaust and possibly injure yourself to no purpose. But you came and you practiced, and you had better make sure that the ballet master did not get the impression that you were losing form . . .

But Ninette watched and made mental notes. She could not at all see how the cat was going to make her an *etoile* at this point. Possibly under the Paris system, yes. If the theater owner, the ballet master, the stage manager could all somehow be persuaded that she was this mysterious dancer she was supposed to imperson-ate . . . yes. It could be done. Even if she came with nothing but the clothes on her back, it could be done.

But here? She had no assistants, no scenery, no

music ... and even if she somehow conjured these things up, like Cinderella's fairy godmother, out of backstage mice, how could she survive the "booking circuit"? She had no agent, she knew no one and nothing, had no idea what the next city was, let alone how to get to it, find a place to stay, and begin all over again.

That cat only said, *Wait and see.* She counted the money left in her purse, and tried not to think too hard about the number of days it would last.

A barrage of thunder startled her awake, and she sat straight up in bed, her heart pounding. She stared at the window, clutching her blankets up to her throat, seeing the cat sitting there, silhouetted intermittently by the flashes of lightning.

It was a hideous storm. She could not recall ever having seen one this bad in Paris. A violent wind lashed the windowpanes with rain, and thunder grumbled in the distance or crashed near at hand. Perhaps it was that the sea was so near; certainly all the operas and ballets she had been a part of over the years linked dreadful storms with the sea.

This, said the cat, *could not be better.* Satisfaction permeated every word.

"Why?" she asked.

You'll see. The cat could be absolutely maddening sometimes. But at the moment ... silhouetted black against the lightning-filled sky, with that sure tone to his words ... she felt her irritation slipping away, replaced by a kind of superstitious fear. What *was* he, anyway? This beast that spoke in her head, that controlled her like a puppeteer, that had taken her away to a strange land? What did he want from her? True, he had been kind so far but—he couldn't want her body. Could he be after her soul? *Les Contes d'Hoffman,* in which she had danced the part of one of Guillietta's attendants, immediately sprang to her mind. Could this cat, this creature, be a servant of the Devil?

Oh, don't be silly, the cat said, calmly. *Whatever would I do with your soul? I don't want it.*

"Then why are you doing all this?" she whispered.

Because I am interested in you. Because I take pleasure in clever tricks. But above all, it might just be only because I am a cat. She could almost hear him laughing. *That alone is reason enough. Now go back to sleep. I will be waking you about dawn.*

Well that was unlikely to bring her any sleep.

Wake up, Ninette.

The voice penetrated the soft, dreamless dark. She tried to bat it away, like an annoying fly, but it persisted.

Wake up. It is time.

It couldn't possibly be time for anything important.

Four sharp needles pierced her big toe and her slumbers. With a gasp of outrage and pain, she sat straight up in bed, now quite well awake.

"You *bit* me!" she hissed indignantly at the dark shape at the foot of the bed.

I scarcely broke the skin, the cat replied. *You weren't moving, and we have very little time. Get up.*

"Time for what?" she demanded, but the cat wasn't answering.

Put on that cut-up dress over your best underthings, he told her. *And your cloak over all. Don't bother taking anything else. We're going out.*

In the darkness, she gaped at him. "But—"

When this has all settled you can send someone for your things or come for them yourself. But right now, all you need is that dress and your cloak.

"It's still raining!" she protested. Outside, the storm

had turned into a steady, slow rain without any thunder
or lightning, but she had no doubt that it was terribly
cold out there—and why was she going out in a gown
slashed to ribbons?

*I know. I told you I was waiting for something. This
was it. The storm. Now come on!*

Maybe if she hadn't been half-muzzy with sleep, or
if she wasn't more than half convinced this was just a
surreal dream, she might have protested more. Instead, she did as she was told, and stole down the stairs,
letting herself out at the kitchen door, following the
silent cat.

Of course, the face full of wind and cold rain that
she got woke her up thoroughly, but by then it was too
late. And the cat was pushing against her ankles, herd-
ing her down into the street.

"What is this all about?" she gasped.

*You are about to become the victim of a dreadful ship-
wreck. Can it be a shipwreck if it is only a yacht? A yacht-
wreck doesn't sound quite right.* The cat ran on ahead,
pausing in a circle of lamplight to look back at her.

"A *what?*"

*A shipwreck. Remember I told you that we were going
to borrow someone else's reputation? You will be Nina
Tchereslavsky, Russian prima donna. She has never performed further west than Berlin. You look enough like
her photographs to pass. She speaks French almost ex-
clusively outside of Russia, although she does know
some English, and I will arrange for you to learn Russian in the same way I arranged for you to learn English.*

"But how does this—"

*Let me finish. You—that is, Nina—decided to come to
England on holiday, possibly to arrange a tour as well.
Possibly to stay. You are certain there is no dancer half so
good as you here. A friend with a yacht arranged to bring
you. In last night's storm, the boat was wrecked, your*

friend is presumably drowned, and you have lost all of your possessions.

"But I cannot see—"

I will arrange the rest. You have only to remember your name and the storm and the wreck and act dazed. Speak French. I will take care of the rest. The cat herded her quickly down the street to the seashore. By that time, her hair was soaked, the rags of her gown and her cloak were soaked, and with her hair straggling into her eyes she was certainly going to present a convincing imitation of a shipwreck victim. As she staggered along the sand, the sky was just starting to lighten in the east, and the piers of the boardwalk loomed darkly above her head. She had not yet been down to the boardwalk, although she gathered that there were all manner of places of amusement built on it. Out of the holiday season though, most of them were fairly desolate.

Here, the cat said, finally. *Wait here. Try and keep warm. When you hear me tell you to, lie face-down on the sand. Remember, you are Nina Tchereslavsky. Nothing else is of consequence.*

And then the cat whisked away, leaving her at the foot of the piers, shivering, in the dark.

Was this scheme mad enough to actually work? Well she had no choice now.

The automobile chugged and rattled, the headlights doing little to illuminate the cobblestone-paved street ahead. Fortunately the streetlamps were still well lit, extravagant electrical things that they were. Nigel Barrett gripped the steering wheel and was grateful that this was an enclosed auto. And cursed the fact that the storm had chosen last night to break over their heads.

"Why you insisted on dragging us out this early in the morning, Nigel, I do not know." Since this was roughly the tenth time Nigel Barrett's traveling companion Wolf had voiced this particular complaint, Nigel did not bother to repeat his answer.

But his other traveling companion, Arthur Gilbert, did so for him. "Because if we are going to get to Manchester in time to see this singer at the matinee, we have to leave now, Wolf. Nigel's only told you so a dozen times."

"Nine," Wolf replied, with immense dignity, from the rear seat of the enclosed motorcar. "And I don't know why *I* had to come along."

"Because you are the one writing the music for this extravaganza," Nigel replied, carefully negotiating the narrow street in the semi-darkness. Once again, he asked himself why he lived in this part of Blackpool, where every time he wanted to take the motorcar out, he had to negotiate a maze of medieval lanes. "You have the final word on whether I hire her or not."

"Arthur knows what I like," Wolf said tartly.

"Arthur is only the conductor of the orchestra," Arthur himself replied. "And you know your best work comes when you're inspired by a particular singer or dancer. I can't possibly tell whether or not you'd be inspired." He reached around over the seat and gave the wool-shrouded cage a pat. "Don't worry, we won't let you get into a draft."

"I would be much more inspired if you'd let me write an opera," Wolfgang Amadeus said fretfully. "I am *tired* of those ridiculous tinkly ballads you like so much. Sweep! Scale! A challenge! That's what I need!" The African Grey Parrot pulled the wool covering of his cage aside with his beak, and one beady black eye peered out at them accusingly.

"And opera isn't going to fill the seats, Wolf, you know that," Nigel responded without taking his eyes off the street. "And with these moving pictures coming on, pretty soon variety won't either. Don't worry, you'll get spectacle and sweep to fill with music. I've seen the future of the stage, and its name is *The Ziegfield Follies.* Shows with a theme, a regular bill of stars you can count on seeing, that's what will keep the seats full, even when motion pictures take over the music halls."

"I know you keep saying that, Nigel, but you haven't really explained yourself." Arthur Gilbert, a slight, fair-haired man with the build of a whippet and nerves of steel, raised an eyebrow at his employer. "I should think people would get tired of seeing the same thing night after night."

"Do people get tired of seeing William Gillette as Sherlock Holmes?" Nigel demanded. "Or Henry Irving as Hamlet? Or Ellen Terry as Portia? And what about Maude Adams as Peter Pan?"

"Well . . . but those are plays!" Arthur replied, tucking the woolen blanket in around the cage again. "And that's in London!"

Wolf snorted. Or made a sound like a snort.

"And that's the genius of the thing," Nigel said with enthusiasm. "We take everything that people like best about a play—that is, a nice, light story—we add in the kind of music they like, which is where Wolf comes in, but without turning the damned thing into an opera, because last of all, we fit in the best sorts of acts from music hall. We rehearse it all and open it in the slow season, and that's when all the locals will come. When they get tired of it, we'll be in holidays, and the holiday-makers will pack the hall. By the time they leave, the locals will be ready to see it again, and when they're gone, it will be time for the Christmas pantos. That's when we put together the next show, start rehearsals, and open again after the end of panto season. It's brilliant!"

"I don't know, Nigel—" Arthur began doubtfully, when something dark and fast and seemingly as big as a panther dashed into the street in front of them.

Arthur swore, Nigel swore and jerked the steering wheel, narrowly missing the animal, and Wolf swore in German as he was knocked to the bottom of his cage. The brakes shrieked as the motorcar slid to a stop. And the *thing* leapt onto the hood of the car, every hair bristling, eyes like saucers full of fire.

Help! Help! the creature "shouted" into their minds. *My mistress is dying! You must come save her!*

Which Nigel, because he was an Elemental Master, Arthur, because he was an Elemental Magician, and Wolfgang, because he was Wolfgang, all heard with perfect clarity.

"Where?" Nigel shouted across the windscreen.

The shore! Follow me! replied the cat. It leapt down to the ground again, and raced down the street. Nigel fed gas to the motor, which fortunately had not stalled, and raced after it.

They broke out of the maze of streets to the broader roads and followed the cat at last to the Promenade that paralleled the seashore as the sun rose dimly behind the clouds and the rain slacked off to a thin drizzle. The cat dashed across the Promenade and down one of the wooden staircases that led from the boardwalk to the sands. Nigel slid the motorcar roughly to a halt and threw open the door, dashing after it, with Arthur closely behind him.

Hurry! the cat screamed into their minds. For a moment, Nigel couldn't see where the creature was. But then he caught sight of a dark shape just under the pier at the waterline and he raced towards it, grateful that the sand was wet and packed solid enough to run on. The closer he got, the clearer that shape became—a woman, hair down and dark with seawater, sprawled under what was left of a cloak as if she had crawled up on the sand, exhausted, a rough piece of broken timber a little way away from her.

He dropped down beside her and turned her over; she was as cold as ice, pale, and her eyes fluttered open and looked at him, dazedly.

"Miss! Can you speak?" he asked urgently, patting her cheek with one hand to revive her a little.

She answered him in French, which he spoke tolerably well. *"Where—"*

"Blackpool. England. Who are you?" Arthur asked, as he pulled off his coat to wrap around her. Her velvet gown was in tatters.

"Nina. Nina Tchereslavsky," she murmured. *"The yacht—my friend—"* Then her eyelids fluttered closed again.

She is a dancer. A great dancer. A genius, the cat said, dancing with anxiety. *She wanted to emigrate to England; I tried to dissuade her, but she thought she could be a greater star than she already is once she performed on your stage. She sold everything and persuaded a friend with a yacht to bring her here. You must save her! Her father was an Elemental Master, he charged me with protecting her when he died—*

Ah, that explained it then. This was no cat, it was an Elemental Spirit in feline form. "Don't worry, we'll take care of her," Nigel said, lifting the slight girl in his arms. Well, she was certainly built like a dancer. She weighed hardly anything. A dancer. And Russian. . . .

She was cold, certainly, and exhausted, and probably everything she owned had gone down with that ship . . . but if he was any judge of such things, and as an Air Master he was rather good at telling how healthy someone was, she was in no danger of dying any time soon. Dancers in his experience were robust, hardy. They had to be; life for a dancer was anything but easy. As he carried her to the motorcar, already his mind was racing.

Russian dancers were very much in vogue ever since Diaghilev had brought them to London in his Ballet

Russes troupe. This young woman would certainly be grateful to her rescuers. And now she was stranded here with nothing. . . .

"What's happening?" Wolf was shouting from the back seat as he approached the motorcar with his burden. "What's happening?"

"We seem to have rescued a young dancer, Wolfgang," Arthur replied, pulling a warm lap-robe out of the boot and wrapping it around the girl in place of his coat as Nigel set her carefully down on the back seat, and the cat jumped in beside her. "And I think that we won't need to go to Manchester today after all."

Ninette had not needed to feign confusion and weakness. She had lain so long on the sand that all of the heat had leeched out of her body. At first she had shivered and shook and her teeth had chattered so hard she thought they were going to break, but then a kind of lethargy overtook her and she actually started to feel warm. And sleepy.

Dimly she knew that this was a bad sign, but she just couldn't bring herself to care at that point. Fortunately that was the moment when she felt herself being turned over and something warm being wrapped around her. When she managed to open her eyes, she saw a blurred face, a man's face, looming over her. She had just enough wit to remember her story and her new name, to gasp out that name and a few more words, and then the effort just became too much and she let her eyes fall shut again.

When she next came to herself, she was in a huge bed, engulfed in it, in fact, lying on what must have been a feather mattress and covered in eiderdowns, with hot bricks all around her and the cat sitting smugly on a pillow next to her.

"Ah, she is awake," said a voice in English, and another man, this one an old one, in a dark suit, with a full white beard and moustache, loomed over her. "Drink this," he ordered, putting a glass to her lips as he raised her head with the other hand.

It proved to be hot brandy rather than some nasty medicine; she sipped it cautiously, then blinked at him as it went almost straight to her head. "You'll do," the man said with satisfaction, and looked off to a part of the room she could not see without sitting up. "It is a good thing she is a dancer," he said in that direction. "They may look fragile, but in my experience, they're strong as horses. I doubt anyone without that kind of strength could have survived a wreck in that storm last night. But with some rest and good food, she'll be as right as rain in a few days."

"Glad to hear it, Doctor Lambert," said the voice she remembered from the sand. And a moment later, the man who owned the voice, face no longer a blur, came to the side of the bed. *Do you know where you are?* he asked in French.

"Somewhere in England?" she replied.

"You said your name was Nina," he prompted.

"Nina Tchereslavsky, yes. I am a dancer, a ballet dancer. So many Russian dancers have had great success in the West, and I am tired of the snow of St. Petersburg. I asked my friend Nikolas—" it was the only Russian name she could think of *"—if he would take me on his pretty little boat to England. I thought I could find a good company here. My reputation—"* here she raised her chin a little, in haughty imitation of La Augustine *"— should more than suffice."* Now she faltered. *"But there was a terrible storm. A terrible storm. The boat began to break apart. We went into the water and I lost Nikolas—"*

Unbidden, the memory of her *Maman* lying, slowly dying, wasting away with fever in the cold of the garret came to her mind, and she burst into tears.

The man, an earnest fellow with brown hair and eager eyes in a round face, patted her hand awkwardly. *"Now don't give up hope yet!"* he said, even though his face told her that he didn't have any hope at all that the imaginary Nikolas would have survived. *"A tiny thing like you survived, there's plenty of hope for him."*

"But I am all alone!" she wailed. *"All alone, and I have nothing and no one—"*

All of that was true enough, and gave force to her fear and grief. "That will be enough of that for now, Mr. Barrett," the doctor said with authority. "Let her sleep. The powder I put into her brandy should be working any moment now."

And indeed, even as she raised her hand to wipe the tears away with a corner of the soft, soft sheet she lay under, the room did a kind of spin, and she found her eyes closing all by themselves.

Nigel Barrett was in his element, reporters clustered about him, shouting questions at him. This was a good setting for him too, the opulent sitting room of his apartment, fitted out in the latest and most expensive style. He beamed at them all, impartially. Not only were reporters from the Blackpool, Liverpool, and Manchester papers here, there was even a man come up from London. London! There was nothing, nothing that he could have concocted that could have produced this windfall of publicity!

Knowing a good yarn when he heard one, Nigel had rung up the papers once he knew the little dancer was going to be all right. The story of the wreck and its lovely survivor had spread rapidly thanks to the telegraph and the telephone. Everyone wanted to hear the story first hand. Nigel and Arthur had concocted something that they thought would suit—be romantic

enough and plausible enough to pass muster. Because
certainly they couldn't tell the truth. . . .

Instead, the cat, Thomas, had been, much to his disgust, imbued with all the qualities of the most devoted
of dogs. Some of the reporters were even considering
having their papers give him a lifesaving medal. At least
one probably would.

Now the story ran that the cat had run up to them as
they paused the auto for a moment near the piers to
wait for someone to cross the street. Never mind that
their real route would have taken them nowhere near
the piers; Nigel had conveniently not mentioned why
they were out at that hour in the first place. The cat sup-
posedly had jumped onto the hood of the motor, and
when Nigel had gotten out to chase him off, had jumped
down and grabbed Nigel's trouser-leg in his teeth. Then,
doglike, he had tugged until Nigel followed them, leading them to the girl. No, the cat hadn't then been the
girl's pet—all of them had reckoned that having a cat
swim to shore from a sinking yacht would be rather too
much to be believed. Yes, she was adopting her savior—
that was to forestall any newspaper scheme of having
the cat adopted by a reader lottery. Yes, he was watching over her now, it was immensely touching—that, of
course, was to strike the proper note of sentiment. Yes,
they intended to offer Miss Tchereslavsky their hospi-
tality until she was well enough to decide what she
wanted to do—true enough on all counts.

Finally when he thought they had all heard enough,
he ushered the reporters out with orders to his butler to
make sure they all got a good brandy before they left
"to ward off the cold."

Only then did he return to his sitting room where
Arthur and Wolf were waiting for him.

"Did it pass muster?" Arthur asked anxiously, as he
closed the door behind him.

"No reason why it shouldn't," Nigel replied, settling into his favorite armchair and propping his feet on the fire grate. He accepted a brandy from Arthur with a sigh of satisfaction. "Good gad, old man, Americans couldn't have manufactured something this sensational! Wolf, do you think you can write music for a dancer instead of a singer?"

The parrot snorted, and took a dainty bite out of a hothouse grape. "At least it will be slightly more of a challenge than writing music to fit: *"Charlie, my Charlie, oh do tell me true / Am I still your sweetheart, your dear Alice Blue? / Will you take me to church, will you take me to town / In my dear little Alice-blue, Alice-blue gown?"*

"That was a hit!" Nigel reminded him, and the parrot groaned. "The costermongers and newsboys were whistling it in the street!" he continued. "You must have sold thousands of copies of the sheet music!"

"A bit, a bit," Arthur said complacently. "Kept you in fresh peas, Wolf."

But already nebulous plans were unfolding in Nigel's fertile imagination. He remembered a production of Shakespeare—*The Tempest* it was—and the sensational effects managed on the stage as the curtain rose. He could do that. *They* could do that. "We'll have to manage to get a shipwreck into the plot," Nigel said aloud, causing both of them to stare at him.

"Whyever for?" Arthur said after a moment. "That would be a dreadfully expensive set to create."

"Because we're going to have the dancer that was saved from a shipwreck as our star turn!" Nigel shook his head at their surprise. Couldn't they see it? It was a fine thing to capitalize on saving her in the first place, but better to remind the public of the great story in two or three months and capitalize on it all over again. "Half of our publicity is already done for us, and the locals and the holiday people alike will fill the stalls to see the 'shipwreck girl' saved all over again."

"You don't even know that she'll stay with us," Arthur protested mildly. "Nor that she will be in the least interested in performing in a mere musical show."

"This is a ballet dancer, Nigel," the parrot said, drawing himself up with great dignity and looking down his beak at the music-hall entrepreneur. "And a prima donna to boot. An *artiste.* She'll be looking for a ballet company, mark my words—"

"You mark mine. First, she's indebted to us. Second, she's the daughter of an Elemental Master—where else would she go for people who won't think she's balmy for talking to a cat? Third—" he grinned. "Ballet dancers like money too. Loie Fuller wasn't too high-nosed to appear at the Moulin Rouge. She'll make a lot more money with us than with some ballet company." He stood up and began to pace. "Elemental Master—that gives me an idea. We need a story with magic in it. That way we can hire old Jonathon, who has the Kung Chow act—always good to have another of the company about—"

"Kung Chow?" Wolf said in dismay. "I am *not* going to substitute for one of his wretched doves again! Really, Nigel, this is going too far—"

"No one is asking you to substitute for a dove, Wolf," Nigel said, pacing faster. "We should make this a real *Arabian Nights* story. Shipwreck our girl in Arabia, have her taken to a harem, that way we can bring in all the variety acts as things to entertain the sultan! And have an excuse to put her in as little as we can convince her to wear. And there are plenty of girls in our chorus who wouldn't blanch at doing a harem dance. Have her escape with the Court Magician's help—"

"Oh good lord, why don't you just steal the plot and music from my *Abduction from the Seraglio* and have done with it?" Wolf said in disgust.

"Why don't I—Wolf! That's brilliant!" Nigel turned towards the parrot and conductor with a smile lighting up his face. "Perfect! You adapt the music for our show, we can tout it as 'Based on *Abduction from the Seraglio* by Wolfgang Amadeus Mozart.' Make the print just large enough that the punters won't notice and the high-minded will. The punters will get their nautch dances, and the high-toned will tell each other how fine it is to listen to classical music while they gawk at the nautch dances from behind their pince-nezes. It's brilliant! I love you!" As Wolf growled in startlement, Nigel swooped him up, kissed his beak, and put him back down on his stand again.

"Brilliant! Brilliant! I'm going to go look up the libretto of this opera of yours and see what I can keep out of it. Arthur, help Wolf with some catchy lyrics. We'll need at least one love song, of course, and one song about being homesick. And one from the sultan about making the beauty his slave for all time—" Nigel strode off, heading for the music library.

Behind him, Wolf sighed. "Well," the parrot said in resignation. "At least I won't have to make up any little tinkly tunes this time."

5

NINETTE sat up in the bed, curled her arms around her knees, and listened in astonishment to the cat. Thomas posed on the foot of the bed, looking precisely as if he had always belonged there. Somehow over the last few hours he had transformed without essentially changing, from the rakish alley-prowler to a creature of great elegance.

And he had been listening to her hosts while she had been sleeping, then come back to report to her what was transpiring. "They are planning the production around *me?* But—but—but they have not yet seen me dance!"

You have seen what passes for a dancer in these music halls, the cat said, with a touch of arrogance. *Did you not say yourself that you would make the best of them look like a pony doing tricks?*

"Well, yes, but—" But these girls weren't dancers, not really. Oh, they might have taken some lessons, but they clearly had not been trained as Ninette had been trained. Ballroom dancers with a few tricks and high kicks, and one or two of them could teeter about on their toes, but they were not trained dancers as she knew training.

And you know all of the applause-garnering turns, the passages that make people leap to their feet, yes?

Ninette considered that. Yes, she did. The thirty-two *fouette*-pirouettes from the Black Swan pas de deux, Kitri's exuberant solo, full of leaps where her heel touches the back of her head from *Don Quixote,* the mad scene from Giselle, the character solos from *Sleeping Beauty, Le Corsair, Swan Lake,* all of these things. She had rehearsed them over and over again, against the day when she might actually be called upon to dance them. These were the sorts of pieces that the great dancers dismissed as "tricks" or cursed the need to perform, but that audiences adored.

I very much doubt that they will have a choreographer as such. So you will be making up your own dances. I would advise you to make them as showy as possible and steal liberally from anyone you think audiences would like. Loie Fuller, for instance. The cat sniffed derisively. *By now so many have stolen from her that one more will not matter, and everyone loves seeing yards of fabric being tossed about under colored lights.*

And by now, everyone in the dance world knew how Fuller manipulated her lights and silks, despite her attempts to keep such thing secret. There was even a kind of name for it, the "serpentine dance," or "skirt dance" by which such things were advertised on playbills. That gave Ninette some ideas . . . the best thing she could do, if she was going to have a show built around her, would be to manage pieces that looked very impressive but involved short passages of flashy footwork interspersed with a great deal of stage effects. A skirt-dance would certainly fit that bill. Now, she had seen some Swiss and Finnish girls in France performing a kind of dancing-gymnastics with long ribbons, balls, hoops and clubs. She could certainly do a piece with a ribbon, and perhaps another with a hoop or a ball.

The rest she could certainly lift whole from the ballets she had learned. "If they are going to create a show around me—" she began eagerly.

Stop right there, the cat commanded, fixing her with his gaze. *You are doing precisely the wrong thing. You must not be the eager one. Think of La Augustine! Would she fling herself at someone who was creating a show around her? Of course not. She would be amused. Perhaps condescending—this is only music hall, after all. Then, perhaps, she would allow herself to be interested. She would let herself be coaxed and courted and only gradually would she be persuaded. Once persuaded, of course, she would fling herself into it. La Augustine is nothing if not a professional. But she would never give the impression that it was she who was the eager one.*

Ninette nodded, slowly. The cat was right, of course. As long as they believed she was what she said she was—and there was no reason not to—the coaxing should come from them. She shivered a little; this was heady stuff, and she was not at all sure she was going to be able to deal with it.

That is why you have me. The cat curled the tip of his tail around his feet and looked smug. *I shall be your impresario. I brought you this far, did I not?*

That was certainly true. And "this far" was impressive indeed. She thought about her last few hours since waking after a refreshing sleep. First there had been the long hot bath, attended by a maid who washed, dried, and put up her hair for her, before tucking her attentively back into bed. Now she looked about herself, at the opulently appointed guestroom, at finest bed she had ever seen, at the gorgeous embroidered and ribboned and laced nightdress that the maid had helped her into, at the remains of the wonderful breakfast on the tray beside the bed. Three kinds of eggs, ham, sausage, grilled tomatoes, beans, toast, oatmeal . . . enough for three people. She had left a great deal of it, though it troubled her to do so. She hoped it wouldn't go to waste.

"All right, then I should be—"

Distressed. Your imaginary friend with his mythical yacht is still missing. You must ask after him, first thing, any time anyone comes in here. I doubt very much that they will trouble you for a few days. When it is clear that "all is lost" you must be sorrowful. But not too sorrowful. You must not let them think this imaginary fellow was more that just a casual friend. Tell them you need to work to get your mind off it, and allow them to find you a rehearsal pianist and a studio space. Then work. They plan to ask you if you wish to stay here, in Blackpool. They mean here for now, although, trust me, in a very short time propriety will ensure they get you an apartment of your own. Say yes, immediately, and burst into tears and say that you are all alone in the world and how kind they are.

That wouldn't be difficult. They *were* kind and she *was* all alone except for the cat.

Eventually, about the same time that they will think you should be in your own establishment, they will broach the subject of working for them. I will be right with you; I will tell you what to say.

She frowned a little at that, because she rather thought she would not need the cat to put words in her mouth, but let it pass. So for right now, she should simply lie back and be pampered. That would not be bad. She thought fleetingly of her belongings at the boarding house, inventoried them in her mind, and reluctantly, decided they were not worth going back for. Though poor Madame would wonder what had become of her . . .

I will get your keepsakes, the cat promised. She nodded. That would do. There wasn't a great deal she
wanted; a little left of her mother's "jewelry" consisting
of a jet rosary, a jet bangle, and a silver locket, a few letters and her mother's marriage license.

*I can get those. Leave it to me. You will have to find a
place to hide them, though.*

That was easy enough; it would be even easier once
she had a private place of her own, but for now, thanks
to any number of overheard conversations and the plots
of any number of sensational operas and plays. "I will
ask for a Bible and paste the papers inside the cover,"
she said. The jewelry would probably escape notice. The
marriage license, however, would give her age away.
Fortunately dancers tended to look ageless so long as
they did not put on weight. She should be able to pass,
easily, for being ten years older than her real age. Old
enough to be the real Russian dancer.

"How did you manage to talk to these men?" she
asked, finally. "I thought you could only talk to me."

The cat grew tense. *That . . . is an excellent question.*

She waited, but the cat remained silent. "Well you
ought to answer it then," she said impatiently.

I am thinking. The cat washed an ear with one paw.
You believe in magic by now. Yes?

It was her turn to hesitate. Did she? Real magic, not
stage magic? The thing of fairy tales? How else could she
be talking to a cat?

"I . . . suppose . . ."

*The two gentlemen that "rescued" you are magicians.
That is why I can talk to them too. There is no need to go
into much detail, but talking cats are the least of the astonishing things in their world.*

She stared at the cat, who began washing his other
ear. "But I'm not a magician!" she protested. "Am I?"

True, you are not. But your father was. He . . . charged

me with taking care of you, you know. And some things, like being able to talk to magical creatures, come with the blood.

"But I never did before!" For some reason, she felt indignant, as if this sudden ability was an imposition. "Why is it that I have not been talking to magical creatures all my life?"

They would have had to be willing to show themselves and talk to you first. Could a cat smirk? It sounded like he was smirking. *They don't display themselves before just anyone. If you are a magician, you can coax or coerce them, but if all the power you have is to speak to them, they are likely to stay in hiding. Except for the ones you would not have wanted to see. Those, I kept away.*

That gave her pause, and she bit back the irritated retort about snobbery she had been about to deliver. "There are bad creatures?"

So bad, you would have spent all your life in terror.

In that case she certainly did not want to see them. "So these men are magicians?" She thought about that. The cat certainly had known, well in advance, what he was doing. He'd gotten her onto the ferry, across the Channel,. And across England to this specific town. "Did you plan for this all along?"

I have planned for this for months, among other plans. The cat hesitated a moment. *I have been planning for your future for most of your life. I had hoped you would become an etoile at the Paris Opera, but as that plan fell to pieces, this was my second. Clearly this one is riskier, resting as it does on deception, and my ability to cozen these magicians. If this had fallen to pieces, I had a third, and a fourth, although neither of those were as desirable, and they did not make as much use of your dancing. I am more familiar with Britain than I am with France, so when the first plan fell apart, it was here that we needed to come.*

"Did you come to France with my father?" she asked, now very interested.

In a sense. That is not important now. I am engaged in a deception with these men. It will not hold forever. I am certain that at some point they will learn the truth, but at that point you will be their great star and it will not matter. They are showmen, first and foremost; it is the show that matters. Do you take my meaning?

Ninette nodded. That was always true to a greater or lesser extent in the theater. The great stars were as much publicity and showmanship as talent, with the exception, maybe, of amazing talents like the Divine Sarah Bernhardt and Eleanor Duse. Even then . . . would they have been quite so acclaimed if they had not been so eccentric?

"Do I need to be eccentric?" she asked.

Hmm. A good question. Let me think about that. The cat hunched down over his forepaws, eyes half closed. *I think, eccentric in simplicity. Elegant simplicity, not all bare feet and scarves like Isadora. But we will have plenty of time to work on that. First, let me drill you on your mythical yacht-person.*

Needless to say, Ninette knew nothing about yachts. But she did know a great deal about the rich old men in fur coats who would be expected to own a yacht. Together she and Thomas concocted a plausible story for the apocryphal Nikolas. He could not be *too* rich, or one would expect a hue and cry about his missing state. He could not be titled either, for the same reason. So it was to be a very small yacht, something a bourgeoisie merchant would have bought to impress young dancers and singers. And Nikolas would have been Nina's friend, but not her *particular* friend. She would have been ready to accept favors, but not yet ready to let him into her bed.

Over the course of the day her two rescuers found many excuses to check on her progress. Soon, she was calling the two of them by their first names.

And the cat drilled her mercilessly on her story in between times. So when they finally asked her questions, she was able to weep and cry, "Poor Nikolas! Poor old man!" in a way that left no doubt in the minds of her benefactors that she had very little emotional investment in "Nikolas," and that in all probability he had offered this trip in order to impress her enough that she would take him as her protector.

This cheered both of them up immensely, even as they tried to comfort the weeping "Nina." This was understandable; a dead lover was a terrible complication, but she would probably be able to put Nikolas behind her in fairly short order if he was only a "friend" from whom she had perhaps accepted a few gifts.

In the late afternoon someone from the Royal Lifeboat Service arrived, resplendent in a uniform, to talk to her about the sinking. She almost panicked, but the cat soothed her, and quietly coached her on what to say. As she sat between her two benefactors, wrapped in an elegant dressing gown, the officer remained standing, looking acutely uncomfortable.

It was not difficult at all to seem upset, because she was upset, but her visible efforts to calm herself seemed to earn her some respect from the Lifesaving Officer.

"We are trying to learn where the ship might have gone down, miss," the officer said in English.

She blinked at him. "My Eenglish, not so good," she said, and gestured to him gracefully. *"Parlez-vous francais?"*

"I do," Arthur spoke up, and turned to the officer. "I'll be translating; sir, it's not uncommon for Russians artists to know French, but not English."

The officer grumbled a little about "foreigners," but nodded. "All right then, how many were on this yacht?"

"Myself, and Nikolas, and five others," she said carefully, coached by the cat. "It was a motor yacht. Two of the men took it in turns to steer it. There was one man who was Nikolas' servant, and the other two did things, took care of the pretty boat, cooked, cleaned. Nikolas had just bought this yacht, and he did not know much about these things, I could tell, but he pretended that he did. I wanted to go to London, but he said, no, no, we must sail all around England that you can see all of it and then decide."

The officer groaned. "Gentleman yachtsmen. Does she have any idea if he registered at any ports?"

When Arthur translated, she shook her head.

"Probably not then." The officer sighed. "The name of this vessel then?"

"*Yvgenia*," she replied promptly. "Nikolas was alone in the world," she added, as the cat prompted her. "He did something with speculation . . ." She shrugged. "I never could understand it. He laughed and said that Yvgenia was the name of his mother, who was always happy to see him leave."

"And how is it that the young lady came to shore?" Now that was a dangerous question and one that Ninette had been hoping would not be asked. She would have to tread very carefully here—

Drop your head, the cat ordered. *Don't look them in the eyes and speak very slowly. You don't remember a great deal.*

She repeated that verbatim in a hesitant voice.

The storm came up suddenly, the cat continued. *You were asleep. One of the crew came to wake you, and tell you to get dressed. You had never been on a boat before and you were afraid of the violence of the storm. You tried to make your way to the deck, when there was a great crash and you were thrown into the water. Fortunately you are a strong swimmer, but you could see noth-*

ing in the storm. You found a plank to cling to for a while, and you thought you saw lights and began to swim towards them. You were determined to live and that was all you could think of. You remember crawling onto the sand, and that is all.

"She must have wrecked just off the North Pier," the officer said, and shook his head. "Though why we weren't alerted—"

"A yacht that small? In a storm like that? With an inexperienced owner?" Arthur exclaimed. "The Lifeboat Service is hardly to blame, sir. No telling if she was even storm-worthy."

"Well that does account for some flotsam that came ashore," the officer muttered.

"Really, I cannot imagine anyone holding the Lifeboat Service to account for this. You'll have to notify the Russian Ambassador of course." Nigel nodded sagely. "Miss, do you remember the names of the crew?"

"Nikolas Petrov Vladisky," murmured Ninette, as the cat dictated. "One pilot was Sasha, I do not know his last name. The other was Ivan Bolodenka. Nikolas's man's name was Borya Fedorovich. I never knew what the rest were called except their first names, Dimitri and Yuri."

Now cry, the cat ordered. She was so nervous about being found out that it wasn't at all hard to do as he ordered and start to sob.

Alarmed, the officer patted her hand clumsily. "There, there, now, miss, you're a good, brave girl. I'll let the embassy know these people were lost."

She looked up, impulsively, and he flinched.

"Let the maid take you back to bed," Nigel said, beckoning the servant over. She waved the maid away; the girl curtsied and left the room. "No, I shall be all right. Is there any sign of—" She looked up again at the Lifesaving Officer, and he winced.

"Tell her that we probably can't hold out any hope at this point," the officer said. "If they wrecked off the North Pier, we probably won't even find bodies; they'll be taken out to sea by the tide and turn up in Ireland, if at all."

Arthur translated the first part of that, but not the last. She dropped her eyes.

"Thank you, miss," the officer said ponderously. "*Merci, mademoiselle.*" He coughed. "I'll be on my way, then. I doubt very much I will need to trouble the young lady any more, she's been most helpful."

"You expect to hear anything from the Russians?" Nigel asked in a low voice.

The officer shook his head. "One bourgeois speculator, related to no one, and a handful of sailors who might or might not have been no better than they should be? Probably not. And this young lady might be a good dancer, but I misdoubt anyone from the Embassy will care unless she was the Empress's particular pet. I'm afraid you'll have her on your hands unless you find someone else to hand her off to."

"Hand off my golden goose? Not likely." Nigel winked, as the cat curled up around Ninette's feet and purred. "I'll show you out, then, sir. Care for a brandy against the cold?"

"Shouldn't drink on duty—"

"Nonsense, it's medicinal—" The two left the room as Ninette wiped her eyes with a handkerchief.

As soon as they were out of earshot, though, she turned to Arthur, holding tightly to the scrap of cloth and lace. "And how is it," she demanded in French, "that you can hear my cat?"

"HA! I warned you!" came a third voice, one she thought she remembered from the auto, although she jumped when she heard it. "Didn't I warn you? I told you she would be a clever little thing, all the dancers I ever knew were!"

"Yes, Wolf, you told us," Arthur said with resignation.

"Who *is* that?" Ninette asked, heart still in her mouth, looking back over her shoulder and seeing nothing but a parrot in a cage, sitting on a swing.

Then the parrot reached over to the bars of the cage, and to her astonishment, unlatched the door and flew over to the back of the couch. "I am Wolfgang Amadeus, who for my sins has found himself stuck in the body of a bird," the parrot said mournfully. "It probably has something to do with *The Magic Flute.* I was warned not to write a Masonic opera. I, who once visited the courts of Europe and wrote music for Emperors, am now reduced to sitting in a cage, begging for green peas, and writing tinkly little melodies for music hall performances." He sighed, and tilted his head down, eyeing Thomas evilly. "And don't get any clever notions, cat. You might be an Elemental Creature, but my beak can still make an impression on your nose."

I wouldn't dream of it, the cat said with immense dignity. *Just what do you take me for?*

"Hungry," said the parrot, and fluffed out all his feathers. Ninette stared at him, and then looked at Arthur.

"Is he really—?"

Arthur shrugged. "He's my Elemental Familiar, so only heaven knows. I'm only a magician, not a Master, so I can't tell these things."

"Even the Master cannot tell if Wolf is telling the truth or making up grand tales," said Nigel, returning to the room. "All I can say is that those 'tinkly little melodies' he hates are quite popular, so I say it doesn't matter. But you, my dear, are not a mage yourself—"

But her father was, and he left me in charge of her, the

cat replied. Tartly. Ninette eyed him in surprise. *I told you that already. Really, if you are going to make me repeat things . . .*

"I beg your pardon, *Monsieur Chat,* most heartily," Nigel said with a bow. "Well, I expect we'll have to look out for you now, Miss Tchereslavsky, since those of us Elemental magicians that actually get along without fighting each other tend to be a close-knit group here in Britain."

"Mind, there are far more who *don't* get along than those who do, idiot lot that they are," the parrot added sardonically. "Imagine! There are a goodly number that refuse to even speak with me just because I'm a bird!"

Intolerable, the cat drawled. *The Philistines!*

Wolf glared at him.

"I am afraid I have nothing," Ninette said, looking down at her hands. "All my fortune was in my jewels, and those are at the bottom of the sea."

"Don't worry about that for now," Nigel replied, leaning down to pat her hand. "You just think about getting your strength back so you can dance. You'll soon be on your feet again once that happens. And I'm sure we can find a way to make that happen. Right, fellows?"

He winked at her, but she didn't miss the glance that passed between him and Arthur. She glanced down at the cat, who looked as smug as, well, he deserved to be.

What did I tell you? the cat asked. *Just do as I say, and you'll be so successful that La Augustine will read about you in the papers and envy you!*

6

THERE was something comforting and universal about a rehearsal room.

Always the same. Broad expanses of glass on two walls—windows on one, mirrors on the opposite. Practice *barre* stretching out along the mirrored wall. Piano in one corner. Dust always hanging in the air, rosin dust, and dust shaken out of cracks in the wooden floor by the pounding of countless feet. Depending on the time of day, and whether or not it was raining again, sunlight might or not be streaming in through the window, filled with that dust, which would then sparkle like fairy dust.

Rehearsal pianists were always thin, always earnest, always homely, usually bespectacled. They always wore dusty black. This one was thin, earnest, homely, bespectacled, and female, her hair put up in a tight little arrangement of braids wrapped around her angular head. She also spoke French, an asset.

For the first time in her life, Ninette had a rehearsal room to herself. For the first time in her life, she was not being put through her drills by an instructor or a ballet master. She had to remember it all herself.

She punctuated her requests for tempi with *s'il vous plais* and *merci*. After all, rehearsal pianists might utterly forgettable and generally ignored as a kind of extension of the piano itself, but they were still human beings. But in between the *please* and *thank you* she concentrated on getting her body back into something capable of a performance.

Despite all the exercise of walking she had done, she had not been doing any dancing since she had left France, and her muscles told her so. Everything had to be taken slowly. Each group of muscles must be warmed up, stretched, and tested. Then the entire body had to go through the same procedure. Only then was she prepared to try a solo, and a not very demanding one, either.

She wished she had a partner. She wondered what the odds were of finding one.

"*La Sylphide,* first solo, *merci,*" she said, and proceeded to work through that first piece, where the mischievous Sylph first invades James' home and finds him sleeping in front of the fire. She interrupted herself often, asking the patient pianist to repeat a phrase, drilling herself mercilessly until her forgetful body got it right again. Oddly enough, there was peace in this. She might have been in Paris; this might have been what she would have been doing had she been lifted to *etoile* status. Outside this room there were talking cats and men who claimed they were magicians, a stolen name, a life that was not hers, and a fabrication she had to maintain. In here, there was only the music, the relentless tyranny of the choreography, and the discipline of shaping a reluctant body into the graceful movements of the dance, without pause, without faltering.

How strange that the one thing that she had thought

she would like to escape was the thing she now fled to
for comfort.

"Nigel."

Nigel looked up from his desk. This was the first day
since they had rescued Nina that he had spent a normal
morning, and there was a lot of work piled up at his
desk here at the Imperial Music Hall. None of it was an
emergency, or someone would have made sure a messenger got to him at his flat, but it took up all of his
morning and looked as if it was going to stretch well
into the afternoon.

He'd gotten so deep into it that he had lost all track
of time until that familiar voice at his door took him out
of his trance of work as he dealt with letters from booking agents, descriptions of acts, complaints from the
stagehands, requests for materials . . .

He looked up, and blinked at Arthur. "Band-call over
already?"

"Yes, and you should get some luncheon inside you,"
the parrot said from his perch on Arthur's shoulder.
"We've made arrangements for Miss Tchereslavsky. We
checked around at the performers' lodgings and found
a full flat open over at Breckenridge's."

Nigel brightened up at that. Alfie Breckenridge owed
him a favor, and a big one. Nigel had loaned him the col-
lateral to buy the set of lodgings in the first place, when
Alfie had retired from the stage. His wife Sarah was a
sharp one, and they wouldn't *give* him the flat, but—

"What's the terms?" he asked.

"They'll let her have it—knowing it's you that's paying for it for now—at a quarter the going rate until the
show is in production and she can pay for it herself."
Arthur looked understandably pleased at that. "Alfie
told me it's too dear for most of our performers anyway,

and it went vacant half the time, so he won't be losing
that much by it. He was thinking of cutting it up into
rooms, but if our scheme works, Nina will be there in
permanent residence. Care to walk over and cast an eye
on it after we eat?"

"Anything to get from behind this desk." Nigel grate-
fully cleaned his pen and pushed his chair away. Arthur
tucked Wolf away inside his coat with the parrot's head
sticking out under his chin, and off they went.

"You should get a secretary to take care of that,"
Arthur observed, as they left the building via the stage
door, turned up their collars against the drizzle, and
headed in the direction of the Dial, which was the name
of the Imperial Music Hall version of the pub that
sprang up in the vicinity of every theater Nigel had
ever seen. Not for the benefit of theater patrons, no.
For the benefit of the entertainers. It generally would
take a great deal of effort on the part of a casual the-
atergoer to find these pubs, tucked in as they were in
backstreet corners, generally behind the theaters themselves.

And always no more than a few yards from the stage
door. They pushed open the doors to a place that had
not significantly changed in decades, except for electric
lighting instead of gas. A fire burned on the hearth, and
the air smelled of tobacco smoke, woodsmoke and
bacon. Wolf popped out of Arthur's coat and took his
usual place on Arthur's shoulder.

Yellowing playbills and fading autographed photos
adorned the walls of pubs such as this. The bill of fare
was plain, cheap, and always available. It was clean, but
it had seen better days . . . probably its better days had
been about a century ago. It was generally run by someone who had once been in the theatrical trade himself—
seldom long enough to have garnered a name of his
own, but long enough to have gotten a fair notion of

what players and acts and musicians needed—or would put up with.

In the case of the Dial, the proprietor was a benevolent sort. The food was decent, the service prompt, the prices reasonable, and people tended to look the other way if your trained animal came in with you as long as it was well-behaved. Champagne was available, something you didn't find in many pubs, because theatrical folks had a taste for it.

The place was full, since morning band-call was over and everyone that didn't have another place to go had crowded in here to get a bite between band-call and afternoon rehearsal. Most of the people in here were the stagehands, who greeted Nigel, Arthur and Wolf with genial respect. Wolf generally took care to act like a bird around them, and confined himself only to the very occasional clever comment audible to the room. Nigel knew that Arthur's companion had an ongoing prank though; at quiet moments the bird would lean down and mutter something in Arthur's ear to try and get him to laugh.

Not today, though. There was only so much time until the early afternoon rehearsals started; Arthur was needed there and Nigel liked to watch the acts for signs of trouble. Performers were kittle cattle; some were reliable, stable, and would go on until they dropped, giving one solid performance after another. But most weren't. There was always the ongoing curse of the showman to contend with; the life of a performer, gypsy-like as it was, was not a good one for making and keeping friends or lovers. Performers' egos being what they were . . .

And then there was that ongoing curse of the showman, the bottle. Performers being performers, none of this would show when the time came for the curtain to go up. But cracks would appear at afternoon rehearsals, particularly if they weren't going well. Nigel liked to slip into the back of a box—never the same twice—and watch. Especially now, when he had his prize, his leading lady, for this new kind of music hall idea. Now he wanted to get a solid lot of acts to fit into this show, and he needed to know he would be able to depend on them for most of a year. That meant no missed performances for being drunk, no replacement of partners for infidelity, no screaming fights backstage, no trouble. They would have to comport themselves like the big theatrical and operatic companies did in Europe, where everyone was permanent, you knew who the stars were, and everyone had to get along, at least marginally. Music hall performers were hard workers, but they weren't used to that.

Nigel and Arthur ate quickly, but quietly, with Wolf helping himself to what he liked off both their plates. Most of the stagehands were finishing up just as they did, and there was a little awkwardness at the door, quickly settled as Arthur stepped aside so Wolf could climb back into his coat.

Like most music halls—except, perhaps, in London—this one was also surrounded by buildings given over to theatrical lodgings. These were, as might be expected, of variable quality. Some were actual boarding houses, where the lodgers could expect at least two and sometimes three meals along with their room. Some provided little more than a cheerless, shabby furnished room. Some had actual flats that included rudimentary kitchens. The one thing they all had in common was that the landlords expected the tenants to be there for no less than the week of their engagement, but not much more, and anticipated they would have nothing more with them than would fit in a suitcase and prop-trunk.

Alfie Breckenridge was unusual in that he and his wife had both been in the theater before retiring to run a theatrical lodging. Most of the house was a classical boarding-house. Sarah kept a good table and their rooms were always full. Breckenridge was able to pick and choose his lodgers, and as a consequence, there were usually no unpleasant folks in his house.

Two houses, really; he and Sarah had done so well they had purchased the building next to theirs, put in a passage between them, and converted the second from flats to suites of two and three rooms.

Arthur rang the bell of the first house; Alfie must have been expecting them, since the door flew open, and it was Alfie himself standing there rather than the maid. "Gents! Glad you could make it before rehearsals started! Nige, Sarah's been asking after you, wonderin' when you were comin' for a good dinner. She don't half fret about that cook of yours."

"She's the one who recommended Mrs. Graves, you know," Nigel said with a grin. "Surely she doesn't think so poorly of her own judgment."

"Oh you know, Sarah, always second-guessing herself." Alfie chuckled. "Made her a good partner for my comic-patter though. Well, right, let's show you these rooms an' we'll see if you think they're good enough for your bally-dancer wench."

He led the way through the communal sitting-room to the passage that had been cut in the wall between the two houses. "When we got the place, I had the notion I wanted to set things up for them as wanted a bit more privacy and a bit more space. House was four flats, I sectioned it up into bed-sitters with one or two bedrooms, so people that had an act with family could lodge together and couples—" here Alfie winked, and Nigel smiled, since he knew Alfie was not in the least concerned if the "couples" in question were married or not "—could have a bit more privacy. But we left the flat at the top alone, thinkin' mebbe we could let it out

to them as stay longer than just a week or so." He
shook his head, leading the way up the stairs. "Happen
you didn't book a lot of those, and it's a bit of a journey
from here to, say, the Opera House. I was just about to
call in the carpenters and give the orders to cut it up
too, when Arthur rang me up. And here we are!"

He stopped at the top landing, took out a key with a
flourish, and opened the door.

Nigel stepped inside and looked around. He nodded
with approval. The rose-papered sitting room had
clearly been furnished by a woman, Sarah probably.
Light, airy, and comfortable. Plain, but good furniture
upholstered in dark rose. Small fireplace with a wooden
mantel, and a mirror over the mantelpiece. Electric
lighting, which was far safer than gas. Not as ostenta-
tious as his own flat, but he *was,* after all, the theater
owner. "Let's see the rest of it."

"Got a small kitchen here, bit of a pantry, but Sarah
an' me are figuring your gel will want us to cater her,"
Alfie explained, throwing up the door on a doll's
kitchen, with a tiny stove and oven. "This's enough for
her maid to cook her up an egg and a bit of toast and the
like, or keep dinner warm in the oven for her. That's
what everyone else in this flat has done, sent down to us
for real meals and all. Some of them even come down to
eat around the big table with the rest." He opened the
next door. "This'd be the maid's room, I reckon. Last
person that let the place was a family act, they had their
daughter in here."

A small, neat, plain white bedroom with a thick blue
coverlet and blanket on the bed, blue china washbasin
and pitcher on the stand, with a blue-curtained window
looking out on the backyard seemed adequate enough
to Nigel. It didn't have a fire, but maids' rooms seldom
did, and it did share the wall with the kitchen, which
should keep it warm enough.

And then he got a glimpse of something, out of the corner of his eye. A small, clever-faced little gnome with a kindly sparkle to his eyes.

An Earth-Elemental, one of the benevolent ones. A brownie. Interesting. Had it been here all along, or had it come in response to the movement through the invisible workings of the Elementals themselves who said Nina was coming here?

He would have liked to question the creature, but obviously he couldn't, not with Alfie there. It saw him looking at it, gave him a saucy wink, and vanished.

Pity. As an Air Master he couldn't actually call the Earth creatures; they would only talk to him if they felt like it.

"An' here'd be the gel's little nest," Alfie said, opening the final door. Again, it was an airy, bright room, this time with a big four-post bed of the old fashioned sort with curtains around it. Not a bad thing, when the winter winds came roaring off the sea, and to drive off the damp from the ubiquitous rain. There was a good fireplace here, and it was as clean and neat as anyone could want. Walls papered in cream, rose, and brown, coverlets, curtains, and furnishings to match. The room was warm without feeling stuffy. "Nice little dressing-room and bath through there," Alfie continued, pointing at a door in the far wall. "Hot water up from a boiler in the basement, modern as you please. Maid can use the bath on the second floor, or this one if her mistress ain't particular. Even put a telephone in. Reckon this'll suit?"

"If she's got any sense, she'll think she's in cream, Alfie," Nigel replied with satisfaction. They concluded the bargain, Nigel sealed it with the first month's rent, and he and Arthur and Wolf headed back to the theater. The street was quieter now, people settling back into their businesses after the rush about for lunch.

"Nigel," Wolf said, with uncharacteristic seriousness,

as they made their way on foot through the back streets, "I have a concern."

Nigel glanced down at the little gray head peering out from Arthur's coat. "Then I would like to hear it."

"Do either of you have any attraction to this girl? Are you likely to?" Wolf's shiny black eyes looked at him piercingly. "You know very well she is quite likely to have some sort of attraction to you, one or both, if only the attraction of a young woman to a man of means. She's in shock *now,* but when she gets over it, she does not strike me as the sort to go without a gentleman for very long."

Nigel laughed. "She'll have plenty of those—"

"You *know* what I mean," Wolf said severely. Arthur sighed.

"The bird has a good point, Nigel," he said reluctantly. "We rescued her, after all. That tends to make a young lady look at you in a different sort of way. It could be a complication unless we are careful about how we treat her."

"Hmm. Then the sooner we get her established in her own rooms, the better." Nigel found the dancer attractive enough, and had she been anyone other than one of his performers, he would have had no qualms about pursuing whatever seemed appropriate ...

But she was one of his performers, and he had always had a strict rule for himself about that. That is, his female performers were not under any circumstances to be socialized with in *that* way. Invite them to parties, yes. Have them at dinners, yes. But only in a party with other performers and nothing outside of the same sort of thing that he would offer to his male performers. It was just too much of a risk. He'd seen this happen to owners in the past; let a star performer become something more, and the next thing you knew, they thought they could dictate the running of the theater to you. He was going to showcase this girl as his star turn. He was *not* going to allow her to turn it into "her" theater.

Wolf made the sound of a sigh of relief. "Good. As long as you keep that in mind."

"Oh, I will," Nigel said fervently. "Business and pleasure shouldn't be mixed. Ever." Besides the other considerations, the last thing he needed or wanted was an entanglement at a time when he wanted to have the upper hand in negotiating with this young woman.

He would give her a fair offer, but he was not about to treat her on the level of someone who could fill entire concert halls just on the basis of their name on a playbill. She was an unknown here. To an extent he could use her European reputation, but English audiences would make up their own minds about her. And he could certainly use the romantic circumstances of her shipwreck. But none of these things were going to compensate for an outrageous salary, especially not in the beginning. He was taking a risk, and he knew it, on this new sort of musical performance. What worked so brilliantly in America might not work here.

By this time they had reached the Music Hall, and Nigel made up his mind at that moment that he was going to do something a bit different today. "You and Wolf keep an eye on the rehearsals, would you please?"

"You have something in mind?" asked Arthur.

Nigel nodded. "I think it's time that I talked to Jonathon Hightower."

"Kung Chow?" Arthur nodded. "The plot I have outlined for this production makes very heavy use of him. I can't think of a stage magician better suited to this."

"Just as long as he doesn't want me in his act," Wolf added, with a shudder. "Really, I don't like bird acts at all. Filthy things, and no conversation. Now, Jonathon, however . . . he is excellent company. Good taste in music too."

Nigel repressed a smile. Wolf would think that; Jonathon was a great aficionado of Mozart.

"I can't think of an Elemental Mage I would rather have here," Nigel responded, thoughtfully. "Something just occurred to me, you see. What if that storm and the yacht sinking weren't an accident?"

Arthur paused just outside the Stage Door, and two heads, his and Wolf's, swiveled to look at Nigel. "You think someone was trying to stop her from coming here?"

"Or merely was getting revenge on her father," Nigel replied, and opened the door for them. "He created that cat as a guardian for her. You would assume he had a reason to think she would need one."

Arthur let Wolf out of his coat. The parrot clambered up to his shoulder. "In that case, there might be more such attacks," Wolf pointed out, as Arthur nodded agreement.

The three of them paused for a moment in the area just past the backstage porter, where the mail was left for performers. There was no one here at the moment, although the sounds of the orchestra warming up for rehearsal were just beginning, and from one of the practice studios came the sound of a piano.

"If the sinking wasn't an accident, yes. I want Jonathon here. There is nothing like a Fire Master to discourage meddlers." Nigel shrugged. "I could be alarmist. But I had rather not find out that I wasn't when the scenery collapses atop someone. Or a rope snaps and a sandbag breaks our star dancer's neck."

Arthur shuddered. "Touch wood that you are being alarmist. But Jonathon can certainly tell us. I think it is probably time for you to find him the fastest way possible."

Nigel grinned. "I was hoping you'd say that."

Nigel locked the door to his office—another reason not to have a secretary—and flexed his fingers. The "fastest way possible" was very fast indeed for an Elemental Master. Whereas an ordinary theater manager would have to rely on a call to Hightower's booking agent, and then a telegram to whatever theater the magician was playing at, Nigel could be a great deal more direct.

He opened the eastern window to his office, rolled back the Persian rug laid over the carpet, and exposed the very special design woven into the flatter carpet beneath.

It was an Invocation Circle, for Air, specifically. Every Elemental Master had his own way of calling his Elementals; Nigel just happened to have one that was uniquely suited to his profession, and the reason why he and Arthur had met in the first place.

In fact, it was probably the reason why the Grey Parrot that claimed he was the incarnation of Wolfgang Amadeus Mozart had flown in this same window ten years ago.

From a locked drawer in his desk, Nigel removed a glass flute.

From the time he was a boy, Nigel had used music to call and communicate with his Elementals. The patterns of the notes just seemed to fit the patterning of the magic. He was not a brilliant musician, not in the way that Arthur was; Arthur could play virtually ever instrument in the orchestra, and do it well enough to fill in any vacant position if he had to. Nigel had never been good enough to pretend to being a professional musician, but he was more than good enough to master something like the flute. For a long time he'd used a metal instrument, but that hadn't quite gotten the effect he had wanted. Finally, on a whim, he had asked a glassblower to make him a glass flute, and the results had been everything he could have hoped for.

Even better had been when Wolf had arrived in their midst. The parrot had volunteered to write little melodies for virtually every summoning purpose that the three of them had been able to think of.

This time, when he raised the flute to his lips and felt the first stirrings of his magic in the tingling of his fingers, he began the melody that Wolf called "The Messenger."

The first soft, breathy notes broke the silence of the office. He felt power swirl around him in a cool, crisp whirlwind of pale blue energies. He hadn't played more than three bars when the curtains billowed inward, and the transparent, laughing face of a sexless child winked at him once from the zephyr that circled him, riding the waves of power.

With a smile he put down the flute, and the elemental spun into shape, a fluttering, translucent bird-child with big eyes and a knowing smile. It waited for his request.

"Please go to Jonathon Hightower," Nigel told it, giving it, as he spoke, the kind of mental "signature" of the Fire Master. "Tell him that I want to speak with him immediately."

And to reward it, he reached for the energies of the air and conjured up a sparkling, dancing, animated spark, a kind of elemental toy that would last as long as the Elemental he gave it to had interest in it. With a crow of delight, the creature seized the offering, and with a shake of wings, sped off through the window, and out into the sun.

Nigel closed the window, rolled his rug back and went back to his desk. Nothing now but to wait, so he might as well get some work done while he did.

7

NIGEL had not gotten a reply by the time the curtain rose on the first performance, and by the time the curtain fell on the last act, he was alternating between concern and irritation. After all, Masters never used Elementals as messengers frivolously, and Hightower of all people ought to know that if Nigel had done so it meant there was some urgency to the request.

Wolf, who was always backstage during performances, flew down from his perch in the flies and landed on Nigel's shoulder as the latter cursed the Fire Master mentally.

"There could be a dozen reasons why Hightower hasn't contacted you, Nigel," the bird said quietly into his ear. "Chief of which is that he is a performer, with his own act to rehearse and perform. Unlike you, he does not have the luxury of a private office in which to conduct rites."

"There's nothing out of the ordinary about sending a telegram," Nigel replied, with irritation. "Nothing that difficult. Step around the corner to the post office and—"

"But why should I do that, when I can come here in person?" said Jonathon Hightower, stepping around a gaggle of little chorus dancers. He grinned, and they tittered nervously; Jonathon looked very much like a caricature of Satan, minus the horns, and he played on the resemblance by cultivating a slim moustache and goatee, and wearing a scarlet-lined black evening cape and top hat whenever possible.

Amazingly this seemingly Satanic appearance translated seamlessly into his stage persona of the mysterious Chinese magician, Kung Chow. Very few people outside the theatrical world connected the flamboyant Hightower with the secretive Kung Chow, and that was the way Hightower liked it.

"Jonathon, you *wretch*—" Nigel exclaimed.

Hightower laughed. "Now how could I resist coming here myself, after all the newspaper stories about the beautiful Russian dancer you rescued from the briny deep?" He lifted an eyebrow significantly. "Had to come see her for myself, don't you know."

Nigel looked at him with exasperation. "Come back to the flat with me, and you can meet her yourself."

"Oh, really?" Jonathon grinned. Nigel gritted his teeth.

"Obviously she had nowhere else to go, Jonathon," he said. "She'll be moving into her own establishment shortly."

Jonathon kept grinning as Nigel passed Wolf over to Arthur and made his round of the backstage before leading him out the stage door. But once outside and away from anyone likely to overhear them, he rounded on his friend.

"First of all, there is nothing going on with that young woman," he said fiercely, as they walked to where he had left his auto parked, moving from patch of gaslight to patch of gaslight. "I have a new sort of musical theater I am planning, I intend to make her the central figure in it, and the last thing in the world I am ever going to do is mix my personal pleasures with the business of my theater!"

Jonathon sobered immediately. "Look, old man, I—"

"And secondly," Nigel went on, without losing a bit of his heat, "The girl is one of *us*, or at least her father was. Enough of a mage that he was able to create a protector for her. What else was I to do but take her in? For heaven's sake, it was her cat that summoned us to aid her!"

By that point, they had reached the auto; Jonathon got in, silently, and remained quiet while Nigel went through the complicated little ritual that the auto demanded to get it started. Only when they were well down the street did he speak again.

"Well, I feel a right fool."

"You should," Nigel snapped. "Now the reasons I asked you to contact me in the first place are part of all that. I want to engage you for a full year at the least, and I want to make you the other star attraction of this production. Now here is what I have in mind—"

He explained his plans for the new sort of musical theater as the auto chugged down the street. Jonathon said nothing, only nodded from time to time, but Nigel could tell that he was interested.

"Well," Jonathon said, as Nigel pulled his auto into the carriage house that now served it as its garage, "I'm equally torn by two questions, one mundane, the other arcane. The mundane one is rather simple; would you rather cast me as the villain of the piece, or sympathetic?"

"Well, I suppose that would depend on how sophisticated we think the audience will be, wouldn't it?" Nigel closed up and prudently locked the carriage house doors. That was the grand thing about having an auto; no horse to feed or stalls to clean out. One could talk all one wanted about the romance of horseflesh, but the amount of cleaning up and caring for—he had far rather pay the mechanic once in a while to fix the motorcar than keep a stableman day in, day out.

"If we thought they would be capable of it, we could write something that casts you as the villain but redeems you in the end," Nigel suggested, as they made their way into the foyer of the building, brightly lit in the newest fashion with fine electric fixtures. "Say . . . your character has a change of heart and helps the girl escape, staying to face the wrath of the sultan?" Nigel's flat was on the third floor of this rather posh establishment, reached by a modern, brass-caged elevator, although stairs were available. It was self-operated, although the owners of the other two flats in the building generally had their servants do the operating.

"I must say, I like that idea," Jonathon mused, as they both strolled into the anteroom of Nigel's flat, to be met by a servant who took their coats. "By the way, I took the liberty of sending my things here . . ."

"I *do* have more than one guest room, you know," Nigel pointed out. He turned to his manservant, who was bringing drinks for both of them, knowing, as he did, what Jonathon's preference was. "Asher, I am perishing. Could something be arranged?"

"I anticipated your requirement, sir, and took the liberty of having a late supper prepared for you and Mr. Hightower." The manservant nodded in the direction of the dining room, and Nigel and his guest lost no time in settling themselves in there.

Discussion of plots continued over the Welsh rarebit, eggs, bacon, crumpets and broiled tomatoes, Nigel secretly gloating the entire time. For all that Jonathon could be an irritating fellow, he was also entertaining and the best illusionist that Nigel had ever seen. And he had a good sense of storytelling. All his suggestions were sound ones.

"Am I missing something, or have you neglected to cast a romantic male lead in this venture?" Jonathon asked, as they moved their discussion and their whiskeys back into the library, where they each took one of the comfortable Windsor chairs.

"You are not missing anything; I haven't. I am not sure that I want to." Nigel tapped the side of his glass thoughtfully. "There is the inevitable problem of finding a dancing partner for her if we do. How many male dancers do you know that are in variety that were trained in ballet?"

Jonathon shook his head.

"Whereas if she doesn't have a male romantic lead as such, we can just have some of the fellows do the lifts, and maybe assist in her turns. Lads trained in the usual sort of stage dance can do that," Nigel pointed out.

Jonathon laughed. "*I* can do that," he replied.

"Well, then, I'm not at all sure we need a romantic lead for her. Might be more interesting if your magician character starts out being a villain, and then gets won over and sacrifices himself so she can get away." He pondered. "Or at least it looks that way. You've always wanted to do a spectacular escape trick; how about if the Sultan takes the magician prisoner and he makes a showy escape?"

Jonathon got a wicked gleam in his eye. "Can I make the palace collapse on the Sultan and all his evil minions? Or set it on fire?"

"If you can do it under budget." That was Arthur, being shown in by the manservant, a whiskey already in his hand.

"I'll set it on fire. That will sell a lot of tickets," Jonathon decided. "Besides leaving the ambiguity that maybe the magician was secretly something like

Mephistopheles all along, and sent to bring his master the soul of the Sultan."

"Good idea!" Wolf exclaimed from Arthur's shoulder. "Makes the whole thing less sticky-sweet. I could even write music for that—"

"No arias!" All three of the humans exclaimed at once. Wolf fluffed his feathers in indignation.

"All right, that takes care of that. I think we have a pretty strong book for this, and once we know what acts we'll be putting into it, and how often our star can perform over the course of it, we'll know exactly what music we need." Nigel tossed back the last of his drink and refilled it from the decanter himself. "Now, as for the other reason why you in particular are here, Jonathon, let me tell you what we know about the young lady."

"And her cat," Wolf added sourly. "Let's not forget the cat. *He* certainly won't let you."

"Cat?" Jonathon looked at them all quizzically.

"Let me start at the beginning," Nigel replied with a laugh, and did so.

When he was done, Jonathon was unexpectedly silent. After waiting for some sort of reaction, and getting nothing, Nigel finally asked, "What are you thinking?"

"That it is certainly interesting. I'm not at all familiar with the Russian Masters. Actually, I don't think much of anyone is; we have a lot of contact with the French and Italian ones, a little less with the Spanish, but . . ." He shrugged. "It does sound as if her father must have come to an untimely end, probably at the hands of another Master. And if he left such a guardian for his daughter, that suggests he expected whoever his enemy was would come after her as well."

"It wouldn't be the first time," Arthur said quietly. Both Nigel and Jonathon grimaced a little. Arthur's grandfather had run afoul of a bad-tempered Scottish

Master, who had pursued not only the old man, but the man's son and grandson. It was only at the death of the Scottish magician that the persecution had ceased.

"Russians are notorious for temper." Jonathon tossed back his own drink. "On the other hand, I am not exactly weak. And Fire magic is rather well suited to combat. Unlike Air, and no slur intended, Nigel."

"No offense taken. Air is the weakest, offensively and defensively. But when it comes to gaining information—" He shrugged. "Short of finding a way to live without breathing, you can't shut Air Elementals out."

"Well, don't underestimate your ability to add to my power. Air feeds Fire and never forget it." Jonathon set his glass down and steepled his fingers together. "Whatever might come after this young woman, I think we will be prepared for it."

"And that is *exactly* why I wanted you here," Nigel said with satisfaction. Well, there it was. The tacit agreement to make all of this a reality, and to protect Nina from whatever it was that threatened her. If Jonathon had not actually come out and said he was going to help out with this enterprise, it was certainly written between the lines. And he would not *say*, not yet, for a magician's words were binding. He wanted to be sure, and Nigel could hardly blame him.

"But I want to meet her before I make any decisions," Jonathon continued, and measured Nigel with a stern look. "No offense, Nigel, but your weakness has always been a damsel in distress. I'm not so easily gulled, and my stock-in-trade is illusion. I want to see her *and* this cat of hers. I want your promise that you will hold by my decision as well. Do I have it?"

Nigel shrugged. He knew Jonathon was right, and although he liked Nina Tchereslavsky quite a bit, well ... he had to face the fact that if she was pulling some sort of deception, there were other singers and dancers he could base his endeavor around. And he had to keep reminding himself of that. She might appear to need rescue, he might want to rescue her, but there was always the possibility that it was all part of some grand confidence game. Not everyone was worth rescuing.

They are talking about you, said the cat. He sat near the door of Ninette's room, with his head cocked to one side. She put her book down in her lap and regarded him thoughtfully.

"They? Nigel and Arthur and Wolf?" She had heard them come in, but had thought it better not to intrude, since it sounded as if they were having a discussion of business.

And someone new. Another Elemental Master. The cat was very still, staring at the door with his tail curled around his feet. *A Fire Master. I think I know him, or at least, his reputation.*

Another magician? "Why is *he* here?" she asked.

I gather Nigel asked him to come. Hmm. Well, it seems he is not only a Magician, he is an illusionist as well. Nigel wishes him for this theatrical production. He is suspicious of you. I suspect he is a very sharp gentleman.

She bit her lip. That was the last thing she needed. "What if he finds out—"

The cat shook his head. *He won't. Or at least, he will not until it no longer matters. What he expects is that you have some purpose other than dancing, perhaps that you intend to get Nigel to marry you.*

She giggled. Nigel was not the sort of "rich" she expected for a protector. He was very careful with his money, and when she found someone to keep her, she wanted it to be a gentleman who liked to show his appreciation lavishly. "But could he find out I am not who I say I am?"

He is hardly an expert on either ballet or Russians. He admitted the latter, and as for the former, he seemed to be under the impression that just any ballroom dancer could partner with you for lifts and turns.

She snorted. If *that* was what he thought . . .

"Should I go out?" she wondered. "Face them now?"

It would be a good idea. They are not expecting you. They think you are asleep.

She got up from the chair in which she had been sitting, reading . . . she did not read easily—it was not deemed necessary for the little ballerinas to be very proficient in ordinary school lessons—but she enjoyed it, even if it was very hard work. For some reason, Nigel had a large collection of French novels, and she was making her slow way through them when she was not practicing.

She set the book aside and smoothed down her skirt with a feeling of great satisfaction. Nigel had been more than generous in the way of clothing. Since she had none, he had arranged for the costume mistress of the theater to take her measurements and get her a good wardrobe. Ninette doubted that the woman had sewn these garments herself, but she undoubtedly had friends or relatives that were seamstresses themselves and could use the work. And the work was very fine. Not the equivalent of a boulevard atelier, much less a great fashion modiste of the sort that someone like Nina Tchereslavsky would patronize, but it was finer than anything Ninette had even seen, much less worn. Even the underthings were exquisite, with lace and ribbons and embroidery. Nor had the wardrobe mistress limited herself to Ninette's ordinary clothing. Her practice skirts and tights were of silk tulle and knitted silk. Her pointe shoes were of the sort that the *etoiles* wore.

In short, ever since the cat had come into her life, things had taken such a turn for the better that she still woke up thinking it was all a dream. And she did not want to lose this. So if the cat said to face them, then face them she would.

She raised her chin, put on the mask of the great *prima,* and sailed out into the hallway. She followed the sound of voices to Nigel's library. The door was ajar, which she interpreted as meaning they did not mind being disturbed. She took a deep breath, looked down at the cat at her feet, and pushed it open all the way.

Nigel, who had clearly been just about to say something, looked at her with a startled expression, his mouth hanging open for a moment. He swiftly recovered though, and stood up.

"Mademoiselle Nina, were we disturbing you?" he asked, in French.

She shook her head. "Not in the least," she replied in the same language, and then smiled. "I 'ave been studying zee English, but it marches better when I am hearing it." She looked around the room as if she were the one that owned this flat, and not Nigel. "You 'ave brought a friend from the theater, oui?"

"This is Jonathon Hightower, a great illusionist," Nigel said hastily. "Hightower, this is Mademoiselle Nina Tchereslavsky."

The stranger rose, took her hand, and bowed over it. She accepted the accolade with pleasure, but also with an air that it was only to be expected. Exactly as La Augustine would have.

And what am I, an old boot?

"And this is the cat, Thomas," Nigel added hastily.

Hightower, who looked altogether like a modern version of Mephistopheles from the *Faust* opera, looked down at the cat, who had sat down regally just to Ninette's left.

"Maybe you should make *him* disappear," Wolf put in, turning one evil yellow eye on the cat.

Really now, what have I done to deserve that sugges-tion? The cat glared right back. *That's rather rude.*

"Well, you might stop looking at me as if you were deciding how many meals you were going to get out of me," Wolf retorted.

I am a cat. I have certain instincts. If you will insist on fluttering and setting off those instincts, you have only yourself to blame. While the parrot fluffed his feathers angrily and glared, the cat turned his attention back to the newcomer. *Greetings, Fire Master. Am I to presume you are not here by chance?*

"Possibly. My friend Nigel had a business proposition he wished to discuss with me." Hightower's expression was as bland as could be. Or rather, he had no expres-sion whatsoever that Ninette could make out. His faintly sinister, yet decidedly handsome face made an excellent mask for whatever it was he was thinking. Ninette had seen many opera singers with superb stage presence who used their faces in exactly that way. In fact, they were never really *off*-stage whenever they might be seen in public.

"Perhaps it ees about zis oh-so-mysterious theatrical venture he has hinted about?" she replied archly. She took a seat, remembering to do so as if she was center stage, with all eyes on her.

"Perhaps. You seem very much recovered from your tragedy, Mademoiselle." The abrupt change of subject might have startled her if she had not already been wary of him.

She hesitated, then sighed. "You will think very badly of me, I suppose," she said, slowly, as if the words were being drawn from her reluctantly. "And I feel very badly for poor Nikolas. But I did not know him perhaps as well as you presume I knew him. He was an admirer, yes. And he wished to be more, yes. But many gentle-men are my admirers, and many wish to be more. I have not had—" she hesitated "—I have not had a *particular* friend for many months now. I wished to go to England, where the winters are not so cold as Russia, and not France, where there are dancers in plenty, nor Italy, where the audiences prefer opera. I said as much where several of my admirers would hear me, and Nikolas had his new yacht, and I allowed him to persuade me to let him take me here. But I did not allow him to persuade me to do anything else. I wished to see if his company would be something other than tedious." She sighed, and looked down at her hands, and stole directly from La Augustine. "I am an artist. My friends are artists. When they gather in my salon, the talk is not of stocks and bonds and commodities. I have had my fill of *particular friends* who cannot or will not understand this talk, and demand that I give up my friends and my gatherings because such talk makes them feel stupid. I did not know that poor Nikolas was such a man. I did not know that he was not one. So taking this journey in his company was to discover if he was or was not, because I would be overjoyed never to face another angry confrontation with a man who could not see the value in things he himself did not appreciate." She made the corners of her mouth turn down. "For many of my admirers I am exactly like a painting. If it is famous, and if others will admire it, and admire the owner for having it, then it is worth collecting. But they do not think that I am not like a painting, that I have a mind, and friends, and I do not particularly wish to be collected and put on display to excite envy in others."

She looked up, with a melancholy little smile. "I hope that does not make me less in your eyes."

The illusionist was unfazed. "Well, Mademoiselle, it does puzzle me that you should come from this wreck des—"

"Destitute?" She gave a bitter little laugh. "Monsieur Illusionist, you will think me foolish perhaps, but one does not trust Russian banks if one can help it. All my life I have kept my fortune with me, in the form of jewels and gold. I take it with me wherever I go. And now it has all sunk down to the bottom of the sea."

The cat had been drilling her in this role until there were times when she wasn't sure which of her was the real one, Nina or Ninette. She sometimes wondered if he was putting memories into her head the way he was putting languages, because she could swear she had mental images of buildings in Russia, the Imperial Palace, Theater Street, the stage of the Imperial Ballet ... she had never even, to her knowledge, seen a sketch or a photograph of these places, and yet they were as real to her as the Eiffel Tower and the Paris Opera.

For that matter, was he slipping Russian language into her mind too? Only today, she had mis-stepped in practice and nearly twisted her ankle, and had sworn, not *sacre bleu!* as she had thought she would, but *blin!*

At any rate, with these things, these images and thoughts at the front of her mind, it was a great deal easier to "be" Nina.

The illusionist shook his head. "Tell me that you will not be doing that anymore," he half-scolded. "It was only a matter of time before *something* or *someone* robbed you of your fortune."

She hesitated. "It was not ... a very big fortune," she said after a moment, and laughed ruefully. "I am too fond of pretty gowns, jewelry, champagne, and caviar, and I am not so very famous that merchants will give these things to me in hopes that I will tell others where I got such-and-so. It is bad of me, I know but ..."

"But there will always be another *particular friend,* who will buy you these things, hmm?" The illusionist raised an eyebrow and she flushed, but raised her chin defiantly. It was Nina and Ninette together who answered him.

"And who does that harm?" she asked rhetorically, speaking of her imagined old man in a fur coat. "I make my friends happy, they make me happy. I deceive no one and no one is deceived by me. I do not pretend to love, monsieur. Love is not for my kind, and I make sure my friends understand this."

The illusionist unexpectedly softened his voice, and a hint of understanding, faintly shadowed with cynicism, colored his words. "Then you are wise beyond your years, mademoiselle, and I am glad to hear your honesty. I believe you. So. Have you any notion just who or what your father sought to protect you from by giving you this guardian?" He nodded at the cat.

With true bewilderment she could only shake her head. "Thomas has advised me and guided me, and seldom has his advice miscarried. It was he who urged the move to England upon me."

There was another prima ballerina at the company, the cat said, "speaking up" unexpectedly. *Nina attracted attention from the wrong quarters. Shall we say,* Imperial *attention? Rather than end up with more than just an artistic rivalry, I advised her to remove herself to somewhere far enough away that the lady's hand could not scratch her.*

All three men chuckled, and even Wolf snorted.

"Our own prince has generated trouble of that sort himself," Nigel said, with a shake of his head. "But that wasn't why your Master created you."

No, it isn't. There was no specific threat at the time. Only the need to provide his daughter with guidance he would not be there to give.

"So whoever did this to him—"

Did not survive the spellcasting, the cat said, abruptly, *so there is no immediate threat. This is not to say that there may not be one in the future, but there is not one now.*

Ninette looked from Nigel to the illusionist and back again, and bit her lip to keep from saying anything. The cat, it seemed, had surprised them both. That was interesting to say the least.

"Well, in that case," Nigel said carefully, with a glance at both the other men, "I think we are in a position to speak with you—and your advisor—about a prolonged theatrical engagement."

Ninette closed the door to the guest room quietly, but once alone, could hardly restrain her joy. "Thomas!" she whispered, taking a few dancing steps, then whirling around in a pirouette, "I am an *etoile!* I am a prima! *Prima ballerina assoluta!* Think of it! The production to be built around *me!* My own apartment and a maid! And fifty pounds a week!"

You should have gotten double that, Thomas grumbled.

"That is more than La Augustine—"

But not more than Nina Tchereslavsky. Ah well. When the receipts start coming in, we will re-negotiate. And you knew all of this before. I told you. Well, not the apartment, but that was only to be expected.

"You told me, but I did not believe it, not really." She sat down on the bed, and examined the hem of her gown with deep satisfaction. Lace three inches deep, and there would be more, many more, gowns like this to come. "I did not believe it until Nigel himself said it, and there were contract papers to sign."

This will be hard work, the cat warned.

"And what I have done up until now has not been?" She sniffed. "The difference between then and now will be that I will not have to rehearse on an empty stomach, nor go home to a garret with no heat."

Well, take care that no one else ever hears you say that. Thomas the cat paced up and down her rug, restlessly.

That Fire Master is altogether too sharp. Normally Fire Mages are the impulsive sort, ruled by their emotions. I suppose he must be the exception that proves the rule.

"He *is* very sharp," she replied, sobering. "I will be careful around him. He frightens me."

He should. Fire is the most powerful of the four Elements in the material world. It is also the most emotional. It takes tremendous control to become a Fire Master, and more still to regularly command the Elementals. They react poorly to coercion. I know of this man; he is very clever. Cleverer still to have come up with a way to make a living that enables him to work in plain sight and leave every ordinary person who sees him assuming he is working some sort of trickery.

"Will he use any of his real magic on stage?" she asked, watching the cat pace up and down the rug.

I expect so. Nothing powerful or important, just—fireworks, amusement for the audience. Pay attention, and you might figure out which thing he does is illusion, and which real magic.

Well, she would do that. It would be fun.

You should sleep now, the cat commanded.

She shivered with delicious anticipation, then rang for the maid to help her undress. The cat was right. Tomorrow she would be moving into her new apartment, all her own. She was going to need sleep.

8

ELEMENTAL Masters needed a very particular kind of servant. To be precise, they must either be Elemental magicians themselves, or have been aware that magic, *real* magic, was in the world, for most of their lives. Often enough, their servants came from a close-knit group of people who had been serving Elemental mages for centuries.

Or, as now, the servant came with a recommendation.

"So," Nigel said, looking up from the letter the girl had presented to him. "Sean McLeod says here that you are a Sensitive." She was a pretty little thing, was Ailse McKenzie: carrot-red hair, green eyes, and clearly as tough as she was tiny. She had good credentials though; she'd served as the ladies' maid in the shooting season at Sean's hunting lodge; his guests were all Elemental Masters and magicians and their offspring. She had wide ambitions though, and according to Sean was not content with doing general servants' work when there were no ladies present. Neither he nor Nigel could blame her; the privileges and pay of a lady's maid were considerably more elevated than that of a parlor maid.

"If that means I see the wee cratures you gents can call up when ye've a mind to, then aye." The girl's Scottish accent was not so heavy he couldn't understand her. Though it might prove difficult for the other party in this equation. Nina might find it difficult to understand her and that could prove a great hindrance. Sadly that was a mark against hiring her.

On the other hand there were many more points in her favor. Nina needed a reliable maidservant, and maids who had experience with magic were not all that thick on the ground. While it was true that Nina herself did no magic, Nina had a talking cat. Eventually a maidservant would notice something odd about the mistress's pet. If she actually overheard what the cat had to say and believed her "ears," she would probably run screaming from the house. If she did not actually hear it speaking herself, sooner or later she would notice her mistress having one-sided conversations with her pet.

Then there was the matter of self-defense. This was something every Elemental Master needed to consider if he or she was wealthy enough to employ more than one or two servants. When enemies came calling, they generally did not offer advance warning, nor did they scruple to ask whether or not anyone in the vicinity was an innocent bystander. You could be killed just as dead by Elemental Magic that you could not see and probably would not believe in if you were told about it.

Miss McKenzie would be able to see it, and might have some defense against it. When it came down to cases, anything that had been sent after Nina probably already had her "scent." If the storm that had wrecked her yacht had been sent after her. . . .

"Mademoiselle Tchereslavsky may be . . ." he paused delicately, ". . . hunted. We are not certain, but the storm that sank the yacht she was on might have been sent to harm her."

Not entirely to his surprise, because the Scots were a tough race, Miss McKenzie raised her head on her slim neck and looked defiantly down her nose at him. "An' ye think, a'cause I have never th' magic of my own, I canna hold my own?" Her eyes blazed fiercely. "Aye, a horse-shoe and a right pair of hobnailed boots will send most of those cratures packing!"

"Miss Tchereslavsky does not speak much English, you know," he said tentatively.

"Lor' bless ye, sir, three years in a row now, I tended a lady what never chattered in anything but French, and we managed all right," the girl said proudly. "I'll find a way t' understand her, make no mistake."

One final thing. "She has a protector," Nigel said. "It's her cat."

"Does it talk?" the girl wanted to know.

"After a fashion."

"An' will it talk to me?"

"That, I don't know. He might."

"Well!" Miss McKenzie said in triumph. "There you are, then."

Nigel blinked. Somewhere the conversation had just taken an abrupt turn, and he had missed it. "I beg your pardon?" he ventured. "What exactly did you mean?"

"If it talks," the girl explained, patiently, as if he was a very slow child, "then she can tell the cat what she needs, and the cat can tell me."

"Ah." That very practical application had not occurred to Nigel. "Very well then, your services will be required." He swiftly negotiated her wages and privileges, and sent her on to the flat with instructions to have the landlord show her in and get everything in readiness for Nina. He then wrote a note to his man, instructing him to pack up Nina's things and send them to the flat.

As usual, the dancer had gotten up at an hour that would have satisfied the harshest stage director and gone straight to the rehearsal hall. There she would work until noon, stop for a bite and a stroll in the sunshine, then return to the rehearsal hall until dinnertime.

However, he proposed to change that schedule today.

As the hour approached when she usually stopped for her midday meal, he went upstairs to catch her before she left. She was just going through some complicated faradiddle involving a lot of fast, intricate steps, and he paused in the doorway to watch. And not because her short rehearsal skirt showed her legs, either; he saw more than enough of his fill of legs backstage. No, this was the first time he had actually watched her doing anything other than exercises, and he indulged himself in a moment of self-congratulation. He was no judge of ballerinas, but he knew his audiences, and she was by far and away the best dancer that *they* would ever likely see.

She finished the sequence and came down flat-footed in that way that dancers had when they were practicing something and not actually in front of an audience. And only as she was turning around did she catch sight of him in the mirror.

She jumped, her hand going to her throat. *"Blin!"* she exclaimed. "You startle me!"

"Your pardon, Mademoiselle, I certainly didn't mean to—" he began, but she waved her hand impatiently.

"It is good you are here," she said in French. *"There is something I wish you to see."*

She ran to the corner and got what looked to Nigel like a rod of some sort, and nodded to the pianist. "Spring song, *s'il vous plaît,*" she said, and as the pianist began what Wolf would surely have snorted at as a "tinkly little melody," she unfurled a long ribbon from the rod and began to dance with it.

Actually there was a great deal more twirling the ribbon in intricate patterns than there was dancing, but Nigel could easily see that this would be no great concern for his audiences. The eye was drawn to the streamer of silk, which was yards and yards long. It seemed almost alive as she made it draw circles and spirals, twine around her and create elaborate figures in the air. And he could just imagine it with some special stage lighting on it too. . . .

When the pianist ended with a flourish, and so did she, he applauded. She caught up the ribbon and began carefully folding it, looking both flushed and pleased.

"*Bien?*" she asked.

"*Tres bien,*" he assured her. "I don't think our people have ever seen anything done like that before."

"*Oh, it is nothing but a little trick, and I could not do the throws and catches, the ceiling here is not high enough. But it looks grand from a distance,*" she replied in French, putting the ribbon and stick up carefully. "*There was a troupe of girls from Switzerland, I think, that performed these things. There is also a hoop, and a ball, and I think both will serve in your production.*"

"Anything that looks good from the balcony will sell tickets, Mademoiselle," he said with pleasure. "Now, I am going to ask you to please forgo your afternoon practice, if you will. I'd like to take you to luncheon, and then to your new flat. It's all arranged, I've had your things sent over, and I just hired you a fine maid to take care of you. She'll have set everything to rights by the time we get there."

To his pleasure, she clapped her hands like a child given a sweet. "Monsieur, you are too good to me!" she exclaimed. He flushed, but smiled.

"Save the praises for when you see it all," he cautioned. "After all, you might not like it!"

The little Scots maidservant answered the door, already looking as if she had been in this place since it was built, her crisp black and white uniform immaculate. "Sir," she said, with a nod of respect to Nigel. "This would be m'lady then?"

Nigel nodded. "This is Mademoiselle Tchereslavsky. Mademoiselle, this is the young lady I hired for you, Miss McKenzie."

Ninette elected not to imitate La Augustine this time; the dancer was horrible to her servants. Instead, she gave Miss McKenzie a friendly smile as she stepped for the first time into her own parlor, and made sure the door was not shut in Thomas's face. Then she looked around, and felt a thrill of sheer delight.

In times of fanciful dreaming she had imagined living somewhere like this. When she daydreamed about being the pet of a rich old man, she had pictured herself in a place virtually identical in every way. Everything about it spoke comfort, not just that the furnishings looked comfortable, which they did, but unlike the boarding house (which was comfort attainable only so long as the money in her purse lasted), or the luxury of Nigel's flat (which was his, not hers), this place whispered a little message to her. *You will never be cold or hungry again.*

"Beggin' your pardon, sir, milady," the maidservant said once the door was closed, "but there's a Brownie in the pantry. Did ye wish me to do sommat about him?"

A—what? Was Ninette's reaction. What was a Brownie? Some sort of mouse? Or worse still, a rat?

It's quite all right, McKenzie, I invited him, said the cat.

"Oh well, it's all right then. Your pardon for interrupting you," she said, without turning a hair. "Your pardon, but I was preparing m'lady's lunch. I shall be in the kitchen if you require me."

"And I'll show you about," said Nigel, looking just a trifle smug.

But Ninette wasn't ready to be shown her new flat just yet. "She heard you!" she said, in a tone of accusation.

Of course. Monsieur Nigel would not have hired an ordinary servant for you. That could have been a problem. Correct, Monsieur?

"Very much so," Nigel replied, and turned to Ninette. "Miss McKenzie is not a magician, but she is able to see the same things that you are. We refer to her abilities as being a 'Sensitive.' You will not need to hide anything from her."

Ninette nodded, with some relief. At least she was not going to have to explain the cat away! "But—how?" she asked in English.

"Our sort of folk need servants, servants we can trust, after all," Nigel chuckled. "I simply let it be known I needed a maidservant for my famous dancer, and one was forthcoming."

Somehow she doubted that it was *quite* that simple, but she was willing to let that pass. The tour of the flat took very little time, although the enjoyment she knew she would have in a more leisurely examination of its delights would occupy her for a while to come. When they were finished, Miss McKenzie had a really admirable luncheon laid out for them, which they sat down to enjoy.

"Excellent, McKenzie," Nigel said, when she had cleared the last of it away.

"Och, well, that would be due to our landlord, sir," McKenzie replied. "'Twas he that brought it all up; I just needed to keep it warm for you."

"Ah, now that reminds me," Nigel said, and began explaining the various meal arrangements she could make. "It's all because this is theatrical lodgings, you see," he concluded. "Players eat at odd times, they generally don't know enough about the matter to keep a good cook, and they don't stay long. Not as a rule, anyway."

Ninette shook her head. It all seemed so irregular to her. "We change programme," she said, finally. "Not theater."

"A more sensible way, to be sure." Nigel nodded. "At any rate, if you want company, you can go down and dine with the others. If you don't, they'll send it up, or McKenzie there can arrange something. The meals will be plain and simple, so if you're longing for beefsteak, or pheasant, or anything of that sort, you'll have to send out for it."

She nodded; it was definitely a sensible arrangement, if a trifle peculiar. But it made sense.

"I'll leave you to settle in," Nigel said genially. "You can skip practice for one afternoon, I should think?"

She nodded, and McKenzie showed him out.

Now the work began in earnest.

Ninette spent all of one afternoon, on a day when the theater had no matinee, showing Nigel, Arthur, Jonathon, and Wolf all of her little "tricks." These were, of course, the sort of things that dancers like La Augustine despised—dancing with the ribbon-wand, the ball, and the hoop, skirt dancing with yards and yards and yards of the lightest silk fabric to make ever-moving curtains that light could be played against. And she showed her other tricks, the showpieces that dancers like La Augustine did *not* despise, although they might pretend to; the solos from *Swan Lake* and *Tales of Hoffman,* from *Bayadere* and *Giselle,* from *Don Quixote* and *Corsair.*

All these things the men loved, and when she was done, exhausted and dripping with sweat, she looked out into the empty theater to see the four of them chattering away like so many rooks, planning what tricky bit should go where in their story.

Wolf was now supposed to write music—or at least adapt it—for all of this, but he seemed to be in a frenzy of delight, and no one ventured to trouble him or Arthur as they sat at the piano, Wolf dictating the music without a pause until they were both often found slumped over the keyboard, the parrot standing with one foot up and head hunched down, on the nape of Arthur's neck.

Nor was Jonathon idle, concocting a tremendous stage-business for the Sultan's burning palace, as well as adapting or reviving several more of his feats of illusion.

Nigel was busy filling in the spaces between Ninette's performances and Jonathon's with other acts. They had to be steady, reliable, and with a minimum of traits that might bring them into conflict with others. This would not be a case where in two weeks, each would go his separate ways. These people, like the theatrical and dance companies she knew, would stay together for months. Little irritations could escalate into harassment, into all-out feuds. It was Nigel's job to see to it that the people he invited to this production were not the kind to escalate.

The plot was a simple one. In the Prologue, a ship would be caught in a storm; they had determined that only a segment of this ship would appear on stage, tossing on the artificial waves. There would be cries of "man overboard" and a dummy of her would be tossed down into the waves. This would not be the first nor the last appearance of the hapless dummy. . . .

She would do a skirt dance among the waves to make it appear that she was drowning, or at least, swimming for her life. She would clear the stage, and then the ship would sink.

In the first act, she would be lying on a "beach," unconscious, and the Sultan's men would find her. They would carry her off, and the curtain would rise on the Sultan's palace. This gave the opportunity for several acts to come on stage to entertain the Sultan. Chief among them, of course, would be Jonathon. He would play the Sultan's Vizier, who enforced the Sultan's edicts with his magic. He would make some poor wretch turn into a chicken or some such thing—they hadn't quite decided what animal they would use, perhaps even a dog—and then the new harem captives would be brought in. Nigel would have to hire dancers for this, but he had some experience with hiring actors and dancers for something called "the Panto," so she expected he could manage that.

Then it would be her turn. Begging and pleading with the Sultan to send her back to her people, she would be refused, and ordered to dance. This is when she would do her hoop, ribbon, and ball dances.

There would be more entertainment for the Sultan, interspersed with a very clever idea on Nigel's part. A scrim would drop down between the audience and the Sultan's court, and everyone would freeze in place like a *tableaux vivant*. Then the lights would come down on the Sultan's Court. Then two footlights would come up, one on a ballad singer, and one on her, apparently gazing out of a window. The ballad singer would perform a number about England or home, while she sighed in her captivity. Then the lights out front would come down, she and the singer would exit under cover of the darkness, and the lights would come back up on the Sultan's Palace.

The Sultan would demand for her to dance again.

This time it would be one of the ballet solos she knew so well. Then the Sultan would begin courting her.

"Now why," Wolf had demanded, "is he going to *court* her when logic says he could simply *take* her?"

"Fairy tale logic, old bird," Arthur had replied absently, "She's a virtuous English girl and therefore the only thoughts that enter the Sultan's head are those of honor and decency." Then he had made that little exclamation that meant he had puzzled out what he was working on. "Try this out for your hoop-dance," he had said, and began to play a melody. As she went through her planned choreography in her mind, everything else was forgotten.

After that, she would stand up to the evil Vizier, who would have a change of heart and agree to get her out. Nigel had the notion for her to do a "naturalistic" dance portraying Anger and Defiance at that point, in bare feet and legs and a little tunic, as Isadora Duncan did.

Next, she and the chorus dancers would do a nautch dance in the harem. She wasn't at all sure about this, as she had never actually seen a nautch dance, but she supposed she could adopt one of Aspica's solos from *The Pharoah's Daughter.*

Then back to the Sultan's court, where, growing weary of her refusal, the Sultan would attempt to force himself on her.

"Finally!" Wolf had exclaimed at that point, making them all laugh.

She would break away and perform a skirt dance with red and yellow lights on her for fire. The Sultan would be frightened, call her an Efrit, and demand that the Vizier do something about her. The Vizier would make her vanish from an open platform.

The last scene she would be in would be where she said farewell on a beach to the Vizier, who would send her away in the custody of a dozen British tars, who would, of course, do a dance with her in the middle of them.

But the last scene would be all the Vizier's, where he would be dragged up in front of the Sultan for helping her to escape, and he would bring the entire palace down in a barrage of fire and vanish out of the midst of it. Jonathon was quite excited about this, for it meant not only a spectacular illusion, but an escape from chains as well.

In general, in fact, everyone was enthused about the production.

It was at that moment that she had realized there were two things she needed. A choreographer was one. A teacher was another. Try as she might, she was unable to put together sequences of steps that seemed at all interesting. She understood this instinctively; something in her compared, say, the Petipa choreography from one of the *Sleeping Beauty* variations, which were by no means his most inspired, to what she was doing, and she fell far, far short. And as for a teacher, she understood that she needed correction, and also understood that she was not going to get that correction working on her own.

Finally she broached the subject to Nigel, whose brow furrowed at her request. "I'm not sure I understand correctly," he said, finally. "I thought it would be no problem for you to put together your little numbers. And aren't you beyond taking lessons?"

"A dancer is never beyond taking lessons," she replied solemnly. "There is always something new to learn. It is hard to practice and look for faults at the same time."

Nigel nodded at that. "Come to think of it, I'm going to require someone to teach all those chorus dancers their parts, and handle them as Arthur handles the orchestra." He pondered this for a moment. "Let me see if the booking agents have anyone of this sort."

Not three days later, he turned up again at her rehearsal studio, and with him was a man she did not recognize. "Mademoiselle Tchereslavsky, this is Monsieur Ciccolini. He will be your teacher, he'll be doing the choreography, and he'll be keeping the chorus under as much control as possible."

"That will not be the easiest proposition," the gentleman said with a smile. He was a tall, lean man, hair once black, now going gray, but continuing to be handsome in that ageless way that only Italians could manage. This was not the "Roman-Italian" whose statues adorned theaters and government buildings everywhere; he definitely had a dancer's build and a dancer's way of moving, but she could tell that his knees pained him. "Young ladies being what they are, I can only promise that they will turn up to rehearsals and performances on time, and come up to my standard, or they will find themselves replaced." He bowed a little. "Mademoiselle, if I may be so bold as to come back with you to your rehearsal hall? I can then get some idea of what lessons you may need."

She was only too happy to take him there, and was very glad that she was already warmed up. He took over the room as if he had been there all his life, addressing the pianist, and taking charge of it all. He instructed her to warm up anyway, which she did, while he scrutinized her. Then, as he set the tempo of the pianist, he called out steps for her to perform.

This was something she had sorely missed. It was one thing to dance a sequence from one of the many ballets that you had memorized, or a sequence that you tried to make up in your head to try and stretch your abilities and all the while watch yourself in the mirror for any flaws. It was quite another to dance a sequence as it was called out by the teacher, and to rely on the teacher to watch for flaws while you concentrated on the dancing.

He ran her through several such sequences, at varied tempi, his long face growing more and more thoughtful. Finally he waved her to the barre. "Mademoiselle," he said heavily, "I am only an old man from Milano, with two bad knees and some ability to teach little English chorus girls to stagger about on their toes and not disgrace themselves. You are better than anyone I have ever taught. You are better than anyone I have ever danced with. You may be better than anyone I have ever seen. There is nothing I can teach you."

Ninette listened to this with growing astonishment. True, in the past several weeks she had completely forgotten about captivating rich old men and had concentrated on her dancing as never before. But surely that had not made that much of an improvement! Surely he was mistaken. Or flattering her. Or—

Perhaps testing her. She raised her head. "Monsieur, whether or not any of that is true, a dancer never stops learning. You have learned at one school, I at another. Another technique is always worth learning. And you choreograph, which is something I have never done. True?"

"True," he admitted.

She smiled. "Well then, pray help me with this first of my dances for this production, for I confess I can think of nothing to make it particularly interesting." She fetched the hoop from the corner. "It is to combine ballet with the hoop-exercises of the Swiss girls—"

"Ah yes!" he exclaimed with recognition. "I saw them. Well, then, let us begin."

By the end of the afternoon, he had turned a rather lackluster little piece into something amusing and interesting. It was true that he was no Petipa, but he had a good eye and a sound instinct. Being able to make clear improvements in her dance raised his spirits as well; by the end of the afternoon, he was issuing orders and tapping out the tempo with his instruction wand, and using it too, to reposition a foot or a knee—

He was one of those teachers who used a long wand, nearly as tall as he was, to point out problems with the feet and legs. She had only had one such teacher, at the Paris Opera, and he had been prone to using it to thwack little ballerinas across the back of the calf when he did not like what they were doing. Perhaps Ciccolini was naturally more gentle than that, or perhaps he simply deemed her too old for such correction—or maybe he feared that in a temper she would snatch his wand and break it over his head! At any rate, he did no such thing to her.

It was a relief to think about something besides magic, to concentrate entirely on her dance. It was very odd to think that a few weeks ago, she would have been perfectly happy to find herself *not* dancing! This was real, solid, something she had known all her life, something she understood. Magic, she did not understand. How could a cat talk? How could there be little creatures like the Brownie living right under everyone's noses?

Dancing was better. But—there was something lacking even with her dancing.

But she needed something more. She needed—

"Mademoiselle," the instructor began, breaking her out of her reverie. "This looks very fine in this room. But to judge whether or not it will serve on the stage, you must take it *on* the stage. And to judge whether or not it pleases an audience, you must take it before an audience."

She thought about that for a moment, and realized what it was that she had been feeling the lack of.

An audience.

She had not, until that moment, realized just how much she had missed that aspect of dancing. The audience! Not just potential suitors, but all of them, from the little girls at their first ballet to the old balletomanes. She wanted to hear applause, feel their presence, drink in their attention.

It was very strange . . . when she had danced the *Sylphide,* she had not even considered the audience, and yet now, that applause had been like a drug. And she wanted more of it.

"I quite agree with you, Monsieur," she said with a nod. "I will speak with the director. There is no reason why I should not start performing. Same time tomorrow, then?"

He nodded. "I fear my mornings will be filled with teaching people who have perfect figures and an imperfect sense of where to put their feet or how to execute a few steps. In other words, I will be instructing the chorus."

"Very good, Monsieur," she replied—the old man bowed to her, and took his leave. The pianist began packing her music away, and Ninette retired to the little changing room just off the rehearsal room. She changed into her street clothing, and went straight to Nigel's office.

He looked up as she tapped on the doorframe, for the door itself was open. "Mademoiselle?" he said, looking worried. "That Italian chap not to your liking? I'll find you another teacher if you must—"

"No," she said swiftly. "No, he is excellent!" She took a deep breath. "However, I grow uneasy that you support me and I do nothing."

Nigel laughed. "You are in rehearsal. You are earning your salary—"

She shook her head. "I have never performed before an English audience. I need to see what they are like. Now is the time to try some of my dances, to see if they respond to me. Sir, I would like to perform in your show. Not the one we are creating. This 'music hall' that you are presenting."

The look of surprise on his face made her smile.

"If you're certain," he said, finally, "I'm sure we can fit a dance or two in."

"I am certain," she said, firmly. "And Monsieur Ciccolini believes this is a good idea too."

"In that case, I would be the last person to argue," Nigel replied, giving in with good grace. "We'll start you next week, on the new playbill."

She smiled and thanked him. The conviction that this was exactly what she needed remained with her all the way back to her flat.

9

NINA Tchereslavsky regarded the dead old man in her bed with a remote regret. Regret, because he had, after all, offered so little sustenance, and now she would have to find another admirer with a great deal of money, but it was tempered with the knowledge that she really did look very chic in black. It was a great pity, but he had to be devoured. He had been getting restless, eyes beginning to rove—which was how she had gotten him in the first place. But Nina left nothing for any other female creature, human or otherwise, when she was finished with a man. That little pale-haired girl in the back of the chorus would just have to go hunting elsewhere.

So farewell to Herr Klaus Obervelten, the farm-tractor tycoon.

But it would not do for him to be found here.

With a twist of her mind, she summoned a herd of the kobolds that were as much slaves to the power she granted them as they were her allies. Being very much part of the material world, they came scampering through her open bedroom window rather than manifesting in any other way.

"Take that to its home," she said, pointing a languid finger at the corpse and wrapping her silk-velvet robe more tightly around herself. "Put it in its bed." With another twist of her mind, she showed them where her benefactor's home was, and where his bedroom was in that house. Without a word, the little mob of kobolds had hoisted the body onto their backs, and a moment later, were scampering out the window with it. They would go over the rooftops, of course; it was night, and the sun wouldn't hurt their eyes. It certainly would not do for a policeman to see a dead, rather naked body being carried through the streets by things invisible to his eyes.

That would be unfortunate.

Nina closed the window and stretched. That was that, sadly. No more presents, and the heirs would likely very soon cut off the monthly rental payments for this very expensive flat.

No matter. She had enough to live on for a while until she found another so-called "protector." It would not take long. The magic and energy she took from her old men was sufficient to allow her to keep this form as it was when she had devoured it and moved into the girl's life. She looked not quite twenty, in that ageless way of ballerinas everywhere.

She had chosen her victims very carefully, not at all at random. The original Nina had been well on the way to becoming a great dancer, and had attracted a great many followers at the point where the creature that became her had taken her, but few of them had been the sort that would have done her any good. She was forever attracting starving poets, who would write wonderful things about her, but did not pay the rent on a nice flat. She had been very wild, and rather wanton, and threw herself away on these beautiful, but impecunious fellows. Evidently she had not taken the lesson of *La Boheme* to heart; she had doted on *La Dame Aux Camellias* instead. Her talent for dancing and her fine body had been wasted on her silly little soul.

The creature had swiftly changed all that. It had been easy. She simply assumed the form of one of her own victims, who had been an exceedingly beautiful young man, and Nina had happily let the creature seduce her. Once in her bed, it was only a moment until Nina was absorbed and the creature became Nina.

She had spent all the rest of that night getting used to the dancer's body and memories. In class the next day, she had been clumsy at first, occasioning some giggles from the other girls, but she joked and laughed herself about "a little too much champagne" and they all put it off to a hangover. But the creature had a great deal of practice in mastering forms, and by mid-afternoon she was actually dancing better than the original. This was not as hard as it might seem. For one thing, she was able to concentrate as Nina had not been. For another, her body did not tire or hurt as Nina's had. The beautiful movements of ballet, the creature now knew, were performed more or less in pain. Well, the creature did not generally experience that sort of pain; as long as she could drain others to heal or sustain herself, she would not ever suffer, either.

By the evening's performance, in which Nina was a soloist, the creature was ready. Backstage, all the beautiful but impecunious boys found themselves relegated to the back of the crowd, as Nina concentrated on the old and rich and not at all beautiful. By morning, Nina was wearing a fur coat, a diamond bracelet, and was about to be installed in a fine little flat complete with maid. Her benefactor had been an aging count, well used to keeping pretty little ballerinas, and if he had a taste for cruelty, well, he did not last long enough to in- dulge himself in it too much. The next man, a highly suc- cessful wine merchant, was easier to deal with, and just as generous.

For some reason, dancers attracted old men. Some much older than the ones that pursued opera divas. This was exactly as the creature that had taken the dancer's form and place liked it. Old men were prone to dying from a thousand and one causes, and Nina's benefactors were all very old men, and she was discreet. Most of the time, unless the old gentleman himself wished to flaunt her, as Herr Klaus had, no one knew there was a liaison. As for the ones who paraded her like a trophy, no one thought twice about it when Nina lost a few lovers in such a fashion, since not a single death was directly con- nected with her. Herr Klaus would be found in his own bed, with no indication that he had been with her last night. Nina's servants, who were rendered blind and deaf when she chose, could not have told anyone other- wise even if they wanted to.

Perhaps she should go to the Bohemian quarter and find herself a starving artist or tortured poet. Or two. Or three. And it was a very good thing that she was leaving to dance elsewhere; she could take another old man or two there without the rumors of the previous ones fol- lowing her. She would choose ones who needed to be discreet; that way no one would be the wiser when she consumed them.

The creature had taken the forms and shapes of many beings over the years; an elemental creature of earth, it had first been conjured and inexpertly bound some three hundred years ago by an Earth Master who relied on instinct rather than learning, and whose self- confidence was nothing short of hubris. He was the first human that the creature had devoured; up until then, it had confined itself to lesser Elemental beings and animals. But once she had absorbed the magician . . . that was when things began to change.

Her talent, which had caused the magician to try to bind her in the first place, was that not only could she kill anything by absorbing its essence, she could then imitate it flawlessly afterwards. So once she discovered that, having absorbed her erstwhile captor, she was able to stay on the Material Plane, there was no turning back for her. She had taken on the form of that foolish Elemental magician for quite some time before his life bored her, and when she was ready to move on, it hadn't taken a lot of effort to find someone else to be.

The creature—the first mage had called her a "Troll"—went back to bed. When the body was found, which it would be soon since the sky to the east was getting brighter, "Nina" needed to be in her bed, alone. She might not be *sans peur et sans reproche,* at least in the eyes of the world, but having him die in her bed might excite the suspicions of the wretched police. There were Elemental Mages everywhere They could, and would, banish her back to her previous existence. Or worse . . .

She wrapped the silk sheets around herself and settled into the lovely, soft bed. It had been a good day when Nina Tchereslavsky decided she was going to use magic to get the attention of a certain beautiful young poet who was not interested in her. The current Nina judged that this was a very foolish thing to do; not only would most love spells not have worked on someone who was devoted to someone else, there had been a dozen equally beautiful young men clamoring for her. As for the dancer, she had been prepared to throw her entire life away on a succession of these beautiful young men, none of whom would have done her a particle of good, had any money, or ever likely would have any money.

Whereas the creature that had taken her place had made her great. A much, much better use of the gifts that had been given her.

With these thoughts in mind, Nina drifted back off to sleep, fully expecting to be awakened by the maid bewailing the death of the old man.

Instead, she was awakened by the maid bewailing nothing, only bringing her the morning pastry and chocolate, and an envelope, a letter from the impresario of the theater in Salzburg at which she was expected to perform. She frowned at it before opening it. She really hoped he was not canceling her engagement. She needed to move away from Hungary altogether; too many men had died around her, and this last one might start some talk. Germany, that was far enough. She would be discreet. It wasn't hard to be discreet when you knew what to look for.

Provided this impresario wasn't having second thoughts.

But instead, what fell out was a note and a newspaper clipping.

I trust this note will reach you where you should be, the note read, *because you cannot perform in my theater and one in England at the same time.*

Swiftly she caught up the little cut-out bit of paper. It wasn't much, only a note that Nina Tchereslavsky was performing at some music hall in Blackpool and that she was to be the star of an upcoming and very ambitious project by the owner of that theater.

At first, Nina did not grasp what this meant.

Then she flew into a rage.

When at last her initial anger was expended, the bedroom was virtually destroyed. The furniture was in splinters, the bedclothes and curtains in rags. The servants knew better than to approach her in this mood; she likely would have killed them.

Not that this would have mattered to the world in general. Her servants were not human.

She stood in the middle of the wreckage, trying to think.

This . . . girl . . . was impersonating her. It did not matter that she was off in some provincial little city in England, where no one would see her but farmers in smocks and thick boots. What mattered was that this girl was stealing the reputation that Nina had built. Stealing her identity.

She had stolen from Nina. No one stole from Nina.

Her skin flushed with rage again, just thinking about it.

She would go to England. She would find this girl and kill her. It could not possibly take any time, and it should be pathetically easy. She would do what she had done with the original Nina, she would take on the form of a beautiful young man . . . or if that did not work, a very rich, old one. She would seduce the girl, and then kill her, and leave it to look as if she had been murdered by her lover. And of course, that lover would no longer exist. Nina could change to another form, and leave the country, all in time to make her debut at Salzburg.

She finally felt her anger cooling, and even managed to smile. Amid the chaos, she found the pull for the bell, and rang for her maid. The servant opened the door a crack, timidly.

It was so frustrating that she was fettered to this solid form! If she had not been, she could have been in England within a day, moving in the secret ways of the Earth Elementals, swimming through the very crust of the earth itself. She could change her form, she could work Earth Magic herself, but she was still as bound to the laws of the mortal world as if she was mortal herself.

"Clean up this mess," she ordered. "Then have the others pack my trunks. Tell Yuri to order my car and get tickets to England." How fortunate that the ballet sea-

son was over! "And you, cancel all my engagements and
send for some new furniture; have this room repaired
and re-furnished while I am gone. There is nothing here
I need to deal with that cannot wait."

"Hold very still," ordered Jonathon, as he closed
Ninette into the cabinet. "And don't be afraid. Nothing
you see is going to harm you."

"But—" she began, as he closed the door. He didn't
open it again, and she stood there, in the dark, in what
felt very like a coffin, wondering what it was she was
going to see that might—

And then the entire box was engulfed in flames.

Terror overwhelmed her; she shrieked at the top of
her lungs. She tried to bring up her arms to beat on the
door of the box, but it was too narrow, and she couldn't
move. There was no fastening on the inside of the box;
she tried to get up her foot to kick and couldn't even do
that. The flames were everywhere, and—

Suddenly she realized, in mid-scream, that she wasn't
even warm, that her clothing was not on fire, that she
didn't smell smoke, that the inside of the box was not
even warm to the touch.

Whatever Jonathon was doing, this was *not* real fire!
And she was quite ready to kill him at that moment. He
might have *said!*

That was when the trap door beneath her that she
had been told about opened, and she dropped down
onto a pair of soft mattresses. Her knees automatically
flexed as soon as she was falling, so she landed lightly.
But fuming.

She stormed across the space beneath the stage and
up the stairs to the backstage; her face must have
looked like thunder, because even the stagehands scuttled out of her way. With hands balled into fists, she

stalked across the stage to where Jonathon had just opened the cabinet with a flourish to show it was empty. At the sound of her feet thumping across the stage—for a ballerina can walk *very* heavily if she chooses—he turned.

"Now that is the kind of scream I—*ow!*"

She had kicked him in the shin before he could finish the sentence. He looked at her in astonishment. She kicked the other shin.

"Ow!"

"You might have said!" she shouted. *"Merzavets! Lopni tvoya selezenka I ospleni tvoy glaz, nechistaya sila!"* The Russian simply poured from her lips without thinking, and she would have been surprised if she had not been so furious. "You frightened me to death!"

"I am a magician! You *know* it couldn't have been real!"

Oh yes, and she very much doubted that this was any illusion or stage trick. Those flames had to have come from his powers as an Elemental Mage. But she could not say that, not in public, so instead, she kicked his shin again.

"I would have known if you had warned me, but you did not!" she retorted. "You close me in a coffin, and then, fire! How was I to know it was not some terrible accident?"

"You would have heard someone shouting *Fire!*" Jonathon barked, heatedly.

"I would have heard *nothing!*" she shouted back. "I was *screaming!*"

Silence descended on the stage. Finally Arthur chuckled from his position in the orchestra pit. "Admit it, Jonathon. You wanted her to scream. You gave yourself away when you said that was the kind of scream you wanted."

Jonathon flushed and looked away.

"Oh!" she spluttered, and kicked his shin again before stomping off the stage.

Behind her, with some satisfaction, she could hear him swearing.

The cat was waiting in the wings, and walked back with her to her dressing room, where she slammed the door closed, sat down, and looked at him.

That was very bad of him, the cat observed. *It's a naughty schoolboy trick.*

"He is quite old enough not to play such things," she said severely. "I am doing my best to be a good assistant to him, and he should not play such things on me. Stage fire is not funny."

Especially not when you are trapped in a box. The cat sighed. *He hasn't changed. He drove off more young ladies with his pranks than you could imagine.*

She looked at the cat oddly. "You know him?"

His assistants, the cat said hastily. *The stagehands talked about it.*

Ninette turned back to the mirror of her dressing table, but considered, and not for the first time, that the cat sounded as if he knew, or had known, the Fire Master in the past.

But it could be when my father lived here, she thought. There was no reason why the cat should not have been with her father before he came to Paris. Though why the cat should want to conceal this fact, she could not imagine. Thomas was full of mysteries. How had he known to come here, to Blackpool, for instance? How did he know that there was a theater owner here, moreover, one who was looking for someone very like her? But she was not going to pose these questions to him. If he had not told her these things before, there was no reason to think he would do so now, and she was not in a position to force him.

Are you going to rejoin the rehearsal? Thomas asked.

"When I think I have been away long enough to have made my feelings clear," she said firmly. "That was not funny, and I do not intend to put up with any more such pranks. I am not an assistant that has no choice but to endure that sort of thing."

Well put. And about time someone taught him that schoolboy tricks are very unwelcome when played by an adult man.

She waited a few moments more, then came out of her dressing room and returned to the stage, where Jonathon was fussing with his apparatus. She cleared her throat and he jumped.

"You aren't going to kick me again, are you?" he asked, turning to her with a grimace.

"I shall, if you do any such thing again," she said stiffly. "I am not your hired assistant, who must endure cruelty in order to collect her pay, and if you play more tricks on me, I shall kick you somewhat higher than your shin."

His eyes widened. "You'd do it too, wouldn't you?" he said with grudging admiration.

"Yes, I would." She looked up at him defiantly. "Now, I believe we have an illusion to rehearse. I take it you wish me to scream in a terrifying fashion when I see the flames?"

He nodded speechlessly. She returned to her "spot" and knelt, arms behind her back as if tied there, then nodded to Arthur, who took that as the cue it was, and lifted his baton.

This time the illusion proceeded in a professional manner. Jonathon locked her in the cabinet, when she saw the flames, she shrieked, and if she let out a bit more anger with her screams, well, no one was the wiser. The trap-door released, she dropped onto the mattresses, then made her way back up to the wings.

They ran through the trick three or four more times

before Jonathon pronounced himself satisfied. "You are a capital screamer, though," he said, apologetically. "I should have told you what was coming, since I can clearly see you would have done just right if I had warned you."

She raised her chin. "I am a professional," she said.

"I can see that." He looked uneasy. "I am sorry I frightened you."

She sensed that was the closest she was going to get to a real apology, and nodded. She was *not* going to apologize for kicking him, even though she was fairly certain that he now had four round little bruises on his shins.

"I think that the illusion is ready to use tonight," he continued.

"I think so too. I will have just enough time to change after my ribbon dance." She couldn't help but smile at that. The ribbon, hoop, and ball dances had, with some more adjustment by Monsieur Ciccolini, been quite popular with the audiences.

"That's a nice bit of business, that ribbon dance," Jonathon said awkwardly, then paused. "You know, I have an illusion that makes a handkerchief fly about the stage. You might do a dance where you chase it. Or dance with it."

"I would prefer a combination of the two," she said after a moment. "I begin by chasing, then stop and dance to see if it can be lured, and lure it into dancing with me."

He laughed. "That is a good notion. Let's go talk to Nigel and Arthur about it."

She nodded, and the two of them headed up to Nigel's office.

Arthur was with him, as they both expected, going over some last-minute changes to the bill—just a little rearranging of the acts, since it was proving awkward to

get the performing dogs off the stage in time for the ragtime dancers to enter, since they had to come in from
both wings. The acrobats were going in after the dogs instead, since they could enter from one side while the
dogs left on the other.

Jonathon explained the idea for the new illusion, Nigel
approved it, and Arthur made several suggestions for
music until they finally settled on a piece. Only then did
Ninette ask the question that had been in her mind since
her shock. "What *were* those flames?" she asked. "They
were not even warm, but they looked so real!"

Jonathon chuckled. "Pure illusion, not stage magic,
but one that ordinary folks can see. As a Fire Master I
know everything there is to know about Fire and its
creatures, and as a consequence, I can call up real
fires, or summon up what is nothing more than the illusion of fire. That's how I intend to burn down the
Sultan's Palace at the end of our production, except
the fires will be partly my illusion and partly stage-
craft."

He held out his hand, and a moment later, there was
a flame dancing on the palm. "Don't touch that one,
that's real," he said cautiously. He held out the other,
and a second flame sprang up, but with the two side-by-
side, she could see that there were differences. The illu-
sory one was paler, and rather than flickering and
moving randomly, this flame kept the same side-to-side
motion, as if it was some sort of clockwork pendulum.

"That's the problem with illusions," Jonathon continued, turning both hands into fists to banish both flames.
"Unless you concentrate all you have on it, you always
wind up with a second-rate imitation of the real thing.
Still, it wouldn't do for me to burn down the stage, or my
apprentice either."

She smiled slightly. As witticisms went, it was rather

feeble, but she was determined to hold the high ground
and not show any further displeasure with him.

"By the way, Mademoiselle." Arthur said thoughtfully, "How did you know about Jonathon's regrettable
tendency to make his assistants so angry at him that
they leave his employ? He must go through two or
three in a year."

Jonathon flushed, and Ninette restrained a smile. She
guessed that Arthur was also tired of Jonathon's pranks,
and was using that question as a means to show the magician that his behavior had not gone unremarked.

"The stage hands," she said, after thinking quickly
about what the cat had said. "When he did not arrive
with one, they talked about it. Frankly, they did not
seem surprised, only anxious that one of them not be
dragooned to serve as his victim in the illusions."

Jonathon flushed with embarrassment, which well he
should, given the circumstances. Whether the cat had
known about it from some previous acquaintance and
had lied, or it really had been the stagehands, it was
rather unpardonable behavior.

"I well, I suppose I am notorious," he said, with an artificial laugh. "Do you think we can get a spot of something to eat before the performance?"

She almost said something, then changed her mind.
"I'll send one of the boys out for something," Nigel
replied "I wanted to talk with you both about whether
or not you'd—noticed anything, or anyone, that seemed
too interested in Mademoiselle Nina."

They exchanged a glance. "I am not certain I would,"
she said, finally, and shrugged. "You should ask
Thomas."

"I did. He looked inscrutable. By which I think he
means that he has sensed something, but that it is
nowhere near. Certainly not in Blackpool, probably not

in the county, Possibly not in England. But I suspect that whatever it is, it will be here soon. So I suggest we plan for its arrival."

Ninette could only look baffled. She could not imagine who among the circles of Elemental Masters good and bad, could be holding a grudge against her.

"All right. I suggest that you and I, Nigel, have our creatures watching for any other new Master that enters the city," Jonathon said with a nod. "Now, the Master *might* be able to conceal himself to a greater or lesser extent, but Elementals gossip, and that's something no Master has ever been able to break them of." He grinned. "Even if he has Wardings on him, he'll still cause a ripple in his element just by existing, and the other Elementals will sense that."

Nigel nodded.

"Then what?" Arthur asked.

"Then we wait for him, or her, to do something," Nigel replied. "We cannot act against him, there are rules about that, and I don't want to face someone like the Old Lion for breaking the rules. Besides, unlikely as it seems, we might get another Master in here just as a visitor to Blackpool, and it would be very unwise to launch an attack of some sort on some hapless stranger."

Jonathon shuddered. "The Old Lion would fry us for that."

"Besides, if you are clever, he will not know that you are there, or that you know what I am supposed to be," Ninette said, after a moment of silence. "I think it would be wise to wait. No?"

Yes.

All eyes turned to the window, where the cat sat on the sill, although he had not been there a moment before.

Our enemy does not know about me, either, Thomas pointed out. *"Laying low," as our American cousins would say, is the wise choice here. But be prepared, because it is possible an attack will not come from magic, at least not at first.*

Ninette stared at him.

"Perhaps I should round up a solicitor then," Nigel replied, half in jest.

That might be wise, replied the cat, not at all in jest.

NINETTE stopped in astonishment at the door of her dressing room. It was full of flowers.

She had been dancing in the performances for two weeks now, and had been acting as Jonathon's dancer and assistant for one. Last night she had added a fourth dance to her routines, a skirt dance with special colored lights playing on it, a la Loie Fuller. Sure that had not been the occasion for all of this!

There were bouquets of every size and color, from a little nosegay of violets on her dressing table to an enormous creation that practically required a table of its own. Her maid, Ailse McKenzie, had collected the cards and arranged them on her dressing-table. She opened each one, to see messages of admiration ... and five different names. Well! It seemed she had a suite of admirers!

For a moment, she felt a warm glow, and a smile passed over her lips. This was wonderful! This was exactly the sort of adulation that the *etoiles* enjoyed, and it was a harbinger of more substantial offerings to come.

From flowers, the tributes usually rose to flowers and fruit, then flowers and chocolates, then flowers and jewelry . . . or they did, if several men were vying to become one's benefactor. Of course, there was no telling how rich any of these men were. It was nearly summer, and flowers were not as dear now as they were in winter. She didn't know enough to tell which were in season in England, and thus inexpensive, and which were not and thus expensive, but these extravagant floral tributes could represent the limits of extravagance of any or all of them. A starving poet could and would spend his last farthing on a bouquet for one whose looks excited his imagination. Poets and other artists were hardly the most practical of creatures. Still! It would be wonderful to have the men that had given her all these flowers crowding her dressing room after the performances, and even nicer if one of them took her out for dinner afterwards. . . .

"I'll be accepting visitors after the show, Ailse," she said, slowly and carefully, for Ailse did not always understand her heavily accented English.

"Gemmun visitors too, ma'amselle?" the girl asked.

She nodded. The girl nodded, though Ninette thought her face showed a trace of disapproval. That was only to be expected. She had never served theater people before, and likely had no idea that the dressing room of a principle served as a kind of drawing room for the *etoile*. Or perhaps she did not think that Ninette should be encouraging so many men.

Well, she would have to get used to it. Ninette reckoned that if the maid could get so accustomed to a Brownie living in the pantry that she put out a daily bowl of milk and plate of bread for it, she could get used to Ninette's admirers, and perhaps, a benefactor. Eventually.

Not that Ninette expected to find the sort of benefac-

tor that La Augustine enjoyed here in this city. That was
highly unlikely. It did not seem to run to rich men, or
nobles with both titles and money. Nor did she expect to
see such men in this sort of theater; she had never yet
seen the kind of men she hoped to attract, the sort that
became the protectors of *etoiles*.

Or at least, they would not come here until Nigel's
real show began, if there even were such in this city.

Then . . . well to be realistic, the ones who came would
probably not be the nobles with both titles and money,
nor the ones whose great-grandfathers had been both
wealthy and genteel. Rich men, newly rich, with fast
motorcars, who like jazz and ragtime . . . yes, perhaps.
That sort had come to the opera now and again, but
they tended to favor the dancers at the *Moulin Rouge,*
and then, they did not keep any one woman for very
long. Why should they? Dancers at the *Moulin Rouge*
were not devotees of art and culture, they had simple
tastes and seldom took thought for the future. A ballet
dancer, an opera singer—they knew that their days
were numbered on the stage, and they took thought for
the future. They looked for men who would give them
presents that would support them when they could no
longer dance or sing—things like not just a flat, but the
entire building the flat was in, or presents of money
without asking where that money was going.

The great courtesans understood this, as did their
benefactors. Ninette had actually been present one day
when some fanatic street preacher had accosted one of
those great ladies outside the theater and chided her for
her "irregular life." "My good man," the lady had said
with a laugh, "My life is a great deal more regular than
that of your wife." And everyone had known that was
true. The street preacher's wife could never be sure of
what her household allowance would be, nor when it
would come. The courtesan, however, had arranged for

all such things to be negotiated ahead of time by her factor—often an older female relative. She had a dress allowance, her foodstuffs were charged, her rent was paid, she had an allowance for when she entertained her own friends or went out to the theater alone, she knew that she would be taken once a year to Monte Carlo or some other holiday spot, so many times to the races, so many times to the theater, and so forth. All negotiated very carefully, nothing left to chance. The sort of men that Ninette wanted understood all this.

The *Moulin Rouge* dancers—and she was far closer in position to them right now than to La Augustine— never thought of the future if they could help it; when they got presents of money, they spent it, and they would not know what to do with a building of flats except to allow all their friends to move in and stay for nothing. They were happy with the flashy jewels and champagne suppers of the bold, rich men who drove big, fast motorcars. This was the way that such men liked things. And those men were not old. Nor were they often very kind. In fact, from what little of those sorts of men Ninette had seen, she judged them to be very demanding, very arrogant, and often difficult to deal with. They *wanted* and what they wanted, they generally got. They also had very little regard for wants or needs not their own; they expected to be the ones being pleased, and not the ones giving pleasure. When they gave a gift, it was with the expectation that it would be displayed so that everyone would know what a fine gift they could give. They seldom took their kept women to the theater, to the opera, to places where the "respectable" might go. The lives of *their* women were very irregular indeed.

She considered these things as she carefully and expertly applied her stage makeup, and as Ailse helped her into her costume. All things considered, she decided, if these were that sort of young man, she would not give any of them particular encouragement. She would accept their flowers and other gifts, but give them nothing other than the opportunity to display to each other how important they were, and to vie for her undivided attention.

And it was always possible that these were merely romantic young men for whom sending several bouquets of flowers to a dancer was the acme of extravagance. And since she had far more in common with Manon than with Mimi, she did not propose to live on love in a garret. So she would enjoy their attention and their flattery, but give them nothing to hope for beyond that she would allow them to give her attention and flattery.

Besides, the audience gave her that . . .

And with that in mind, she hurried off to the wings to give them every reason to grant it to her.

The house was full, the holiday-makers' season in full bloom, and it was an audience that expected to be pleased, was prepared to be pleased, and was happy to show that it was pleased. Her dances with the props, the huge skirt, and the colored lights brought oohs and ahs from the audience. Then she changed from the skirt costume to the simple long Grecian-style dress she wore for the first of Jonathon's turns, the trick with Jonathon where she chased his dancing handkerchief. It was never quite the same twice in a row; she played the part of a young girl that Jonathon was trying to make smile. He would pull the handkerchief out of the air, make a little puppet of it and make the puppet dance. She would chase it, and it would elude her, popping in and out of a bottle to keep her from capturing it. Then she would decide to trick it, go off to the other side of the stage, and dance wonderfully intricate ballet passages cribbed from the solos from *Les Sylphides*, the Chopin ballet that had no plot, as opposed to the *La Sylphide*, which had been her triumph and downfall. The handkerchief would become curious, come closer and closer, and finally end up dancing with her. That brought delighted laughter.

Then she ran offstage and quickly changed into her "captive slave" costume, for the trick where she appeared to be burned alive; as ever, even through her own screams, she heard the gasps of horror. It was a particularly good evening. It almost seemed to her that she could feel the audience's pleasure, as well as hear it. She had actually shivered in the cabinet at their gasps of horror, feeling some of that horror herself.

And when she returned to a dressing room full of more flowers, she found it also full of both passionate and impoverished young men and brash and demanding wealthier middle-aged men. And as she had expected, the older men were all the *nouveau riche,* motorcar-driving, ragtime-loving sort. *Not* the sort from which one would get proper support.

For one moment, she almost fled, despite her earlier thoughts. She was *not* the great dancer she pretended to be. She was only a little creature from Paris Opera Ballet, not an *etoile,* a bare step up from *coryphée.*

But then she steeled herself, cast her mind back to La Augustine, and sailed into the dressing room with a smile and a tinkling laugh. This, too was a performance, and she would give it her best.

Nigel came by, looked surprised and then pleased by all the attention she was getting, then went on his way. Well, he was surely counting his receipts with great pleasure tonight. Arthur waved, and Wolf flapped his wings at her from the door, but they were clearly on their way somewhere else—home, perhaps.

Then Jonathon appeared, and when he saw the crush, he looked absolutely black. But he did not stay either; he looked daggers at the men, then stalked off. She wondered what reason he thought he had to look so evilly at her visitors. Surely none of these men, not the shallow, showy ones with money, nor the young and romantic ones with nothing, should give him any cause to be concerned. The idea that any of *these* could be a magician with murderous intent was too laughable even to entertain for a moment.

In the end, of course, she sent them all away with laughter and flattering words that sounded like promises but were not, and once she was sure they were gone, she changed to her street clothes, and set out with Ailse on foot for her flat. Through the rain. Again. Did it never stop raining here? At least the street lights were electrical, and remained on during the rain. Blackpool was allegedly famous for them.

Dinner had been left to stay warm in the oven for her; she smelled it as soon as she opened the door. The Brownie, of course, could be counted upon to keep it from burning or drying out. It was a lovely beef dinner; the English seemed to eat a great deal of beef. She and Ailse shared it, she savoring every single bite, slowly and with infinite pleasure, thinking how like paradise this was. Only a few weeks ago she was eating the last of her cabbage soup and stale bread. Now she feasted on roast beef, new potatoes, the first of the spring asparagus, and a splendid chocolate cake to follow. She would sleep in a bed with sheets and warm blankets, and awake to tea and toast and wonderful currant jelly served to her in that same bed. Then she would stop downstairs for another breakfast of eggs and broiled tomatoes and a little sausage before going to the theater. Someone would surely take her out to luncheon, or Ailse would bring her something from the nearby theater pub. She never went without a meal now, and a good one—just as well, because she was rehearsing morning and afternoon, and performing every night. Master Ciccolini was proving a better instructor than he thought he was, for his eye was very good and caught all the little places where her balance could be improved, a turn could be made more beautiful, a line more graceful—and what was more, he knew how to position her to get those things. They were working on the choreography for the big production of *Escape from the Harem* in this way, bar by bar, trial and error. What she could not lift wholesale from other ballets, that is. It was hard work and she needed the good food. She had never felt better, healthier, happier in her life.

Ailse glanced once or twice at her with curiosity, but was too good a servant to ask anything. "Food," Ninette said into the silence, "is a kind of art. Like all arts, it can be simple, or it can be complex, but one always knows when the artist who created it is great. And great art deserves respect and attention." She smiled. "It goes without saying that our hostess is an artist in her own kitchen. Everything she makes is as perfect as it can be."

" 'Tis uncommon good, aye, m'amselle," Ailse ventured, winning another smile from Ninette. And there was another thing. Although she had a heavy accent, and her conversation was unexpectedly sprinkled with Russian phrases, her English mysteriously improved each night. Was that the cat's doing? It must be. She could not imagine any other way in which it could be happening so quickly.

In short, life was wonderful, even without a rich old man to shower gifts and fine living on her. She was beginning to wonder if she really needed such a man after all. . . .

But as Ninette went to bed, she wondered something else; what about the crowd in her dressing room had made Jonathon Hightower look so annoyed?

Nigel's Air Sprites fled from his office without warning, so he was not entirely surprised to see Jonathon come in wearing an expression like a thunderstorm. Nigel went on counting the receipts. "Good house tonight," he remarked.

"Full of idiots," Jonathon growled. "But I suppose that is just as well. Easier to deceive idiots."

"They seemed to appreciate your act."

Jonathon frowned. "I wish she would show a little less leg."

It seemed a non-sequitur, but Nigel was tolerably familiar with the way that Jonathon thought. *Aha. That is the way the wind blows, is it?* Nigel coughed. "If I recall correctly, your last female assistant wore tights and a Merry Widow—and not much more—"

"My last assistant was a trollop," Jonathon all but spat. "This dancer of yours needs to be more careful. Some people seem to think that showing your legs on the stage means they'll get to see more of those legs up close if they just bring enough flowers."

Ah Jonathon—the magician, so far as Nigel was aware, had been notoriously indifferent to his assistants, although it was quietly understood that being his assistant on stage meant sharing living quarters for the tour offstage. And if they objected to that, they were replaced. To Nigel's knowledge only one or two ever had been, at least in mid-tour, and not for that reason. Jonathon's relentless drive and his acid wit, however, had driven more than one of them to quit at the end of a season. He was rather a hard taskmaster, and his sense of humor, as Nina had discovered, was just a trifle cruel. Nigel was actually proud that she had stood up to him over that one incident. Jonathon didn't care for shrinking violets. He respected her now.

Respects her enough to not care for a dressing room full of potential rivals . . .

"She's a ballet dancer. They spend most of their lives half-naked. I doubt she thinks anything of it, no more than you think of spending half your life with false hair plastered on your face." He decided to obliquely change the subject. "Has anything turned up looking to harm her?"

Jonathon frowned at that. "That's the other thing I wanted to talk to you about. My sentries are uneasy. There is definitely *something* in the wind, but whatever it is, they haven't been able to exactly find it. You know they have some limited ability to see into the future?"

Nigel nodded. Fire Spirits and Water Spirits were particularly good at that, Air Spirits *could,* but tended to be so flighty they had trouble concentrating, and Earth Spirits were . . . well . . . very dense when it came to the future, keeping all their attention solidly in the present.

"There is threat to her. And the origin of that threat is here, in this country. That is all they can say." Jonathon's frown deepened. "Do you suppose that whatever or whoever it is knows that she is being guarded?"

"Wouldn't you?" Nigel countered. "We daren't underestimate this foe. Her father was powerful enough to create Thomas, and yet *he* lost out to this person—or persons. For all we know, there could be more than one enemy. And if there is, and they have separated, that could also cause confusion for your spirits."

"Curse it, you're right," Jonathon growled. "And curse them, too."

"Indeed," Nigel replied dryly. "How *dare* villainous cads be as clever as the heroes?"

Jonathon looked at him in shock for a moment . . . and then they both laughed.

Once her rage cooled—and the journey to this "Black-pool" place was accomplished, not by uncomfortable train, but by luxurious steam yacht, giving her plenty of time for her temper to cool—Nina, the real Nina, had gone from livid to calculating. And she realized that there was a very good reason, an excellent reason why the imposter had chosen *her* identity to steal. In the girl's place, she might have done the same.

Eastern Europe, and the Russian Empire, were a very, very long way from England. The English knew only what came to them, visiting *their* shores from out of those remote climes—Pavlova, Nijinsky, Diaghilev, Stravin-sky—and did not care to learn anything more. No one there had seen Nina dance. A few balletomanes would have heard of her name, that she was a great prima with the Imperial Ballet, but aside from a few sketches or blurred photographs, which could have been of virtually any ballerina, there was nothing to tell the imposter from the real thing. "Nina Tchereslavsky" was the perfect per-son to impersonate.

And aside from those few balletomanes, no one would know who, or even what, she was. The imposter was already on the metaphorical high ground, having established herself as "Nina Tchereslavsky." Any chal-lenger would have an uphill fight against someone who had fans, adherents, and the backing of an impresario. Claimants to a throne already being held usually did not fare well.

Perhaps an oblique approach, at least at first.

So, rather than sail that very expensive steam yacht directly into the harbor at Blackpool and excite all manner of interest among those who might wonder who was aboard, Nina ordered it put in to the harbor at Southport, then hired a motorcar and spent a leisurely and very private journey up the Liverpool Road to Preston, eating at the best establishments, sleeping at the best hotels, crossing a river known (she thought rather hilariously) as the "Ribble", and from thence to Blackpool itself. She took lodgings in a fine little hotel under the name of "Anna Vronsky," another joke, since she rather doubted any of the insular and culturally illiterate English would ever recognize the names of Tolstoy's famous hero and heroine of the great master-work, *Anna Karenina*.

Nor did they. And generous payment in advance practically guaranteed discreet silence about the myste-rious Russian lady, though according to her servants, ru-mors flew about the dining room that she was a duchess, even a grand duchess, or at least a countess.

Having established a headquarters, she went about obscuring her magical existence, for a very brief foray into the Elemental realms told her that the imposter was somehow involved with both a Fire Master and an Air Master. Discretion was definitely in order, and cau-tion, and a great deal of covering her tracks. She had plenty of practice in that. There was not an Elemental Master on the planet that would be happy about one of the Elementals achieving what she had done in escaping her bonds. They would be even less happy if they knew how she was sustaining herself outside the Earth Realm. Dangerous. Very dangerous.

That took several days. One more thing was needed; knowledge. This was not her land, nor her language, nor were any of those she had absorbed familiar with Eng-land, much less this particular city. She sent out her maid one night to find and bring back someone who would not be missed.

It took only a moment to absorb the ragged street urchin, who gave her a street-urchin's command of the English language, and a street-urchin's knowledge of the city. Only then was she prepared to go and have a look at her imposter.

And she did not do that as "Anna Vronsky," either.

It was a very good thing to have servants that were not human—and were totally under her control. There was no curiosity to contend with when she sent out her maid to buy a second-hand men's suit, nor when she assumed the face and figure of one of the poets she had consumed. Carrying a stack of empty boxes, as if she had just made a delivery, Nina left the hotel by the service entrance without anyone looking at her twice.

Then it was a simple matter to dispose of the boxes and make her way to the theater where her imposter was dancing. She bought a cheap balcony seat, and sat, unsmiling and unmoving, through the entire performance.

Grudgingly, she had to admit that the little trollop was good. Quite good. And it was clear that she was an audience favorite. Of course, the mobs of holiday goers in the theater were quite prepared to be pleased with just about anything they were given, provided it was novel and amusing enough. And it was quite clear just who and what the girl had purloined her dances from, even if most, if not all, of the audience had never seen Loie Fuller or Isadora Duncan. Nor had they even heard of the dancers except as the subject of articles in newspapers.

After the performance, Nina went back to the stage door, and loitered, listening to the gossip among the stagehands. Here her knowledge of the language was perfect; she fit right in. And her knowledge of backstage life allowed her, eventually, to slip around to the theater pub, pay for two bottles of cheap champagne, and get in backstage by pretending she was a delivery person. One bottle was destined to be delivered to a woman who sang popular songs, and the other to a comedian, both with notes of congratulation and an unreadable signature attached. But having them gave her all the excuse she needed to linger backstage—

She learned that the imposter was very popular with the backstage workers. That was awkward, because by her nature, she had a great many limitations as to what she could and could not do. She could easily influence someone whose mind was already tending in a direction she wanted it to go, but it was the next thing to impossible to influence them in the opposite direction. There were also disadvantages to being tied up in very mortal form; she could not manifest in the girl's flat and simply absorb her. She would have to somehow get within embracing range of her, and remain private with her for as long as it took to absorb her. There would be no finding allies back here, and the girl was too well-guarded to think of a direct approach.

She also learned that the imposter had so thoroughly ingratiated herself with the theater management that an enormous production was being planned solely around *her.* So there would be no hope in disenchanting the management with her, either. . . .

Nina would have to think of an entirely different plan of attack.

With that in mind, she left the bottles of champagne with their surprised and gratified recipients, and returned to her hotel. Once there, she got the boxes from where she had hidden them, then applied at the service entrance for admission to her own suite. The room was rung for permission, the maid gave it, and Nina took herself back up to her quarters and assumed her rightful form.

Once there, she paced like a caged lion, restlessly, trying to think of a way to undermine the girl. She could not do so on the basis of talent, that much was clear. The girl had made far too many friends in that theater to do so there, too. Why could she not have been a scheming, vituperative shrew? Why hadn't she been arrogant, cold, heartless? Why had she spent time and money distributing little favors to the stagehands? Why hadn't she had furious arguments with the orchestra?

Furthermore, there were not even rival lovers to set against each other, nor was there a hint of scandal to excite the interest of the press and outrage the public! Why hadn't the girl had the decency to take up with a married man as his lover? That sort of thing was shrugged at on the Continent, even expected, but it could have brought her down completely in so-proper England!

Well there was no use in lamenting what had not happened. Nina needed to think of something that could.

Well ... there was the possibility of creating a scandal out of nothing. She could find someone utterly unsuitable who *wanted* to be the girl's lover, make him think that the girl reciprocated his feelings, then inform the wife ... that would take time, however. And a great deal of effort.

Well it would certainly do to at least start that project. She could begin by finding such a man. One of the imposter's many admirers, who crowded her dressing room, no doubt, was of the proper stuff to turn into a man obsessed.

But in the meantime ...

She shook her head. She was famished, and not for mortal food. She had not drained anyone since that street urchin, and he had been relatively unsatisfactory. There had not been a great deal of life in him; it had gotten beaten and starved out of him by the streets. There were two kinds of people that provided her with a satisfactory repast. First and foremost were those rich old men, who were fat with abundant living and experiences. All those memories, all the things they had accomplished—it was like a multi-course meal created by the finest of chefs.

And then there were the young men, full of passion,

dreams, hopes, and desires. Everything about them was sharp, new, flavored with high emotion. She could not have said which were her favorites. . . .

But tonight, on such short notice, it would be much, much easier to find a young man.

She summoned her manservant. Tonight she would be taking another long walk.

11

THE show was coming together.

In fact, it had progressed far enough that the entire score was complete, and Arthur was rehearsing the orchestra in their parts, Maestro Ciccolini and Ninette had finished their choreography and Ninette was rehearsing her numbers, as well as dancing in the evening. At first, Ninette had been worried that her act would get stale—music hall audiences were used to seeing a different bill every week, after all. But Nigel assured her that Blackpool, at least in holiday season, was very different. The audience changed every week, so to them, the revue was entirely new. And he was right.

Ninette's admirers had gone from a handful to a young army. None of them were what she was looking for, but then, she was no longer looking very hard. It seemed that the more she danced, and the more audience acclaim she had, the more she craved the applause. It was no longer thinkable that if she ever *did* find a protector, she would give up dancing. She might have felt alarm at this, except that she came off the

stage every night feeling invigorated rather than
drained.

Not that any of the gentlemen who filled her dressing
room with flowers were the sort to offer the kind of
arrangement that suited her. Still, some pleasant things
came from all these admirers. Not just flowers, which
were delightful and kept her flat scented sweetly—there
were some more permanent presents. Nothing spectacular, nothing so enormously expensive that accepting it
would have implied certain expectations that would
have to be fulfilled . . . no, these were pretty, but more
modest tokens. A pair of garnet and tortoiseshell combs,
a handsome set of enameled gold necklace, bracelet and
earrings in the Egyptian style, any number of less remarkable pieces of jewelry, pairs of gloves, fans, lace
handkerchiefs—all tokens of esteem, mute pleas for
preference, but not demands for attention. The one time
a rather remarkable sapphire bracelet had appeared on
her dressing table, it had been very firmly given back to
the one who had proffered it.

There were also many pleasant suppers, and a few
parties—all of them in the company of other members
of the company, of course. Usually Nigel came along, in
fact. And if she was not the first to leave these affairs,
she was certainly never the last.

Certain members of the circle of admirers remained,
men who lived and worked in Blackpool. Others appeared, only to vanish: those who were not residents.
The two sorts were easy to tell apart, and Ninette and
Ailse had a little game between them, of how long it
would take for these birds-of-passage to understand
that money could not necessarily purchase everything
their hearts desired. She wasn't worried; the one and
only time a "gentleman" had gotten a little too demanding, she'd broken his instep for him. Ballet dancers
might look fragile, but dancing built muscles.

He had been the exception though, and she had felt so little threatened at the time that she did not even bother to tell Nigel and have him barred from the theater. In the first place, his broken foot was going to keep him safely confined to his hotel until it was time for him to depart back to whatever grim industrial town had spawned him. For another, he had learned his lesson rather sharply. No need to get Nigel involved.

But Thomas the cat was not happy. And neither was the magician, Jonathon Hightower, but Thomas was someone she could actually *talk* to. The magician would only look annoyed, sullen, or angry, and tell her to leave the magical business in his hands.

"What on earth is wrong?" she finally asked the cat, after his prowling and peering out of windows on what should have been a quiet evening finally got on her nerves. "We had a delightful supper, the house was almost full, tomorrow the theater is dark and we have that dinner party—and I have not seen a sign of this inimical, invisible enemy you think I have."

She didn't add *an enemy that you made up in the first place*, because Ailse was in the room, but her brief glare at Thomas said it for her.

But the cat had other ideas. *There is something out there, and it is no friend to you. I just cannot figure out who or what it is, nor what it wants.*

She blinked a little in surprise. So this wasn't part of his elaborate ruse?

"I can't imagine why—" she began.

That's the problem. Neither can I. He sighed gustily. *I suppose I will have to investigate this. Jonathon—*

She frowned. "I would not take anything Master Hightower says to be an indication of anything at all other than his overactive imagination. He sees a bit of rope and sees a serpent, a shadow and thinks it is a spirit."

He has reasons to. Sometimes a rope is a serpent in disguise.

She flung up her hands. "Have it your own way then! Is there any reason why this mysterious something you both sense must be planning on me as its victim? What about Nigel? Arthur? Wolf? You? Even Jonathon? All of you are far more likely to have collected magical enemies than I!"

The cat hesitated. *I suppose that is possible . . .*

"I would say it was far more likely." She sniffed. "The only enemy *I* am likely to have would be the sort that would put ground glass in the toes of my shoes, or cut the shoulder-straps of my costumes." She surprised herself with a yawn. "I am going to bed. You may stay up and watch all night if you please."

Hmm, was all Thomas would say.

After a great deal of thought, and a great many discarded plans, Nina decided to attack obliquely by attacking not the girl herself, but the theater. If the physical building was gone, she would have no place to perform. If she had no place to perform, she would be cast out on her own, without a salary, and be easier to get at. At this point Nina had decided that she *would* absorb the girl. Not just out of revenge, but because it could be useful to have a second identity ready and waiting to step into which provided such fruitful rewards for her kind.

So that was her plan. Attack the theater, destroy it, and flush the quarry.

As for how that was to be done . . . although fire obviously was not Nina's Element, fire was the easiest, and that was what she would try first.

Jonathon Hightower watched the Salamander twine around the fingers of his left hand, and frowned. Strictly speaking, Elementals could not see the future, not as a human clairvoyant could, at any rate. But they could sense when something was going to happen a short time before it actually did, and they reacted to that.

This one was agitated. Very agitated. Enough to make it come to Jonathon without being invoked, which was something Fire Elementals rarely did. All he could discern from it was the sense of danger, danger and destruction, coming soon.

Wait— No, he sensed something more. The danger had to do with fire.

Fire was always a theatrical nightmare. Everything about a theater was a fire hazard. The scenery, made of canvas painted with oils, the curtains, the dry wood . . . it was worse in the days of limelight and gaslight of course. There were terrible stories of performers getting too close to the lights and going up in flames. That was why there were buckets of sand, and sometimes water, tucked unobtrusively away everywhere in the wings.

Finally, the Salamander grew frantic, and he decided he was going to take a walk.

His present lodgings were, in fact, the guest bedroom that the dancer had just vacated. Nigel saw no reason for him to take his own lodgings, and every reason why he should *not*. Here, among Nigel's trained servants, accustomed to mages and magic, he could do whatever he chose to do and not so much as a raised eyebrow would occur. Outside of these walls, however, was a land of nosy landladies, curious fellow tenants, and a wealth of horror stories about what had happened when an ordinary person stumbled into someone working magic. And truth to tell, for all his apparent misanthropy, Jonathon liked the company of others well enough if his companions were intelligent.

One certainly couldn't fault Nigel, Arthur, or even Wolf on that score. Besides, this saved him money. Power as a mage did not translate into wealth, and not every, or even most, Elemental Masters were independently wealthy. Nigel had made his fortune honestly, by gauging the public's tastes and meeting them, but he was no more the norm among Elemental Masters than he was among ordinary folk. Jonathon had chosen a path that would probably never make him rich, although if he was careful, he could retire comfortably one day. So living off Nigel did not bother him one whit, since it meant that much more of his salary could be tucked away towards that end.

Staying here had other advantages—one of which was that he could stroll out of the flat at two in the morning without making an excuse to anyone, and know that no one would be poking a nose out to find out where he was going. More to the point, he could return when he pleased and not have to answer to anyone, nor face being locked out.

So off he went, after choosing an inconspicuous coat and old cloth cap to wear in order to blend in with the locals.

The Salamander vanished, leaving a sense of relief in its wake as it did so. Whatever he was doing must have been right.

The streets were dark and quiet, even here in the theater district. They were, however, very well lit—it was bad for business if your customers fell and broke a limb on the way to the theater, and worse for them to be the victim of a cutpurse or felon. For once, there was no rain. At this time of night, one of the most important things to do was to walk briskly and with purpose, so that any policeman that spotted him would be certain that he was a man with a duty and a destination, and would not hinder him. He passed by two such on his

way to the theater, and only when he reached it did he
pause, slow down, and drop into the shadows.

And chided himself for such a melodramatic action.

Still . . .

He slipped around the side of the theater and paused,
still staying concealed in the shadows, as he stood with
his back against the wall, considering what could and
could not be seen, trying to become invisible. Once he
had regulated his breathing again, he *listened*. . . .

And that was when he heard it. The unmistakable
sound of someone striking a match in the darkness of
the alley.

Carefully, slowly, with his hand shielded by his arm
and the breast of his coat, he called up a tiny flame in
the palm of his hand. "Show me what you see," he
breathed, the simple words calling up a spell of as much
intricacy as a piece of fine lace. He stared into the flame,
willing it to show what that fire struck in the alley was
surrounded by.

As if reflected in a mirror, he saw a shabby boy, cap
pulled down over his forehead. He was striking a match.
The flame that Jonathon was looking through was some
little distance away, a tiny fire of the spent sticks of the
matches piled there.

The boy set fire to something. Something like—a tail?

That was it. He was lighting a bundle of straw and lint
that was tied to—

A rat's tail.

As the rat squealed in fear, he opened the door to the
cage, and it dashed out and into the ally.

Jonathon in his turn, leaped around the corner, only
to see the bobbing ball of fire that was just out of reach
duck down a grating into the sewer.

"You!" he shouted. "You there!"

The wrong thing, of course, though it had been a calculated risk—would the boy freeze in place, or try to run?

He ran. And he knew these streets better than Jonathon. Within moments, he was gone, and Jonathon was left staring into the darkness that had swallowed him up.

Dammit.

Had that been the only rat the urchin had turned loose? He dared not take that chance.

He dashed back to where he had seen the boy crouched, and to his dismay, found a dozen empty wooden live-traps—it had been a live-trap that he had mistaken for a cage. In a moment of rage, he kicked them, scattering them across the alley, splintering several.

But temper was not going to fix what had been done. He was going to have to work quickly. There were an unknown number of rats scrambling about this area, trailing fire behind them. Rats that could get into anywhere ... but most especially, between walls and under floorboards.

Quickly, he summoned a circle of protection about himself; it glowed on the slimy cobblestones of the alley with the deep red-orange of coals in the heart of the fire. Once there, he had his own little mantra for summoning—where Nigel used music, he drew.

With a wand of fire pulled out of the element itself, he drew in the air around himself, sigils and symbols in what would look to an outsider like a hopeless jumble, but which were, in fact, precisely placed. They glowed, yellow-hot, hanging in midair around him. The boy had turned loose a dozen rats, not less, possibly more. For good measure he scribed the desire for two dozen Salamanders on the wall of air around him.

With a push of his power, he set the final sigil. Then he sent his wand back to where it had come from, opened his arms, and Called.

The symbols around him flared, blurred, pulsed with the power he gave them, and then vanished in a blinding flash.

And Jonathon swarmed with Salamanders. They danced all over him, wreathing around his arms, threading in and out of his jacket, as he explained to them what they needed to do.

"A boy was here," he told them, and showed them with his thoughts. "He set rats loose with fire tied to their tails. I don't know where they all went; *you* have to find them."

He got their answer more in impressions than words. Agreement. Fire? That was what they *were*. Of *course* they could find the rats.

"*All* of them."

Of course. That went without saying. And then what?

"You must follow and eat every bit of fire they leave behind them. Then when you find them, you must eat the fire tied to their tails."

Glee. They were not often permitted to devour real-world fire. This would be like candy to them. But . . . he did not expect them to eat the rats, did he?

"No, that is not necessary. But go! Those rats could be setting anything on fire!"

Agreement.

And then they were gone.

They flashed in a dozen different directions at once, leaving him standing alone in the alley, lit only by the light from his circle of protection. Wearily, he dismissed it. The Salamanders had been alert and focused; there were times when he had trouble with them, but this, evidently, was not going to be one of those times.

They did naturally what he would have had to do magically and at greater physical expense; they were tracking the rats by the "scent" of fire, and their "noses" were better than a bloodhound's. He knew he could leave them here to do their work. When they were done, they would simply go back to the Elemental Plane of Fire, sated and happy. They had been "paid" twice: once in the magical energy he had given them, and once in the feeding they would have.

He wanted to lean against the wall in fatigue, but it was cold and damp and very dark here, and none of those conditions agreed well with a Fire Master. Instead, he trudged back to Nigel's flat. He knew the others were sound asleep by now, and with the crisis averted, he reckoned that morning would be soon enough for them to hear what had almost happened.

Nina tore the vagrant she had found in the gutter limb from limb in her rage, then sent the pieces off with her goblins, to be dropped into the sewers all over the city. And then, she went back to her hotel, climbed up the wall and in through the open window, and shed her blood-stained clothing. She set the maid to cleaning up the mess while she flung herself down into her bed and brooded.

What wretched luck that there was a Fire Master associated with the theater! She wondered what had brought him there tonight? Was it only restlessness and an urge to walk, or had he somehow been warned of what she was doing?

She was just glad she had been trying something without the taint of magic to it. This trick had come out of the annals of ancient sieges—sending animals into a city or an armory to set it afire. Rats were the favored vehicle for this—small and agile, they could carry the fire into the heart of the building. And she had paid the rat-catcher who served the building specifically for these rats and no others. Terrified, in pain, they would run to the place they thought of as home, dash through their secret ways in a futile effort to lose the thing that was hurting them, the fire tied to their tails.

It had been a good plan. Too bad the Fire Master had shown up to ruin it.

But she, at least, had gotten away. And he had no idea she was anything other than a mad little street urchin with a penchant for setting fires.

One good thing had come out of this. Now she knew the face of the possible opposition, or part of it, anyway. She would have to be cunning, careful.

She settled herself in her bed, and began to think.

"He *what?*" Nigel spluttered.

"He was tying bundles to the rats' tails, setting them on fire, and—" Jonathon paused. "—and turning them loose."

"That is an ancient siege trick," Wolf said unexpectedly.

Jonathon did not ask the bird how he knew that. Wolf was always coming up with unexpected bits of information.

"Well what are you waiting for?" Nigel asked, regarding him angrily. "Is it Nina? Is this someone attempting to attack her? Is this what we should be looking for?"

And now Jonathon had to hesitate. "I don't know," he said, finally. "There wasn't anything at all magical about what was going on. It was just a street-boy, and it wasn't as if he was actually trying to start fires that I could make out—more that he was just tormenting the rats for the fun of it."

"But?" Arthur asked, watching him closely.

"But I don't like it. If Nina's enemy is clever, he could have paid the boy to do this. There would be no telling that it was the work of a mage." He got up, all his interest in breakfast gone. "I just don't know. It seems almost diabolically clever. But the storm—that is the work of someone who just doesn't think. And yet—"

"All right, Jonathon," Arthur said, finally. "What we can do is to be on our guard. The fact that your Salamander came to *you* before we had a burning theater means that they seem to have rapport with you we can probably count on."

He nodded. That was reasonable.

"In that case, we should assume it was the work of Nina's enemy, and that she's been discovered," he replied. "Whoever this is, he's very subtle. So we should assume spies, attempts to lure her out somewhere alone, and indirect attempts, like on the theater."

"Humph." Nigel put his fork down and frowned. "I wonder, if it is Nina's enemy, what he'll come up with next."

"Clearly we have to think in terms of things that are not magical," Jonathon pointed out. "Whoever this may be knows very well that there are Masters here, and he is not going to make it easy for us to find him, or stop him."

All three of the others, Wolf included, nodded. "We must think like a saboteur, or an assassin," Arthur murmured.

"And not just that," Jonathon replied grimly. "We must think like a clever one."

Nina still thought that burning down the theater was the best plan. The question was, how to do so without showing her magical nature. Her second attempt was more straightforward in execution but devious in planning.

Taking on the look of one of the ruffians she had absorbed, she went in search of the sort of pub where unsavory deals could be made. Then, once she found such a pub, she let it be known that her employer had a building she wanted removed from the property it was on.

It was not long before she was sharing drinks with someone who thought that might be arranged. He was a little surprised to discover the building in question, but it was just a brief flash, and then he was all business.

Nina was relieved to discover that he did not *want* to know why the theater needed to be burned. She did not offer said explanation. She merely paid him what he asked, and settled back in her suite to await the results.

But the results were disappointing. There was no fire on the stipulated date, and the next day the sensation of the morning paper was that a known arsonist had been caught red-handed, and he was expected to be spending the rest of his life in prison.

Credit for the discovery was given to a young police constable, but Nina cursed, knowing in her heart it must have been that wretched Fire Master.

She made one more attempt, but her heart wasn't in it; like the first try, she used an animal to try and carry fire into the building. This time it was the starlings that nested in the top. She gave them matches and twists of oiled paper which they carried up to the roof and tucked into their nests; she intended to do just a tiny bit of magic to ignite the matches themselves. That failed as the first had; one of the wretched birds dropped its burden on a passer-by, and the next thing Nina knew, the building was being scoured and the poor starlings lost all the nests they had started.

She also looked for ways to lure the imposter out away from anyone else; if she ever managed that, the result would be that the imposter would be absorbed, and Nina would change into her clothing and take her place. At least for a little bit—just long enough to have a great row with the theater owner and flounce out.

But the girl wouldn't accept invitations of that sort. No "I have something that might be to your advantage," no supper invitations from handsome young men, no— nothing.

In fact, the girl led a life so cloistered that it gave Nina pause. Not the work—Nina herself did the work of a dancer, and a good one too—but the sacrifice, that was unprecedented. No little téte-a-téte dinner parties with select gentlemen. No afternoons off for a picnic. No afternoons off shopping! That was what truly astonished Nina; every other dancer she had ever known was an inveterate shopper!

It was a pity too, since shopping would have been the ideal way to take her. Become a helpful shop girl, suggest there were better things in a back room. Take her there—and become her. No one the wiser.

There would be a complication of course, because it was possible that she might just decide to stay here. That impresario in Germany . . . she could cancel the appearances . . . but then she would have to eliminate him, too, or return his money. If she didn't he would probably sue for breach of contract.

All right. It was time to play to her strong suit. Use her own Element.

Ninette limbered herself backstage at afternoon rehearsal. She had taken the ball, hoop, and ribbon dances out, and had put in two pure ballet solos. Both, had she been asked, were blatant copies of two of Anna Pavlova's dances—"Waterlily" was a copy of her "California Poppy," complete with bringing the petals of her skirt up around her at the finale when the stage went dark, and "Fairy," which was a copy of Pavlova's "Dragonfly." But Anna Pavlova was far away and unlikely to ever get to Blackpool, and people were actually coming to Blackpool for their holidays to see *her!*

Of course most of that was due to her miraculous "rescue" that spring. But still. . . .

"Those dances are rather good," Jonathon said from behind her.

She shrugged, and bent over to touch her forehead to her knees and hold the position for a moment. "I copied them from Pavlova," she said frankly.

"I know," came the surprising reply. "I saw 'California Poppy' and 'Dragonfly' in Monte Carlo."

She straightened so fast she almost hurt herself. "What? And you said nothing to Nigel?"

It was his turn to shrug. "He wouldn't care. I know I don't. A dance isn't like a magic trick. I don't think you can ever say 'that's mine' once you've done it in public."

"I suppose so," she said, dubiously. She hesitated, but anything she was going to tell him was lost as the trained dog act suddenly saw Thomas, and idiotically forgot all of their tricks. Thomas headed straight for the dressing room with the pack in full cry behind him and the frantic trainer right behind them. Ninette let them all run— she knew very well that Thomas was more than a match for a hundred dogs—but Jonathon swore and raced after them all. Perhaps he was concerned for the dogs.

But that was the moment when things began to thaw between them.

12

NINETTE was keeping her muscles warm in the wings when the female half of the dog-training act dashed up to her, face white. "Have you seen Nigel?" she asked, breathlessly. Ninette stared at her, perplexed and alarmed, all at once, and pointed to stage left, where Nigel's sleeve was just barely visible behind a piece of scenery.

The dog trainer—Ninette strained to remember her name since the act went by the name of "Harrigan's Amazing Hounds"—rushed across the stage in a blatant violation of all the rules of performance. *Thou shalt not cross the stage during someone else's act in rehearsal—* dress rehearsal, of course, not band-call.

The act she ran through was, thank heavens, that of the character-comic, who was a good-natured old fellow, even if he did partake of the bottle a bit more than he should have. He kept right on, like a trouper, even as the female trainer seized Nigel—literally!—and began an urgent speech that started off quietly but very, very rapidly ascended into the hysterical.

She spoke too rapidly for Ninette to understand her, given that for Ninette, English was still very hard to comprehend unless people spoke in a leisurely manner. She got a few words here and there—*accident* and *broken legs.*

She rushed back across the stage again, her agitation visible, her eyes seeing nothing but the way out. Ninette kept warming up. No matter what, the show went on. It always went on. Only the death of a monarch would close down a show.

But in just exactly the time it took for someone to cross from stage left to stage right through the back-stage area, Nigel appeared at her elbow. "Harrigan somehow fell into a hole in the street and broke both legs," he said grimly. "I hate to ask you to—"

"I will put back the ball, ribbon, and ring dances," she said instantly. It was not as if they were great effort to perform. Not like the *Black Swan* pas-de-deux. Not like *Giselle's* Mad Scene. Not like the *Corsair* solos. They were, in fact, full of little pauses, rests, where she could catch her breath before going on to the next difficult passage. And they were done on *demi-pointe* rather than full *pointe.* She would have to change her shoes, but that was no great difficulty, and if worst came to worst and the ribbons wouldn't unknot, she could cut them off and Ailse could put new ribbons on while she danced *en pointe.*

Nigel nodded with relief and gratitude. "I'll be in my office; I should have a replacement act by tomorrow."

She shrugged. "So long as the audience is not bored with me, I can dance the extra solos for as long as you need me to."

He just said something that sounded like "You're a brick," and dashed off to his office. She was left shaking her head. It was going to be a long and strenuous night.

She went looking for her ball, ring, and ribbon music.

At least the band knew it. And at least the hole she would be filling was in the middle of the bill. She'd be well rested by the time her skirt dance came up.

By band call the third day after Harrigan broke his legs, if Nigel had been any other impresario, he would have been tearing his hair out. Because by that time, it was beginning to look as if the Fates had targeted him for disaster.

This was a very desirable venue for most performers; a six-week engagement at minimum meant it was possible to relax, unpack, mend things, take in the local sights. It was, after all, the audience that changed during the season in Blackpool; virtually a new audience twice a week. Nigel usually had far more acts auditioning than he had slots for them.

But now . . . first Harrigan, who had fallen into a hole that his wife swore literally "opened up in front of them" and broken both his legs. It was a good thing for both of them that Nigel knew a doctor who was also an Elemental magician, though not a master. He did not care to think of what a butcher's job an ordinary doctor would make of such a patient. So Harrigan was now splinted and resting comfortably surrounded by wife and dogs, a stone's throw from the doctor's office. Nigel was keeping him on wages, partly because it seemed the right thing to do, and partly because he wanted the Hounds for the big show, and when Harrigan was well again, he would certainly feel a debt of gratitude to Nigel.

But the next day brought another unpleasant surprise.

Three of the acts just . . . quit, with four more weeks to run on their contracts. They wouldn't tell him why, nor would their agents, but he suspected that a rumored Australian impresario with a supposed "golden tour"

was to blame. On the one hand, he viciously wished all
of them to perdition. On the other ... he knew how most
of these things turned out—with performers stranded in
the middle of nowhere with no money and no prospects
of getting any, sick with heat and tropical disease and
bitterly regretting the decision that had brought them to
that pass. He had already made up his mind that he was
not going to ask these acts to stick for the big show, but
still, he needed them *now*. He was not going to ask Nina
to put in another turn, and anyway, she could hardly
make up for half the show missing.

As it happened, though, Nigel was the rare sort who
always assumed some disaster was going to overtake
his shows, his theater, or the season, and planned accordingly.

He regularly made forays into the countryside and as
far as Liverpool, looking for people with talent who had
not yet "caught on." Two fast trips in his motorcar
yielded him a perky little singer with a genuine gift for
comic timing and a "novelty" juggler and his partner, a
fellow who impersonated a drunken "toff" with an impertinent maid who kept piling things into his arms
when he came home after a night on the tiles. He rushed
them to the theater in time for a quick rehearsal; to fill
the last slot, Jonathon put in an act he seldom performed anymore, a Hindoo fire-eater. It was all *real*
magic, of course, and as such it was something of a risk.
If there was an untrained Elemental mage in the audience, Jonathon's performance might "wake him up."
And there were those who hunted Masters as well,
though usually feuds were of a personal nature.

Jonathon, however, swore that there were precau-
tions he could take, shields he could set up. Nigel was
disposed to believe him, but he wanted the act safely
tucked away as soon as possible. He simply did not want
to take any chances when there might be someone

hunting for Nina—why give a hunter an opening for an attack?

So a morning on the phone and running back and forth from the telegraph office to London netted him a brother and sister "minstrel" act from America; the idea of a woman in blackface playing a banjo and tap dancing seemed to have put some booking agents off. But on the basis of an enthusiastic report from one of his scouts, which he trusted, he pursued the lead. He learned they were starving in London; he engaged them on the spot and arranged for the agent to advance them money so that they could buy train tickets to Blackpool.

All three of the new acts were enthusiastic and terribly grateful for the opportunity to play in one of the "big" halls. All of the acts were solid, if not brilliant. By the weekend, the programme was full again, and Jonathon and Nina were able to drop their extra turns, and not a moment too soon. It was clear that the extra work had just begun to wear on them.

Nigel watched the two of them from the wings as they ran smoothly through the "evil magician" turn, feeling unspeakably grateful that they had both come through without a murmur of complaint. No matter what else could be said about this Russian girl, there was no doubt in his mind that she was willing to work, and work hard. She was an imitator rather than an original, but no one on holiday in Blackpool and spending time in a music hall was likely to have seen the originals, and the girl gave you a good show for your money. Who did it harm, that she borrowed Loie Fuller's serpentine skirt dance without a blush of shame? How did it matter than she turned Pavlova's "California Poppy" into her own "Waterlily"? Was Pavlova losing money by it? Had Pavlova ever even heard of Blackpool? Would Fuller ever set foot in this city? Since the answer to all of these questions was "no," Nigel didn't see that anyone could have any quarrel with the girl. In fact, he thought she ought to be commended. She was probably the first ballet dancer most of these people had ever seen. And having seen, the holiday-makers might choose to have a look-in on a real ballet corps. Who could tell? They might even become regulars at the theater.

It wasn't as if she was claiming to be Pavlova, after all. In the theater, nothing was new, and the only people that ever successfully kept the secrets of how they did things were magicians.

He watched her with the eye of a critic rather than a showman as she went through her paces in Jonathon's act. She was certainly graceful, but that went with being a dancer. She wasn't much of an actress, but then, she wouldn't have studied acting. Nigel didn't know much about ballet, but he had the vague notion that the dancers were far too busy keeping track of their steps to do much acting. She didn't have to be much of an actress anyway; the audience for Music Halls was not one for subtle nuances. They liked showy tricks, melodrama; they wanted to be thrilled and amazed; they wanted to laugh and be dazzled. The Divine Sarah and Eleanor Duse had no place in the music hall. Little Tich, however, dancing in boots that were as long as he was tall . . . that was what they wanted.

He continued to watch. She was good. The audience liked her. Part of that was her youth, part her apparent fragility, part the romance of her rescue these several weeks ago. She connected with the audience too, she had an instinct for that. Performers had been a success on that alone.

One thing he didn't get from her was that . . . spark, that something special, that he felt from people that really *were* geniuses. He was hardly an ignoramus; he made a point of going to London when he could, to see what the world considered great. And there was a magic, a special something, in those for whom the stage was a kind of home, that the rest of theatrical humanity just did not possess. Ellen Terry, Henry Irving, they had it, and the audience reveled in seeing it displayed. He'd gone to ballets as well as the theater; he had seen Nijinsky, Pavlova, and Isadora Duncan too. They had it, they had it and made the stage sing beneath their feet. Eleanor Duse. The Divine Sarah, dear God, *she* had it, she could make you believe she was anything she chose to be, and you would completely forget that she was not fourteen years old as she spoke tremulously from her balcony to Romeo, that she was not the courtesan Marguerite Gautier and dying of consumption, that she was not even a woman, as she donned the breeches of Hamlet.

Nina Tchereslavsky did not have that gift. She had another, a gift for evoking emotion, and for giving it back, and she was good. She would never be immortal.

On the other hand, the people who had that spark often didn't do well in life. It was almost as if having been granted this enormous gift, the Fates decided that you had to make up for it in other ways. Those who had it seldom prospered in love; those who had it often drank to excess, or dosed themselves with morphia or hashish or some other drug. Those that had it knew that their gift was a jealous mistress and would tolerate no others.

Besides the people that came to music halls didn't want to see genius. Genius wasn't comfortable, it didn't actually care about what an audience wanted. Genius didn't set out to entertain you; if you were entertained by genius, that was incidental. Genius burned, and if you weren't careful, you burned with it. Genius didn't want you to forget your troubles, make you laugh, make you gasp. Genius wanted to take your troubles and make art out of them, which was all very well, but made it cursed uncomfortable to live around genius.

No, for his purposes, he didn't want genius, he didn't want art, and he certainly didn't want artists. He wanted entertainers. He wanted people who lived for the sound of applause and would turn themselves inside out to get it. People like that tended to be troupers, and when something bad happened, they pulled together to make sure the show went on. Genius regarded an audience as a sometimes-inconvenient thing that insisted *it* should be the judge of what it was shown. Genius only wanted to show the audience something that would make it go away and try very hard to think. Of course, people who lived for audience approval could be trouble too, craving that approval to the exclusion of everything else, making a dreadful pother about themselves offstage and hogging the limelight when on. In fact, there didn't ever really seem to be an *offstage* for them. They played to the people around them as if they were always in front of an audience. In their own way, they were going to always be lonely, for there was no room in that place for anyone who was not audience.

But after all this time, Nigel was fairly good at recognizing that sort, and he generally did not extend their contracts unless there was absolutely no helping it. He knew Jonathon; Jonathon craved that applause but was far too cynical about it to recognize it for anything other than what it was—the momentary pleasure and approval of people who were prepared to like you, so long as you weren't appallingly bad. Jonathon enjoyed tricking them—in the sense that he was, at least once in his act, performing real magic right in front of their noses.

And Nina seemed to be level headed about it as well. He was happy to see how much she desired that short-lived accolade, though, because it meant he wasn't going to lose her to one of those fellows who thronged her dressing room after the show.

That was always a worry with a pretty young girl, a

solo act. After a while, they got tired of moving from town to town, never staying longer than six weeks in any one place. They wanted to settle, and he didn't blame them. And if one of those fellows with their motorcars and champagne and jewelry offered to take her off the boards and set her up in a neat little nest with all the modern conveniences and all . . . well, you couldn't blame a girl for taking them up on it.

That was what the brilliant thing was, from a player's point of view, about this scheme of his. It was going to be exactly like one of those ballet or opera companies. The players would stay. It would be the production that changed. Everyone would get to have a home, rather than lodgings. People could stop living out of a suitcase, could acquire things like furniture and dishes, could sleep in a bed they could truly say was their own at night.

And then there was Jonathon.

Nigel smiled a little, watching the magician once again flawlessly execute the finale of his act, the part other magicians called "the Prestige." Jonathon *did* have that spark, but it was not for stage magic.

Sometimes Nigel wondered if he knew his friend better than Jonathon knew himself. Perhaps he did.

Jonathon Hightower, unlike Nina Tchereslavsky, did not live to hear the audience applaud. For him, in a way, the audience was irrelevant. He didn't want to amaze them; he often remarked sarcastically how very easy it was to amaze them. He was thoroughly devoted to seeing that they did not leave unsatisfied at the end of his act, but after that, he really didn't much care.

He said he was more interested in astonishing his fellow magicians, but that was not it either. Nigel had been watching him for many years now, and the conclusion he had come to was one that would probably shock Jonathon.

Jonathon was not a showman. Jonathon performed stage magic only so that he could make a living at a profession that permitted him to be what he was without having to answer too many questions. If he could have done the same thing by being a farrier or an automobile mechanic, he would have done so, provided he'd had the aptitude for either of those things. He needed the sort of profession and living space where odd things could happen without anyone taking notice. Granted most people could not see the Elementals—but they could certainly see the effects of the Elementals. Rains of fish and frogs, crops flattened in patterns, weird lights in the sky—too many of these occurrences and people started to talk. Accidents happened, but when you were supposed to be an ordinary fellow, a clerk or a carpenter, fingers were much more likely to be pointed in your direction than if you were rich, if you lived in the sort of place where everybody knew everybody else's business.

No, stage magic was for Jonathon only the means to an end. What Jonathon really *was*—was an Elemental Master.

Nigel had seen it, when Jonathon talked about Elemental magic, about things he had learned about the creatures of Fire, of the things he had seen. The spark had been there, and no doubt about it. Other stage magicians that Nigel had known over the years had been passionate about the tricks they invented, but not Jonathon. He was careful and craftsman-like about mastering the tricks he had purchased, and he clearly enjoyed the acting part of his turn, but it was only when he spoke of how he was integrating Fire magic into things in a way that made it appear to be more stage effects that he really lit up with enthusiasm.

He had been born to wield the power, to study the power, to learn more about it. But Nigel very much doubted that his friend had figured this out for himself yet.

Then again, he hadn't had the leisure or the space to do any proper work with his power. The designation of "Mage" or "Master" had to do with the amount of innate power and control you had, not how well you had learned how to wield it. In many ways, Arthur, who was "only" a Mage, had more mastery over his Element than Jonathon had. Arthur had other things too, for he was a Sensitive as well as a Mage, and the need to control the one had brought discipline to the other.

But Jonathon had been itinerant for almost as long as Nigel had known him. They had first met when Nigel had been the proprietor of a much smaller "music hall," a place that was mostly intended for drinking with a nod to entertainment, and a Water Master out in Lancashire County had suggested he give the young stage magician a trial. It was very hard setting up proper spellcasting when you were in lodgings, and you could be interrupted at any moment by a landlord who wanted to know what all the funny sounds and lights were about. And that was just for the magics that you could be taught or learn on your own—researching new Elemental spells took a deal more time, space, and effort, and a traveling showman rarely had a lot of any of those.

Of course, once the big show was on, and Jonathon realized he had *settled* in a place, would he realize that it was possible for him to start in serious study of his powers and abilities? Right now, in this building, Nigel had a flat that covered all of the first floor, and Arthur had one of the two that took up the second floor. As he watched Jonathon work, and thought about the kind of house guest he had been, it occurred to Nigel that he would not be at all averse to having Jonathon as a neighbor. That would mean the first and second floors were all taken up by Elemental mages, all in the business of entertainment. No one would make any inquiries about strange lights, odd sounds, or unexpected smells. In fact, no one would think twice about it. "Oh, it's the music hall people," would be the general consensus, and the neighbors would go about their own business.

As for Nina . . .

Star performers had been made of lesser stuff than she was. Now, Nigel did not know a great deal about ballet, but there was one thing he could tell. Nina connected with her audience. She made them want to like her. That was a rare gift; ninety-nine performers out of a hundred couldn't do it. In fact, Nigel had come to suspect that those who were able to enchant an audience in that way might just have some talent of a psychical nature about them. Now, once they got this business of who was after her settled—and he was sure that they would—then there was just one thing to worry about with Miss Nina.

How to make it worth it to her to stay with the company instead of finding a rich man to care for her.

He would have to think about that. There was this much; the girl had a talking cat, and she had witnessed magic, real magic. No one who understood that magic actually existed could ever look at the world in the same way again. She needed to be around people who had seen the sorts of things that she had seen, knew the sorts of things she knew. That just might be enough to hold her.

Add to that, a nice flat of her very own, the accoutrements of a star performer . . . even if she was only the star of one music hall in Blackpool. For some, that might be enough, and Nina did not strike him as being greedy.

He needed to put his mind to it. He knew what Jonathon needed, and soon enough Jonathon himself would come to realize this too. Now he had to figure out just what it was that Nina needed.

Watching these two work together, he could see that he could set any number of shows based around them . . . they didn't have to be fairy tales either, or at least not ones with working magic in them. Already an idea was forming in his mind . . . there were all those popular operettas based around minor royalty from tiny little European monarchies that no one had ever heard of running away to pretend to be peasants and falling in love . . . The person in question was generally a prince, but what if it was a princess? A princess who just wants to dance on the stage? Who runs away because she's about to be married off to some other minor prince she has never even met, gets a job with a musical theater, falls in love with the stage magician . . . Yes, and when her parents come to collect her, the stage magician reveals himself as the prince she was supposed to marry, who *also* ran away because he couldn't bear to be shackled to some girl he had never met . . .

Yes, that would be an excellent plot for their second production. It wouldn't do to get too bound to fairy tales. Variety, that was the way to go.

Now he just needed to deduce what would keep Nina happy and contented.

The genuine Nina knew the signs. People were starting to eye the mysterious Russian with a bit less awe and a bit more suspicion. This was taking longer than she had thought it would.

Sabotaging the theater had not worked. It was impossible to get at the girl directly. None of the men that flocked to her dressing room came up to the mark for causing scandal.

Well, she needed to find a place to live, a place where there would be room enough to work some real magic, and where no one would be looking askance at the comings and goings into the night.

A few moments with the concierge elicited regrets

that she was leaving and the name of a reliable agent. Within half a day, the agent had found and taken her to view three suitable flats. She rented the first one, which came furnished. More importantly, it was on the ground floor, and had a separate servants' entrance which was *not* overlooked by any of the other flats in the building. She could come and go whenever she liked without being seen. It also included the cellar, which meant her Elemental slaves could come and go without needing recourse to any outside entrances.

She wrote the impresario in Germany, canceling her appearances, and sent payment to him for the cancellations without a qualm. This was war, now, and she was *not* going to lose.

13

NINA had made a major mistake when she first arrived in Blackpool, and now she knew it.

She had assumed that her imposter was just an ordinary, greedy little human being. Now she knew better. The girl had a protector, an Elemental Master, a Fire-Master to be precise. She still didn't know which of the men around the girl was the magician. Humans were infernally good at hiding their powers, if one was bent on hiding them, and most of the clever ones would never come out in the open if they could help it. If a mage was of her own element, she would certainly sense him in the powers when he actually worked magic, but if he was not of her element, he could be conjuring away at removing mountains and she would never know it if he was shielded.

And if he was shielded all the time, she'd not be able to tell him from an ordinary sort of human.

She had made a grave mistake, choosing to attack the building as she had. She had used creatures of her own element—the rats were of earth, of course—to be the carriers of disaster, but it had been *his* element, fire, which would have been the actual cause. Some of these blasted humans were on good terms with their Elemental creatures, good enough terms that the benighted things acted as watchdogs, and that must have been the case here. There was absolutely no doubt what had put out the fires. Salamanders, dozens of them. And that could *only* mark the work of a Master.

All right. This meant that she couldn't go after the girl directly. She would have to be very careful how she did it indirectly. That meant working entirely in her own Element.

It was unlikely there was another Earth mage anywhere in this city; Earth mages felt acutely uncomfortable in places where the ground was paved over, where there were filthy slums and tenements, and where the air and ground were poisoned by the smokes and effluvia of humans living in such crowded conditions. These conditions did not trouble Nina in the least; on the contrary, these were the sorts of things that Trolls thrived in.

So it was unlikely that there would be a mage of her own Element to sense when she was working. And it was very unlikely that the Fire Master would sense it either. He couldn't know who or what she was, or he would have tracked her down by now. So long as she stayed within her own element . . . it was safe to use magic.

So . . . what to do?

Well, the obvious thing was to try to get at her with one of the most powerful weapons in Nina's arsenal.

Illness.

There were all manner of things that Nina could strike her with. And now that she had an establishment of her own from which to operate, she could investigate which might make the best weapon.

The vehicle would be another question entirely. Nina

was not going to trust this to one of her dim-witted underlings, oh no. Nor to any old rat or mouse that she might trap.

Nina was going to make a homunculus, a bit of magic for which the Earth magicians were unusually apt.

And she moreso than a human magician. She needed no implements, no herbs, in fact nothing but a shielding circle—and herself.

She called in her maid. "Is the cellar prepared?" she asked, with an edge to her voice. She had told the creature to have the cellar made ready as soon as she took possession of the house—but had her servant done so? They could be astonishingly thick. It was the problem with the creatures of Earth; they often moved slowly, and they were not very clever. Nina had been an exception even among the Trolls who were the cleverest of the sorts of Elementals that wise magicians did not call up. But that was probably because of the number of humans she had absorbed over the years; it was not just their forms that stayed with her, it seemed that some of their intelligence remained as well.

But fortunately the maid nodded, and Nina felt a moment of satisfaction. They were learning, it seemed. Good. It was about time.

Waving the maid away, she descended into the cellar alone.

She did not need a lantern, nor indeed any light; Trolls could see in the dark as well as any cat. The steep wooden stairs were no trouble to navigate once she rid herself of her clumsy and encumbering human garments and continued on in her shift. What foolishness it was to wear such things! Humans were so stupid sometimes.

She felt the cool and the damp on her skin with a sense of great relief. It was at times like these that she almost regretted giving up her existence in the underground world of the darker Earth elementals. And yet, the life she had now was so rich, so varied, so ... luxurious ... she could not even contemplate giving it up. When she thought about how simple-minded and dull her own servants were ... no. She was never, ever giving up this life.

The cellar was paved with stone, which, fortunately, was all native to the area. That made it ideal in every possible way. The preparations that Nina required were simple; a protective double circle had been deeply inscribed into the stone, with words in the ancient language of the Earth Masters etched between the inner and outer circles. Nina inspected these carefully, until she was satisfied that they had been written perfectly, that there were no flaws in the words, nor breaks in the circles. It was not that she was in any danger of course. These circles were not to keep anything out. Her human body with its Trollish powers was more than enough to take care of anything that might come at her across these circles.

No, this was to keep her power in, to keep from betraying her presence to that accursed Fire Master, and any other meddlesome human mages that might be alerted. The Fire Master *shouldn't* be able to sense Earth power, but ... she preferred not to take any chances. And anyway all the Elementals gossiped, especially the Bright Powers. Let a Faun or Dryad get a scent of her presence, and the next thing you knew a Sylph would find out about it, and from there it was a short step to the ears of those Salamanders that danced attendance on him.

She had not gotten as far as she had by being careless.

She crossed the lines of the circle, knelt in the center, and with a touch, called Earth magic into the carvings. Slowly, gradually, they began to glow a smoky and sullen ochre.

With a whispered word, she raised the power into a dome, arching above her head. Invisible to mortal eyes, though visible to hers, the corresponding half of the dome penetrated deep into the stone and earth of the cellar floor. Now she was walled, shielded, protected from every prying sense. She was invisible in here; even her own servants would not be able to sense her.

She cupped her hands over her belly, feeling the power rise in her now; she concentrated with all her might, for what she was about to do was the closest her kind ever came to giving birth.

And it was just as much work, although the time of "labor" was considerably shorter.

She pulled her own substance out of herself and into her waiting hands, panting and sweating as she robbed herself of her own flesh, and gave it shape and life. She groaned, not with pain, but with effort. And when she was done, there it was in her hands, about the size of a newborn human baby, a faceless, smooth little thing like a dough-man or a wax doll, waiting patiently for her to give it purpose. It was the same color as the earth here-abouts, and it was cool to the touch, with a faint dusting of grit over the surface of it.

She would have liked to lie down at that point, for the effort had been greater than she remembered. But she did not have that leisure. If she did not give this thing its purpose, it would start to merge with her again, and this would all have been for nothing.

So she called up more power with another whispered word, invoked the particular form of pestilence she wished to visit upon the girl, and gave the creature her "scent." With every layer of magic, the homunculus glowed a little more, a dark and angry glow like cooling lava. Finally, when she was done, she set it down on the floor in front of her, feeling weary to death, as she never felt after mere physical exertion like dancing.

The homunculus stood there on its own, nearly vibrating with the need to be off about its purpose.

She dismissed the magic in the protective circles, and the homunculus did not waste a single moment. It sank into the floor of the cellar as easily as if the stone had been water, and in a moment, it was gone. Not even another Earth mage was likely to be able to detect it. Only another Elemental could. That was the beauty of this: since it had once been part of her, it became its own little independent creature. Not quite a Troll, but close enough it should raise no alarms among the other Elemental creatures hereabouts.

Finally, after a long, long rest on the stones, slowly drawing in Earth energy to replace what she had lost, she got to her feet and pulled herself up the stairs.

If all went well, within the week, her imposter would be dead. And she would then be free to decide whether or not to take her place.

There was something going on that no one was talking to her about. Ninette could tell by the way that Arthur, Nigel and Jonathon would look at her when they thought she wouldn't notice. And it wasn't the "we are suspicious of you" look, it was the "we are really worried for you" look. That made her uneasy, and it made her even more uneasy to think that whatever was going on probably had a great deal to do with magic.

She really didn't want to think about magic. Despite that there was a very helpful brownie living in her flat. Despite that Jonathon was producing all manner of magical—the real sort, not legerdemain—effects on stage. Despite the fact that she was half friend and half slave to a talking cat. She just would rather not think about magic at all. Rather than growing easier about it over time, knowing about it, knowing it was real, actually had the effect of unnerving her further. It was as if the solid and understandable world she knew was just a thin shell over something impossible and deadly, something she could not see nor guard against. All her childhood fears of night-hags coming through the windows and demons up through the floor *could be real.* And what was more, *she* had no way to protect herself against these creatures.

It was horrible, every moment of it, and so she thought about it as little as possible.

Ailse astonished her. The little Scots maid was as practical and level-headed as any Parisian landlady, and yet, she not only accepted all of this, she seemed to have no particular difficulty in doing so. She put out a little food and drink for the Brownie every night, and pretended to ignore the shy little creature whenever it happened to get caught in the open. Although she said she could not hear Thomas unless he spoke to her directly, she spoke to him at all times as if to a human being. And Wolf, whom she certainly *did* hear, she flirted with in a sort of dry, ironic manner. The practical and level-headed nature would seem to preclude any belief in magic. And yet . . .

All this glancing and looking worried had begun about a week ago. Ninette finally got fed up with it. It was making her more nervous than thinking about magic. So she decided to accost the one person of everyone in the group that was likeliest to give her the truth.

"Ailse," she said that night, as the maid was combing out her hair, "why is everyone so on edge this past week? And why do they keep looking at me?"

The maid was silent for a good long time. Her hands kept moving automatically, but looking in the mirror, Ninette could see a very thoughtful expression on her face. "Well, ma'amselle," the girl said thoughtfully, "They wouldna like my tellin' ye, but I've been thinkin' 'tis a sin and a shame to be keepin' ye in the dark."

"I knew it!" Ninette said fiercely. "I knew there was something amiss!"

"Well, it's that summon tried to burn down the theater, d'ye ken? And they be thinkin' it has sommat t' do with you," Ailse said reluctantly.

"Me?" Ninette's mouth fell open with surprise, and she turned and took the brush from the maid's unresisting hands. "How could that have anything to do with me?"

"Because, ma'amselle, they're thinkin' it's all of a piece, that you have a strong enemy, a magician—well, not you, but your Papa that's gone." The girl nodded. "They're thinking that the wreck of your friend's wee boat, the laddie that tried to set fire to the theater, and the accidents are all at the hand of this magician, d'ye ken. Because they're unnatural for certain sure. There's thousands as wouldna believe that tale yon Harrigan told, of the hole in the street opening up under his feet, but *I* do, and more's the point, so do Master Nigel and Master Jonathon."

Ninette listened to this with astonishment, not the least because Nigel and Jonathon were hanging their theory on a slender thread indeed. That their entire "chain of events" began with a shipwreck that never really happened—

She bit her lip and was about to turn away from the maid, feeling a terrible load of guilt, when suddenly from the direction of the kitchen a commotion erupted that sounded like a cross between a cat-fight and a drunken brawl, punctuated by the crash of crockery.

Both young women hesitated a moment, then Ninette leapt up from her seat and ran for the door. She stopped long enough to grab a poker from the fireplace tools, and flung open the door of her bedroom.

It was easy to see the cause of the noise. Thomas and the brownie tumbled together on the floor, tangled up with something else, both of them fighting, both of them screeching. The brownie was shouting something incomprehensible, while Thomas sounded like a perfectly ordinary cat in a towering rage.

The thing they were fighting, strangely, made no noise at all.

Ailse went straight for the kitchen, as Ninette stood by looking for an opening in which she could bash the thing with her poker. She couldn't tell what it was; it was a sickly, muddy-earth color, and had four limbs and a head, and that was all she could tell for sure. But as she set eyes on it, she felt a creeping horror, absolute revulsion, and her hands shook as she clutched the poker.

Ailse came back with a big iron pot and a lid. Before Ninette could ask what *that* was for, she shouted, "Stand aside! Cold iron!" and in a flash, both the cat and the brownie freed themselves.

Ninette, who had been waiting for just that, took the opportunity to bash it with her poker. Incredibly, she connected with it. Even more incredibly, she stunned it. And while it was stunned, Ailse clapped the pot down on top of it, then slid the lid underneath, and flipped pot and creature back over. Ninette slid her poker through the pot's two handles, locking the lid down tight.

And a good thing she did so, too, for a moment later the creature recovered, and the pot began gyrating as it tried to batter its way out. Ninette, went quickly to the fireplace, then put one of the fire-dogs on top of it just to be sure; this stopped the pot from bounding, but a furious hammering came from inside as the creature beat on the lid and sides.

The brownie stood there, panting, staring at the pot. "Damme! Wha' be that?" he asked, the first time that Ninette had ever heard him speak.

That, Thomas replied grimly, *is an homunculus, and it*

*means us no good, I promise you. Don't, on your lives, let
it out. I am going to get Nigel and Jonathon.*

Limping slightly, the cat leaped out of the window,
leaving the two young women and the brownie staring
at one another.

"Well," Ninette said, finally. "Do you think we ought
to put more heavy things on top of the pot?"

"I'm thinkin' it wouldna hurt," Ailse said, and went in
search of something heavier than a fire-dog.

An hour later, Ninette sat on the bed in her room,
seething. It was quite bad enough that Nigel, Arthur,
Jonathon *and* Wolf had all come rushing up the stairs to
her flat, acting as if she and Ailse didn't have the sense
the Lord gave a goose, but it was worse that they all but
shoved her maid and herself into this room and barred
the door with a chair to keep them in!

Ailse sat primly in the chair staring a hole in the door.
When she glanced over at Ninette and saw that the
dancer was looking at her, she grimaced.

"You are thinking," Ninette said, and marveled a little at how firm her own grasp of English had become.
Then she shivered. That was magic again. Creeping into
her life, little by little. Making such tiny, helpful
changes—until the moment when some shapeless thing,
some awful monster that was terrible all out of propor-
tion to its size, got into your own flat and—

And what? Why was it here? Preying on the Brownie?
She didn't think so. Something told her it had come for
her. Thomas had said it meant them no good, and she
could well believe it. Had it come on its own? Had it
been sent? If it had been sent, who had sent it?

Was this somehow tied to the person who had tried to
set fire to the theater?

"I am thinkin' ma'amselle, but 'tisna my place t'say—" Ailse said with great reluctance.

She grimaced. "Oh please do speak your mind. I think it will be the twin of my own thoughts."

Ailse looked at the door again. "Men," she said, slowly, and with great deliberation. "Now an' then, they be as a'mighty as they think. But 'tisna often."

Ninette was surprised into a giggle, and some of her nervousness ebbed. "What do you suppose they are doing out there?"

Ailse shrugged. "Some mess of magic, do ye ken. And we shouldna see it on account of we have no magic of our own, and we're puir weak women besides. We shouldna fash oursel'es. Let the braw laddies handle it."

Ninette nodded, flushing. "Forgetting who it was caught it in the first place."

"Aye." Ailse looked back at the door. "But nivver mind. I'd be guessin' we'll find oot soon enoo—"

And at that moment . . . something indescribable happened.

If you could have a soundless explosion, that was the closest that Ninette could come to the experience. She felt the concussive impact of *something* out in her sitting room, even though not even her handkerchief fluttered. She felt as if she *should* have been driven back against the counterpane. She was left feeling slightly disoriented, exactly as if she had been struck by something, and from the look of her, Ailse felt the same.

Out in the sitting room, Jonathon began to curse.

Ninette was feeling too dazed to react, but Ailse shook off her shock and jumped up out of the chair she had been sitting on. She stalked straight to the door and pounded on it. "Ye might as well let us oot!" she said fiercely.

"Yes, yes, all right," Arthur said, sounding distracted— or maybe just as dizzy as Ninette felt. "I'm coming!"

There was a scraping sound as the chair was pulled away from the door; Ailse opened it, and held it open for her mistress. Ninette got up, slowly, afraid to find her pleasant little sitting room in ruins.

But in fact, the sitting room was fundamentally intact, except for the few things the Brownie and Thomas had broken in their struggles with the homunculus.

But there was a very nasty stench in the air, and the iron pot was empty.

"I would be rid of that, if I were you," Jonathon said, seeing that her eyes were resting on the container. "It won't be fit to use for anything for a long time, perhaps never."

"Why—" Ninette began.

"Because this thing was a pestilence-bringer," Nigel replied wearily. "Anything you cook in that pot for a while will make people sick."

Ailse peered closely at him, as if to ascertain whether he was joking or not. "'Twill still work as a trap for the uncanny, noo?" Ailse persisted.

"I suppose it will," Nigel began.

"Good. Then we're keepin' it," Ailse said in triumph. "I'll be puttin' it somewhere safe. But it's no bad thing, havin' a trap for uncanny evil wee things. What was it here for?"

"Not what," Jonathon corrected. "Who. It was here for Nina. And I would very much like to know how she managed to attract the attention of so practiced an Elemental mage."

Her father— the cat began.

"Bosh. Humbug," Jonathon interrupted. "This was a very *personal* enmity, as you very well know, cat. You felt it. We all did. That thing was pestilence and hate, and whoever created it did so for the purpose of being rid of Mademoiselle Tchereslavsky."

"Who sent it?" Ninette whispered, a feeling of terrible dread coming over her.

"Well, that would be the problem," Arthur put in, scratching his head with one hand, while with the other he scratched Wolf's. "It fair disintegrated when we tried to find out. Violently."

"So that is why we would like to know, Mademoiselle, just how you managed to make a personal enemy of so powerful a mage," Jonathon went on. "Particularly as you have no magic yourself, and profess that you do not much care for it . . ."

Helplessly, Nina looked at the cat. The cat shook his head, as if to say, *Be quiet! Say nothing!*

But Ninette was tired of the subterfuge—and she greatly feared that if it went on for much longer, it would get in the way of—well—everything.

"I have been deceiving you," she said with a sigh as the cat looked frantic. "And I am very sorry. But I do not know why a powerful mage would want me dead, because until a few weeks ago I knew nothing of mages and Masters and Elementals. That is because I am not Nina Tchereslavsky, prima ballerina with the Imperial Ballet. I am Ninette Dupond, *coryphée* of the Paris Opera Ballet."

There. It was out in the open. And all of them but the cat stared at her with their jaws dropping.

The cat only groaned and dropped down to the floor to cover his face with his paws.

14

JONATHON took a slow, deep breath, his brow like thunder. But before he could say anything, the cat spoke up.

Don't shout at her, magician. It was all my idea. And I took advantage of the fact that she was light-headed from hunger to persuade her, too. The cat stalked up to Jonathon and looked up at him, tail lashing back and forth defiantly. *I stole money and tickets to get her here from Paris. I told her what to do. I concocted the shipwreck story. It was all my doing.*

Ninette looked into their eyes. Arthur licked his lips. "She's still a first-rate dancer," he said hesitantly. "It's not as if she cheated us that way."

Wolf made a *tsk*ing sound. "People create fantastical stories about performers all the time to puff them up," the parrot said thoughtfully. "They always have, I expect. You should have heard some of the ones about me."

Jonathon still looked wrathful. Ninette stared down at her hands. "My mother was abandoned by her husband when I was a baby," she said, softly, and began the tedious recitation of her misfortunes in a flat voice. She only looked up once when Nigel laughed, on hearing La Augustine's reaction to her grave error in smiling at the *prima's* patron. "It was not funny," she said flatly. "I knew at that instant that it was the worst possible thing that could have happened. It was not that La Augustine was jealous—she did not care a *sous* for whether the old man really loved her or not. It was that in that moment, I threatened her . . . livelihood. I threatened to take away his interest, and thus the flat, the luxuries, the jewels and furs and beautiful gowns. Of course she was in a rage. She was not ready to give him up yet. In fact, I am not sure she was ready to give him up at all. He was an ideal patron, old, unmarried, and no relations closer than a cousin. If he died, he could leave her very comfortable, and a dancer does not have a long life on the stage."

Nigel sobered immediately. She continued with her story, of being cast out of the Opera Ballet, of trying to find a position elsewhere, of determining finally that she was going to go to the *Moulin Rouge* . . . to find someone who would give her money. She did not say for what purpose. She did not need to. She looked up again, to see that all three men had looks of embarrassment and chagrin on their faces.

She thought many things, and with them came a flare of anger. Men never had to face these choices. A man could always find work if he looked hard enough. A man had so many more choices than any woman. *Oh, you do not think of this when you take girls into your beds, or into a room at a not-too-careful hotel. You do not think of them as real persons, who are doing this not because they want to be in your bed, but because they must go there or starve. You give them money and they go away and you never think of them again. They are the amusement of an hour. Maybe, maybe, you ask for them, look for them again. But not too often, for then they might start to make demands of you. But they think of you. They look at the money you give them, and they wish that all the men would be kind, would not beat them or try to cheat them. They count the money and wonder how long it will last them . . . or they count the money and cry because they must give it all to their procurer, and then give themselves to another stranger, who might not be kind. You do not think of these things . . . yet in your hearts, you know them, in your hearts, but your minds shove them away so they will not be disturbed.*

The cat took this moment to jump into the conversation, which was just as well, seeing as she was on verge of saying these things out loud.

When she was all alone, hungry, and facing being put on the street, I knew I must intervene. That was when I stepped in, and I took advantage of her. He then took up the narrative, describing exactly how and from whom he had stolen purses and tickets. Telling how he had herded her onto the Metro, then the boat-train to Calais, onto the ferry, then to the train to Blackpool. How he had found her the boarding house, and how he had devised the little charade of the shipwreck.

When he paused, she spread her hands wide. "And there you have it, for everything else, you know what happened, except that I am Ninette, not Nina."

Ninette, the cat interjected, *who convinced your new ballet-master that she could not benefit from lessons given by him. And you know his credentials are impeccable. Ninette who has been dancing every night, sometimes taking two turns more than anyone else, to increasing acclaim. Ninette, who convinced all of you by her talent to base an entire show around her. Ninette, whose dressing room is thronged every evening by fans and well-wishers, and full of flowers. Who charms the gentlemen of the press and the little girls who give her sticky nosegays of violets.*

Out of the corner of her eye, Ninette noticed Jonathon frown a bit at that. But the magician said nothing.

Nigel ran his hand over his hair. "You have me there," he said. "It isn't Nina Tchereslavsky that our audiences are coming to see. They come to see the dancer they've all heard about, from other people who've seen her. Good heavens, I doubt if one in a thousand has ever seen a real ballet-dancer before, much less an entire ballet, and they don't give a farthing about some 'Rooskie wench' who danced in front of people they openly make fun of, like the French and the Germans and the Russians. It might be different if we were the Royal Opera Company—"

"But we aren't," Arthur said firmly. "We don't have a Royal Circle, we don't have titles and famous writers and famous painters in our audiences. We're nothing but entertainment for the masses. We have Bertie and Mary from Worcester, we have Sally and Tommy from Liverpool, on holiday, looking for a good time and getting it. They see the dancer up there and they know someone who's good, even if they don't know a *jette* from a *plie*. And if we throw Mademoiselle Ninette out on her ear, they'd be tearing the curtains down to hang us with them." He looked from Nigel to Jonathon and back again. "I don't see we have a choice. And I don't see where anyone is being harmed by this. I say let the charade go on. Ninette isn't taking a shilling out of Miss Tchereslavsky's pay-packet, and no one east of London is ever going to know there's two of them."

Nigel grinned. "I'm glad to hear you say that, old lad, because I was going to propose the same thing. But tell me," he continued, turning to Ninette, "How did you learn to speak Russian? For that matter, how did a poor little ballet girl from the Bohemian parts of Paris learn how to speak English?"

Oh, that was my doing, Thomas the cat said smugly. *I just found a bannik in the bathhouse of one Alexei Balonovich that had come over with his master. He and I struck a bargain, and I got him to whisper Russian in her mind while she slept. You might be amazed at all the Russians who live here. Russia is not an hospitable place if you aren't a friend of the Tsar. And as for the English, there are plenty of brownies in England to teach her English the same way.*

Jonathon looked at the cat sharply. "That isn't supposed to work unless you've got some magery in you."

Well, she has. Her father was an Earth Master; that part is true enough. And she has a touch of it, enough for her to hear me, enough for her to learn languages. . . . The cat looked slyly at all of them. *And enough to enchant an audience. And don't tell me you haven't seen her do it. Charm. Charisma. It's magic, right enough, opens up a connection between her and them. It's all there, what they used to call "the glamourie." And that's all of the magic there is in her.*

"Huh," said Arthur, and Wolf chortled. Nigel just shook his head.

"This still doesn't tell us why there's an Earth Master trying to kill her," Jonathon said sharply. "We're no closer to unraveling that particular riddle than we were before."

But at least you won't go barking up any Russian trees, the cat replied. *Nor, I advise you, any Parisian ones either. La Augustine may be a witch, but she's not the sort with magic, and so far as I know, there's not a soul Ninette ever came across that has a jot of magic in him— or her—other than me. I won't say that she never made an enemy, though I don't know of any, but I do know that there was no one around her that I ever sensed that had magic enough to light a candle.*

The men exchanged looks of resignation. Finally Nigel shook his head. "I'm curious about one thing, cat," Nigel said slowly. "Why Blackpool? Why not—Bath, or Birmingham, or Plymouth? I can understand not wanting to try your trick in London, where someone might have seen the real Nina Tchereslavsky, and there are a lot of people there who know about the famous ballet dancers in the rest of the world, but why come all the way up into the North?"

You, Thomas said instantly. *How many impresarios are there that are also Elemental Masters? I had to find someone who could hear me, didn't I? That was the only way to make the trick work.*

"Impeccable logic," Wolf said, and chortled again. "Keep on like this, and I might even start to like you, cat."

Jonathon scowled. "Shall we have done with this love-fest?" he asked. "We need to find out who is behind these attacks, and put a stop to them, before someone—probably our star dancer—is murdered."

Ninette shivered at this timely—and unwelcome—reminder. She kept shivering though, feeling very cold, and rather empty inside. The secret was out, and now . . . now she did not really know what she should do. And there was still someone, some terrible magician out there, who wanted her dead. Ailse got up and fetched a shawl and put it around her shoulders. "There noo, ma'amselle," the maid said in her no-nonsense tone. "Ye've got t'dance tomorrow, an' there's naught going to happen more tonight." Ailse looked at Nigel, Arthur, and Jonathon sternly. "You lads, be off with ye. Worrit yer heads about it all ye like, but not here. Ma'amselle Ninette needs to sleep."

"Gad." Nigel shook his head. "You're right as rain, Ailse. Curse it all though . . . if only we could concentrate on either the magic or the theater, one or the other, and not have to deal with both at the same time."

"If wishes were horses, beggars would ride," Ailse quoted primly. "Go along with you."

Ninette stopped shivering, but immediately felt as if she could not keep her eyes open anymore. Perhaps it was the unreality of the situation; despite how she had felt when she first clapped eyes on the horrid little monster, she could not seem to think of it as menacing, much less life-threatening, now. There had been a strange little—thing— in her sitting room. It hadn't even been as big as the cat. Ailse had clapped a cooking put over it—how absurd was that? So absurd no one would even write a ballet about it. She yawned, stifling it behind her hand, and Ailse pounced on her.

"That will be enough of that," the maid said firmly. "To bed wi' ye. And oot with yon gents!"

A word with you, Jonathon, Ninette vaguely heard the cat say, as Ailse hustled her back into the bedroom. *I'll walk you home.*

For a moment she was moved to protest—she needed Thomas here! Who else would protect her if another of those things put in an appearance? But then she realized that if Thomas wasn't worried, then there probably was no need to worry at all. She followed Ailse meekly into the bedroom, quite as if it was Ailse who was the mistress here, and she the obedient maid.

The cat had had mixed feelings, watching the Fire Master's expressions change over the course of Ninette's confession. At first, Jonathon had been angry at Ninette's deception, that much was clear. Thomas could only assume he was angry because he had been tricked, and not for any "moral outrage." Ninette had only been doing what Jonathon did every night on the stage—tricking people into thinking that what was in front of them was something other than what it was.

Then had come grudging acceptance, as first Arthur, and then Nigel had voiced their own opinions on the subject.

Then, interestingly, when the mention of Ninette's many admirers came up, the cat had seen acute annoyance flash across Jonathon's face. In fact, it was akin to the annoyance that Thomas himself felt.

Fascinating . . .

Of course, if Jonathon was attracted to the dancer, he would do his best not to show it. Not because he had any ridiculous ideas about the moral inferiority of his fellow entertainers, but because he would know how often disastrous flirtations within a theatrical company could be. And Jonathon, from all that Thomas knew about him—which was a great deal more than Jonathon was aware!—thought of himself as a confirmed bachelor.

Nor did Thomas himself particularly want Jonathon attracted to Ninette.

On the other hand, if the choice was Jonathon—or one of those fellows that filled her dressing room—well, then the cat would fervently welcome Jonathon.

All of them made their way to the ground floor, and out the private entrance, without encountering anyone else. It appeared that despite the row that had gone on in Ninette's sitting room, the other tenants had remained blissfully unaware of any unpleasantness. That was good, because otherwise the ruckus would have been very difficult to explain.

When they stepped out into the cool, damp, dark summer night, with the scent of wet brick and growing things on the air, Thomas took the opportunity to glare up at Nigel, Arthur, and that wretched bird. And then he coughed, politely.

Arthur and Nigel took the hint, and swiftly outdistanced the two of them, rapidly moving through the patches of light where the streetlamps stood, until they turned a corner and moved out of sight. Thomas could feel Jonathon's eyes on him, and sensed the frown.

"Well, get on with it," the Fire Master said impatiently. "What is it you wanted to tell me that you couldn't say in front of the others?" Without waiting for an answer, the Fire Master strode out in the footsteps of his friends.

Largely—my motives, said Thomas, reluctantly. *Let us start with the question, "Why Blackpool?" The reason is simple, really. I know Blackpool. I am a native of this area. That was how I knew that an Air Master was the impresario of this particular music hall. Since I came from this part of England, I made it my business to keep track of the Elemental Masters here.*

"You—what?" The cat felt a certain smug satisfaction. He had managed to surprise the magician. Well, there were more surprises to come for Jonathon Hightower. The magician wasn't the only one who was good at keeping things up his metaphorical sleeve.

I said, I know the city because I lived here, about twenty years ago, more or less.

"What a surprise, you hardly look a day over ten," came Jonathon's sarcastic reply. "You are a remarkably well preserved cat."

The cat bristled, the hair on his tail poofing out a little. Like uncle, like nephew. Were all the Hightower men born with acid wit, or did they learn it from one another? *Do not mock me, Jemmie Hightower,* he snapped. *And keep a civil tongue in your head. I knew your uncle, and I knew you when you were still in nappies.*

The magician stopped dead in his tracks and swiveled

to look down at the cat. His voice shook a little. "No one—has called me 'Jemmie'—since—"

Precisely why I used that name with you. You surely don't think I am an ordinary cat.

"Well of course not! You're a magical—" Jonathon stopped, and a dumbfounded look came over his face. "No magical construction could be half as clever as you. Most of them could never even think for themselves, much less some up with the wild plans you have. What *are* you?"

I am a cat, replied Thomas, primly.

"You are as much a cat as I am a Bartholomew Faire conjurer. I say again, what *are* you?" The cat looked up and saw Jonathon's eyes narrow. "Or is the right question not what, but *who?*"

Thomas sat down on his haunches, and wrapped his tail tightly around his legs. *You must swear never to tell Ninette. If you do, I swear I will scratch your eyes out, and pee in all your stage props.*

Warily Jonathon nodded. "All right."

The cat sighed. He hated letting these secrets go. He had hoped to carry them to the grave. *I was as human as you are, and no, I am not reincarnated in cat form, as Wolf claims to have been. I was an Earth Master, and this is a permanent transformation. I lost a magician's duel, and my opponent froze me in the last shape I took. Not surprising, really; she was a truly vindictive and jealous wench, and she never forgave me for running away from her—and even less was she inclined to forgive me when she tracked me down and discovered I had married someone else.* He still remembered the look on Helen's face when he told her. The fury—it had been enough to make him take a step back at the time. And if he had thought for a moment that he might be able to run away from her again, that expression had utterly disabused him of the notion. *They say hell hath no fury like a*

woman scorned ... I am inclined to think they are right.
Kipling also says that the female is more deadly than the
male. I am in a position to corroborate that.

He could almost see the thoughts running through
Jonathon's head as the Fire Master ran through all of
the Earth Masters in the last forty or so years he had
ever heard of that came from hereabouts—sorted out
all the ones that had gone missing or that could not possibly have known his uncle or clapped eyes on himself
as a baby—then eliminated all those too young to be
the one in question—

Thomas recognized the moment when Jonathon put
all the clues together. His jaw dropped.

"Thomas Dupond?" the mage gasped incredulously.

The cat sighed. *The same.*

"But—" another clue floated to the surface, and
Jonathon almost reeled. "But—you must be Ninette's
missing father!"

Now you know why I did what I did. The cat's tail
lashed angrily. *I did not abandon my wife and child! I
was ambushed, and they were threatened. Helen Waring
tracked me to Paris, sent a private detective to find me,
and confronted me literally no more than a block from
my home. She threatened to make life unendurable for
Marie and Ninette, and you know very well that she
could have, and would have, and she would never have
had to use a bit of magic to do so. The only way I could
distract her was to call her out in a magician's duel.
Which, as you must have deduced, I lost.*

"But now we know who the magician that is trying to
kill Ninette is!" Jonathon crowed. Thomas sighed.

You are leaping to far too many conclusions, the cat
told him. *No, in this case, you are quite wrong. Helen
Waring is not the Earth Master we are looking for.*

"Why do you say that?" Jonathon demanded.

Because she is dead, Thomas said flatly.

Silence for a moment. "How can you be sure?" Jonathon asked, after a pause.

Because I killed her.

More silence. Then Jonathon cleared his throat awkwardly. "Ah . . . how did that come about?"

She intended to go through with her threat to torment my wife and child. I expect she had some idea of capturing me as well, but I got over the shock of finding myself permanently a cat a great deal faster than she had thought I would. I crept into the hotel where she had rented a room that same night, Thomas told him, reining in the anger and hatred that still lashed him whenever he thought of that cruel, cruel woman. How he despised her still! Had she been a man, her evil nature would have been uncovered and dealt with long before it had come to this pass by her fellow Elemental Masters, but since she was a woman . . . they had laughed at what they called her "folly," and had never taken her seriously. Perhaps that was why she had obsessed over Thomas; he had taken her seriously. He had known she was, or at least one day would be, a menace. He had realized that she was dangerous to him, when he had begun finding her creatures spying on him. And she had money, a very great deal of it, being the only child of a shipping magnate who had left her his entire fortune, while he was as poor as a church-mouse. She had assumed she could buy him, as she had bought everything else she wanted, including the best of tutors in her magic. It must have come as a tremendous shock to her when she discovered he had fled. *I waited for her at the top of the stairs,* he continued, reliving that night. *And when she stepped out of her room, and was not looking, I ran between her ankles and tripped her. It was a new hotel, in the latest fashion they called Art Nouveau. There were terrible stairs in that place; very steep, beautiful marble with sinuously curving iron railings, and treacherous.*

She broke her damned neck exactly as I intended she should. I was glad I did it and I would do it again.

Another long pause. "But . . . you lost the chance to have the transformation reversed—"

Which she swore that she would never do, Thomas said bitterly. *In fact, her last words to me as she sealed the spell were "I hope you enjoy mice, for you will be living on them from now on." At a stroke she doomed my poor Marie and Ninette to starvation or worse, and me to a miserable existence either running from her, or as her captive. My only regret is that she did not suffer as poor Marie and Ninette suffered. I did what I could for them, but I was limited by . . . well, real life. I stole purses and left them where Marie would find them, but I had to be careful, and I had to make sure it was nothing too generous nor too often. Marie herself would have started to question where they came from, and if she started looking too prosperous, the* gendarmes *would start to ask questions to which she would have no answers.* How well he remembered his horror when Marie decided that Ninette would have to become a courtesan! And to see his lovely wife trading her favors among the artists for the sake of a few sausages . . .

It made him angry, ashamed, and vengeful, all at the same time. It still did.

"I—see," Jonathon said, slowly. "I mean, I do see. I'd have felt the same in your place . . ."

I hated it. And Marie—trained Ninette to think that she must find a rich protector. I hate that even worse, if that were possible. Thomas paused to get a grip on himself. *But Ninette is a good dancer, and I was sure she would be able to make her way without needing to find a—protector. In fact, I had planned to help her rise in the ranks as soon as there was an opportunity. Figaro praised her! That is no small matter in Paris! And when she found herself ejected from the Opera Ballet . . . I did not want her to find a rich protector elsewhere. I still do not.* His mental voice turned fierce. *I want her to never need any such thing. So I waited until she was desperate and dizzy enough with hunger that she would accept such a thing as a talking cat, and set my plan in motion. And you must never, ever tell her who and what I am.*

"I gave you my word," pledged Jonathon. "And I give it again."

Good. Now, I think we must part. I am going to serve as nightwatch. And you must go and try to discover who it is that wants my child dead.

And with that, Thomas stood up, flicked his tail twice, and leapt off into the shadows.

Jonathon Hightower had had a fair number of unpleasant surprises in his life, but this evening certainly should be posted near the top of the list. First, there was the arrival of the cat and his frantic call for help. Then the discovery of just what the young ladies had caught. Then Ninette's confession—

Ninette. He had to admit the name suited her much better than Nina . . .

And now this. It was as implausible a tale as anything in a shilling novel about rags-to-riches newsboys, or American cowboys and savage rustlers. Yesterday he would have called such a story sheer lunacy.

But that was before; now, well . . .

It was the spare, unembroidered way in which Thomas had told his tale that made it the more plausible. He had to admit that his blood had run a little cold when the cat had described so matter-of-factly how he had murdered his tormentor. But then again . . . she deserved it. He remembered stories his uncle and some of the other Elemental Masters in that circle shared over beer or brandies. Helen Waring was not remembered with anything other than distaste—and curses, and the general opinion that it was to be hoped that "she got what was coming to her." Not that anyone suspected she had been murdered . . . she had just gone to the continent, and rumors had returned that she had died. But no one ever was quite sure about Helen Waring, and for all anyone knew, she could appear again without warning. It would be a profound relief to some people in magical circles to learn that she really had gone on to whatever "reward" she had earned.

And he *certainly* didn't blame Thomas for doing his best to keep his child from prostituting herself. In Thomas's shoes—or fur—he'd have done the same. From the tone of the cat's mental voice, it had been agony to watch Marie training the girl for such a position, knowing he could do nothing about it.

But then, there was the deception. He hated being lied to above all things.

He walked back to the flat in a sort of smoldering temper, which was rather the worse for the fact that he could not really fault her very much for doing so. It was not as if she had somehow cheated them; she had worked damned hard for them all, in fact. It was not as if she didn't have talent, for she certainly did. In fact, he had no real reason to be angry with her . . .

Are you angry with her because she lied about her identity, or because you just learned she has been raised to be a courtesan, and she is unlikely to give up that plan?

He gritted his teeth. Well, at least he had an ally in hating *that* idea. The cat Thomas was entirely of the same mind about that . . .

And neither of you will have anything left to fret about if you don't put your mind to discovering who it is that wants to be rid of her and why! the logical part of his mind protested. *Really, you had better set your priorities . . .*

He stopped, then; looked up and blinked in shock. No wonder the pavement had felt somehow familiar—

He had gotten from where he left Thomas all the way to the building that contained Nigel's flat without having any memory of the intervening space.

15

"**W**ELL," said Nigel, over breakfast. "What are we going to do about this situation?"

No one had to ask "What situation?" since none of them had slept particularly well last night. After many attempts to trace the homunculus back to its source, both Nigel and Arthur had to admit defeat. Jonathon had not even tried; "Fire," he had said distinctly, "is not an element conducive to bloodhound work." Nigel had hoped that the Air Elementals might have a memory of the creature's passage, but evidently it had not come out into the open until it reached the building that housed Ninette's flat.

"Guards, for one thing," Jonathon said, slowly chewing a mouthful of toast. "Wards, for another, since I am not sure we can rely on Air Elementals to remember they are supposed to guard her."

Nigel groaned. "Wards. Do you know how much that is going to attract attention to her? We might as well set a beacon on the top of her building! Better yet, why don't we simply just send invitations to every dark mage we know of, and let them all appear at once?"

"Oh come now, Nigel, it isn't that bad," Wolf said, leaning down over Arthur's shoulder and helping himself to a generous bite of Arthur's scone. "After all, I wrote an entire opera that revealed I was an Elemental Master, and look how long it took the dark ones to puzzle it out!" He held the bite in one claw and ate neatly, as Arthur gazed ruefully at the place where all the jam had been until Wolf took it. "Poor Salieri. He went quite mad after that. Convinced himself that *he* was the one that killed me."

"Wolf—it was a disease homunculus that did you in, wasn't it?" Nigel cast the parrot a sharp glance. "I don't suppose it would be the same mage—"

"After all this time?" Wolf made a sound like a snort. "I think not. Besides, the creature was clearly after our dancer, not me."

Nigel sighed, and went back to contemplating his kipper. "Well, nothing is simple, is it?"

"We could set a trap . . ." Wolf continued, wiping his jam-sticky beak on Arthur's dressing-gown, much to the latter's exasperation. "Not anything that would actually *catch* the next creature that attacks her, but something that would allow us to trace it back?"

Jonathon shook his head. "If we were the same power, yes, but for an unlike and an antagonist power? It would take us years to work out how."

"I would rather know *why*," Nigel said thoughtfully. "The girl seems so inoffensive. It doesn't make any sense."

"Then it has to tie back to her father somehow." Jonathon pursed his lips. "I believe I will send some messages out via Elemental to the other Fire Masters that might remember Helen Waring and Dupond. Nigel, you do the same. Perhaps if we can unravel the mystery from that end, we'll be in a position to do something for Ninette."

"It might turn out to be someone that Miss Waring scorned," Wolf said, with relish. "Someone who blamed Dupond for it. That could be very useful actually. So long as he isn't utterly mad, we might be able to show him that rather than being jilted, he had a narrow escape!"

Nigel rolled his eyes. "Trust you to think of that. It sounds like a plot for one of your operas."

"Speaking of which," the parrot said brightly, "I have the plot for Nina's next vehicle! It's very Ruritanian, and if we can manage it, I think we can even get a swordfight into it! It's about a princess who is engaged to marry a prince she's never seen, and only wants to be a dancer instead, so she disguises herself as a maid and runs away to London, where she becomes a sensation."

"And I suppose that the prince she was supposed to marry only wants to become a stage magician," Jonathon drawled sarcastically.

"Not at all. The prince has been going to university here, sees her on the stage, and not knowing who she is, falls instantly for her and begins wooing her. She doesn't know who he is, she only knows he's a very rich student and is probably noble, and doesn't take him very seriously at first." Wolf looked triumphant. "Then we can have an evil cousin who has plans to usurp the throne, and kidnaps the princess to use her as bait for the prince. We can have a grand melee sword fight and end with a triumphant wedding scene when they all realize who they all are."

"I think you have been reading too many sensational novels," said Jonathon dryly.

"Bosh. Let's just make the kidnapping an *attempted* kidnapping so we don't have to change the scene." Nigel looked up, a light that Jonathon very well recognized in his eyes. Jonathon sighed.

"Shall we concentrate on protecting our leading lady and get her *first* show on the stage before we think about her next one?" he asked, exasperated.

Nigel shook his head as if to clear it. "You're right. So. Wards?"

Nina woke from her death-like sleep with a groan. Destroying her homunculus before those cursed Masters could trace it back here to her had been destroying a part of herself. Doing so had left her prostrated on the floor, too weak to move, and she'd just held onto consciousness long enough to get her servants to pick her up and carry her to her bed.

She had saved herself, at the cost of a great deal of power.

At least now she knew what all her enemies looked like, as seen through the eyes of the homunculus. There were two, not one, Masters: an Air Master and the Fire Master she already knew about. There was an additional Air magician, the wretched dancer who had only the power of glamorie, and a girl that was Sighted.

She did not have to ring for her servants as a human would; they knew when she was aware and needed them again. And they knew just what it was that she needed, too. Two of the men each brought a struggling street urchin in, both children so ragged and filthy it was impossible to say whether they were male or female. Not that it really mattered to Nina. She fell on them like a starving dog on a steak. When she was like this, there was no finesse involved, only the hunger and the need to replenish herself.

Literally, in this case. She had lost substance as well as energy, and when she was done there was nothing left of

the children but their rags. Feeling sated and reinvigo-
rated, she stretched and yawned. The servants took that
as their signal to remove the rags and send her maid in.

"Draw me a bath," she said. "I need to think."

What she meant was that she needed to draw on the
memories of all those she had absorbed, on their collec-
tive intellects. Her old men might have been addled by
her spells and her beauty, but most of them were intelligent men who had not inherited their wealth. They had
earned it, every penny of it, and gotten it as ruthlessly as
anyone could imagine. They had been shrewd, calculating, and scheming. All that was hers to call upon now.

As she sank into her hot bath, with her hair piled high
on her head and the scent of musk surrounding her
from the perfume oils and special herbs she always put
in the water, the first thing that came into her mind was
this.

*They know you are here, now, and they know what you
are.*

They might not know *who,* but they would know
what, or at least, they would know that an Earth Master
walking the dark path was hunting their precious
dancer.

*It is only a matter of time before they find another
Earth Master to hunt you.*

It was true that Earth Mastery tended to come to
those who were reluctant to venture into cities, and for
good reason. What human beings did to the Earth in
their cities left it fouled and poisoned, and Earth Masters felt that acutely. Still, given that there was an urgent
need, one could be persuaded in time. It all depended
on how organized the Elemental Masters were, here-
abouts. If they were highly organized, as they were in,
say, Germany, it would not take long at all. If, however,
they were as chaotic and anarchistic as they were in
Russia . . . it might take a year.

So assume that you have between two weeks and six months. Unless . . . you find something else to distract them with.

Thus came the advice of those shrewd old men from their decades of chicanery, backstabbing, Machiavellian schemes. *Find something else to distract them with. They will have a hard time fighting a battle on two, or even three fronts.*

She frowned, pursing her lips. This could be a problem. If she were back on her home ground, she could have had a dozen distractions for them already. And she had already tried making one of the dozens of admirers around the dancer besotted . . .

Wait . . .

She nodded to herself. Yes, that was one thing she had not tried. She had been working with men who were already attracted to the girl. What she had *not* tried was *creating* a crazed and infatuated admirer.

Yes. That would work. But she needed another front to work on. If only she was back east of Germany! Then there would be people who *knew* she was the real Nina Tchereslavsky, and—

Wait—

Of course!

She sank down into her bath with a smile of satisfaction. There would be several cables to send today. She would have to be sure to send them from different offices to avoid drawing attention to herself or to her servants. This trap should come as a complete surprise.

And it should, ideally, ensure that all of her enemies would be so very busy that they would not see her real attack coming.

Because I don't have any hands, nor voice, that's why! the cat said with irritation to Nigel. *If I could work most*

Earth Magic, don't you think I would have done so to make sure my wife and child were taken care of? Maybe some of you can wield your power just by sitting down and thinking hard, but I can't, and I never could. I needed physical implements and I needed the chants I was taught.

"If he can't, he can't, Jonathon," Wolf said with a deep sigh. "I must say, I sympathize. I'm rather in the same pickle." He fanned his wings. "No thumbs, don'cha know. Heaven knows I've *tried,* but when you can't pick up both the wand and the cup at the same time . . ."

See? Even the bird understands.

Wolf gave the cat an evil yellow eye and made sound like a rude little boy.

"Curse it," Jonathon said with passion. "I don't know any Earth Masters."

I was the only one in this part of the country, old lad, the cat said, wearily. *I am afraid this is going to have to be done the hard way. The letter-tree.*

Wolf groaned. Jonathon nodded reluctantly. "All right. I'll do my lot. Wolf, you get Arthur to do yours; I expect he and Nigel know pretty much the same circle of magicians?"

"Identical," Wolf replied, and sighed. "Bother. This could take a month."

"Or more." Jonathon's mouth was set in a grim line. "Once we find an Earth Master, we will have to persuade him this truly is an urgent situation in order to get him inside a city. Only the Dark Walkers like what happens to the Earth inside a large city."

"Truer words," Wolf grumbled.

They were all sitting in Ninette's dressing room, waiting for Ailse to escort her to the theater. It had been agreed that she was not to go anywhere alone from now on. Not that she had done so very much before, but it was even more imperative now. Jonathon had already set the Fire Wards around her flat; Nigel was setting the Air Wards now.

At that moment, the subject of their concern arrived, along with the little Scots maid. And Ailse had a very determined expression on her face that made Jonathon's eyebrow rise. His curiosity was further aroused by the expression of excitement on Ninette's face.

He wasn't the only one to notice. "Do I sense a conspiracy?" Wolf exclaimed, standing up straighter on his perch on the back of a folding chair.

"Summat," Ailse said shortly, and turned to Jonathon. "I'm thinkin' sir, that ye'll be havin' more sense than Master Nigel and Master Arthur. You too, Master Wolf, Master Thomas."

"Sense about what, exactly?" Jonathon asked warily.

"She wants to teach me to shoot!" Ninette burst out, her cheeks very pink now. "I think this would be a very good idea!"

"Shoot?" Jonathon exclaimed, startled. "You mean, a firearm?"

Ailse glared at him "No, a knittin' needle, ye gurt booby!" she snapped, clearly having lost her temper. "Of course I mean a firearm!" She opened her purse and removed one of the biggest handguns that Jonathon had ever seen, wielding it with all the calm of an expert. "This lad, t' be precise, or one like it. Me ald father taught me afore I left home," she added with pride. "And me brother brought me this from America, aye. But 'twas me granny as told them t'teach me. 'There's nothin' dark and fearsome can stand against Cold Iron, Silver or Blessed Lead,' she said, and Father allowed she was right." To Jonathon's dumbfounded astonishment, she expertly broke the revolver and spilled six cartridges into her hand. "Two each," she said with pride. "There be the Cold Iron." She held up one with a business-end of a dull black. "Tricksy, those. I mun be sure they dinna rust i' the revolver, an' this near t' sea, that isna an easy thing. Here be the Silver—" This time the bullets she held up were as shiny as a proud house-wife's best cutlery. "An' those I mun be polishin' every day too. An' this is th' Blessed Lead." These looked ordinary enough at first. "Cast from the lead from the roof of our own kirk, with pastor's own blessin' on 'em, and look—" She turned the bullet to face Jonathon and he saw that the soft nose of it had been cut and cut again "—Saint Andrew's own blessed cross on it, d'ye ken."

Jonathon knew a little about firearms, as did most stage magicians, and he knew about the practice of cutting a cross into the nose of a bullet to make the soft lead spread more when it hit a target. He blinked. "Saint Andrew's own blessed cross" was likely to be hell on earth for anything those bullets struck . . .

"She's very good!" Ninette said, her eyes shining. "Really! I would feel ever so much safer if I knew how to shoot and had a gun!"

Jonathon considered this, carefully, and it wasn't only supernatural entities that he was thinking about when he considered the dancer with a revolver in her hands. Earth Magic was also the magic of animal instincts. If *he* was an Earth Master, and *he* wanted to eliminate a pretty young dancer, one with many admirers . . .

"I am going to argue in your favor," he said carefully, "if you both promise me one thing." He turned first to Ailse. "I want you to make sure that she is deadly with this thing. She cannot afford to miss and she cannot afford to have it taken from her. Do you understand me?"

The Scots girl pursed her lips grimly. "Aye," she replied. "An' that I can do, if 'tis in her t' be a shot."

"And you—" He rounded on Ninette. "You *must* be ready to shoot to kill, without pause, without hesitation, if you ever have to take that thing out. There will be no time for second thoughts, no squeamishness. Whoever this is might well use someone—" He thought for a moment, then decided that being blunt was the only answer. "—might well use one of those men that throng your dressing room as an instrument. If that happens, there will be no question of guilt or innocence, no mercy. You will have to kill, or be killed. Or . . . worse," he added with conviction. "The object might be to carry you off to much worse than simply death. And I do not mean mere rape." Ailse went scarlet with embarrassment at the word, but he went ruthlessly on. "I mean dissolution. Terror. Horror, such as you cannot imagine. These magics that we use are primal forces and as such, they have all the raw power of the tempest, the volcano, the earthquake."

He hoped—in fact, he prayed—that Ninette, child of Montmarte as she was, was near enough to the violence that could be in those streets that she would truly *understand* what he meant, and would be willing, able, to be just as violent to ensure her own safety.

Her eyes became very thoughtful, and a bit distant. He sensed she was looking deep into her memory. Her expression darkened, and he felt hope.

"I am no hothouse flower, M'sieur," she said, quietly. "I am the—the cabbage grown on the windowsill of a garret, so that one might eat. There were Apache-gangs in my street. I have sometimes had to run home very fast to avoid the absinthe-drinkers, the hashish-smokers, the procurers with knives. I know how evil can wear a friendly, even a familiar face. Yes, M'sieur Jonathon. I can shoot to kill."

The cat, silent until now, growled a little. *A few of those limped home when I got done savaging their ankles,* he added. *I may not be a mastiff, but I can probably give her a moment or two more to aim.*

"All right," Jonathon said, with a slow nod. "I will

make sure Nigel and Arthur have no objections. And I myself will go out and get you a revolver." He eyed the monster in Ailse's hands. "But not quite that big. You don't have the wrists for it, Ninette. I won't get you a ridiculous little lady's gun, but I will get you something you can handle."

"An' the bullets!" Ailse said, instantly. "Cold Iron, Silver, and Blessed Lead."

He raised his eyebrow again, and Ailse blushed. "I *am* an Elemental Master," he reminded her. "I think I can manage. Even in so seemingly hardheaded and ordinary a city as Blackpool."

It took relatively little effort to get the Silver and Cold Iron bullets. It was the Blessed Lead that proved to be the sticking point. There were not many churches, even in wicked Blackpool, that were willing to part with a bit of their lead roofing material when someone looking like Jonathon turned up and asked for it. Three times he tried, under various pretenses, and three times he was turned away with varying degrees of suspicion and hostility. And there was no helpful padre, well versed in the ways of Elemental mages, anywhere within the city limits.

He'd have used Ailse's bullets, except that he had already determined that Ninette could not possibly shoot the monster pistol that Ailse wielded with such dexterity. Her attempts at dry-firing the gun would have put bullets into the sky or the ground at her feet, but never in an assailant. And besides, as the afternoon wore on, he became more determined that he *would* solve this difficulty. He had the gunsmith who would help them choose a weapon for Ninette and was willing to cast him bullets of the size needed in whatever material he chose to present. While not a mage himself, he knew mages, and ghost-hunters, and a variety of arcane folk; odd requests like this were routine for him. All he needed was the Blessed Lead.

Finally at wits end, he resorted to chicanery. He found a church with a roof badly in need of repair, hired an urchin to shinny up a drainpipe and steal him some, then salved his conscience with a generous donation in the "Repair Fund" box.

By then it was time to rush back to the theater for the evening performance, something which, in the light of what else was going on, had a distinct edge of unreality to it.

He found himself in the wings during Ninette's turns, and not at all by accident. He watched her closely in the light of his new information, but he could find nothing whatsoever lacking in her skill. If anything, she was better now than she had been when she first started dancing here. That was, undoubtedly, partly practice. But there was something else, too. There was—a sense of joy in her dancing that had not been there before, a feeling that she was *giving* this performance to her audience, generously and unstintingly.

And the audience was giving back to her.

There was absolutely no doubt of this; if he could not actually see the energies, he could sense their effect on the energies of his own magics. It was not a parasitic relationship; it was a symbiotic one. The audience poured over her their pleasure, their appreciation, their support. She gave back to them happiness, exuberance, joy. It was, perhaps, the most remarkable thing he had ever seen on a stage.

There's her magic, the cat said, from his feet, startling him. *There's dozens would give their souls for that sort of power.*

"I can imagine," he murmured. "If she chose . . . if she learns how to reach an entire hall, how to do this when she isn't dancing—"

She could have the world at her feet. Or at least, London. She could fill a lecture hall on whatever subject she wanted, and get people to rush out and support it. She could probably even get elected to Parliament. It's a dangerous power.

"Terrifying, when you think about it," Jonathon said darkly.

But she'll never use it that way, the cat countered firmly. *I know my girl. None of that would make people happy.*

Jonathon snorted. "Once she figures out that she can use this to get even better presents out of those fools that come backstage—"

She's giving the presents back.

The cat's words made him glance down incredulously. "Bosh!"

I'm telling you. Just you drop by and watch. She's been giving the presents back, keeping only the flowers. See for yourself.

"But—why?" Jonathon managed.

'S'truth. I don't care about her keeping the presents so long as she doesn't end up in the bed of some blackguard—but she started handing 'em back about the same time as she discovered this magic of hers.

Jonathon shook his head. He wasn't quite sure what to make of this bit of information. He turned and left the wings before she finished the dance, going back to his dressing room, shared with the patter-comic and the male half of the sentimental-ballad singers, and stared at his own reflection in the dressing-table mirror for a while.

Finally he shook himself out of his reverie and began carefully applying his makeup. Why should he care what she did or did not do with the presents those idiots pressed on her? Although he had to admit, given everything that was going on now, it was a wise decision on her part. He didn't *think,* now that they were all on the alert, that anyone could slip anything magically dangerous past them and into Ninette's hands, but you never knew. And gems and gold were the provenance of an Earth mage, too. If anyone could exploit such a thing, it would be an Earth mage.

Well if she had hit on that dangerous spot for a potential breech in their defenses, good for her.

He ignored the fact that he felt like gloating. Or rather, he ignored it until the moment that it was appropriate for his evil stage-self to gloat and smirk over his captive. He didn't quite realize *how* much he was enjoying himself until she whispered, as she was being locked into the cabinet, "If you cackle, I swear I will not be able to keep from laughing at you."

After a single glance of outrage, he slammed the door shut with a bit more force than was strictly necessary, and locked it up. He wasn't *that* bad, was he?

Yes, it turned out, he was. Nigel intercepted him on his way back to the dressing room. "Just a word. A bit less of the villainy, would you? That's all right for the pantos, but if you do that too often here, they'll start laughing and shouting, 'Look behind you!'"

Chagrined, he savagely wiped his makeup off and headed for the stage door. Or at least, that was his intention.

But his feet had a mind of their own, and took him to the door of Ninette's dressing room. As usual, it was thronged with Lotharios. As he had seen before, they slipped little velvet boxes into her hand or onto the dressing table.

But this time, he caught the by-play with a sense of astonishment, as Ailse collected each box and discreetly gave it back to the giver with a whispered, "Mademoiselle cannot possibly accept this."

Only once did she make an exception to this. The giver was a little girl, who solemnly presented her with a tinsel ring she must have gotten out of a cracker. With equal solemnity, Ninette accepted it, put it on, admired it, and directed the attention of everyone else in the room to it. Nor did she put it aside when the child had been taken off to an overdue bedtime.

Jonathon slipped away before she could notice him.

16

NINA had her fool, and an excellent choice he was, too.

Terrance Kendal had the acute misfortune of having ambitions that far, far outstripped his abilities, and an ego to match. He had been the only child of a deliberately "invalid" mother who doted on him, and a distant father who worked himself to death, leaving Terrance and said mother just enough money for pretensions of gentility, but none of the substance, like the protagonists in a satirical story by Saki. He had been given airs, but no graces. If he'd had wit, he might have found a place as a hanger-on in the circles to which he aspired, but sadly for him he had none.

Terrance was sent away to school, but alas, it was not Eton or Harrow, or even a second-tier school, a fact which was to cause him embarrassment for the rest of his life. He was encouraged by his mother to believe he was a budding genius, and it came as an embittering experience for him to discover that no one else had this impression. He was large enough and coordinated enough that he was not bullied, but he was no one's friend, either. He was good enough at sports to survive, but not good enough to prosper. He thought too highly of himself, and made no effort to hide the fact that he felt himself to be the social superior of the entire school. To his face, he was mockingly called "Your Lordship" and behind his back rather less flattering names. He left school as alone as he had arrived.

University proved as great a disappointment. His credentials were lackluster, his antecedents plebian, his wealth nonexistent, his personality composed of nothing but affectation. He managed to get into a college that housed members of the classes he thought he belonged in, and he immediately set to work proving himself a nuisance. He hung about trying to get himself invited to parties, and when he could not, whenever the chance arose, he invited himself. He tried to drink, and he hadn't the head for it; tried to gamble and hadn't the wealth. He couldn't afford a horse or a motorcar, and the only possibly route to the affections of those to whose ranks he longed to aspire, that is, the road of sport, was a closed book to him. He played neither cricket nor football well enough to make the teams, and he could not even pull a decent oar. The true wealthy and titled students were unimpressed with his scribblings and poetry; those who had the wit and learning recognized it for the pathetic dross it was, and the rest laughed to scorn the notion that a "real man" could find any interest in such nonsense when there were things to shoot and things to ride, things to play and things to cheer on, things to acquire and things to display.

Thus disappointed, Terrance returned to the maternal bosom in Blackpool to sulk on what he increasingly viewed as a "pittance."

He had never felt affection for anyone, not even his adoring mother. His love-sonnets were as flat as uncorked champagne. So when Nina began her work on him, it was to persuade him not that he was violently in love with the dancer, but that she was violently in love with *him*.

Nina began her campaign with excellent box-seat tickets to the performance, and although under any other circumstance he would have scorned such entertainment as "too common," this time he was persuaded. Partly because the tickets were sent, ostensibly, as a belated birthday gift from one of the few Cambridge men who had not utterly scorned him, and partly because of a rumor—entirely untrue—that the hall was going to be graced that night with the presence of the Crown Prince.

So he went, and seated in the next box, Nina went to work. She took care to work her magic in a very subtle manner. He was one of those sorts that could not go to a performance of any kind without nibbling and drinking throughout it, and before his (fashionably late) arrival, she had gotten into his private box and carefully laid out a little buffet in miniature for his pleasure, all of it bearing the magic she intended to become a part of him.

The magic she wove was compounded of half lust and half hallucination. It was easy enough to incite the lust; the hallucination was subtle. Terrance was made to believe that the dancer spent the greater part of her performances looking at *him*, winking at him, smiling at him, gazing coyly at him. By the time the evening was over, Terrance had more than half convinced himself that the dancer would be his in a moment, if he but raised his little finger and beckoned to her. He congratulated himself on his conquest, smugly. Not that he would have anything to do with so common a creature as a music-hall dancer of course but this was not a real music hall dancer, this was a *ballerina*, and a Russian to boot. So it was all right. Her devotion was acceptable; in fact, he considered that it was his due.

By the end of the performance he was basking in the imagined attention he was getting, and traveled homewards in a taxi in a state of self-congratulatory satisfaction. Of course, he did not deign to join the crowd attempting access to the dancer's dressing-room; not only was he above that sort of plebian behavior, he had every expectation that the lady would come to *him,* and not the other way around. Like Charles the Second, he would summon; like Nell Gwynne, she would answer, overawed with the honor he bestowed upon her. If he chose to summon, that is. He had to be sure she was worthy of his attention.

And so for several nights running, he made his observations. He took care never to take the same box twice, but always she somehow intuited where he was, and bestowed her flirtations on him. His mother complained mildly after the second week of this, of the expense of box seats every night, and could he at least share the box and the expense with some chums? He stared at her in fury; then the next day, in a rage, he went to the safe-deposit box at the bank, substituted her rather fine pearls for imitations, and sold the former. Thereafter there seemed to be no expense, so his mother's nagging tongue was stilled. He told himself this was his right as the head of the household. Besides, they were to come to him eventually, and what need had she for pearls anyway? She hadn't gone out in decades, except to funerals, and to those she properly wore jet, not pearls.

But that awoke him to a possible difficulty. He lived at home, with his mother; he could not bring a mistress there!

But a trifle of research on the part of the hall-boy eased his mind. The dancer had a flat of her own, with an entrance both private and discreet. So there would be no difficulty, and thankfully, no expense. The most he would need to provide would be a pretty trinket now and again, and the safe deposit box contained many tokens belonging to his mother than he imagined would be suitable.

With all these things settled in his mind, he decided the moment had come for the summons. He wrote it on a small card that he directed the hall-boy to convey to the dancer at the theater one afternoon. Then he took himself to the establishment he had chosen for the first assignation, a restaurant considered both smart and discreet; suitable for a man of wealth and taste to meet his mistress—or one who he was about to make his mistress.

He timed his arrival to a nicety. It would not do for her to appear at a table littered with the evidence of a long wait. He calculated how long it would take the boy to reach the theater, how long before he could deliver the note, and then, because she would, of course, fly out with the greatest speed to answer his invitation, how long it would take her to reach the establishment. He arrived there about five minutes before he reckoned she would.

But of course he made sure to ask the headwaiter if she had possibly preceded him. Having determined to his satisfaction that she had not, he had himself seated in the intimate and secluded corner he had reserved, ordered a brandy, and sat back to wait.

After some fifteen minutes, he was concerned. At half an hour, he was irritated. As the hands of his watch told him an hour had elapsed, he began to grow angry.

By the time he left the place, nothing in his stomach but overpriced brandy, he was in a towering rage.

Exactly as Nina had desired.

"What is that?" Ninette asked Ailse, who had answered the tap at the door of the dressing room and come away with a single card in an envelope with nothing written on it. "I hope it is not another invitation to teach some poor child how to totter about on her toes. Monsieur Ciccolini already has as many pupils as he cares to take."

For some reason, the wealthy of Blackpool seemed to think that she had so much time on her hands that she would be overjoyed to teach their children to dance. Not with an eye to going on the stage, of course! No, the doting mothers in question had more of a vague notion of a dainty little tot in a fairy dress, flitting about on the lawn to the strains of Mendelssohn for the entertainment and admiration of garden-party guests. The normal sort of display that one trotted out on these occasions was a daughter singing or playing, or more rarely, the dramatic rendition of "The Lady of Shallot." A dancing daughter, provided she was not yet nubile, would be a novelty. And it seemed that every good entertaining mama in Blackpool had conceived of this same novelty all at once. Ninette must come and teach the ball dance, or the ribbon dance, the hoop dance or the skirt dance.

Fortunately, Ninette had a stock answer for this. Ailse had written it up on cards, so it was ready-made and at hand, and needed only to have name and address added.

Dear (blank): I cannot tell you how honored I am by your invitation to teach your offspring. Alas, I fear your confidence in my ability is not matched by my competence as a teacher. I am, myself, still very much a pupil. However, I commend to your attention my own teacher, Monsieur Ciccolini, who has given me the skills you so admire. Sincerely, Nina Tchereslavsky.

Ciccolini now filled as many hours as he cared to, teaching these poor things the discipline of the ballet. Of course, it would do them a world of good. Knowing they would never get beyond flitting around a garden in a fairy dress, Monsieur Ciccolini did *not* put them into pointe shoes or stretch the little muscles to the aching point. Instead, he gave them exercises that would make them graceful, taught them the *demi-pointe* steps of the "white ballets" before toe-work became commonplace, and choreographed charming little diversions that would at least not cause garden-party guests to have to stifle yawns.

And he did so with great and abiding patience, patience that was justified by the very high fees he was charging. Nina found it all rather amusing. These women saw nothing wrong with expecting *her* to do the same thing for free, but Monsieur Ciccolini could command a handsome fee for his labor.

Then again, Monsieur Ciccolini did not stand to profit as highly as she did from the upcoming grand production, *Escape from the Harem.* There was no doubt in Nina's mind that she was going to be worth every farthing, but the total still dazzled.

"'Tis not another one of *those,*" Ailse replied, her brow furrowed with puzzlement. "Canna make out what, exactly, this laddie wants . . . looks like he is inviting ye t' tea, nobbut he writes like he's invitin' ye t' Royal Audience."

Ninette took it from her, read it through, and began to laugh. "Oh my!" she chuckled. "That is exactly what it is. Have you ever heard of this fellow?" she asked, handing the card back to Ailse.

The maid shook her head. "What with all the cards and flowers and all, a body would think ye knew every name that wasna already in the papers," she said dubiously.

"Exactly." Ninette chuckled. "This is nobody, but he thinks very highly of himself. I expect that this is not tea he is inviting me to. I think this is an audition to have the honor of being his mistress. And if I pass, he will *permit* me if you will—"

Ailse went scarlet, although Ninette could not tell if it was from outrage, amusement, embarrassment, or a combination of all three. Although she suspected the latter.

"Now," Ninette continued thoughtfully, "it *might* barely be possible that this is someone of great importance masquerading behind an unknown name."

"What?" Ailse gasped. "The Prince? Prince Edward? But—"

"But I think it highly unlikely." Ninette serenely counted off the reasons on her fingers. "First, the royal yacht is nowhere to be seen, nor the royal car on the rails here. Second, Prince Edward was reported by the papers yesterday to be in Monte Carlo. Thirdly, should the prince seek to hide behind an unknown name it would be the name of one of his gentlemen, and he would *not* send a plain-jacketed manservant with dusty shoes to deliver the note. And what is more, anyone he sent would stay for an answer, because as royalty knows, the answer might be 'no,' and it would not do for a Prince to be loitering even in a private room of a common chophouse."

Ailse breathed a sigh, half of relief, half of regret.

"And I do not intend to answer the invitation of someone who clearly regards himself as no less than royalty who is, in fact *not* royalty." She turned to the dressing room mirror. "Particularly not when we have so much work to do. If this man had even the faintest idea of what my life is like, he would issue an invitation for a late supper, after the performance, not an afternoon tea. Toss it away, Ailse."

"We are shooting today, Mademoiselle," Ailse said firmly.

"I know. Nigel is sending his automobile in an hour.

And in the meanwhile, I intend to practice the solo from *Giselle*." Monsieur Ciccolini had the choreography from that ballet memorized so well that he probably could have taught it had he been blinded, and although Ninette was hardly performing the classical repertoire anymore, she intended to continue to learn it. One never knew. Perhaps, one day, if only to indulge her, Nigel would stage a real ballet. She felt faintly guilty about claiming to be a ballerina, and yet never actually doing real ballet.

With Ailse keeping careful track of time, she had just enough time to leave the studio garbed in a most peculiar costume and jump into the back of the auto before the driver became impatient.

"Hoy!" Jonathon said, looking at her in astonishment. "I thought I was taking Mademoiselle Ninette to shoot!"

"So you are," Ninette replied, pushing back the boy's cap on her head. "And this is a much more practical costume for shooting than any gown I own."

She had put her hair up in the ballerina's bun, and clapped a tweed cap, purchased from a shop that sold boy's hats, over the top of it. She wore a shirt, rather than a blouse, of very severe cut; this had been purchased from a shop that sold the sort of things that ladies who typed wore to their offices. There were no lace cuffs or frou-frous to get in the way. On her legs, Ninette wore the contraption known as a "bloomer skirt"; admittedly, she could have gotten the sort of divided skirt some ladies wore to ride or play tennis in, but from what she understood, there was going to be a great deal of clambering over rocks, and she wanted her legs as free of encumbrance as she could manage. "I wish I could have gotten boy's trousers or even knickers to fit me," she said wistfully. "But on such short notice, it wasn't possible."

She was scarcely embarrassed, seeing as she had worn

far, far less onstage for a very long time now. Jonathon's lips quirked in a ghost of a smile.

"Allow me to congratulate you on your good sense, mademoiselle," he said. "There are females who would have expected me to carry them to where we are going to go."

Ninette sniffed scornfully. "Then you are accustomed to dealing with females who are fools," she said. "Nigel said it would be a wild part of the coast; I took him at his word, and I dressed to suit. You and Ailse are doing me the favor of teaching me this. It would be sad if I were to play the fainting maiden now."

Jonathon chuckled, then turned his attention to putting the automobile in motion and sending it down the street.

The auto trundled its way parallel to the ocean, passing the boardwalk, the beaches with their holiday families and bathing machines, all the little businesses that catered to the enterprise of sea-bathing and beach-picnicking. It was a rare day, without a cloud in the sky and without any prospect of rain. The famous electric lights that had made Blackpool a household name at the turn of the century were festooned everywhere. They passed the famous Tower, and Ninette made a private vow that when this was over, she was going to see all of these things she was missing. The Tower, the Winter Gardens, the boardwalk, the illuminations, the Opera House and all of the other theaters that Nigel competed with. The road narrowed and became more primitive, the ride a bit rougher as the macadam turned to gravel, and the beach on their left turned to rock flats.

Finally, at a place where the worn grass showed that other people had left vehicles, Jonathon turned the auto off the track and parked it, nose facing the sea. "Here we are," he announced.

"So it seems. Why here?" Ninette asked.

"Chiefly because this is where a good many people already come to practice shooting," Jonathon said. "The local folk know this, and stay well away to avoid the odd stray bullet by a beginning marksman. This is far enough away that the sound of gunshots will not excite any interest in the holiday makers, nor is there anything of interest here for the hiker or the sea-bather. We shall be quite alone."

"Good!" Ninette applauded. "I should not like to be responsible for shooting someone's ear off by accident."

She hopped down out of the car without waiting for Jonathon's aid, and walked as far as the edge of the grassy area. Looking down, she saw why the local folk came here to shoot. Nature had provided a kind of perfect target range; there was just enough of a drop-off down to a beach of pebbles and a mud-flat that it was unlikely stray shots would go anywhere other than into the earth or out to sea. The beach was not the sort to invite bathers, even though it was secluded. And the scramble down and back up again could only be attempted by the athletic.

Of course, all of them were athletic, and as she was completely unhindered by skirts, Ninette scampered down the crude path as nimbly as a monkey.

The end of the beach, most often used for targets, was a stack of flat-topped boulders, thoroughly pock-marked and decorated with splashes of lead. Glass shards and pottery fragments showed what figured most often as the targets, although three or four bullet-ridden, rusted tin cans showed that there were others who preferred targets that did not break when your bullets struck them.

Jonathon had come prepared with a sort of easel and some sturdy pasteboards with the crude outline of a man on them. These he proceeded to set up without a

word, then came to join the two women at the opposite
end of the "shooting gallery."

He carefully explained the peculiarities of this pistol,
then left it up to Ailse to get down to the particulars.
Since there was no further call on his services, he turned
his attention and his mind back to the question of just
who Ninette's enemy might be.

Thus far, they'd had a singular lack of success in finding an Earth Master. The few that he or Nigel had found
were all too old to come live in a theater in Blackpool,
and even if they were so inclined, they couldn't have
borne the psychic stench of the city for very long.

He expected Ninette to be fearful, and she certainly
screwed up her face and jumped the first few times that
Ailse fired the gun. But then she stepped bravely up,
took the pistol in steady hands, and patiently let Ailse
position her and show her how to squeeze off shots.

They went wide of the mark, of course. That was what
he had expected. But what he had not expected was
how quickly she began to sight in on the target. By the
time they were halfway through the box of cartridges,
she was hitting the target more often than not. By the
time the box was empty, she was confidently firing and
hitting almost every time.

Jonathon was honestly astonished. "You're certain
you've never done anything like this before—" he ventured.

Ninette looked at him with a twist of her lips. "I think
that if I had, I would surely remember," she said wryly.
"But recall what I am. Dancers must have very good
control of their bodies. Well, stand up—"

He did so, wondering what on earth she could be
thinking. She stood quite close to him for a moment,
measuring him with her eyes. It was a very calculating
look, and he couldn't imagine what she was going to do.

That she *was* about to do something, he had no doubt. He had seen that look in her eyes before.

She settled her feet in their stout little walking shoes a moment, and then, like lightning, she made a tremendous jump and high kick, higher than he had ever seen her make before. The sole of her foot flashed within a hair of his nose, and hit the brim of his hat, knocking it cleanly off his head.

He stared at her. She shrugged. "A cabaret trick," she said calmly. "The can-can dancers and washerwomen at the Moulin Rouge do it all the time. Usually when the gentleman is drunk; the gentleman gets a look up her skirts and she keeps his hat until he ransoms it back. But be sure, if I had wanted to kick your nose and not the brim of your hat, I could have."

He looked at her soberly, without anger. "Better still?" he suggested, "Aim for the chin. You could break a man's neck that way. At the worst, you would knock him flat."

She blinked. *"Mais oui?* That is something to remember, then."

He licked his lips, considering. "Practice it," he suggested. "It's better than the pistol. We can't explain away a bullet, we can explain away an unfortunate fall."

She nodded, and for a moment, the sun seemed to fade. Then they all shook off the mood, and scrambled back up the rocks to the auto.

This time, Ninette sat up front with him as he drove back to the theater. "I am thinking you like me a little better now," she said, over the noise of the motor.

"I was disposed to be very angry with you when you told us how you had lied to us," Jonathon replied, after a long moment of thought.

"But?" she persisted.

He answered honestly, but reluctantly. "Well. You *are* a good dancer, a very good dancer. There is no doubt that you are very popular with the audiences. And there is also no doubt that you work as hard as any of us. I don't think anyone gives a hang whether you're Russian or Red Indian, the point is you give them good entertainment. But still, you lied to us . . . I don't like being lied to."

"*Mais ouis.* But . . ." She looked out the windscreen, her mouth in a small pout of melancholy. "Would any of you have listened to me, let me audition for you, if I had not come with this story, this lie?"

Jonathon grimaced. "To be honest, no."

"Then I should have starved. Or jumped into the river. Or gone into many men's beds." The matter of fact way she said it made him flush uncomfortably. "I did not want to do any of these things. And actually, I think I really did not know I wanted so badly to dance, either, until the people began to pay attention to me."

"It's a drug," he said quietly. "That admiration. It's a drug like any other, as bad as absinthe. You want it. You can't do without it. And once you've had it, you'd rather die than give it up. At least—" he added honestly "—it's that way for some."

"It could be for me, I think," she admitted. "I am taking care, I hope. You understand me? I am trying not to believe that I am so wonderful. But I feel something, out there—"

He debated a moment. "It's magic. You have a touch of it," he told her, deciding to make a clean breast of it. "You're not like me, or even Arthur—you're more like Wolf. You'll never have more than that touch of it, never work spells, but this much is yours. When you dance, when you give yourself to the audience, when you forget about everything and try to please them, you feed them. You make them happy. Your magic makes them forget that the tinsel isn't gold, that the props and scenery are only painted canvas and wood. And when you feed them, they feed you. Don't you always feel stronger and better when you come off stage?"

"Oui!" she exclaimed. "And I could not understand it! I never used to feel this way when I danced! I was exhausted! And then, after a while, here, I began to feel so full of energy when I came off the stage! Sometimes I need to settle and quiet myself, for otherwise I could not sleep! And you say this is my magic?"

He nodded. "It's you feeding them, feeding them something to take their minds out of themselves for a little while, and then they feed you. It wouldn't be enough to keep you going for hours and hours," he warned. "But I think that all the dancing that Nigel has planned for you in his big production will ultimately be no problem for you."

But with that, she laughed. "Poo! You have not seen a great ballet, then! The prima is onstage for almost all of it! *Swan Lake, sacre bleu,* nearly every scene! It would have been no problem without this magic . . ."

But then she smiled. "Still!" she added cheerfully, "With it, things will be very good indeed."

But as he wound his way through the streets to the theater, something occurred to him. What if *this* was what her unknown enemy wanted, this rare "performance" magic?

The attacks, then, would not be so much directed at her, as they would be to take what she had away.

Well, it looked as if he had some research ahead of him. It was going to be a long night. But, he hoped, a fruitful one.

17

NINA had wound up her first distraction and let him go. Now for the second.

They would be looking for Earth Mages; her use of the homunculus betrayed her origin. Very well. She would give them some. Or at least, she would give them something that *looked* like an Earth Mage.

She chose her decoy candidates very, very carefully, for they had to appear to be Earth Mages of the vilest sort, right up until their protections were exploded. The more plausible they were, the better. She could, of course, find mortals that ardently desired the powers of an Earth Mage, and who had just enough of the Gift in them to counterfeit Mastery without ever having anything more than what she granted them. But firstly, that would be wasteful, and secondly, she knew from past experience that such people were dangerous. They got ambitions, and they thought they could take what she would not give them. Such, in fact, had been her original summoner. When mortals got ambitious, things got . . . messy. And while she was not at all averse to mess, she knew that in this case, it could betray her. So she would set up the unknowing as her decoys, in a way that could not be traced back to her.

Her first choice was a natural one: a particularly nasty brothel-keeper of the lowest and most brutish sort. His customers were the same, and as for his "wares," well, they were in no condition to think about much of anything. His girls were all addicted to the drugs he gave them, most were Chinese, and he kept them in nasty little cells lining the corridors of his building on the waterfront, cells a mere six feet by eight, with nothing more than a pallet and a blanket, and a rag or two for clothing. They plied their trade, ate, slept, were drugged, and eventually died in these little "cribs," as they were called. For pure misery, his establishment had to be high on the list of those creating negative energies, and Nina, surprised by the amount she was able to make use of, made a note to try this particular method at some time in the future. But for now—all she needed was her decoy.

She set herself up in a dingy room in the building next door, wearing the form of one of her vagrants in order to rent it and its noisome contents for a week. There was no lock for the door; she was forced to make do with a chair wedged beneath the knob. She worked swiftly, and without a protective circle, but within shields. A Circle where none should be would only attract attention, and besides, there was not much in the Earth realms that would dare take her on now.

She tapped into the energies boiling out of the brothel next door; siphoned off a cornucopia of rage, hate, shame, lust, and pure despair, and used it to create some of the most powerful Earth-shields she had ever built. Carefully she placed them around both the brothel and the building of flats she was in now. This would further serve to confuse the matter; it would not

be clear whether the "Mage" was to be found in the flats
or in the brothel. When she was done, she was satisfied;
the shields were like stone walls; if they had been the
walls of a fortress, not even the guns of a naval warship
would be able to break them with a single shot. She
added a "tap" to keep those shields supplied from the
never-ending stream of soul-sickening darkness. Anyone who saw shields that strong would assume that the
Mage inside them was stronger still. Unfortunately for
them, this was hardly the case. She left the shields per-
meable to herself alone until she left the building. Then
she closed them even to herself; the perfectly ordinary, non-magical people who belonged there would
have no difficulty in crossing, but any creature of magic
would be stopped dead in its tracks. This, of course, now
included her.

Now what would happen when those shields were
broken by a concerted, unrelenting attack? Nina
wasn't entirely certain. Perhaps nothing. Or, perhaps
the power would backlash on those who were supply-
ing it. In that case, it would backlash on the girls; in
their weakened mental states, that might drive them
mad, or it might kill them. If the latter—well, that
would be delicious. It would mean the oh-so-noble fellows guarding the imposter would be personally responsible for the deaths of up to two dozen girls who,
at least in the sense of harming *them,* were innocents.

She walked away from that place with a grin on her
face that made people who saw it cross to the other side
of the street. Nina liked this plan so much that she decided to repeat it.

A few hours' worth of walking in similarly unsavory
neighborhoods netted her more of what she was looking for; by nightfall, she had found two more establishments in which to do the same. The first was a gin
palace, the second, an opium den. In both, she was able

to rent rooms in which to do her work, undisturbed, once she had purchased, respectively, two full bottles of "blue ruin" and a pipe and sticky ball of black-tar opium.

She used the gin palace first, pouring the poisonous stuff out of the window, then getting to work. It was a trifle more difficult to set up a "tap" here, since the people who were systematically destroying their health, their lives, and their brains with the stuff didn't actually live there. But she got the notion of putting the "energy sinks" into the benches that they sat on, and that worked admirably.

The next day, it was the turn of the opium den; she mashed the drug into a crack in the floor where it was indistinguishable from all the other muck collected there. What had served her well in the gin palace served her equally well here; this time she put the "sinks" into the bunks that those who could not afford a room stretched out on to fume their brains into drifting, benumbed pleasure. This was trickier than the brothel or the gin palace. Unlike alcohol, the opium did not admit the mind to anger. No, the emotion she siphoned here was bleak despair. Beneath the drug, there was the fear of not being able to raise the money for the next debauch, there was self-loathing, and more often than not, the wish that this time, the drug would end the struggle for existence. Then, of course, there were the addicts that appeared without money, suffering the agonies of withdrawal from the drug, so desperate for it and in such pain that they would do anything at all to get it.

Anything.

She walked away from the opium den with a feeling of smug cleverness.

In order to return to her new home without exciting comment, it was necessary to make a few stops and

changes of clothing, going from the poverty-stricken vagrant, to a lower-class workingman, to a simple servant,
to a lady's maid, and finally, to herself. The last two
changes of clothing she had concealed in order to effect
the change, one in the backyard shed of a nearby house,
the second in the tiny carriage-house of her own set of
flats. She walked straight in from there, as casually as if
she had merely gone for a stroll for the sake of the sea
air. As it happened, there was no one there to note her
coming in, as there had been no one to note her leaving,
but she had learned over the years that remaining unde-
tected and unmolested required the careful management of such details.

Her maid let her in, and she ordered several of her favorite foods at random and ate and drank hugely. She
was surfeited on the dark energies of misery, but for the
last four days her body had been subsisting on dubious
sausages, doubtful cockles and oysters, and suspicious
eel pies, and it craved wholesome, toothsome food.

With body and "self" satisfied, she flung herself down
on a settee and watched the plump, red-faced throng
parade under her windows. It amused her no end to
think how little these holiday-makers that flocked to
Blackpool in the season were aware that brothels,
opium dens, and gin palaces existed mere streets away
from where they were strolling. These, she could never
feed on. There was simply too little there. One part ig-
norance, three parts complaisance, five parts smug self-
congratulation, and a touch of anxiety that one day it
might all go smash ... thin stuff, and bitter, and flimsy as
the paper they wrote their letters home on to save on
the postage.

No, they had no idea that this pink pleasure-palace
of a city had a dark and rotten heart. They only saw
the façade. But of course, only the middle class and
upwards could afford to take a holiday at all, much

less one in another city. The middle class preferred to keep these sordid things at a considerable distance. The middle class did not want to know about what lay underneath the surface of anything. And it particularly did not want to know about the impoverished and desperate. It might be persuaded to part with the odd penny or two at Christmas to supply Christmas cheer for the "deserving poor," but on the whole, these were things it was better not to think about too carefully. The middle class liked their impoverished class to be in the newspapers, not underfoot, and particularly not underfoot when the middle class was bent on enjoying itself. Opium dens had their place in sensational literature, and one could get a delicious thrill when a lecturer thundered sternly about the evils of white slavery, but when one went on holiday, one preferred to think of the city one visited as an endless panorama of delights and ignore the cockroaches that would appear if one took down a panel of the pretty scenery.

"Fools," Nina muttered, and turned away from the window.

Having constructed three of these decoys, Nina knew that her labors were not at an end. Oh my, no. The hunters might not be lured by something so obvious. She turned her mind to more subtle decoys; something that would serve exactly the same purpose as her blatant works, but would not trumpet its existence for anyone with the eyes to see it.

Even if they took the first bait, she actually didn't think her targets would be fooled twice, but you never knew, and the hollow shields were in any event the easiest and fastest to create. They bought her time. Let the enemies waste their time stalking the premises, trying to determine who among all the vile inhabitants was the Mage, and then destroying the shields. While they were distracted, she would be stalking the dancer, and when she finally struck, they would never see her.

She brooded about what to do for three days, then worked out something that would serve. The next set of decoys was going to be a deception within a deception. Instead of creating obvious shields, she used the same principle of using the energies of despair to fuel the magic, only this time, it was to hide, rather than protect.

Once again, she stalked the streets of Blackpool, a nondescript ruffian, looking for the best places to use for her loci. After two days of testing the energies, looking for sustainable concentrations of despair, she found what she was looking for. A workhouse provided the first source, an orphanage the second.

The workhouse was fairly ordinary as such things went. People only came there because they had been wrecked on the reef of debt and financial ruin, and yet had some small hope that they could, with hard work, get themselves and their families out of it all. They quickly found, of course, that they could not; that the workhouse offered the barest of living on starvation rations, but the only place you could go from the workhouse was into the street, where there would be no food, no roof, and nowhere to go. Families were separated, men from women, children from parents. Despair there was in plenty, but it was the dull despair of those who had been pounded on the rocks of life until there was little spirit left in them.

The orphanage, however, was actually very difficult for her to give over to her intended plan, as it was such a huge generator of senseless death. Infants were swaddled and stacked like cordwood on beds in cheerless rooms, to remain in their increasingly soiled wrappers until the scheduled time for feeding and changing. Never were they allowed to move freely, and the thin skimmed milk they were fed was not enough to sustain the majority of them. They were so starved and dull they failed even to cry—this was pointed out to visitors as an example of how "good" they were.

They were not "good," of course. They were dying, most of them. Pneumonia and flu, chicken pox and measles, whooping cough and diphtheria . . . these childhood ailments would carry off battalions of them at a time. The infant wards could go from full to empty in a matter of days. The death rate was nearly ninety percent.

Children too old to be swaddled were left tied to bedsteads with no toys and little or no exercise, and fed equally inferior food of more skimmed milk, gruel and bread. As soon as it was possible to put them to work, they were rented out to mill owners. Not one in four lived.

It was delicious. All those little lives, cut short so soon . . . every life fraught with unrealized potential. She determined then and there that she was going to begin looking for an orphanage to patronize once all this was sorted out. It would be delightfully ironic to be seen as the Lady Bountiful to the little orphans in public, while in private she battened and prospered on their deaths.

All that took less than a week to set up. And meanwhile she was carefully watching the progress of her toy, Terrance Kendal.

He had come away from the failed assignation in a rage, but rage cooled too quickly, especially in a bloodless thing like him. He had, in all of his life, never sustained anything like passion for very long. Passion required commitment to something other than one's own self, because it required being focused on the object of passion, rather than one's own self. She needed to engender more than rage, she needed him to tip over the edge of sanity into obsession. If she had been forced to wait for it to happen naturally, she might have been waiting long. However, she had a number of resources she could use to manipulate his mind.

To begin with, dreams.

Dreams were very useful. They existed outside of logic, outside of normal behavior, and cut straight into emotion and instinct. Mortals did and experienced things in dreams that they would *never* think of doing, much less actually do, when awake.

Now to give a human dreams was not as easy as it might seem. The ordinary sort of human, without any magic to speak of, was singularly resistant to the any touch of the arcane. The sheer power of his disbelief was astonishing to someone who had never come up against it; the inability to See the creatures of other planes and other realms only reinforced that. This disbelief created a wall between a human mind and anything that might try to force it via magic. What a Mage had to do in order to infiltrate a human's mind—rather than just cracking it open, which was rather damaging and not at all subtle—was to find out just what it was he *did* believe in.

Fortunately, in the case of Terrance . . . he believed in God and the Church. Not, of course, the kind of honest and open-hearted belief that would also have protected him . . . no, indeed. He believed in the comfortable, dozing-in-the-pew sort of orthodoxy that promised him Heaven in return for the weekly offering and an occasional high tea for the clergy. He liked his clergymen modern—that is, a fellow who would talk to him about hunting and dogs and fishing, and not about uncomfortable things like the state of the poor and the exploitation of the mill-worker, or abstract things like morals and conscience. He certainly was not comfortable with those who took too close an interest in the state of his soul, but preferred those who reassured him without actually saying anything that his soul was in good repair and a place waited for him in Heaven—a Heaven populated by Cambridge men who would see his worth at a glance and give him the respect and deference he was simply was not getting here on earth. That this Heaven would also include plebeians who would fawn over his every word and beg to serve him went without saying.

So Nina put on one of her male guises and went to visit him dressed in the clerical dog collar.

She appeared round about tea-time, knowing that if a clergyman presented himself at that hour, it was a given that he would be invited to share it by Terrance's mother.

And so it was. Within two minutes of sending in a card, "Father Martin" was seated on the best horsehair sofa across from Mrs. Kendal and a rather bored-looking Terrance, nibbling on a watercress sandwich and drinking rather insipid tea. It was such a typical example of a stolid, middle-class sitting room that it could have been photographed and framed as a representative of its kind. The wallpaper was mauve, with great cabbage-roses climbing all over it. The woodwork was dark and shining with wax. The furniture was covered in mauve plush; there were small tables crowded with "curiosities" everywhere a table could be put, hand-embroidered firescreens, hand-embroidered cushions, hand-embroidered footstools—evidently Mrs. Kendal had a great deal of time on her hands and from the paucity of books in the room, did not care to pass it in reading. Mrs. Kendal was one of those blonde women who looked like roses in their youth, but faded rather quickly, like a printed chintz that has been washed too many times. She was thin— Nina rather suspected she lived on tea and toast and the occasional bowl of broth—her hair was now an indeterminate shade between silver and straw, her eyes were the pale blue of a sky with a thin haze of high cloud over it, and her voice was scarcely louder than a whisper.

Even her gown seemed a faded black, rather than

the uncompromising color of full mourning. If there had been any less of her, she would have been a ghost herself.

Nina had long experience of reading mortals, and with the thoughts of those she absorbed, and it was easy to categorize this woman. Very pretty, by nature docile, she had been taught that was all she had to be in order to achieve the acme of all possible goals, a Good Marriage. She had been schooled and catechized within an inch of her life in the most rigid form of religion, and frightened by a nanny and teachers and clergymen into a petrified fear of ever "being naughty." And because of this, she made a modest social success of herself. Her looks eclipsed her timidity, and her fear of practically everything was interpreted as shyness and an attractive modesty. She went where she was led, did what she was told, probably responded to her suitor's proposal of marriage with "All right." Once married, she was bullied by husband, parents, siblings, teachers, and son, and probably by her own servants.

She was as afraid of a social faux pas as she was of a sin, and to feel anything at all strongly, to break the surface serenity of the household, was the worst of all social faux pas. Every household book, every tome on proper wifely duties, preached this. This was at least partly where Terrance got his own cold-bloodedness; she had never had a passion in her life, or at least, she had never dared to allow herself to feel one. And life escaped her because she had never dared to grasp any of it; not youth, not joy, not love or romance. The only thing she had felt strongly enough about to try to hold it was her son, and she clung to him like a strangling vine, which made *him* all the more determined to shove her aside. This, of course, she refused to see. In her world of sentimental ballads and mottoes, the few tomes of what passed for fiction that she got from the lending library, this was how it was. Terrance was her "darling boy" who must, of course, be devoted to his invalid mother. He would never do anything to upset her. She had, after all, devoted her life to him, delicate as she was. She had no idea that every time she spoke those words, she increased his distaste for her company.

This was not helped by her pathetic conversation; the small gossip of the ladies of her charity-sewing group, timidly ventured opinions on the state of the world that she immediately discarded if Terrance frowned, complaints about all the "foreigners" in Blackpool, tales of woe about the servants.

As Nina listened to her nervous chatter, she thought to herself that there must be hundreds of women like her in Blackpool alone, and that they would be absurdly easy to exploit and devour. A little kindness, a bit of attention, and the right word at the right time would turn women like her into devoted slaves, who would passionately defend their chosen idol against anyone that criticized him or even failed to worship at his altar. It would have to be a man that attracted their devotion, of course. That sort of interest in another woman was "unhealthy" and highly suspicious, for no real woman could be so strong as to deserve the slavish devotion of others of her sex.

Like the orphanage, Nina filed that away in the back of her mind as another rich source of sustenance. The disadvantage would be that she would have to be a clergyman, of course.

But a few complaints about the indifference of Mrs. Kendal's doctors made her revise that. A doctor . . . that had a number of advantages. A doctor with a new scheme for invalid women—something pleasant, rather than extreme, like vegetarianism, or cold water baths, or cereal flakes for every meal. Something involving a great deal of tea. And sweets. And perhaps opium-laced cordials . . .

But for right now, her attention was on Terrance. With patience and skill, she insinuated into Mrs. Kendal's mind the idea that "the men" had important things to talk about, things that she was neither clever enough to understand, nor worldly enough to bear. Yet at the same time, Nina managed to insinuate that Father Martin did not feel these things, though her son might; Father Martin only feared that these matters were too weighty for a creature as delicate as she, and actually considered her to be the wisest and most gracious of women.

So, when it was clear that there would be no more afternoon visitors for tea, Mrs. Kendal pled her fragile health and left them alone. That was when Father Martin heaved a sigh, and leaned forward towards Terrance in a confidential manner, his expression turning earnest and grave.

"I would not for all the world have wanted your dear mother to hear this," "he" said quietly, "But I must ask you something, man to man. What do you know of that dancing woman, the Russian? The one all the papers had stories about—the one in that shipwreck. You know of whom I am speaking, I know."

"Nina Tchereslavsky," Terrance said automatically, flushing. "Nothing much, I've seen her act at the music hall a few times. I read the stories in the papers. She's accounted to be a handsome enough woman, I suppose, but certainly—really, Father Martin, she is a dancer in a music-hall who shows her limbs to anyone with tuppance, when it all comes down to it. Our paths are scarcely likely to cross, and if they did, I should hope she would know her place. Why?"

Father Martin heaved a great sigh. "Because, Mr.

Kendal, the woman is a Jezebel, and I have reason to believe she is interested in *you.*"

Terrance's eyes lit up, and his brow grew moist, but he probably thought he had schooled his features into indifference. He shrugged. "Me? I don't believe I have been to the music-hall more than twice or thrice in my lifetime. Whatever do you mean?"

He did not ask what a less self-centered man would have asked, which was "How do you know that?" He did not ask what a cleverer man would have asked, which was "Why should someone like that be interested in a man who has never so much as sent his card backstage?" And he did not ask what practically anyone else would have asked, which was "What business is it of yours?" He did not ask these things because he was under the impression that the comings and goings and doings of Terrance Kendal were naturally the interest of all the world. He had a fine appreciation of himself, and took it for granted that everyone else should. If anything, he took this as the signal that the world was finally paying him the sort of attention that it should.

Father Martin made a *tsk*ing sound. "I make it my business to keep an eye on the creature, since she ruined a good young man of my parish. I have learned her sordid history on the Continent."

Terrance made a kind of shrug that said, without words, "Well! The Continent! What would you expect?"

Father Martin nodded at the shrug. "You would think that someone as fairy-like as she would have a kind heart, a sweet nature, but no. She is steeped in black evil."

Terrance laughed, a bit uncomfortably, and wiped his brow with his handkerchief. "Oh, come now, padre, I think that is coming a bit strong for what must be the paltry sins of a young lady no better than she should be."

"Oh no. I use the phrase with full knowledge," Father Martin assured him. "She makes it her business to find good young men of fine breeding, like yourself. She smiles at them from the stage, lures them into coming to her dressing-room, first in the crowd, and then alone. She makes them fall in love with her, she exploits them for every blessed penny they have, and when they have exhausted their resources and are one step away from the workhouse, she casts them off."

"Oh surely not—" Terrance replied, looking guilty and sweating more heavily.

"I have the proof," "Father Martin replied. "She has left a trail of tragedy behind her from Russia to Blackpool; madness, suicide, poverty. I attend her every performance now, and I noted her interest in *you*. I came to warn you. Shun her! She will devour any young man that comes into contact with her as the spider devours a fly."

To Terrance's fascinated ears, Nina poured out a wealth of tales of "the dancing Jezebel." The more she told him, the more his anger grew, especially as she waxed eloquent on the material possessions the dancer had seduced out of her suitors. He said nothing, but she read him like a book. *Now* he knew why she had never answered his note! Somehow she had discovered that he was not the possessor of such wealth as she required, and had spurned his advances. She deemed *him* not worthy of *her* attention, the hussy! The brazen slut!

When Nina was certain that the fish had taken the bait and the hook was well and truly set, she took her leave. She had what she needed; the entrée into his mind.

Now for the dreams.

She left Terrance with his rage newly roused. He would go to bed tonight in a fever of indignation made stronger by the fact that he had no one to speak to about this. If he'd had a friend, they could have commiserated over brandy in the library, or even over a pint at the pub . . . but he had no one, and as a result, he would stew over this and fall asleep after tossing and turning for at least an hour.

Nina had come away with something from that house: Terrance's handkerchief, which he had patted across his flushing brow and left on the table. Now she had the link to him she needed, as well as the way into his mind.

So she waited until well after midnight, and then set up her preparations; small ones, so as not to cause any great ripples in the currents of magic. Just the handkerchief, a mirror, and herself, full to repletion of power siphoned from another round of vagrants. As before, she worked without shields or containment circles, putting out no more ripples to the currents of power than some serving-maid trying inexpertly to create a love-charm. In fact, that was the genesis of this spell, an Earth-magic love-charm.

She stared into the mirror, holding the handkerchief, and sent a tendril of magic across the city from herself to Terrance. When she saw his image in the mirror, sleeping fitfully in his stuffy bedroom, she knew she had him.

With a smile of satisfaction, she began weaving her dreams, sending them into his sleeping mind. Image piled upon fevered image, all of them reaching deep into his mind, past all of the conventions, the manners, the morals and into the deepest, most primitive parts of his mind.

In them, the dancer featured, tantalizing, tempting, seductive. The dream-Nina did more than seem to smile at him from the stage; she beckoned, winked, quirked an eyebrow. This time, Terrance went backstage, where the dancer, no more than half clothed, whispered promises, and allowed him certain liberties.

She did not go too far into the realms of sex, because she was quite sure Terrance was still a virgin. But she certainly made the dream-Nina exercise all of her wiles on the dream-Terrance—in his dreams, he grew heated, restless, and aroused. Yet the dream-Nina never got beyond promises and poses, while the dream-Terrance sweated and lusted.

And then, the rejection. And worse, the laughter.

The rejection took place at a grand party. Dream-Terrance was treated with contempt and denied entrance to a gathering to which he had an invitation. The invitation said "fancy dress" and yet everyone else was in evening dress, further increasing his humiliation. To hide his discomfiture, he kept his domino-mask on. He pushed past the servants at the entrance, who turned up their noses at him, to find Nina in a ballroom, surrounded by attentive males. They were all laughing uproariously about something. As he neared them, all too conscious of his inappropriate garments, the stares of the other party-goers, he overheard something. His name, followed by a roar of laughter.

"And so I told him 'fancy dress!' " she crowed. "And look! There he is, the pathetic fool! What a guy it is!"

Then dream-Nina turned, and looked at him fearlessly. "You are useless to me, little dog," she said mockingly. "You are of less use to me than a pet monkey. The monkey, at least, is amusing. You have no money, though you pretend to it. You have no breeding, though you would like us all to think you are loftier than the Prince of Persia. You are stupid, and never did more than middling well in any of your schools. Your head is stuffed with commonplaces. You don't know music, you don't know anything about art, and you don't understand more than half of what is going on around you. You are *a bore,* with your middle-class ways and middle-class morals! Shoo! Find someone else to put to sleep! You cease to amuse."

And with that, she turned away, leaving him the center of a circle of people pointing at him and howling with laughter.

In the mirror, he woke up in a cold sweat. And Nina smiled. She was rather fond of that dream, and he would continue to have it once a night from this moment on.

If that didn't tilt him over the edge, nothing would.

18

NINETTE sat sidesaddle on a chair and hooked her chin over the back of it, her hands resting just underneath her chin. She watched Jonathon as he sat on the hearth-rug of her bedroom, carefully crafted a working circle and summoned the shields, all without using anything other than a candle and his index finger. And she could not see a thing.

Well, perhaps a little. A kind of vague heat-shimmer in the air. Maybe. Assuming that wasn't her eyes being very tired after a long morning rehearsal, a short after-lunch revision of choreography, and a matinee and two evening performances.

These "Bank-Holiday" things were *terrible*. Everyone got a holiday, it seemed, except the poor performers and entertainers.

"Are there supposed to be flames?" she asked, doubtfully.

"Not really, no," Jonathon replied absently. "It is more the abstraction of Fire, the energy that *is* the Plane of Fire, represented here—" He looked up at her, and smiled suddenly. "I am boring you to sleep, aren't I?"

"No, I am only dreadfully tired," she replied, and eyed Jonathon's work with longing. "Please tell me you will be done soon?"

"Very soon," he promised. "But good shields take time, and I have learned a trick or two over the years. I don't think a creature of any Element will be able to pass these if it's one of the nasty sort."

I hope you're right, lad, because none of us have gotten much sleep lately, the cat said, from his perch on Ninette's bed.

And if he's not the nasty sort? The Brownie suddenly appeared in the door, arms folded, looking daggers at Jonathon. *Oh, it's like you lot, forever casting us out of our homes and—*

"No one is casting anyone out of his home," Jonathon snapped. "Have done, will you? This is tricky enough without a lot of critics standing about."

The Brownie snorted, but the cat just curled his forepaws under his chest and half closed his eyes, waiting.

He did not have long to wait. No more than five minutes later, Jonathon grunted in satisfaction, and then made a complicated gesture with his fingers.

For a moment—so short a moment that Ninette was not entirely certain she had actually seen anything—the walls of faint heat-shimmer flared a hot yellow-red, like the heart of a burning log. Then she felt something rush through her, taking her breath away for a moment.

The Brownie's eyes were as big and dark as the bottom of a bottle of ink for a moment. He took a deep breath in a gasp, and in that moment, Ninette found she was holding her breath and did the same.

Bollocks! the Brownie exclaimed.

"I told you it would be strong, and I told you that you would be all right," Jonathon said with a smug look of self-satisfaction about him. "Maybe you'll believe me next time."

The Brownie snorted, and vanished into the kitchen. Jonathon stood up, brushed off his trousers, then picked up the candle and blew it out. "There," he said. "That should take care of any magical intruders. You may take your rest, Mademoiselle." He bowed a little from the waist, and she giggled a little tiredly.

"And if they are not magical?" she asked, in all seriousness.

"Then you may summon a policeman by screaming out a window," the magician said carelessly.

"And if they are magical and still pass your boundaries?" she demanded.

"That," he replied, already on his way out the door, "is why you have the pistol."

It had been a very good day. Jonathon had gotten a very tricky piece of stage magic equipment that he had bought from an old and retiring performer to work properly at last. Of course, he'd been forced to replace every spring in the wretched thing, and then work out what tension they *should* be set at, but it had been worth it, in the end. The panels popped closed so fast that even if you were looking for it, you wouldn't see it happen, and the noise was easily covered by the band playing a crescendo. People weren't used to seeing mechanical things accomplish anything fast, and in the uncertain stage-light he would have for this business and a burst of a flash-pot, they'd never realize what had happened even though they looked straight at it. Which they wouldn't, of course. He'd have his distraction going. Though he had cursed himself many times for buying the wretched thing in the first place in the end, it was worth it. The audience would see a young lady vanish before their eyes, and reappear across the stage, and all without use of a trap-door in the stage. He hated trap-doors anyway. Unreliable things, they were always sticking, and you had to depend on stage hands to be sure the mattresses were in place under them, and even then it was possible to fall wrong and break an ankle. During his apprenticeship to a fine old stage magician, the fellow's young nephew had done just that, and had gone on and walked his way through the rest of the act on an ankle that was months in healing. And of course, you weren't just depending on the trap door to work, you had to hope the lift at the other end was also working . . .

Not to mention what a disaster it would be for Ninette to break an ankle.

No, this was better, and now it was working. He could hardly wait to try it out. Magicians' assistants were always on the small and lean side. But Ninette was exceptionally small and lean even by those standards. *And* agile. He was so excited by the whole prospect it was all he could do to set the trick aside and not demand she cut short her morning lesson with Maestro Ciccolini to try it out.

He pondered what he should do to fill his time.

For a moment, he toyed with the idea of calling up a few Elementals and sending them out on a search for the person that had sent the homunculus after Ninette. But—he'd done that several times already, and they had been unable to find a trace of the magician. They still hadn't found an Earth-Master, who *could* do that sort of thing—where the blazes were they all, anyway? Was there some sort of official Earth Master holiday going on? He had woken up this morning in a particularly frustrated state of mind for just that reason.

But Nigel had had an idea over breakfast. As the maid dished them up eggs and sausages and broiled tomatoes, he had looked rather smug.

"Much longer and you'll be licking the cream off your whiskers," Arthur had said, finally. "What is it that has set your brains afire, old chap? Is it another idea for the musical production? No? A new act you've hired? Not that either? Well, what, then?"

"I have a nephew of an old chum who's a Water-Master who's going to join us," he'd said. "And I'm Air and Jonathon, you're Fire."

"Go on," Jonathon had urged. "You're stating the obvious and being obtuse, old man. Don't torture us any more, I beg you, or we'll be forced to fling buns at your delicate cranium."

"Well look, with three of the four Elements all inside one Work, what we can do, is we can pool our resources and look for places our magic is excluded from. That's where we'll find Earth-based power operating." He looked at them all in triumph. "It will probably be shields that we see, but that's fine. We'll know where he is, then."

Jonathon had sat there blinking for a moment, and Nigel had gotten worried. "What is it?" the impresario finally asked. "What is it that I am missing?"

"Only that I thought *I* was supposed to be the clever one," he'd said, full of admiration. It was a beautiful plan, and had all the virtues of simplicity. If they hadn't been needed for band-call, they probably would have still been at the table turning ideas over and over to see what the undersides looked like.

So, as soon as this Water-Master arrived, they'd be trying to ferret out where this renegade Earth Master was, and deal with him.

Jonathon went to take a turn around backstage, where he watched the brother-and-sister dance act without really seeing it. It would be a great relief all the way around to get this thing dealt with, hopefully incarcerated somehow. Mind, all this only fed the fire of a long-held conviction on his part, that the Elemental Masters who were not actually gone to the bad *ought* to be organized enough to know each other from one end of the country to the other and be able to work together on a regular basis. They *certainly* should be able to call upon one another for help at a moment's notice! Good heavens, there was a Minister for practically everything else in the government, there damned well ought to be a Minister of Magic! Even if it meant revealing to the Government that magic was real, and that terrible things could be done with it.

But of course, trying to get the notoriously reclusive and fiercely independent Elemental Mages to agree to anything of the sort was rather like trying to, in the immortal words of John Donne, "get with child a mandrake root."

Well, as it happened that little poetic image Donne used wasn't *impossible,* not for an Earth Master with the right set of skills . . . at least, that was what some of the grimoires he'd been reading over the years suggested. So maybe it wasn't impossible for the Elemental Masters to get organized. Maybe if something threw a big enough alarm into them they finally *would* organize.

The right place to start might be with the London crowd. Oh, yes, they were all peers of the realm, or most of them anyway, and as a consequence they all chummed around together, had hunting parties and concert parties and balls and all that Social Register fol-de-rol together anyway. And they had the other sort of Hunting Party when they thought it was needed, like the old medieval lords, banding together to go slay a dragon or depose a king. It was more or less in their blood . . . maybe he could get them to step up and take charge of all of the Elemental Masters in the British Empire, not just their own "set." He could appeal to *noblesse oblige.* He could suggest they reach out to the

Masters in London first, just as an experiment, then go
further if the experiment proved fruitful.

But that would be later, when all this was sorted out.
And in the meantime, he could start writing to people,
and asking for addresses of their friends, for the one
thing he could do would be to make certain that the
story of Ninette's father got spread far and wide. Not
that he'd been turned into a cat, of course. That was a secret, and he wouldn't betray it. But all the rest of it—
that much was important for other mages to know
about. They needed to realize that it didn't take invok-
ing a Greater Demon on Salisbury Plain to make another Elemental Mage dangerous. All it took was being
ruthless, bad, and willing to do anything to have your
way, because once you started having your way, what
you wanted gradually became larger and larger, and af-
fected more and more people. This little campaign
would take time, but moving slowly in this case was a
great deal better than running about waving one's
proverbial arms and shouting about a danger no one
else could see. Better to just tell the story, and let people figure it all out for themselves, so that not only
would his fellow mages begin to see how dangerous it
was to keep on the solitary paths they had been, but also
how dangerous it was to disregard the power of one
overlooked person when it became obvious that she
was going to use that power wrongly.

And it was equally important for the good gentlemen
to realize that their womenfolk had the potential to be
even more dangerous than most of them imagined in
their worst nightmares. They were all the more dangerous because they weren't taken seriously.

"Hell hath no fury," indeed.

He realized with a start that the song-and-dance
turn was over, and the dumb-show comic was running
through his paces. The man himself was affable

enough, but Jonathon didn't much care for that style of comedy. Shoving his hands into his trouser pockets, he went off to the stage door, thinking vaguely of some fresh air.

There was an odd sort of fellow, lurking there. Not the sort one found at a stage door; *desperately* middle-class and trying not to look it. Cambridge tie, but one of the more obscure new colleges; one of those that, the fellows at Trinity would say, looking down their long noses, "Oh, they're open to *anybody*." As if that were a sort of veiled insult. Egalitarian, they were not. Jonathon, who had, in fact, gone to Trinity, and could, if he chose, hold his own with the best and worst of the blue-bloods, found himself both exasperated and in agreement with the attitude.

Because often enough the "anybody" was someone like this chap, who had not gotten a good education because he hadn't gone to Cambridge to get one. He'd gone to get affectations, and social connections, and to collect reflected glory because for whatever reason, he failed to produce any himself.

"Hoi," he said, as the fellow mopped his face with a handkerchief, "anything I can help you with?"

The fellow started, and turned piggy eyes on him. "Ah, er, not really," he said, turning the good and useful word into "rahlly" as he aped the upper-class drawl, "Just curious, don'cha know? Stage door, is this?"

Jonathon knew very well that no one outside the company would recognize him for the sinister magician of his act, so he slouched a bit and leaned up against the wall. " 'Tis," he said, hands deep into his pockets, as he felt for his matches. "This here's a musical variety hall. Very posh, popular with the toffs."

The stage-door porter, who guarded the door like a mastiff, looked as if he was going to laugh at Jonathon's "act."

"So," Jonathon continued, guessing shrewdly what had brought the man here. "I ourta warn you, there's no messin' about with our star-ladies, if that's what o-*casioned* you to be here. In-vee-tation only, that's the word. We don't allow no loiterin' about in the halls, in 'opes of getting into the dressing room, neither. This is a *respectable* house. You go on down t' Shipley's, if that's your game."

The fellow perspired more. "No! No!" he stammered. "Just passing by! Just curious! No harm meant!"

And with that, he fled the scene.

The porter looked after him, mouth a little open in surprise. "Wot th' hell was he on about?" the man finally gasped.

Jonathon shook his head. "Probably thinking he'd wait until one of the girl-acts came out, and see what he could get. I can't think of any other reason for someone like him to turn up here. His sort generally don't take holidays at Blackpool, and they don't go wandering in-quisitively down alleyways to see what's at the back of the buildings. He knew what this was, and he had something planned when he got here."

The porter turned red-face. "A masher!" he said wrathfully. "Bloody 'ell! If he cooms here agin, I'll send 'im packin', see if I don't!"

Jonathon chuckled. "You might just have a word with the Reicher brothers instead," he suggested, naming the "strong-man" act that used their two sisters as their "props." It made for a very interesting and surprisingly graceful act, actually. The young ladies took beautiful poses, poised on tiptoe in the palm of one brother's hand. Then they would collapse bonelessly into his arms to be tossed to the other like a ball. "You might let it be known that the fellow was asking after their sisters."

The porter looked at him sideways, then broke out into an enormous grin.

Jonathon strolled away, whistling.

Nigel had not mentioned that the Water Master in question was one of the youngest Masters in the country. It usually took an Elemental Master decades to come into his full power; Alan Grainger had done so before his twenty-first birthday.

Now, partly that was because Alan had applied himself to the study of his Element and its magic with the devotion of any artist to the art that consumes him, whether that be music, painting, or the crafting of words. Part of that was because he came early into his power, calling and playing with Undines before he could actually talk, swimming before he could walk. And part of that was to his teachers' credit; his parents were great Water Masters in their own right, and two of the best teachers Nigel had ever heard of.

Alan was the rarest sort of bird there was; raised by kind, clever people, he was kind and clever himself. Having seen that there were powers he would never command, he was modest. The pliant nature of water was his; flowing around obstacles whenever possible, but implacable in force when there was no other way.

He was also astonishingly good looking. Had he not been so modest, Nigel often thought, he could have made a fortune on the stage. But as self-effacing as he was, nothing would induce him to, as he would say, "make a guy of himself in public."

It was a very good thing that he was clever, but not brilliantly so. He did modestly well in school, then at university. Then again, he didn't need to be a brilliant scholar. His family owned a fine whiskey distillery in

Scotland. He would, in due course, run it. He enjoyed
the work, understood it, and would be happy in it, and
his studies in history were something he had under-
taken because he enjoyed history, not because he expected to have to make a living as a teacher or a scholar.

It was the "astonishingly good-looking" part that
caused Nigel the most amusement. He expected that
Ninette would find him attractive. He also expected that
something would then occur with regards to Jonathon.
Either he would take the same interest as any friend
would—and if he had any sense, and the attraction was
mutual, he would urge Ninette to pursue that attraction—or he would react with jealousy. In either case,
this would be good for Jonathon. All this restless vacil-
lation was distracting everyone at a time when they
needed to be anything but distracted.

As for the little dancer, well, there was no telling what
the girl would do—except that Nigel was fairly certain
she wasn't the sort to deliberately break a fellow's heart
and lead him on. Plus, she was French, and French
women, in his experience—if they were the good-
hearted sort—were honest in their *affaires de couer*.
Mind, he didn't think that *she* actually knew what she
wanted yet. She had plenty of life experience in seeing
amour as a business transaction, but was pretty heart-
whole in that department herself.

Women tended to be fascinated by Jonathon, the
wretched dog. It was the stage persona partially. Women
were attracted to dangerous men, and even though
Jonathon was no more dangerous than any other confirmed bachelor, and rather *less* dangerous than confirmed womanizers, he *appeared* dangerous. Partly it
was the challenge; here was a personable man, well-
educated, well-spoken, at the top of his trade, who could
not possibly care less about women. Several of his assistants had, over the years, fallen into an infatuation with

him. Always he revealed something to them that made them decide that there were better prospects elsewhere.

On the other hand, he'd been treating Ninette in a way he had never treated another woman before. He gave her more respect than any Nigel had seen with him before. Alan's mere presence might wake him up to the fact that here was a rival that could compete with him on his own ground.

If there was a fault that this paragon had, it was that Alan was, well, *mild.* He never became passionate about much of anything. That might have been his youth, but Nigel suspected it was his nature. This was no bad thing in a Water Master, though Nigel sincerely hoped that one day he would find something he cared deeply about, be it a cause or another person. Nevertheless, this was what they needed right now. Alan would not get upset or agitated; he would simply apply his mind to the problem at hand and keep at it until they had solved it.

Furthermore, Alan had the luxury of being able to devote his entire mind to the problem. He did not have tricks to work out, choreography to create, dances and acts to practice, a theater to run, or an orchestra to keep under control.

Last of all, he had the advantage of coming to it with a fresh set of eyes and thoughts.

A tap at Nigel's office door caused him to look up and smile broadly. "Alan, my boy, good to see you!" There was the young man himself: lean and fit, a good six feet tall. He had a chiseled face with handsome, angular features, frank blue eyes, and hair just a little untidy.

"Sir, if I may interrupt your work—" Alan began in that Scots burr tamed and softened by his terms at university.

"None of that," Nigel interrupted. "There will be no 'sirring' here. You are our peer in power and it is high time you got used to thinking that way."

The young man's mild blue eyes lit a little, and he

smiled. "Very well, Nigel. 'Tis true enough my people at home treat me in that way, but I never expect it outside our walls. My uncle said only that you had a rather nasty problem, and a dangerous one. What can I do to help you?"

"Close the door, then come sit down; this will take some explaining."

As Nigel laid out the situation that faced them, he noted with approval that Alan was actually paying close attention; he interrupted from time to time, and asked Nigel to explain some things further.

Finally Alan sat back in his chair and absently swept his sandy brown hair off his forehead with his thumb, then rubbed his eyebrow a moment. "This is a puzzler," he admitted. "You're all right, though, a good place to start would be to hunt for places where our Elements are excluded, and I have just the tools for that particular task."

"I was hoping you'd say that," Nigel said with relief.

"Just one more question, and this one is personal, so you can tell me I'm an impertinent brat if you like and that I should keep my nose out of your business." Alan paused a moment, but on getting no reaction from Nigel, went on. "Why are you spending all this time and effort to protect this girl? She's nothing to you, and from what you've been telling me, she has scarcely enough magic to qualify as such. She lied to you from the beginning, so why are you repaying deception with trust and protection? I tell you now, my uncle would likely have turned her out the moment she revealed her falsehoods."

"Good questions." Nigel had been prepared for something of the sort. "For one thing, we like Mademoiselle Dupond. She might have begun with a lie, but other than her wild tale of how she arrived on these shores, she has been completely honest and aboveboard with us. She says that this was all the idea of the cat, the cat says the same, and I for one believe them. It's not as if she were a Princess Caraboo, Alan. The imposture harms no one so far as I can tell, and she *is* a very fine dancer. You'll see that for yourself. She's thrown herself whole-heartedly into this company, and stepped into the breech when we lost a few acts earlier in the season. That's one reason. For another reason, she *is* a legacy."

Alan nodded at that. A "legacy" was the offspring or spouse of an Elemental Master, especially if they had been left without that magician for whatever reason. The other Masters—at least those in the circles that Nigel traveled in—regarded such people as the particular responsibility of all other Masters. This was doubly so if those left behind had no magic of their own. Granted, few Masters had any sort of feuds going that would extend to the next generation—yet such a thing had been known to happen.

"Point taken," Alan agreed. But Nigel was not yet finished.

"Last of all, I will admit to you that I have not only liking for her, I have a very solid pecuniary interest in her. She has talent. She is probably not as good a dancer as the greatest of our time, but she is a fine performer, and she knows how to charm an audience. Well! Heaven knows Loie Fuller was no kind of dancer, either, and like Loie Fuller, our Ninette gives every bit of value with every atom of talent she has. And she works hard; performers are rather lazy dogs, in my experience—this girl is not. I expect to build many shows with her as the star turn, and I expect she will be grateful enough to remain here in Blackpool, take what I can give her and not what other, more wealthy impresarios will offer." He nodded at Alan's uplifted eyebrow. "Oh yes, I readily admit to you that I am prepared to exploit her as far as she will let me."

Alan smiled crookedly. "You mean you will exploit her as far as your own good conscience and her good sense will allow. But I can understand a motive like that, I *am* a Scot, after all. Very well then, I am prepared to accept her as you have and give her the benefit of my abilities. Well! When can I meet the rest of our little group?"

There was a flutter of wings that made Alan start, and Wolf landed on the perch beside Nigel's desk. "You can meet two of us now," the parrot said, tilting his head over sideways. "So this is the Water Master. A child prodigy, I am told?"

"You should be familiar with that, Master Wolfgang," Alan replied, recovering quickly. "Quite familiar, in fact." The bird clicked his beak delightedly.

"So I am! Well, do not emulate me by dying too young. And here is Arthur, who hasn't got the benefit of wings to whisk him through the backstage."

Alan stood up and turned around as the conductor entered the room, and shook Arthur's hand heartily. "A pleasure, and I wish this were under better circumstances," Arthur said, taking a seat of his own.

Alan shook his head. "Our kind always seems to be meeting under unfortunate circumstances," he said, sitting down again. "I met Nigel when he was assisting my uncle with a bad bit of business about five years ago."

"In Scotland?" Arthur asked, and at Alan's nod, continued, "Yes, he told me a bit about that. Very ugly doings. Someone should have done something about that old man long before he got to be a menace. It's deuced easier to prevent a disaster than it is to clean up after one."

"Well, we like our freedom and our privacy, north of the border, and we don't care to meddle in a man's business if he wants to make a hermit of himself," Alan countered. "The worst that could be said of Auld Geordie was that he was a misanthropist and generally had a quarrel with anyone to cross his path, but up until that last, he had never done any soul any harm. We had rather leave our eccentrics alone; we've had more than enough of witch hunting in the bad old days. It's only when the eccentric goes and calls up ancient evils because his neighbor's a better fisherman than he that we feel we need to *do something about him,* d'ye ken?"

"Yes, but the general populace saw the damned thing, and might well have gotten *eaten* by the damned thing if the Masters hadn't acted," Arthur protested. "As it is, Loch Ness is going to have a notoriety I much doubt the natives will care for!"

Nigel snorted; having been up there, he was well acquainted with the hard-headed nature of the natives, as well as their sly sense of humor and the ability to wring a penny out of stones. "Being Scots, they'll find a way to exploit it and make money off the Sassenach," he said. "Without a doubt."

Alan smiled crookedly. "I expect so," he replied comfortably. "When a Scotsman butchers a pig, he uses everything but the squeal. When presented with a monster, he'll find a way to make *someone* pay to strain his eyes looking for it. I'd be very much surprised if this didn't make the papers, or at least, the pages of the annals of fantastic occurrences. Once that happens, every landlady and publican will be re-chalking the order boards with new prices for those who come to gawk." Then he laughed. "And every man jack of them will be lamenting that the little castle by the Loch is too ruined to rent out, and crying pity that you can't charge for taking or painting pictures of it."

Nigel turned to his friend. "Did you manage to pry Jonathon and Ninette away from the new trick?"

Arthur rolled his eyes. "Pry is nearly the right word. Something or other got misaligned or malfunctioned or something, and Ninette was trapped in it for a bit."

Nigel frowned. "That couldn't be—"

"No, it was *not* caused by magical interference," Wolf assured him. "Jonathon and Arthur both made sure of that. It was nothing more sinister than the usual business with one of Jonathon's contraptions. Evidently when he tested it, he hadn't allowed for the weight of someone inside."

Nigel shook his head. "Poor Ninette."

Arthur shouted with laughter. "Poor Ninette! Poor Jonathon, rather! He had every stagehand and half the acts clustered around him while he tried to get her out, all of them offering advice. We had to restrain Bob Anderson from hacking the thing open with a fire-ax. I swear to you, a vein was throbbing on Jonathon's temple by the time he got her out."

"Ninette wasn't helping, either," Wolf said merrily.

"Well, it is a *very* good thing that Ninette is not afraid of the small places," said the lady in question, causing all the men to rise out of politeness. "It was not *tres amusant,* but at least I was not feeling that my breath was being stolen." She shook hands gravely with Alan before taking a seat. The cat promptly curled up at her feet and watched the newcomer with unblinking eyes. "I am Mademoiselle Dupond, as you know, and this is the cat, Thomas."

They had only just gotten settled when the last of the party showed up. Nigel immediately felt sorry for him. Poor Jonathon, indeed! The magician's collar was half off and unfastened, his shirt sleeves rolled up, and the knuckles of his right hand were scraped and a little bloody. "Damn genius mechanics to perdition!" he swore bitterly. "Give me an honest craftsman who isn't too concerned with being clever!" He offered his right hand to Alan. "Forgive my shabby appearance, but I have been wrestling with someone else's Muse."

The Muse almost won, the cat remarked. *I was begin-*

ning to think Bob was going to have to use that fire-ax after all.

"If I hadn't got the catch to turn, *I* would have been the one using the ax," Jonathon replied.

"All is well as ends well, *n'est ce pas?*" Ninette said calmly. "You have discovered the trick of it, and I was able to abuse you most amusingly and you could not touch me!"

Jonathon shook his fist at her and scowled fiercely and she laughed. "You frighten me not at all, magician! Where else would you find an assistant of my sort? But we should not waste this good young man's time with our silliness," she added. "*Pardon.* Now, you are the Water Master, yes? And good Nigel has told you of the plague I have brought upon his house?"

"I am and he has," Alan nodded, and Ninette smiled warmly on him. "And I have some ideas I would like to share with you all—because this will *need* you all before we are through."

"Then say on," said Wolf, bobbing his head rapidly. "You will never have a more attentive audience."

19

NINA reflected slyly that one of the many, many advantages of being what she was, and *not* a human dancer, was that she never had to trouble herself with the tedious work of classes and rehearsal if she didn't care to. Of course, when she was dancing with a ballet company, she had to attend the company rehearsals. It would have looked odd had she not. She had not gotten as far as she had by slipping up in so careless a manner. She faithfully attended all company rehearsals and all rehearsals with her partners, but her mornings, given by mortal girls to round after round of endless classes and exercises and the solitary practice of tricky parts in the ballets then being performed, were entirely free. Ostensibly, as the great *prima,* she was taking very private lessons and doing her exercises in her own comfortable studio, well lit, well ventilated, warmed by good stoves in the winter and catching cooling breezes through opened windows in the summer. And of course, she always took care to have such a studio, with a gramophone in place of a pianist. All very grand. But of course, she never used it.

And now, thanks to the fact that she was *not* a frail little mortal, she was able to devote all of her time to the battle with the imposter, when a human would have been forced to continue those classes and lessons in order to stay at the top of her form.

But all Nina had to do in order to restore muscle strength, tone, and flexibility was to assume the form she had stored in her memory, of the ballet dancer she had taken when the girl *was* at the peak of her abilities and in the best of health. In fact, once, on a lark, when the season had concluded and other dancers were taking concert venues and tours, she had decided to truly indulge herself. After all, she had been between benefactors, and she had never yet tried the so-called "sin" of gluttony. So during the glorious month of June, she had spent the time getting enormously fat, eating every good thing she ever cared to try. And of course, when the company gathered together again, she was back instantly to her slim, trim self, with never a hint that she had ever so indulged. Gluttony, she thought, was overrated. These things were pleasant to eat, but they gave nothing like the rush of feeling and power when she absorbed a victim.

So it was without the need to dance or to attend rehearsals that Nina assumed the schedule she preferred; sleeping until noon, rising late, and going out to pursue her various tasks and needs by night.

She had chosen her dwelling with an eye to being able to get in and out without any of the neighbors noticing, especially at night. In a way, this was turning out to be one of the most comfortable times of her life, in all truth. She was able to hunt and consume whenever she wanted—which was nightly—without worrying about a protector catching her away from the luxurious flat he was keeping her in. Or worse, catching her at her feast. She had no performances to concern herself with, so she could hunt from sundown to sunup if she chose. She had the wherewithal for the luxuries she had grown fond of, and the leisure to enjoy them without rehearsals taking up her time, or protectors hovering over her. This was, in many ways, a glorious life of freedom that she was actually enjoying. It occurred to her more than once that the girl had actually done her a favor, waking her up, shaking her out of herself, reminding her of what she truly was. It was so easy to get immersed in a human life, to think of it as the be-all and end-all, rather than the means to an end. Sometimes she too was very foolish.

And the truth was, if the imposter had not stolen her identity, she might well have had done with "Nina Tchereslavsky" in the not too distant future. Human life-spans were very short, and the practical life of a dancer shorter still. What injuries or illness did not cut short, simple old age generally did. She had already begun attracting a few comments, mostly spiteful and from those who wished to take her place in the limelight, about how *well preserved* she was. It was very likely that within the next two or three years, she would have been forced into counterfeiting her own death as she had so many times in the past, and assuming a new persona.

That was the awkward part of this; curse it. *She* did not age, naturally, but mortals did. The first and best way to be noticed in an unpleasant fashion was to seem not to age. She had always been able to find a way to transfer her accumulated wealth and goods to the new persona before but—

Well, this time it was going to be awkward. She was well known; if she died and left her possessions to someone no one had ever heard of, there would be questions. Worse, if she died and the bulk of what she had owned turned up missing, there would be even more questions. She had been looking into the fabrication of a distant relative—

But now she would not have to. No one knew her here in this country. For all they knew, she was no older than the twenty years she appeared to be, rather than the forty that Nina would have been if she were actually alive.

Furthermore, she had two strings to this bow. If she could manage to get the girl alone, for just long enough, she could simply assume *her* appearance and identity. That was the riskier of the two, because the Masters protecting her might be able to tell the difference *before* she killed them. Or, she could do what she had come here to do in the first place: expose the imposter for what she was, and use the notoriety to engineer herself a brand new career in England, where no one knew her history, and where she could go on dancing and attracting wealthy old men for at least twenty or thirty more years. By then, she could establish a "daughter," and in due course the "daughter" would inherit her famous "mother's" estate.

A shy, retiring daughter . . . plain, studious, the sort that attracted no male attention of her own. The sort that preferred to remain closeted up with her books and not be seen too often. Short-sighted, with enormous glasses. Calf-clumsy, and ill at ease in company. No one would wonder why she was so seldom seen.

There would have to be a husband, of course; that was easily arranged. And the husband's tragic death soon after the "birth."

How to arrange a baby . . . buy one, of course. A fat bribe to an orphanage, a false name, and it would be done. No need for messy things like a human birth.

Then absorb it once the fiction had been established; no one of any consequence wanted to see babies or infants. They were messy, noisy, unregulated creatures best left to the attentions of wetnurses and nannies. That would hold things for at least three or four years, until the child would be presumed presentable for brief moments of time to adults. At intervals, then, she would get one of those workhouse children, trot it out for inspection, and absorb it when she no longer needed it. A teenager she could counterfeit herself—and easy enough to arrange rare appearances when her mother was supposed to be sleeping, or dressing, or otherwise not immediately available for company . . . in fact, the whole art would be to find a way to present herself that would not arouse sympathy, but would, at the same time, make it clear just why her putative child was never seen in polite society. Rabbity little red eyes, she decided. Big, thick glasses, and rabbity little red-rimmed eyes. She would say that the light bothered her always and gave her headaches. No, not say it. She would whine it.

For a few moments more, she found herself so immersed in the details of her next life that she forgot there were the details of this one to sort out before she could move onwards. It was only when the maid-creature brought in the morning mail, which included a large, flattish box postmarked from her flat that she gave herself a mental shake and attended to the present.

The contents of this package were going to provide her with the makings of the last distraction. And it would be one that they would never, ever anticipate.

She smiled as she cut the string and opened it up, to make sure that her servant-creatures had not left anything out.

Michael Peterson was not the sort of solicitor that was accustomed to seeing handsomely and expensively dressed women in his outer office, and he could not account for the one that was there now. His clients were more apt to be balding middle-class gentlemen with querulous dispositions and uncertain stomachs, apt to take offense and equally apt to fire off a slander or libel suit, or a breach-of-contract case when sufficiently roused by real or imagined slights.

Michael encouraged them in this; after all, he got paid whether or not the case had any merits. Such things could stretch on for some time, particularly when he and his opposition were in collusion to make them stretch on.

It was not, however, the most rewarding of law-practices. There were times, as now, when he would look across the road through the window of his chambers to the chop-house with longing, knowing that he would have to satisfy his hunger with the cheese sandwiches he had brought with him. And furthermore was the penance that tonight he would either have to boil an egg and make toast in his room, or manage to get through whatever glutinous stew-like creation his land-lady had concocted: greasy, vegetables boiled to bits, and with only a nodding acquaintance with meat. His clients at the best of times would not bring in the sorts of fees that supported beefsteak dinners and tidy flats with a cook and a housekeeper. Now they were in a litigious lull, and that was not good for him.

So when the lovely woman dressed in garnet-colored silk responded to his invitation to enter his office sans appointment, he truly did not expect that she was going to offer him work—truth to tell he thought she was from some charity and looking to get a subscription from him. He would not be rude to her no matter how insane her charity, because some day she might be the cause of him getting more work. No, he would be polite, let his barren office speak mutely for him, and beg her forgiveness for not having brass to spare for her cause . . . and at least he would have had the pleasure of the company of a stunning woman for half an hour.

So it was with growing astonishment that he listened to her outlining, not the plight of abandoned orphans or sheepdogs, or African savages, but the whole of a fascinating and wildly unlikely tale.

She was so stunningly beautiful so he would have listened to her no matter what she said. She was small, dainty, with a mass of dark hair done up in some complicated braided style that looked like a crown and penetrating eyes that seemed to change in color as her mood changed. Her nose was just a trifle too long, but that made her face interesting rather than merely pretty.

If she was to be believed, and was not wildly insane, it was the most sensational case that *he* was likely to get his hands on!

For this woman claimed—and the papers she brought with her seemed to bear her story out—to be the *real* Nina Tchereslavsky, and the one currently performing at the *Palais Royale* was—an imposter! A fraud who had stolen this prima ballerina's name and reputation, and was battening on both.

Who was the fraud really? This woman did not know. Michael vaguely recalled the stir when the girl was washed up after a shipwreck, speaking nothing but Russian and a bit of French, so it did seem that these two dancers were, in fact, both Russian. And that seemed too much for mere coincidence. This woman only asserted that her imposter was someone *she* did not know.

It seemed completely impossible, for first of all, how would an unknown Russian dancer come to Blackpool in the first place; why not go somewhere that there were proper ballet troupes, like London? Secondly, why should she claim she was someone of whom Blackpool knew nothing? The cachet of being a Russian ballerina was not that impressive, particularly not in a music hall. And in the third place, why enter music hall at all? Why not attempt to get a part with a ballet or opera company? There was an opera company, at least, in Blackpool; why hadn't she gone there? And that brought them full circle again: why here, and why not London?

And yet, because it seemed so outrageous, so unlikely, it conversely became, to him, the more believable.

But by itself, it would hardly impress anyone, much less a judge. Michael turned over the documents that had been presented, one by one. It was a fairly thick portfolio. Together they formed a curious collection.

The first lot were press-clippings; interesting, but not particularly useful in and of themselves, since the photographs could have been of almost anyone, and the sketches were of someone who had no real distinguishing features to say the least. And how difficult would it be to assemble such a collection? One could subscribe to bureaus that collected these things for you.

The documents in the second set were more useful; personal letters from various men of wealth and rank. The problem was, though all of them began with "Nina" and ended with the gentleman's name, they were all in foreign tongues. And where he was going to find someone in Blackpool who could reliably translate Russian, he did not know. There were plenty of Russian exiles, but whom could he trust to give him accurate translations, and not merely write down what they were told to say?

And again, how difficult a thing would these be to counterfeit? If they were love letters it would be one thing; it was unlikely that she would dare present such a thing and very likely they would be repudiated, but a simple letter of admiration for her skill in dancing? No man would really care. And no gentleman was likely to make the long trip to Blackpool England merely to verify that the letter was genuine.

So, while interesting, these were of no particular value.

The third set, however. . . .

It was the habit of people in these days to buy photographic portraits of particularly beautiful women to ornament their walls with. Now, many of these were of young women who had no particular thing to recommend them *except* their beauty; they were, in fact, known as "PBs" or "Professional Beauties," and all they were required to be was lovely, amiable, with impeccable manners, and of at least moderate breeding, enough so that they could reasonably be invited to elite social gatherings to add sparkle, like a bouquet of exquisite flowers. That the Crown Prince generally at least made the effort to add them to his ever-growing collection of mistresses went without saying, though not all of them succumbed to him.

But others among the much-photographed were professionals of the stage; actresses mostly, but dancers were included, and even a few opera singers.

And the last set of these photographs were of the dancer Nina Tchereslavsky, in costume as, so far Michael could tell, various fairies, harem girls, spirits, and princesses. At least he guessed by the tiny crowns that they were princesses. For all he knew, they could have been aquatic waterfowl, or flowers. These photographs were plainly labeled, some in the queer letters the Russians used, but most in good lettering readable by civilized people. *Mlle. Nina Tchereslavsky, Odette. Mlle. Nina Tchereslavsky, La Sylphide. Mlle. Nina Tchereslavsky, Raymonda.*

Now these could be counterfeited, too, but it was less likely. Those costumes had to be fitted to each dancer, and it wasn't likely that someone would have all these things sitting about in a wardrobe somewhere. So although the photographs were designed to show off the legs rather than the face, still, the face was clear.

So taken all-in-all, the entire portfolio argued powerfully that the owner was in fact the real dancer.

"I wouldn't advise you to take this into a court of law, Mademoiselle," he said, finally, closing the portfolio.

She looked startled, and a little angry. "But is that not what you do?" she snapped. "This—this *creature* has taken my name, my place! My reputation! I have been forced to cancel a contract because of this! I had to pay an enormous sum! Is this not a thing for the courts?

"I should have said, *not yet*, Mademoiselle," he soothed. "We will eventually, of course. But our first strategy should be to take this to another court entirely, that of public opinion. We should make a sensation of this, so that when it does get into court, it will be noticed."

"And this would be good?" she asked doubtfully.

"Oh very good, very good indeed," he told her earnestly. "And I know just the newspaper too."

And in truth, he did. He had used them before on other cases. But of course, there was no competition between a case featuring a balding old man and one featuring not just one beautiful dancer, but two.

"And this will help me?" she persisted.

"Better than a trial." Her folded his hands atop the papers and peered earnestly at her. She stared at him for a moment, and for some reason, suddenly, her eyes seemed very cold, very alien. Despite the fact that her eyes should have seemed lovely.

But they weren't lovely. They were cold.

Ah, but that did not matter, What mattered was in

this portfolio. "We will take your story to a newspaper," he continued. "They will place the truth before the public, and the public will see. This imposter will be routed. There may never need to be a trial, but if there is, many of the jurors will have seen these photographs and they will know the truth."

"Very well," she said finally. "You may call your newspapers."

Nina was not nearly as reluctant as she had seemed. She was, in fact, not at all interested in going to court. A lawsuit seemed to her to be an inordinate waste of time and effort, although the threat of one would take little effort on her part, yet would agitate her enemies no end.

But this, the idea of using sensation-craving newspapers to hound her foes—this was sheer brilliance. It was all she could do to keep from insisting the solicitor run straight out and bring in people from these newspapers on the spot.

Instead, she curbed her impulses and pretended reluctance. This was not unlike allowing a protector to "acquire" her. She would make them court her, coax her; she had ample practice in being the one sought after.

She allowed the solicitor to "persuade" her, and to arrange a meeting with a newspaper reporter for the next day. She "reluctantly" allowed him to keep her portfolio. There was only one thing that she was annoyed about; she had been certain she would be able to persuade one or more of her devoted adherents to make the journey to Blackpool to verify her identity, but they all sent regrets. It seemed that her hold over them was not strong enough at a distance to cause them to abandon good sense and speed to her rescue. It might not, in fact, hold them at all. She had never really had occasion to test it. It had always seemed to her that human mortals, the men in particular, were easily manipulated and entranced.

Well it was an annoyance, and something that could be worked around.

What she could do, easily enough, and in fact had, was to order her servants at home to bribe and browbeat one of the stagehands into coming to stand surety for her identity. It was difficult for a poor man, especially one who was no longer young, to look at more money than he could earn in twenty years and not turn it down. So this man, a common fellow named Jannos Durzek, was already on his way here by train and boat. She would have to find a translator, of course. She would have to find one anyway, for the Hungarian and Russian and Czech letters.

All this was running through her mind as she arrived at the solicitor's office for her meeting with the newspaper man. She had put forth a great deal of effort to look her best, and at the same time, to look every inch the *prima*. There must be no doubt in this man's mind that he was in the presence of a great dancer, even if he had never heard of her nor had any ideas about ballet.

The man in question was sitting in the solicitor's office when she arrived. He took his time about getting to his feet, eyeing her with an insolence that made her seethe. If she had not needed him, she would have slapped that expression from his face, then ambushed him in the night and absorbed him. Perhaps she would anyway, when she no longer needed him. He was a very unprepossessing man, no longer young, yet holding himself as if he felt he were much younger than his actual years. His suit was slightly rumpled, and though hardly of the best quality, was definitely of the most modern cut. Most gentlemen would have considered it a touch too loud. He did not remove his hat, of the type known as a derby, in her presence, a fact that she resented. Perhaps he was ashamed to; his mousey brown hair looked rather thin, and needed a trim badly. His face wore what looked to be a perpetual smirk, as if he considered himself ever so much more intelligent than most of the people he encountered. His complexion was starting to show the effects of hard drinking, and his eyes, narrow and shrewd, were just a little bloodshot.

She allowed him, reluctantly, to shake her hand, then took a seat. Immediately he began going over the papers in her file, one by one, asking her pointed and detailed questions about all of them. Some of his questions were impertinent, and she felt her temper rising. He seemed to be amused by this, and the more amused he became, the more she was determined to give him the punishment he so richly deserved when she no longer needed him.

Finally he shoved her portfolio of papers aside. "I like this story," he said, bluntly. "I'll take it on."

He would not be pinned down to how soon he intended to publish the story—or rather, what would probably be the first of several stories. "This will be a fight," he warned. "They are not simply going to say, 'Oh dear, you caught us, it's a fair cop,' and reveal the girl's true name. They are going to demand proof. What you have here—" he tapped the portfolio "—is good, but hardly conclusive; it could all be fabricated and I expect them to point that out. But I'll think of something you can do, I am sure."

He was so arrogant! Assuming that she would not be able to think of anything for herself! And how on earth was he remaining proof against her magic-enhanced charm? That baffled her as much as his attitude infuriated her.

She would kill him. She would not merely absorb him

as she did with most of her victims, taking them unaware and rendering them unconscious first; she would
do it while he was aware and conscious and she would
do it slowly.

Oh how she wished she did not need him!

She parted company with him and with the solicitor,
once again leaving the portfolio, this time in the reporter's possession. She was stiffly correct, and as she
shook hands coldly with the man, he dared to grin at
her. "You don't care for me, miss," he said baldly. "Well,
I don't care much for you. I expect you're accustomed
to men dancing attendance on you, and being your lap-
dogs. You're told what a tremendous artist you are, and
all of that tommy-rot. Well, to me you're the same as
that girl that you say is using your name, and you're
both of you no better and no worse than the can-can
dancer on the boardwalk. All three of you pull up your
skirts and kick and show your legs—you and that girl
just pretend it's more refined, which, to my mind, makes
the can-can dancer the more honest of the three of you.
But I know a story when I see one, and this one is worth
chasing after. You need me, and I need you, so you may
glare all you like, and I'll sneer all I like, but the story
will still get printed, and we'll see what kind of a dust
up we can start."

Rigid with anger, she left, the solicitor at her elbow,
apologizing for the reporter, babbling almost, about
how his manner was rough, but he was the best in the
city, how dogged he was in pursuing facts, and how
fair he was in laying them out. The solicitor kept up
this babble all the way to the street, where he hailed
a taxi for her. As he handed her into it, Nina finally
spoke.

"If this were Saint Petersburg," she said wrathfully, "I

would horsewhip him until he bled from a hundred cuts. He is an ignorant peasant. But he has a peasant's cunning, and I believe you when you say he will write the stories to expose this imposter. But keep him from me. *You* deal with him. I would rather feed pigs with my own hands than speak with him again."

Notions of increased fees doubtlessly dancing in his head, the solicitor hastily agreed, and she directed the taxi back to her flat.

The first thing she did when the door was shut and locked tightly behind her was to transform to her true form with a roar of rage. Her garments did not so much tear as burst asunder with the sound of shredding silk. Her servants already knew what to do; they had surely felt her anger for the last hour at least.

They performed exactly as she expected them to. They had clearly prepared for her, and now they fled before her, and opened the door to the cellar with cringing deference. She stood on the top step as they closed the door behind her, and listened to the whimpering of terror from below.

The Troll bared her teeth in a parody of a smile. Her servants had chosen well. Not one, but three victims cowered in the corners of the cellar, trying to somehow become one with the rough brick walls. Her eyes adjusted to the darkness, and she assessed the two slatternly women and the man awaiting her pleasure. By the tattered finery and the display of cleavage, by the too-loud, cheap suit and the air of a bully who finds himself in the power of someone unexpectedly stronger than he, she had a good notion of who her servants had plucked off the street for her. Two prostitutes, and she supposed the man was their procurer.

"Mistress," one of the servants said through the door, "we brought the women here. The man followed; he broke in and threatened us, and demanded money." She smiled. Good. She would take him first.

And she would make him last a long, long time. This was going to be no simple absorption. Tonight she was going to *feed*.

20

NINETTE was summoned in the middle of her exercises to Nigel's office; puzzled, because she could not imagine what could have warranted such an interruption, she quickly toweled herself off and threw on her dress without bothering to tidy her hair or take off her rehearsal tights and demi-pointe shoes.

There she found Nigel, Arthur, Wolf, and Jonathon, all bent over something on Nigel's desk, and the humans, at least, looking rather grim.

"What is amiss?" she asked, feeling uneasy, as they all turned to look at her.

"We have an unexpected problem," Arthur replied, stabbing his finger down at what was now revealed to be a folded-back section of a newspaper. There were several more like it on the desk; Arthur picked this one up and handed it to her.

The first thing she saw was her own publicity photograph, taken in her costume of the Tudor Rose dance. *Dancer Revealed A Fraud!* shouted the headline.

Her heart in her mouth, she skimmed through the arti-

cle as best she could, wrestling with the English. Quickly
she got the gist of the matter. The real Nina Tchereslavsky
had turned up—and how had that happened?—and the
reporter was trumpeting the fact that Ninette was an
imposter. He did not quite go so far as to claim her
shipwreck story was the fabrication they all knew it
was, but it would not take much for people to wonder
about that, too.

At the bottom of the article was the photograph of
the real Nina Tchereslavsky, in a costume of the Rose
Fairy from *Sleeping Beauty*. Ninette stared at it, numbly.

"All right. What are we going to do?" Nigel demanded. "It is not exactly a front page matter at the
moment, but if there is a day that has not got a lot of
news in it, the story very well could soon be there.
Should we—"

You are going to brazen it out, said Thomas the cat,
strolling into the room in a leisurely manner, eyeing the
top of the desk for a moment, before leaping up to it in
a lithe bound. *Take a look at those photographs. Do you
think I chose that particular dancer at random for
Ninette to impersonate?*

Five heads bent over the newspapers, all of them an-
alyzing the two pictures. As Ninette's panic started to
ebb, she looked over the two, side by side, and after a
moment, she nodded. She looked up to see the same
conclusion in the faces of the rest.

"All things considered, there is not a great deal of difference between the two of them," Nigel admitted.

All ballerinas tend to look a great deal alike, the cat
pointed out. *That's out of necessity. They have to be petite, light boned, thin. They tend to have very large eyes,
and stage makeup exaggerates that. That newspaper man
made a grave mistake in choosing to echo Ninette's Rose
costume with the other woman's; the pictures could easily be of the same dancer in different costumes. So the ob-*

vious course here is to make the counter-claim that this woman is the imposter.

Nigel stared at the cat. "You're not joking, are you?"

I never joke. I sometimes make witty remarks, often sarcastic ones, but I never joke, not where Ninette is concerned. No, I think you should brazen it out. Claim that this woman is the imposter.

"What possible motive could she have for impersonating Ninette? I mean Nina?" Arthur ran his hands through his hair. "This is very confusing. . . ."

The cat raised his chin. *Ninette is very successful here. She is one of the main attractions to this theater, and when your new musical play is finally performed, that popularity will only increase. Now remember if you will that people are insular. It does not matter to a Londoner that a performer is popular in New York. He might go once to see the man, but unless all London decides he is good, the average Londoner will not go a second time.*

"What are you saying?" Arthur asked, puzzled.

That we should forget entirely what anyone in Berlin or New York or even Paris thinks. That we should forget what a balletomane thinks. Ninette's audience does not go to ballets, and does not care what the rich people that do would have to say about this. We need to concentrate on what Blackpool thinks.

"I see what you are saying," Nigel replied slowly. "Blackpool thinks that what Blackpool says and does and has opinions about is of the first importance in the world."

The cat nodded with satisfaction. *Precisely. So when we go and speak to your friends in the newspapers here, we must be firm in saying that our Nina is the real one, and that this imposter's attempt to take her place is motivated by the greed for the position Ninette has achieved here. What dancer would not wish to be in that position? That any sensible person from outside Blackpool or knowledgeable about ballet would find this laughable has no bearing. This will not even be a ripple in the London papers, but it might well move into greater importance here. Perhaps, as you yourself pointed out, even a front page story if there are no accidents, fires, murders, or notorious robberies. No, I think that the best thing we can do is respond with affronted dignity and a touch of scorn.* The cat licked a paw thoughtfully. *And one never knows with dancers. They often become hysterical over absolute nonsense. She might indeed decide for herself that what you are building for Ninette is of the primary importance to her.*

"Hysterical over nonsense?" Ninette looked incensed—and then, flushed. "Ah, *mais oui.* The review in *La Figaro*—"

And who knows? Somehow the cat managed to shrug. *We do not know how her reputation is faring on the Continent. It might be sinking. She cannot be young. It might be that to become the star of a music hall in Blackpool has become the height of desire for her. In any event, we very much need to make use of every chink in her armor. Including that.* The cat looked up at them all. *This does have the potential to do us a great deal of good, if we can keep our heads about us, and Ninette can be kind and gracious and say very little about what her life in Russia was like.*

"I can do that," Ninette said ruefully, "since I have no notion of what it could have been like!"

"You should describe what it was like in Paris, only don't mention any real names," Jonathon said firmly. "A dancer's life is always the same no matter where she is from. Only in Moscow the winters are very long, there are heaps of snow, and it is always terribly cold. Make much of that."

Ninette and the cat both nodded. *Jonathon, that is an excellent suggestion. She could contrast our lovely weather with that of Moscow in the winter. Ninette, above all, you must make much of how happy you are, what a fine place Blackpool is, and how much you love the audiences here.*

"That will be of no difficulty," Ninette replied. "It is all true." She looked about her at the men who had become such supporters and friends in such a short time, and unexpectedly, her eyes filled with tears. "One could not ask for better friends than you. I feel as if I have fallen into a fairy tale!"

"Yes, well, fairy tales have ogres," Nigel grumbled. "We haven't conquered ours yet. We don't even know who it is!"

All the more reason not to allow this to distract us. Think of it as a diversion and not any sort of serious difficulty.

"They must have more evidence than just those photographs," Jonathon pointed out.

They may. But they do not have me. The cat looked uncommonly smug. *I will say no more.*

Jonathon gave him a measuring look. "You are altogether too sly, Master Thomas," he said severely.

I am a cat, was the self-satisfied reply.

"I do not know why I ever listened to you," Wolf groaned from under Arthur's coat.

Because I am cleverer than you, the cat replied. All three of the co-conspirators were in a pub opposite the building housing the flat of the fellow who had written the first article. They had discovered, by the simple expedient of buying a few drinks at the pub for his thirsty colleagues, that the man never kept anything he considered to be important at his desk in the newspaper offices. He was not well liked there; he never shared sources, and never put anyone else on to a good story, even if he never intended to follow it up himself. That meant that anything he had gotten from Nina in the way of files and proof would be in his flat.

They were waiting until he left for the evening. They had ensured that he would be gone long, and not in very good condition when he returned, simply by ensconcing Jonathon there in one of his many disguises, and with heavy pockets. By simple expedient of seeming to be a fellow who had won a great deal of money and standing rounds for the entire pub, Jonathon should keep him there, and drinking, for a good long time, without ever raising the man's suspicions by being singled out.

"There he is," muttered Arthur, as the fellow in question sauntered out into the fine spring evening, looking oddly both satisfied and irritated. But from all accounts he was a disagreeable man; perhaps this irritation was his natural state.

They watched as he strode down the street, heading right in the direction of his favorite watering-hole. They waited a good long time, just to make sure he wasn't coming back, that he hadn't forgotten anything, that he hadn't changed his mind. As the dusk turned to darkness and the lamplighters came around—this part of the city hadn't been electrified yet—Arthur and the cat took advantage of the shadows to slip across the street and into the narrow passage between the two houses-turned-flats. Wolf freed himself from Arthur's coat and flew up to the third story to land on a ledge.

"He left it open, right enough," Wolf said softly, and flew back down. "Give me the string," he ordered Arthur in a peremptory tone. Wordlessly Arthur handed the bird a bit of fishing line. Wolf flew up to the ledge, disappeared inside, then emerged again as the string ran out from the coil Arthur held. When the bird was perched again on his shoulder, he took the string back.

"It's around the leg of the desk," Wolf said as soon as his beak was clear. "That ought to be enough to hold one small cat."

It's salmon line, it ought to hold two of me, Thomas replied. He waited while Arthur fastened the straps of a harness around him and Wolf flew up to the ledge a third time, vanishing inside. With the harness fastened to the fishing line, and gloves on Arthur's hands to prevent it cutting into his fingers, the musician hauled the cat jerkily up the side of the building with all four legs dangling limply. They had all thought about having Thomas try and help, but then thought better of it. Only when the cat actually reached the ledge itself did he hook claws up onto it and haul himself up.

The line was easily bitten through by Wolf's sharp beak. After a moment, the line came falling down and Arthur coiled it up and put it in his pocket. Then he waited.

He could hear, very faintly, sounds from up above. Thomas and Wolf had determined, via trials in Nigel's office, that there was very little short of a safe that a cat and a parrot could not get into. What was more, they had decided that they would rifle the entire flat to make it look as if someone had been searching for valuables. Those were probably the sounds he was hearing.

After a very long time, or so it seemed in the darkened passageway, Arthur heard a whistle. And immediately afterwards, a piece of paper, startlingly white in the shadows, came drifting down from above.

Now he was very busy indeed, as a veritable shower of papers came down. They had determined that they were not going to steal only the information about Nina. They were going to take everything that looked to be of any importance. That way the man would not be aware that it was the ballerina's papers that they were after. Arthur had brought a briefcase with him, and by the time the last of the papers was gathered up, it was stuffed quite full indeed.

Finally, after some more sounds of implied mayhem from above, including the tearing of cloth, came what he had been waiting for. *Ready for me?* came the question into his mind.

"As ready as I am likely to be," he whispered back. "Mind your claws!" And he braced himself.

With an impact that made him stagger, the cat landed on his shoulder. He ended up against the wall, breath driven a little out of him.

It isn't me that minds the claws, it is you, the cat replied, with the sense that he was laughing. *I think that is the most fun I have ever had since I was a boy and stealing apples.*

"He's a hoodlum, that one," Wolf said severely, flying down to land on Arthur's other shoulder. "It will be most of a day before that fellow can clean up enough to figure out just what is missing."

"What did you two do?" Arthur asked, easing his way out of the passageway, carefully making sure there was no one in the street to see him when he did so.

"We tilted over and knocked to the floor every book and ornament we could move. We spilled his inkwell. I knocked over the pitcher of water at his washstand. We pulled the covers off the bed. We scattered all the papers that were not in the files, and overturned a chair or two. I uncovered all the food that I could in the pantry and the mice are already at it. But that was not enough for Thomas, oh no. Thomas slashed every pillow and cushion in the flat, tore open the featherbed and the eiderdown, and then shook what he could lift like a terrier with a rat," Wolf said. "And as if that was not enough, he asked me to flap as hard as I could." The parrot could not smirk, but he barked a sound like a laugh. "It looks like a snowstorm struck in there. The man might find a way to clean it all up in a day or two, but it will take a small army of maids to do it."

It took Nigel some patient work to sort Nina's papers out of the rest, but when he was finished, he had a very tidy stack. All of them sat contemplating it.

This could be very useful, the cat pointed out.

Nigel frowned. "But if I use them, they'll know we were the ones that took them." He closed his eyes for a moment. "Let me think about this. If we use them, it has to appear that we had them *before* the real Nina appeared. Now how can I do this. . . ."

They all waited, Ninette holding her breath. Over the time that she had been here, she had seen Nigel say something about "thinking," watched him close his eyes, then come up with something brilliant roughly three times. It had become apparent after the second time that he was not a successful impresario by accident, nor because he used his magic to make himself one. He was a shrewd businessman, with, when he needed to invoke it, the ability to see a way to do something that no one else would have thought of—or at least no one else would have thought of in as short a period of time.

The others all must have been used to this as well, since everyone, even Wolf, remained completely quiet. Traffic noise from the street below came in through the open windows, filtered slightly by the gold gauze curtains there that kept the insects out. A newsboy cried the latest edition from the corner, and that was when Nigel opened his eyes and smiled.

It was to Jonathon he turned.

"I need one of our smartest boys," he said. "Two if you can manage it. They have to be clever, a bit manipulative and sly. Baker Street Irregulars, if you will."

Jonathon grinned unexpectedly. "I know just the lads,"

he said. "I use them myself as often as I can, and I thought—well, this is for later, but I thought we might put them in the act. I could do with a couple of apprentices."

Nigel tilted his head to the side. "You've always said you didn't need—"

"That was when I was going to be traveling about all the time," Nigel interrupted, flushing. "I didn't want to have to keep track of a damned boy on trains and boarding houses and strange theaters. But when this scheme of yours blossoms, we'll be a repertory company. The whole theater will be keeping an eye on them. Never mind that now, you want Scott Merry and Stubbins. They're thick as thieves, those two, and smart as they come. Scotty's the older by about a year. What's the plan for them?"

Nigel was already separating out the material into four piles. "I am going to want them to somehow sneak these into the files at the four major newspapers. I want it to look as if, when we first engaged Ninette, that I sent these publicity materials to the newspapers. By then, the whole brouhaha of her being found on the shore had died down, so this would have been by way of a reminder to them that she was a great dancer on the Continent." He removed folders from a drawer of his desk and wrote Nina's name, the name of the theater, the words *Biographical Material*, and a date on each of them, then filled each folder from one of his piles.

Jonathon shook his head in admiration, and Arthur beamed. "Brilliant!" the musician crowed. "And when *we* go to those papers to say that we have no idea where this imposter came from—"

"They will go to their files, find this, and be convinced we gave it to them long before this woman appeared." Nigel beamed himself. It was an infernally clever idea. "Now, I'll want the boys to put these in *almost* the right place, so that it's logical to have been overlooked."

"Let me get them," Jonathon said, and took off. He returned with two boys somewhere between twelve and fourteen years old. One, taller, with black hair, was obviously "Scotty," which meant the other, a smaller, darker boy with an innocent face until you saw the gleam of mischief in his eyes, must be "Stubbins."

Nigel explained what he wanted, and, to Ninette's astonishment, *why* he wanted it, although he didn't reveal that Ninette was the imposter herself, nor that the materials were stolen.

"Now maybe this seems dishonest—" Nigel concluded, sounding doubtful.

Scotty snorted. "Bloody well it don't," he replied. "No reason t'hev given 'em this stuff before the big show, right, guv'nor? 'Cept now we gots this gel yappin' 'bout how she's the real Ma'mselle. An' if we gives 'em the papers *now,* they says, 'well, y'coulda just got all this anywhere!' an' we're still lookin' bad. But if *they* gots the papers and thinks they gots 'em afore this gel shows up, then Bob's yer uncle!"

"Ain't dishonest," Stubbins mumbled. "Jest puttin' things roight." He cast a sideling glance at Ninette. "Ma'mselle Nina's one uv us, ain't she? So we gotter take care uv 'er."

"All right then!" Nigel said brightly. "Here's the papers, and here's a few shillings for you two—it will probably take all day, and you'll need some luncheon, and money for the 'bus. Off you go! Report directly to me soon as you get back!"

Ninette smiled to herself, knowing that Nigel had given the boys at least twice as much as they needed, and had given them no deadline to meet. He had, in essence, awarded them with a bit of a holiday and the money to make it a rather jolly one at that. She felt terribly touched by Stubbins' mumbled assertion that she was "one of them" too.

"Do you think they can manage it?" she asked Jonathon, who rolled his eyes and laughed.

"Those two? They mastered my cabinet in an hour, and they know more sleight-of-hand tricks than any boys their age should command. It is a good thing that they are fundamentally honest, because they could pick a man's pocket while he stood there looking at them."

"I expect the shillings will run out about dark," Nigel said comfortably. "Expect them back then."

Scotty scrupulously divided the coins between the two of them before they left by the stage door, and they both took a moment to gloat over the windfall. "Cor, Scotty!" Stubbins said with enthusiasm. "Think on it! There's ices, an' bullseyes, an' Kendal Mint Cake, an' catapults each, an' we kin go to th' Tower an'—"

"Job first," Scotty said solemnly. "We gotter do this fast an' smart. Like Sherlock Holmes' boys!"

"Baker Street 'regulars," supplied Stubbins, who read as much or more than Scotty did.

"Right. So t' be smart, we shouldn't oughta do the same thing twice. So how kin we do this four dif'rent ways?"

All the way to the first newspaper office, sitting up on the top of an omnibus, the two plotted and planned like the pair of old campaigners they were. Both had come to the theater off the street as crossing-sweepers; a place like a theater always had need of honest and reliable errand-runners, and the old fellow at the stage door had been directed to find a couple. Both took all their money home to share with enormous families; both were acutely aware of how lucky they were to be where they were. Master Nigel made sure everyone in the theater got fair wages, he didn't demand a share of tips, and he regularly put things in the way of those that needed them. Whether or not he realized it, Master Nigel had engendered intense loyalty in his little fiefdom; there was not a man or woman in that theater who would not have stood between Master Nigel and a runaway elephant. Having been singled out for particular service made the two boys feel rather like a pair of King Arthur's knights, right out of the panto.

This was made even more acute by the fact that the job was to be done for Ma'mselle Nina. Now, there were plenty of acts that had passed through the Imperial acting like they were royalty. Not Ma'mselle. She was, as Scotty put it, "a right'un." Treated everyone fair, said "If you please," and "Thank you," never looked down her nose at anyone, and when she wanted something out of the ordinary, you knew there was going to be an extra penny in it for you. Everyone knew she was going to be the star turn when the Big Show got trotted out, but she never acted like she thought it was her due. Truth to tell, both Scotty and Stubbins were just a little bit in love with her. Who wouldn't be? She looked like a little china doll, pretty as a fairy, and nice as nice . . .

So both of them were going to put a lot of effort into making sure things went right for her—and it made them feel even more knightly. Or maybe like Sherlock Holmes. Or a combination of Sherlock Holmes and Raffles.

The first office they came to was so busy it had been easy for two boys who looked like they knew what they were doing to mingle with the rest of the crowd. There were plenty of boys their age employed in such places, messages needing taken, things needing to be fetched. Careful listening led them to the desk of the fellow that wrote up reviews and other artistic stuff; the boys waited until he left his desk for something, then slipped their folder under a big pile of stuff that was already there.

They left that office no more than three quarters of an hour after they had arrived. One down, three to go.

At the second office, Scotty, who was older, engaged the little girl in charge of putting files away in a mild flirtation, while Stubbins slipped Nina's file in among the rest of those she had waiting. Scotty broke off the conversation reluctantly when Stubbins was finished, and privately resolved to come back when he wasn't on a mission.

Two down. They were halfway done and it wasn't even luncheon yet.

Office number three presented a bit of a challenge. There was a man at the door and it was clear he was there to keep out interlopers. They both eyed the fellow from a distance, Scotty frowning furiously. "I dunno," he said, finally. "This 'un—"

"Got it!" Stubbins crowed in triumph, looking at something or someone just past Scotty's shoulder. He darted out before Scotty could say anything; Scotty turned to see a youngish man burdened with a huge pile of books and papers coming towards the guarded door. In a flash, Scotty knew what was going to happen—

And it did. Stubbins rushed past the young man, brushing up against him just closely enough to knock his burden out of his hands, but not so closely that he ran into the fellow. He kept going as the pile toppled to the floor, as if he was in such a hurry he couldn't be bothered to look back.

Scotty ran out to lend the man a hand. They commiserated on the rudeness of some people, Scotty piled up his arms full of papers and files again, and they parted. Except, of course, the young man now had the third copy of Nina's file in the stack he was so carefully balancing.

Number four was absurdly easy. They arrived just about luncheon-time, and everyone that could was running out for a bite. Scotty merely walked up to the wall of file cabinets, found the drawer for "T," and inserted Nina's file between "Titian" and "Toulouse."

Their work done, they escaped into the sunshine outside, ambling away with their hands in their pockets as if nothing out of the ordinary had happened. Only when they were well away from the building did they look at one another and burst out laughing.

"Thenkee, Mr. Holmes," Scotty said, doffing an imaginary hat.

"Thenkee, Mr. Raffles," Stubbins replied with glee. "Now! About them ices!"

"Reckon we earned 'em, don't you?" Scotty replied.

Stubbins nodded. "Reckon we did."

21

"**I** suppose you're wondering why I called you all here," said Alan Grainger, looking distinctly uncomfortable.

Jonathon, who knew exactly why the young Water Master had called them all together—because the cat had told him—did his best to keep any tone of smugness out of his voice. "Didn't find our Earth-Mage, eh?" he said instead, in as neutral a tone as possible. But he couldn't help but gloat inside. So the young genius hadn't had any more luck than his elders! Hard not to feel a bit sorry for him, especially when he looked at Ninette and flushed. Poor lad wanted to impress the lovely little dancer, and who could blame him?

"I'm afraid not," Alan replied, crestfallen. "Whoever this is, he's infernally clever, and I mean that almost literally. He set traps for us, and they weren't the things intended to catch and perhaps harm *us* either. If we had been gulled by his deceptions, what we did would have hurt perfectly innocent people—well, not *perfectly* innocent, they were actually rather vile." He flushed a deeper crimson. "But they were innocent of any wrongdoing towards us."

"A good job you were being cautious, then," Arthur said in an attempt to console him. "At least we won't have that on our consciences."

"Yes, but I didn't find him, and Mademoiselle is still in danger." He rubbed one temple. "I'm not used to failing."

Jonathon snorted. "Then you aren't trying things that are challenging enough."

To his surprise and Alan's obvious chagrin, Ninette nodded. "The more and harder things you attempt, the more you will fail. You are only guaranteed not to fail if you do not try. *C'est las vie.*"

"We have all failed at this one, Alan," Nigel pointed out. "Whoever this is, he's a step ahead of us."

"He certainly was this time," the young man said glumly, and began to outline just what it was he had discovered.

That was when Jonathon's head literally came up like a dog catching a scent. "Damnation!" he swore. "This is not just a trap. He's misdirecting us!"

"Like in one of your illusions?" Ninette asked, brows creased in a thoughtful frown.

"Exactly. He *wants* us to look for him using magic. He wants us to waste our time doing so. And meanwhile, he is doing something else! But what?" Jonathon grimaced. "What is it that he doesn't want us to see?"

"Whatever it is," Wolf observed, "it can't be good."

"He doesn't want us to see *him,* or rather, to find him." Nigel rose from his chair and began to pace. "The question is—"

And then he stopped, and a look of surprise mixed with annoyance spread over his face. "Good gad. We've been making a fundamental error here. All along we've been operating on the assumption that whoever this is first attacked Mademoiselle with a storm and sank her yacht."

"Nom du nom!" Ninette exclaimed. "That was all a fabrication! It is the red fish!"

"Red herring," Arthur corrected absently. "Exactly. So when we remove that from our puzzle, we need to know when the real attacks date from. And are they centered on Mademoiselle after all? It could just be coincidence, or it could be she was attacked just because she was vulnerable. We might not be looking for an enemy of Nina's; we might just be looking for an enemy of Nigel's."

"I haven't stirred up any trouble that I know of," Nigel said slowly. "But then again, neither has Ninette any magically gifted enemies. But at least we know where to start looking for mine."

"And what to look for." Jonathon pursed his lips. "For that matter, the first attack that we definitely know of came after I had arrived. *I* might be the one that this magician seeks to ruin. And I must say I have made a considerable number of enemies over the years. I am not an easy man to get along with, and I do not suffer fools."

"Surely not—" Nigel interjected, and then stopped. "No, you are correct, old friend."

He began paging through a little book he kept, separate from the larger daybook in which he scheduled acts and noted things down about the day's events in the theater. He had the daybook open too. He looked up.

"Do you suppose—when Harrigan broke his leg, do you think that could have been the first attack?"

All of them stared at him. It was Jonathon that spoke first. "Didn't Mrs. Harrigan say that the street just opened up in front of him?"

Nigel nodded, his lips pressed into a thin line. "Well then, that was the first attack, and it not only came after you joined us, it came after I began letting information on our planned productions get out."

"It does seem to point to the notion that this is an enemy of yours, Nigel," Wolf put in thoughtfully. But then Jonathon saw Alan brighten.

"There is no reason to think that this enemy might have been covering his tracks quite so effectively that far back is there?" he asked eagerly.

"Perhaps. Perhaps not." Nigel regarded the young man shrewdly. "I take it you have a notion?"

"If you know where that hole was, I can probably read what happened in the past," Alan said with a look of determination. Jonathon whistled.

"I don't know of more than one or two Masters that can do that." He was impressed in spite of himself. But Alan only shrugged.

"It's usually more in the line of a clairvoyant rather than a magician, but Water is uniquely suited to scrying," he replied diffidently. "It's more the aptness of the element rather than any virtue on my part."

"Well I think you are very clever to have thought of it!" Ninette said, looking at the young man with admiration. Jonathon scowled a little.

"Will we have to go there?" the Fire Master demanded. "Because that could be deuced awkward even at night. When you start performing magic in the middle of a public thoroughfare, people tend to look at you askance."

"It's not that obvious," Alan replied, "But I do need the exact spot—"

Jonathon rolled his eyes and growled a little, but agreed to take him to the spot. "I will come too!" Ninette insisted. "If need be I can make the distraction."

"You are already a distraction," Jonathon grumbled, but he knew better than to order her to stay behind. She wouldn't obey him and it wasn't as if he had the right to issue commands to her anyway. So the three of them went out into the afternoon—which threatened rain again—as Jonathon led them to the place where the so-called "sinkhole" had been a wonder and a nuisance.

It was filled in now, but that didn't seem to matter to Alan, who looked around to make sure no one was near enough to notice what he was about to do, then pulled a watch out of his pocket along with a small flask, opened the watch so that the cover-plate was resting on his palm, then poured a tiny bit of water into the little dish that the cover made.

Ninette stationed herself in front of him. Looking up at him as if they were having a conversation. Seeing what she was doing, as Alan began to mutter to his little pool of water, Jonathon interposed himself between Alan and the street, his tall form making an effective screen. Anyone who saw them now would only think it was three friends having a peculiarly intense conversation.

Jonathon, of course, could not see what it was that Alan was doing, but he caught some words in a variant of Gaelic that sounded very old indeed.

Alan made a small sound of triumph and spilled the water out of his watch onto the ground. He watched it intensely for a moment, then nodded. "Feel up to a trek?" he asked the two of them, raising his eyes. "I can follow the disturbance in the Water-magic back to the source, I think."

"Nothing ventured, nothing gained," Jonathon observed. "But we should send Mademoiselle back to the theater."

She opened her mouth to protest. He gave her one of those looks that she had learned meant she was going to get nowhere in arguing with him. Then, as he had learned to do around her, he told her why.

"Mademoiselle," he said, in a quiet, firm voice, "we do not know what sorts of neighborhoods we may be going through. I am sure you can defend yourself against a single man, or even two, but we might be set upon by a gang. And someone has to tell Nigel that Alan has succeeded in wringing something from the stones, and is off on the hunt."

Alan was casting entreating looks at her , but she did not look away from Jonathon's eyes. "All right," she replied. "Those are good reasons."

She nodded agreement, but before she could turn to go, Thomas had his own say.

I will be staying with you, the cat put in. *You might need another messenger. You might need for someone to get in at a second-story window.*

"So that you can tear a room apart?" Jonathon snorted. "I think you were an anarchist in a previous life."

Not likely. And I wouldn't have done that if we hadn't needed to cover what we'd stolen.

"I think there has been enough of arguing. Take Thomas, please, Jonathon." Ninette said firmly.

He gave her a firm look. "And what if you should run into difficulties?"

She laughed. "Going back to the theater in broad daylight? Really, I am not so helpless as all that!"

He considered how far she had come with that pistol of hers, and nodded reluctantly. "Just take care."

They parted at the corner, and Jonathon was relieved to see her summon a cab and step into it before he and Alan had moved from their spot. In fact, he let out his breath in a sigh of relief. He should have realized she would be sensible. After all, it was by no means clear that the enemy was actually after Nigel and not her.

He turned to see that Alan was watching him with a very odd expression, as if the young man had only now realized something—thought what that something could be, Jonathon had no idea.

"That is a remarkable lady," Alan murmured.

"Remarkable in that she has more sense than most women," Jonathon replied, wondering what had brought *that* remark on.

Yes, yes, yes indeed, Ninette is a fine creature. Now shall we get on with what we came out here to do? the cat asked in irritation.

"This is going to be aggravating for both of you," Alan said sheepishly. "I have to follow the watercourses, so I will have to go afoot and will probably lead you on a very meandering course indeed—"

"As long as you actually lead us on something, I do not much care," said Jonathon, then softened his tone. He hadn't meant to sound so gruff. "Every Master works within the bounds of his own Element, and I would hardly expect you to conform to a Fire Master's ways. Lead on."

Alan nodded, and the odd little procession moved off.

Alan had not exaggerated. He did lead them on a course that was more akin to a cow wandering a pasture than anyone going directly towards something. From time to time he stopped, pulled out his watch, and allowed a little weight attached to the chain to dangle— Jonathon watched it, though, and watched Alan watching it, and knew within moments of the first pause what Alan was doing.

He was dowsing, that most ancient of means to find water. The pendulum would swing in the direction that they needed to go, and Alan would put the watch in his vest pocket and set off again.

Now normally one dowsed for water. Jonathon thought to himself that Alan was actually dowsing for the direction of the *absence* of water. Or rather, of Water Magic. And he was doing it, not in the present, but in the past. He had found the place in time when what was now a repaired sinkhole had been created. With that mark to guide him, he was following the path of that magic, by tracing where it had in essence shoved everything out of its way in passing.

This was a tour de force that Jonathon knew he would never have been able to duplicate.

He's good, isn't he? Jonathon sensed that the cat was "speaking" for his "ears" only.

Remarkably so, Jonathon thought back at the cat. *I was skeptical—I'm not anymore. Even if—* But he did not finish that thought, which would have been, "Even if Ninette does seem to enjoy his company more than I like."

Well no one can be a young genius forever, the cat said with amusement. *If nothing else, young geniuses become old geniuses, and a newer, younger genius is always coming up, nipping at his heels. Being in those shoes is somewhat less than comfortable.*

Their journey took them long enough that Jonathon's feet were beginning to hurt. He was by no means used to walking great distances; he was, after all, a city dweller, and men of his class took cabs. They would certainly need to take a cab back to the theater to be in time for the first performance. But just when he was about to ask Alan how much longer he thought this would be, Alan looked up and gave an exclamation of mingled triumph and disappointment. Jonathon looked in the direction he was gazing and saw—

A hotel.

"Oh curse it!" he said , annoyed, knowing exactly what Alan was thinking. "I don't suppose—"

"With over a hundred people coming and going from there every day?" Alan shook his head. "There is not a chance I could sort through all of that. Besides, I much doubt that the magician confined his work to a single room. He more than likely expanded it to the whole hotel. *I* would have."

Jonathon nodded. "All right then, we are not completely helpless. I can get a listing of all the people registered to that hotel on that day, as well as the servants and employees. That will narrow our search down from the entire city to at most two hundred people. I call that progress."

Alan reluctantly agreed.

"Now, you may not need to hurry, but I have an act to perform," Jonathon continued firmly. "So right at this moment, we need nothing more magical than the ability to get a cab in front of a fine hotel."

Ninette stepped out of the cab in front of the theater and immediately had the sense that she was being watched.

Or to be precise, she had the sense that there were two sorts of watchers. The first sort were those who were watching her with admiration, varying degrees of recognition, and varying degrees of intent to find out if she could be enticed into a bed. There was a warmth to that which was friendly, even with those who dreamed of her being in their beds. Not even the ones who wanted her in that way had any intention of doing anything other than making her, and themselves, happy. And for the rest, she was something to be admired, like a sunset, or a lovely hat.

This she did not in the least mind. It was the same sort of thing she got when she performed. Even on stage, there were those who thought of her in their beds, and

that only made sense, since her legs were clearly on display, though her bosom was not exactly as generous as
those of the lady that sang "Champagne Charlie." For
the rest, again, she was like a fairy, a magical little creature that they watched flit about the stage so lightly
they were sometimes afraid to breathe lest she break.

That was the good sort of being watched.

No, it was another sort of watcher, a single one, that
startled her and sent a chill of fear down her back. How
she knew this, she could not tell. Maybe Thomas could;
maybe it was simply being around so much magic that it
was rubbing off on her. But she knew, absolutely, that
someone in front of the theater wished her only ill. That
person, whoever and wherever it was, watched her with
loathing.

Was this their enemy? Was this the magician who had
sent all those terrible things to plague them? Had
Jonathon and Alan gone in search of him only to have
him come here?

And which person in the crowd at the theater entrance was it? Her eyes flitted over the crowd, lined up
to buy tickets for the evening performances. They were
all sold out these days, and even the standing-room sec-
tions in the backs of the galleries had plenty of occu-
pants.

She simply could not tell who it was; no one looked
angry, or affronted, or even more annoyed than one
could be with standing in a line on a warm evening.
There was nothing to give her so much as a clue, only
that aura of hate, so with a shiver, she hurried towards
the stage door. Nigel was in there, and so were Arthur
and Wolf. They would know what to do. They would be
able to tell if the person she sensed was the magician
that they were all looking for. She tried to look as if she
was hurrying only because she was a little late, and not
because she knew he was there. If he knew that—there

was no saying what he might do. Once inside that door she would be—

She had only a breath of warning before he was on her, the feeling of rage and triumph, the sound of a footstep in the alley behind her and the sense of *presence* looming behind her. But that warning was enough.

Not enough warning to fumble the revolver out of her purse—but she did have enough to react as a dancer would, sure of foot and aware as if her skin had eyes, knowing exactly where she was, and where he was, and where he was going. There was just enough time to sidestep, turn quickly, and as the man sailed past her, arms outstretched, to kick him as hard as she could in the back of his trousers.

He had clearly expected to grab her, was off-balance to begin with, and the hard kick of a dancer, a well-fed, well-trained, and thoroughly healthy dancer, sent him crashing into the brick wall of the building opposite the theater. He managed to get his arms up in time to protect his head, but that was all. She didn't hesitate for a second as he hit the bricks.

Screaming for help, she picked up her skirts over her knees and ran, her mind on fire with fear as the loathing and hate and rage washed over her, so thick it was a bitter taste in her mouth and a lash to her back, with terror putting wings on her feet.

She didn't remember reaching the stage door, only that she found herself babbling to the doorman and a crowd of people who had run to the door at the sound of her screams. She thought she was saying something about a man attacking her, but her mind was so filled with fear that she scarcely could put two sensible words together. The doorman in his turn left her in the care of the wardrobe mistress and summoned four stagehands, leading them out in a wrath-filled group into the alley while the wardrobe mistress plied her with brandy and water and sent one of the boys for Nigel. The wardrobe mistress, under any other circumstances a crusty old dame with a formidable temper, put an arm around her shoulders as motherly as her own Maman could have been. "Here, sweetheart," she soothed, "now drink this down. Did he hurt ye? Hit ye? Thank God it wasn't dark out there—"

She shook her head and gulped down brandy that tasted salty from her own tears. "He wanted—he wanted—to kill me—" she babbled, as the terror slowly, slowly ebbed.

"I misdoubt it was killing he was after," the woman murmured blackly, but at that point Nigel and Arthur came pounding up, with Wolf clinging like a limpet to Arthur's shoulder. Without a word, Nigel scooped her up, as Arthur gave the wardrobe mistress orders that sent her scurrying determinedly away on some errand.

Things blurred for a moment, and she found herself on the couch in Nigel's office, with Arthur peering into her eyes, Wolf still clinging to his shoulder and peering at her first with one eye, then the other. "Definitely psychic shock," he pronounced, as she gazed up at him in bewilderment. "Honestly it is amazing she didn't just freeze there in the alley and let him do—whatever it was he was going to do. Whoever he was."

"He got away?" she gasped, panic rising in her again. *"He got away?"*

"Ninette!" Wolf barked, and flew down and bit her little finger, hard.

The physical pain snapped the panic, and the fear ran out of her like water from a cracked pot. She clasped her injured finger to her chest and stared at them all, unable to think, benumbed.

Arthur put his hands on her shoulders and shook her gently. "Ninette, it's all right. At least it is for now. Whoever he is, he can't get in here to harm you. Now tell us what happened."

She gulped, reached for the glass of brandy that Nigel held out wordlessly to her and in halting tones, told what little she knew. "I cannot understand—" she faltered. "The horror—the fear—"

Nigel patted her hand, and Wolf rubbed his head apologetically along her wrist, but it was Arthur that answered. "Ninette, there is magic, and then there are the powers of the mind itself. It seems you have something of the latter." He smiled encouragingly. "I do, too. I am about half magician and half mentalist. Tell me, have you been able to tell what the audience feels about you? As if you were feeling what *they* feel?"

She nodded slowly. *"Mais oui.* Since I came here to England, certainly. I am not sure about before—" But now that she thought about it, it did seem to her that she had always had a sense for who was friendly, who was not, and who might even be dangerous. She had just never thought about it very much.

Arthur nodded. "Probably talking with Thomas as you do has made all this stronger. And this man, whoever he is, has a similar ability. I don't know why he hates you so much, but for you it was like someone with a megaphone shouting at you right into your ear. All you could feel was the hate and anger."

"Oui," she said slowly. "It felt like—like a blow."

"It was a blow," Arthur replied, and tapped her between her eyebrows on her forehead. "To your mind."

"My head feels bruised inside," she said, feeling dazed in a way that mere brandy could not account for.

"I am not surprised. Fortunately I have a remedy for that." He smiled down at her. "You are going to take a refreshing little nap, and when you wake up, you will feel quite yourself again." She felt his palm resting on her forehead, and suddenly her eyelids were too heavy to keep open. With a sigh, she surrendered to his will. After all, this was Arthur, and she had nothing to fear from him.

Nothing at all.

Nigel stared down at the sleeping dancer. "I never want to hear you denigrate your powers ever again, my friend," he said soberly. "I certainly could not have done that, just now."

Arthur shrugged. "Well, now we know what it is that she has that holds an audience," he said pragmatically. "And it's not a bad thing."

"Not at all, you'll just have to teach her control. And ethics." Nigel turned away and paced towards the window.

"That's hardly relevant at the moment. Who in bloody blazes attacked her?" Arthur picked up Wolf and replaced the bird on his shoulder. "Was it the Earth Master?"

Nigel shook his head. "No. The Sylphs are absolutely certain there is not a breath of Earth Magic, inimical or otherwise, around this building. Whoever it was has those mental powers, and nothing else, and for some reason he wants Ninette dead." He turned away from the window, as a knock came at the office door. It was the chief of the stagehands, cap twisted between his hands, looking hangdog.

"Sorry, Mister Nigel, sir," he said unhappily. "We lost him. He must've been faster as a ferret an' twice as twisty."

"That's all right, Bob," Nigel replied, though the man winced at the frustration in his voice. "It's hardly your fault. Just tell the lads to be on the watch for him."

"We will, sir," the stagehand replied, and hastily made

his escape. Nigel turned back to face Arthur, running his hand through his hair with agitation.

"First the Earth-Mage, then the other dancer, and now *this,*" he said with a touch of anger. "What next?"

Arthur could only shake his head.

22

NOT needing corsets, Nina never wore them if she could help it. So while the women all around her looked like marble monuments, she was able to undulate rather than walk, and lounge luxuriously rather than sit. This, apparently, was either very attractive to men, or made them acutely uncomfortable. Sometimes both.

The reporter had turned up at her flat—fortunately after she had awakened. Last night had been relatively good, despite the idiocy of her tool. She had decided that she would deal with him later, she had fed, though it was not what she would call a gourmet repast, and she was looking forward to unleashing another round of harassment via the newspapers in the next few days. She received her visitor leaning comfortably back in her velvet chaise, leaving him to take the uncomfortable chair with the itchy horsehair upholstery. She waved him languidly to it, and waited for him to tell her what the next barrage from him against the imposter would be.

But the reporter put paid to that idea.

"You lost it?" Nina said, incredulously, sitting bolt up-
right with shock. "You *lost* it?"

The reporter looked uncomfortable and indignant at
the same time. "More like it was stolen," he protested.
"Along with a lot of my other papers, everything in my
desk but my bills, things I was looking into for other stories. It took me this long to get my place cleaned up to
figure out exactly what was taken. The thieves tore the
whole flat apart looking for something, and it looks like
in the end they settled for taking every scrap of paper
that looked important." He shrugged. "There are some
stories I am pursuing that could cause scandal, perhaps
even divorce. I expect that was what the thieves were
looking for. They'll most likely look through what they
took and burn what they don't want."

"Why didn't you keep these things locked away?" she
snarled, her hands clenching and unclenching as she
strove to control herself. "Are you so completely a fool?
Why were they not in a safe?"

Now he looked angry. "Do I look like the sort of man
that can afford a safe?" he snapped. "And even if I
could, the landlord is so cheese-paring it would probably fall through the floor! Besides, what does it matter?
You can send for more—probably better—bona-fides."
He gave her a superior look. "I told you that we needed
those anyway. This time, get something I can actually
use. Something a bit more convincing than photographs
and impersonal letters." His eyes glittered. "Letters
from *admirers* would be the best. Especially things on
letterhead with a crest. You can't forge that."

She glared at him. Give him letters from *admirers*
now? And if she had been human, that would have been
playing right into his hands. The opportunity for blackmail would be just too tempting—if, in fact, he wasn't already planning on using what she gave him for
blackmail.

She could easily send for things of a more personal nature, of course. But that would take time, and in that time, her enemies might come closer to unmasking her. One thing had already gone wrong with these far-off affairs. Her witness had vanished; he was supposed to be on the train now, but her servant had arrived in Paris without him. She assumed he had been shrewder and more crooked than she had suspected; he had taken her money and disappeared with it halfway between Prague and Paris. It was so maddening, having to rely on her servants so many miles away! They seemed to get more thickheaded with every month.

That was a setback, but, she had told herself, it was a minor one. This was only a skirmish, a feint, not the real battle. She could continue without a witness—and after all, it had always been an uncertain thing whether a working-class foreigner who had to speak through a translator would be believed.

Last night had been more serious. Her stupid tool had taken matters into his own hands and attacked the girl in broad daylight. Now the question was, would this be connected to her? She thought not, and the fool had gotten away, but—if they did, then her position became much more precarious. With the addition of a Water Master, the Elemental Masters had enough accumulated magic to effectively prevent her creatures from getting into their homes, and the theater, and if they tracked down an Earth Master strong enough to hunt her out—

Last night she had convinced herself these were only minor setbacks. There had been no sign that the magicians actually had linked the attack to her.

But now, to hear this—

Was it common thieves, after all? She listened, tight-lipped, to the description of how his flat had looked, and to him swearing he had locked the door securely before going out. It sounded as if it must have been common thieves—she didn't think any of the theater people would have been likely to ransack the place so crudely. The stage magician could easily have picked the locks of course, and relocked them too, but she very much doubted that any of them would have torn open cushions and the mattress. No, that sounded like stupid, petty criminals. But still! Her pictures and other proofs of her identity were gone!

She realized at that moment, that despite her own self confidence, in short, things were not going at all well, and she needed to take it out on something, before her temper snapped altogether and she did something stupid and irrevocable in public.

And then she eyed the man before her, who had gone from being self-defensive to bullying. Every word he spoke, every line of his body, said the same thing. He was a man, she was a woman, he would therefore always know the right way to handle her story. She should be properly grateful for his advice. She should do as she was told, and keep that temper of hers to herself.

He was more and more infuriating by the moment. He had been injudicious enough, this reporter, and bald-faced enough, to come to her flat. He had been stupid enough to come alone.

And she had no further use for him.

She nodded once to her servant, who took the silent order, and left, closing and locking the door behind her. The man heard the click of the lock, and at first, it did not register with him. Then he turned to see that they were alone, turned back to her, smirking, anticipating, no doubt, that she had finally realized what a masterful man he was, and was going to yield to him in more ways than one.

She smiled sweetly at him. Then she shifted to her true and proper form. The smirk froze into a rictus of incredulity and fear when he saw what was facing him. His eyes bulged, and he made a little mewling sound.

"I have no further need of your services," said the Troll, and slapped him to the floor with a single blow of her hand.

She made him last for a good long time, after first choking off his voice by the simple expedient of stuffing his mouth full of clay. He could still breathe through his nose. Her neighbors were awake and about, and it would be awkward to have to explain the screams. She absorbed him a little at a time, taking time out to actually, physically, feed on his flesh, just for the taste and the sensations it aroused in her and in him. She did not, of course, detach the limbs that she fed on. She wanted him to feel it, feel the horror as he watched her feed, and was helpless to do anything about it. Not a drop of blood was wasted; she absorbed it as it dripped from the ruined flesh, as she absorbed his energy, little by little. She savored all the complex flavors of his fear, spiced with despair and hopelessness. Finally, when she could wring nothing more from him, when he was semi-conscious at best, numbed, his mind hiding away from her, from the horror of what she was doing to him, she came to the point where it was time to end the game. She killed him and absorbed the rest of his body. When she was finished there was nothing left but a few bloody rags.

She reverted and signaled to her servants to return and clean up the mess. She was not sated, but her temper had been appeased. Now her mind was clear enough to think. She flung herself down on the chaise again, and allowed her servant to clean the blood out from under her fingernails before it dried there.

This was not going well. She had only one advantage at this point: that the Elemental Masters did not know that the real Nina Tchereslavsky and the Earth Master that was plaguing them were the same person. They did not yet know who she was nor what she was, and her location was still secure. But that could all change in a moment.

Briefly it occurred to her that the safest thing to do would be to abandon this project and go back. She had not yet ruined her reputation as a dancer with that single canceled contract. There were a thousand excuses she could plead; she could manufacture a plausible, even sympathetic reason for why she had not honored it. Or she could simply remain silent on the subject and allow people to gossip; humans being what they were, they would probably assume she was giving birth to a child out of wedlock.

And for a moment she toyed with that idea. She could even admit to it, and carry out the plan she'd been intending to execute here. She could purchase an infant virtually anywhere, call it hers, and bring it back to her home. It was not as perfect as the plan she had made for taking over this girl's place. There would be no marriage, which meant there would be scandal of course, but that hardly mattered to her. It wasn't as if she was hoping to make a good marriage! On the contrary, the more would-be lovers she had vying for her, the better.

Meanwhile she could carry out the rest of the plan. Display the brat at regular intervals. Absorb it when it was big enough that she could counterfeit it, and then play the dual role of mother and child. She would then be her own heir, and "Nina Tchereslavsky" could disappear in some manner.

It could work. It could easily work. All she had to do would be to pack her things and simply leave.

Then the thought of that wretched girl and her meddlesome friends enraged her all over again. She would not leave this battle! The wretched girl would have to pay for what she had done! Once again her hands clenched and unclenched, and the fingernails grew just a little longer, a little pointier, a little sharper.

Besides, now that the Masters knew that she was out there, she could not imagine that they would rest until they identified her. And when they did that—

Her mind shied away from the thought, but she could not escape it. It was the one scenario that actually frightened her. The Masters simply could not permit something like her to exist. An Elemental creature, as powerful as any of them, who could and did walk among them, wielding magic in *their* world with a skill the equal to any of them? To them she was an abomination, a blasphemy, and they would not rest until she was not just banished, but destroyed.

It was sheer folly to think that they would leave the hunt once they had started it. She had inflicted too much damage on them already, and they would not rest until they had gotten revenge.

It was time to end this, end it while she still had all the advantages. The imposter would die, but her friends would precede her.

By the time Jonathon, Alan, and Thomas returned to the theater, Ninette had awakened from her rest, and was in a better state to tell them what had happened. Thanks to Arthur, the incident had lost its immediacy, and she was able to recite those details that she remembered calmly.

None of them knew what to make of it. "All I can tell you is that he hated me with a terrible passion," she said rubbing the bridge of her nose as the memory made her head ache a little. "I cannot tell you *why,* and I do not ever recall having seen him before."

"Maybe we should see if the mad-house is missing an

inmate," Nigel said, half in jest. But Ninette and Arthur both turned to look at him thoughtfully,

"That might be no bad idea," Ninette replied slowly. "The strength of that hate, the lack of anything but hate—it indeed felt like that of a madman."

Nigel regarded both of them soberly, as Arthur nodded. "I suppose there is no harm in making sure," he said, finally. "Very well then. I'll send to the police and ask them to make inquiries."

As the humans discussed just how much it would be prudent to tell the police, Thomas slipped out. There were a few advantages to being trapped in the body of a cat, and this was one. He might not have the nose of a hound, but he could follow a scent-trail, even one as muddled as this one was likely to be. He felt a distinct sense of urgency in this. He could not imagine that this was some random madman who had somehow fixated on Ninette. No, this was linked to the other attacks, and the only way to find out how it was linked was to find the attacker.

Fortunately, the attacker had been kind enough to leave a blood-trail. Faint, but it was there. And it was just as fortunate that he had elected to stagger back to whatever place he deemed safe on foot.

Since his trail took him down back streets and through alleys, Thomas presumed that whatever injuries he had gotten impacting the brick wall had been obvious enough that he did not want to show his damaged self in public.

But this was two long treks across Blackpool in one day, and he was getting very tired indeed by the time the trail ended at the back entrance of a little house with pretensions of grandeur where Thomas's sharp ears picked up the sound of a woman's voice raised in a plaintive tone that was not quite a whine.

Thomas quickly leapt the wall and positioned himself where he could hear every word.

". . . dear, I wish you would go tell the police about those footpads!" said the woman. "Look at your poor face! You might have been—"

"Enough, Mother!" The male voice that answered her was rough with anger. "I am not going to the police, and that is an end to it!" The scent that wafted from the window matched the one Thomas had been following, washed over with the scent of disinfectant. "There is nothing I can tell them; I never saw those ruffians' faces, they simply manhandled me into a wall and fled when they heard someone coming. I am not inclined to open myself to ridicule because I allowed myself to be caught off-guard by a couple of rough laborers!"

"But, dear—"

"I have made my decision, Mother! Kindly do not fret me with it any further! Now, I am going out. Thank you for your ministrations, and do not trouble yourself to wait up for me."

For one brief moment, Thomas panicked when he realized that the man was going to be opening the door only a scant foot or two away from his hiding place.

But then he shook his head, because he knew this fellow wasn't going to do anything except shy a stone at him, perhaps. He was a cat! If a cat could look at a king, then it could certainly lurk with impunity in the shrubbery.

The man opened his own front door, and stalked stiffly out into the street. Thomas gave him a few paces, then followed. But it was with a powerful internal struggle. When he saw the marks on the man's face that so clearly told that he had slammed into the wall, Thomas had no doubt at all that this was his quarry. And it had taken every bit of his self control to keep from leaping on the man in a fury and making a total ruin of his head with teeth and claws.

He hoped that he would gain some clue as to why the man had attacked Ninette, but all the fellow did was to go to a second-class club and proceed to get drunk. He went at it methodically, as Thomas could tell by watching from the vantage point of a hiding place under a sofa, and he went about it silently. He was scarcely popular, that much was painfully clear. No one greeted him, and he greeted no one. Eventually, he passed out in a stupor, empty glass falling to the rug beside him. One of the club servants picked up the glass but left him where he was. Evidently he was no favorite with them, either.

Finally Thomas left, and made his way back to the theater, stealing rides on the backs of cabs; now that it was dark he could do so without fear of being chased off or exciting any comment. He was experiencing very mixed feelings at the moment, but uppermost was unease. This man was a prig, a buffoon and a fool, but he was not mad. Nor did he correspond to the enraged creature that had attacked Ninette. Yet the scent was the same. There must be more, much more, than met the eye here. He thought about it all the way across town, but could come to no conclusions even as he slipped into the theater and arrived just in time to see the end of Jonathon's act.

Ninette performed flawlessly; certainly no one out there in the audience had an inkling that she had been attacked earlier that day. He sensed something more from her as well: an awareness of her relationship with the audience that had not been there before. That awareness seemed to spur her to overcome what had happened that afternoon, to transcend it, to perform a kind of alchemy that turned the experience into something good that she could give them. She wasn't quite managing that—but she was trying, and for that alone she more than deserved the hearty applause she got. Thomas felt irrationally proud.

When she came off the stage, some of the performers and stagehands that knew about the afternoon's attack came up to her to tell her she had done well; unspoken were the words *are you all right?* She must have known this, for she thanked them and took the time to make sure they saw her looking completely normal. Thomas gave her extra scrutiny during this. She seemed to be fine; in fact, he sensed that from being frightened she had gone to being angry. This was good; anger was a potent weapon, and by now, she should have learned something of control. He would, of course, make sure of that.

He followed her back to her dressing room, and sensed at that moment a hesitation and a weariness in her when she saw the usual crowd waiting. But he watched as she straightened her back, put on a smile and went in to deal with her admirers.

But she did not have to deal with them for long.

It could not have been a quarter hour later that one of the boys came with a summons from Nigel. Since even her admirers could not take precedence over the theater owner, they let her go with reluctance and cries of protest, and she made a graceful exit. Thomas followed.

He was debating whether he should say something to Nigel about his discovery, but—something stopped him from doing so. That made him pause, and sit for a moment with his tail wrapped around his paws while he considered his reaction, as the rest of the group in their turn discussed their own results. Jonathon had his list of hotel guests on the date in question, and had already compared that to the current register. He already planned to investigate those that were still in residence as well as the employees, and see what his two imps could find out about those who were gone. Very methodical, but this also seemed to Thomas to be perilously slow.

Nigel was tracking down appropriately powerful Earth Masters. He already had the addresses and letters of introduction to three of them. Also productive—and also slow.

He regarded them all through slitted eyes, and took some careful thought as he weighed them in his mind.

That was when it occurred to him: while they all took this seriously, none of the men, not even Nigel, regarded this as a contest they might lose.

None of them has ever lost before, he thought. *Nigel and Jonathon I know have faced very perilous creatures, but they have never lost. It has never occurred to them that they can. In their world, the good and chivalrous man always prevails.*

Looking at Ninette's sober face, however, he knew that she, at least, was quite well aware that things could go horribly wrong. Probably Ailse was too. Both of them had come from very different backgrounds than any of the men. Both had been poor, and in Ninette's case, she was quite well aware, always, that had things gone otherwise she might well have ended up worse than dead, in a terrible existence as a Parisian prostitute.

But the men had all gone to public schools, university, and if their parents had not been wealthy, they had at least been comfortable. By their own efforts, they had achieved respect and prosperity, and no one had ever seriously given them many moments of concern. When Nigel had faced down the worst of the magical creatures he'd dealt with in the past, it had been when he was much younger, and young men are always viscerally convinced of their own immortality.

So there it was, the reason why Thomas's own instincts were telling him to keep his information to himself for now. There was certainly more to this extraordinarily sane madman than met the eye. If he was dangerous, Thomas wanted to find out in a way that would threaten none of them. Even if he could convince all of them that direct confrontation was a very bad idea, they would still want to spy on the man, and they were simply not going to be very successful at that. Humans were large, and none of these friends was skilled at being unobtrusive. A cat could go anywhere.

Tonight the men put Ninette and Ailse into a cab for the short trip home, and made it clear that Ninette was to take taxis anywhere she needed to go if Nigel was not available to drive her in his motor.

Sensible precaution, and Ninette took it so. Then again, her energy was starting to run low; Thomas could tell from the way she was starting to droop, just a little. He jumped up inside and settled at her feet, and again, the silence between her and Ailse told him a very great deal. She was exhausted, and that was hardly surprising.

It was only when she was tucked into bed and Ailse was out of the room that Thomas jumped up and sat on the foot of it to speak with her. She was trying to read a book, and making heavy going of it, at one and the same time too tired in body and too active in mind to stay focused.

I found your attacker, he said without preamble.

She sat straight up. "You did? But—"

Shh. I did not want to tell the others. There is something exceedingly odd about him. I need to investigate this further, which means I will be out all night. You will be all right, yes?

For answer, she reached under the corner of her mattress and pulled out her revolver.

Good. I very much doubt that anything will happen, but I need to know you are prepared to defend yourself. I intend to share everything I learn with you, Ninette. I do not believe that allowing you to remain ignorant will make you any safer.

She nodded, her expression grimly determined.

I am going to try to find out why he is so deathly enraged with you, why he is obsessed with you, and once we know these things, we can formulate a plan to deal with him.

"That seems a great deal wiser than stalking up to him and asking him why he attacked me," she said dryly. "I never really saw his face, so I cannot even be a witness as to who it is."

Police would take a dim view of a witness that never saw her attacker's face, he agreed. *Very well then. Lock the doors and windows, and when I return, I will simply find a comfortable place to wait downstairs until you awaken. A cat, after all, can sleep virtually anywhere. And our landlords know I belong to you and will give me a handsome breakfast of kippers.* He jumped down off her bed and up onto the windowsill, and from there out onto the roof. He waited until he saw she had locked the window as he asked, then flicked his tail once in the moonlight.

Au revior, cherie, he said, and began making his way back to street level. He had a taxi—several taxis—to catch.

23

THE way that the club's servants treated the man that Thomas was following said volumes about his unusual behavior. Servants could be dismissed on the basis of a single complaint. Very often the level of their personal comfort depended on the generosity of the patrons at holidays or when special requests were supplied.

So to be bundled into the cheapest possible cab, with no concern for his dignity and comfort, to have his pockets gone through and used to pay the hack driver in advance, argued for someone who had sunk so low that the servants expected nothing out of him and treated him accordingly. It also argued that even the ruling members of his own club would take the word of a servant over his.

Rather pathetic. And it made his attack on Ninette all the more puzzling. It was as if this was a real-life Doctor Jekyll, though one without the fictional doctor's better qualities.

Thomas got himself a ride easily enough. The man didn't even notice a cat getting in with him. Thomas tucked himself up as small as he could though, because the jolting of the poorly sprung cab was slowly knocking him out of his stupor. By the time the cab arrived at his home, he was conscious enough to clamber out, curse the driver, and stagger up to his door. Thomas followed a prudent distance behind and watched to see which lights came on upstairs. He noted, as he had expected, the lights—gaslight, he thought, by the way it increased rather than coming on—in the front upstairs bedroom. The back would overlook the tiny scrap of paved yard suitable only for the maid to do the laundry in, and other similar household chores; neither the lady of the house nor the master would care to have that view out their window. The maid—or maids, if there was more than one—would have the attic. It appeared that the man occupied the room of choice, leaving his mother to climb two sets of stairs instead of one. *How chivalrous.*

Thomas noted with pleasure that the passage from ground to windowsill was an easy one for a cat. Plenty of places to climb led to a faux-balcony below the windows, and the night was warm enough that—

There. The maid opened the window for the man, her expression of weary resignation clear from here. All Thomas needed to do was to wait.

Wait he did, as the lights were turned down and then off, as the neighborhood quieted further, until he was fairly certain the man was asleep. Then he scrambled nimbly up to the balcony, squeezed through the railing, and leapt up to the windowsill.

And there he was. Thomas expected sottish snoring, but the sound that came from the man made all the hair on his back stand up and his tail puff out like a bottle-brush.

He was whimpering . . . pleading. Then in the next moment, the pleading turned to an animalistic growling so full of hate that Thomas very nearly leaped down to the street again.

Thomas could not make out exactly what the man was saying, but there was something about it that sounded like half of a conversation. And he would dearly, dearly like to have heard the other half.

Then something else put up the hair on his back. The faint scent of magic. But not just any magic. This was not the magic of an Elemental Master. No, oh indeed not. This was the raw, half-tamed power of an Elemental itself.

And it had the scent of blood to it.

This man wasn't in the throes of a nightmare, he was caught up in a Sending.

Thomas didn't recognize the scent, so it could have been any of the three Elements not his own. Nevertheless, anyone capable of reasoning would reason it was damned unlikely to be anything other than Earth.

Then the man spoke his first intelligible words: "I am coming." He moved then, threw off the bedclothes, reached for his clothing. His eyes were still closed; he was obeying his master's command in his sleep.

For a moment, and a long one, Thomas fought the urge to flee. He wasn't an Elemental Master anymore, he wasn't any kind of a magician, he wasn't even human! He was a cat! What could he do?

But he knew very well what he could do; it was something none of the humans he was in league with could do. He could take his courage in all paws, follow this man, and do it without being seen.

Just so long as he could avoid being detected by other means.

He jumped down to the street to wait, one shadow among many.

Ninette awoke suddenly, her mind preternaturally clear, every sense alert.

Thomas was in trouble.

How she knew this, she could not say; perhaps that encounter with that horrible man had done something to her mind, made it more sensitive or something of the sort. She had noticed it last night when she had awakened in time to warm up for her performance. She had *felt* things more clearly than ever before, from the stage-hands, the other performers, and then, most strongly, from her audience. At first she had been a bit upset and angry, but then she realized that it was not so bad. Feeling how much the audience was enjoying what she did made her think that perhaps this could be useful.

And now she knew without a doubt that Thomas was in trouble. She felt his fear, and she knew that she could use that to find him; it pulled her like the North Pole pulled a compass needle.

She pulled on clothing, the bloomers outfit she wore to go shooting. With her hair under a cap, she would look like a boy, and that should keep her safe enough. She stuffed her pistol into one pocket, bullets into another, money into a third. She went to wake Ailse only to discover that Ailse wasn't in her own bed.

That made her pause; then she racked her brain trying to think of where her maid *could* be, and came up with nothing.

"She's walkin' out with that lad from the hotel band."

Ninette turned to see the creature that Nigel called a Brownie looking sideways at her. She didn't see much of the little fellow, he was shy by nature, and she wasn't a magician after all. But it made her obscurely ashamed that this fellow knew more about what Ailse was doing and who she was seeing than she did.

"I think they went to th' pub," he continued, flushing, "Though I couldn't tell ye which one."

Well there was nothing to be done about it. Ailse was gone, Thomas was in trouble and from the growing urgency she felt, there was no time to try and rouse Nigel, Arthur, Jonathon, and Alan. The best she could do was this.

"Thomas is in danger," she told the Brownie urgently. "Don't ask me how I know, I just do. When Ailse gets back, tell her that, and tell her to get the rest. Thomas was following the man who attacked me; I do not know what kind of trouble he is in, and it could be something I can solve by walking in and claiming him for mine. I know only that he is frightened and I must go to him."

The Brownie nodded. "Aye, I can do that, miss." Then he looked pained. "Wish't I could come with you. . . ."

But Brownies, so Nigel had told her, were very tied to a place, once they settled into it. Literally tied in many ways; unless Ailse or Ninette were to do something that would offend it, the Brownie was unable to physically leave the building.

"Just tell her. I'm sure she'll be back soon." She wouldn't have gone far, not after that madman had attacked Ninette.

But *she* must be thinking that Thomas was still here, and that it would be safe enough to leave Ninette with him standing guard. She didn't know that Thomas was gone.

Ailse could be gone for as much as an hour or even more, and there was not enough time to search through all the pubs within walking distance. This was, after all, an area of boarding houses that catered to entertainers, and even when the barmen had to call "time," they stayed open, serving food and tea while people sipped from their own flasks or made the beer they had bought before time was called last for an hour.

A jolt of fear passed through her. Thomas was definitely in trouble. There was no time to lose.

She snatched up her keys and ran.

"You are a curious creature," said the Troll.

Thomas knew it was a Troll, because he could tell, by scent, that it was not human the moment he had surreptitiously entered the house. Here in proximity to it, inside barriers and shielding, things were very clear. The damp-soil scent of Earth power was everywhere, overlaid with the corruption that was the hallmark of the Dark Element. And the unmistakable signs of something very large and very powerful, besides the lesser boggles and simulacra, meant that the powerful one must be a Troll. The first thing that had occurred to him, and with a jolt, was that he had, all unaware, been the one to find their elusive Earth Master, for only an Earth Master would have an Earth Elemental in thrall. There could not be two such in the city.

The second thing that occurred to him was to run.

Unfortunately, he discovered that he could not.

The whole house was bespelled. Things could get in easily, but once inside, the only way to get out was to be let out. He had slipped blithely inside, following his quarry, only to discover that he was trapped.

All right, put a good face on it. Since he could not go back, he decided to go forward. He followed the man, who whimpered a little as he stumbled along the passageway and up the stairs, heading for the next floor. The entire scene was surreal; outwardly, this was the entry, hall, and staircase of a very well-appointed, moderately luxurious, and utterly respectable home. It had all the right touches, from the scenic photographs and paintings on the walls, to the Turkey carpet on the floor, from the elaborately carved balustrade to the latest in electrical lighting. But the aura of dark corruption that hung over everything, and the tortured face of the man climbing the stairs as if he was ascending the Matterhorn, made it feel more like something out of a nightmare.

Thomas followed, knowing that there was no way he could have escaped detection, even if the master of this place hadn't done anything about him yet. So he acted as if he had intended to be in this position all along. *When all else fails, try a bluff.* Mind, that particular philosophy had not worked all that well for him in the past.

Then again, that could mean the odds were good for it finally working. Right?

The man paused at an open doorway. Then Thomas got a second shock, when the voice that called out to them was female.

"Come in," said the voice, and paused. "Both of you."

The man shambled in. Thomas followed.

And got the third shock, although part of his mind was saying, smugly, *This should have occurred to you, you know.* He knew the woman lounging like an odalisque on her sumptuous chaise.

It was the real Nina Tchereslavsky.

Or rather, a Troll wearing her shape.

The Troll made a contemptuous gesture at him, and he found himself frozen in place. Which was not quite as bad as it could have been, however, because the Troll's primary attention was on the man.

"You have failed me," the Troll said, looking down her pert nose at the man. "You stupid ass. What sort of an idiot attacks someone in broad daylight? With witnesses? Within reach of help?"

The man's mouth worked, but no sound came out. The Troll's words, curiously enough, were in good English, with a slightly upper-class accent. Thomas wondered how that came about, if she was supposed to be Russian.

Then again, she was a Troll, and magic was a part of them. He supposed . . .

But wait. There was something else wrong here. Where, exactly, was this creature's Master?

"Never mind that, I will tell you," the woman continued with contempt. "A brainless, over-educated, under-schooled fool, who has been certain all of his life that he is *entitled* to the finer things, yet has never worked to achieve them."

This did not sound like any Troll that Thomas had ever heard of. Most of them could scarcely manage more than a grunt.

"So, given that you are a brainless, over-educated, under-schooled fool who has just ruined any chance he had of getting *near* that imposter, what do you think I should do with you?" she continued.

The man stared at her dumbly, and tried to mouth words, but nothing came out.

"Fortunately for all of us, your *dear* mother does not know you are here. In fact, she does not even know you have left the house. No one knows you are here—" she looked down at Thomas "—except this cat. And I doubt he will be able to go running to the police, or anyone else. So, really, there is nothing to prevent me from doing exactly as I please with you." She smiled. It was a smile that made Thomas's tail brush out again.

That was when she changed into her normal form. Yes, she was, indeed, a Troll . . .

Her head brushed the ceiling; she looked now like a crude doll made of gray clay, and she smelled like a combination of sour earth and rotting flesh. She reached forward and embraced the man. It would have been funny, if his face had not been contorted into a silent scream of anguish.

Then came the horrible part. When he had been human and a magician, Thomas had read about Trolls doing this, but he had never thought he was going to see the *absorption* process up close. Certainly not this close.

With the victim paralyzed and able to move only his eyes, the Troll pressed him into her chest. *Into* it. Little by little, he sank into the clay, and in a way it was a relief that his face went in first, because at least Thomas didn't have to look at his expression anymore.

And this could have been still worse, really; in some accounts, a Troll would dismember and partly eat a victim, rather than merely absorbing him. It was said that they grew to like the taste.

But where was the Troll's master?

Thomas curled his tail tightly around his feet, and pretended to watch with interest, all the while trying to detect a human, *any* human, anywhere in this house. Well other than the victim.

Nothing.

No, he thought, aghast. But the conclusion was inescapable.

There was no Elemental Master here. There was only—this thing. A horror, a blasphemy, something that should never have been. An Elemental that had been given form and substance on the Material Plane and gotten loose. A creature that did not belong here, turned loose and left to work its will on humans. Any humans.

He thought he knew now where it had gotten its relatively high intelligence and cunning. It must have begun absorbing humans right away, and with that had come more wit, more ability to think. With that, too, had come enough memory to tell her of the dangers of living among humans. So now there was a Troll that could *think,* plan, and carry out those plans. A Troll that could keep its identity hidden. A Troll with patience.

That last might have been the worst.

Thomas thought quickly, because in a few more moments, the Troll was going to finish absorbing her prey, and then she was going to turn her attention to him.

He cleared his throat as the last of her victim vanished, with a little dry cough of the sort that sometimes preceded a hairball. *Very good,* he said gravely. He couldn't manage approval, but at least he could sound serious. *No point in wasting him, but no point in allowing him to continue wasting air either.*

The Troll reverted to the form of the dancer. Had there even been a real Nina Tchereslavsky? Probably, but judging by the Troll's looks, she hadn't been very old when she fell afoul of the creature.

For a moment, she looked puzzled. Then her lips curved in a cruel smile. "Wasting air. I like that. You seem very calm for someone who has just discovered that what he walked into, he cannot again walk out of."

But what if I don't want to walk out? Thomas asked, calmly. *What if I intended to meet and speak with you?*

The Troll's mouth gaped. "Speak with me? Why?"

Thomas sniffed. *I should think that would be obvious. You are clearly more clever than the theater people. You are obviously stronger. You know who they are, but they still do not know where you are, much less what.*

"So you—"

I came intending to negotiate with you, yes. It is prudent.

"But you would be deserting your mistress, her friends—"

I am a cat, Thomas replied, hoping against hope that the creature would not look past his words. *Cats are by nature selfish.*

Because if the troll had any inkling that he was something more than he seemed. . . .

"A good point," the troll replied, thoughtfully. "So, you think to join the winning side?"

I know the winning side when I see it, Thomas replied.

Fortunately, walking around Blackpool so much had given Ninette a good sense of the city, so she didn't walk blindly into trouble-spots. Those were not *just* places where hooligans and thieves lurked, hoping for some drunken toff that could stagger by, be coshed on the head and robbed. And what would happen to a lone girl would be worse still.

She took cabs where she could, ran where she couldn't, until her sense of *danger/fear/danger* brought her to a rather posh neighborhood indeed. No flats here, these were all fine townhouses, all built of identical stone, all with identical front façades. From the street, in fact, it could look like one long building, exactly like the front of a government building, for instance. Only when one looked closely could one see the narrow passages dividing building from building.

Her sense of trouble took her to the third from the corner. After a quick look up and down the street, she slipped around to the back, and tried her hand at the door.

It opened at her touch.

Saying a silent prayer that Ailse had returned home at last, that the Brownie had told her that Ninette had gone after Thomas, that Ailse had in turn gone for the men, Ninette slipped inside.

She waited while her eyes adjusted to the light. This *should* be a kitchen area—and at this time of night, there should be no one in it.

After a moment, she saw that she was right on both counts. That was a relief.

She fumbled the revolver out of her pocket. She had not dared to take it out in public or in the street; she was fairly certain she would have gotten into immense amounts of trouble if anyone had seen it.

She crept across the floor, revolver in hand, and peered through the doorway, while allowing the emotions to come to her. Thomas was definitely here—upstairs somewhere, and afraid for his life. But there were other things too, things that had the same *sense* to them that the little homunculus had had—not quite living, in fact, with less actual life in them than a house-sparrow, and nothing in the way of emotions—and one *thing* that actually did have thoughts, feelings, emotions. Very strong ones too, and all . . .nasty. Just brushing against them made her want to throw up.

Thomas was in the same room with the thing.

I must say, Thomas said, looking up at the thing that was calling itself Nina Tchereslavsky, *I have heard about you Earth Elementals, but I never heard of one as powerful or as clever as you.*

He considered that he was very lucky that cats had no expressions to read. And that the Troll could not actually read thoughts either. "Nor will you," the Troll said, puffing up a little. "I am unique!"

I can see that. Is it true that you can change shape? I mean, change it to something other than your native form and this one? I had heard that some of the most powerful of Elementals can do that, but I have never seen it. He paused. *Truly, I was thinking it must be some kind of myth.*

"I can take any form I care to, as long as I have absorbed the original," the Troll boasted, straightening, the pride evident in its voice. "Watch."

In truth, Thomas would rather *not* have watched, but he didn't have much choice. Watching the Troll shift forms was a very uncomfortable experience. Its body rippled in a stomach-churning manner, and the way the skin and hair seemed to crawl—it was entirely unnerving, and Thomas would have sworn until now that he had unshakeable nerves.

The Troll went through the forms of a dozen different people, all of whom must have been its victims, before Thomas shook his head in mock-admiration. He wasn't admiring her, of course. What he was doing, after he got a grip on his own discomfort and mastered it, was studying her. When she changed shapes, she changed the clothing as well. So the clothing was a part of her. If you ripped it, would she bleed? Feel pain? He could see how she could counterfeit the living flesh, but how had she managed to learn to duplicate the clothing? Did she *always* wear this sort of "clothing," or did she make use of an ordinary person's wardrobe as well?

Then he realized that she must, because she *was* a real dancer. She would have changed costumes, changed into practice clothing.

How had she counterfeited being a real human all this time? Elementals generally did not understand humans. If she hadn't been so evil, he would have been lost in real, not counterfeit, admiration.

That is amazing, he said. *Can you take on the form of anything other than a human?*

"If I choose," the Troll replied smugly.

Thomas blinked, and the Troll's form writhed, thickened, and instead of a human looming over him, there was a bear. It was a black bear, of the sort that often was taken from town to town by traveling entertainers and made to "dance" for thrown coins. In England they were usually not seen outside circuses, but on the Continent, such creatures were sometimes kept by gypsies. It balanced adroitly on its hind legs, looming over him, staring down at him from its tiny, shiny eyes, and growled.

Then it went to all fours, and writhed again, this time taking on the shape of a tiger easily the size of the sofa behind it.

Thomas got up and prowled around the beast, as if he

was astonished by it. *Amazing,* he repeated. *And you are, for all intents and purposes, the beast. Correct?*

The tiger nodded.

I can see where these forms would be useful, the cat said thoughtfully. *If you wanted to hunt someone, but did not want to chance the blame falling on you, all you would need to do would be to get him alone, take on the animal, and—*

The tiger made a snickering sound, nodded, and the shape writhed again, and Thomas found himself staring up into the long tusks and whiskered cheeks of a walrus. *I cannot imagine how that shape would be useful,* he said doubtfully.

The troll returned to the shape of Nina. "Then you have never fallen off a ship in winter," she said, with an air of superiority. He wondered about that statement. Had she fallen—or had she been pushed? He'd have bet on the latter.

I will take your word for it. Can you become a bird?

"Of course. But—" She frowned more deeply. "I do not care to do so for long. There is only so much thinking so little a head can do." She made gesture of impatience. "So, why is it you have come to me, cat? Have you no loyalty to your mistress?"

Thomas snorted. *I am a cat. When is a cat loyal to anything but his own best interest?*

The feral smile that greeted that statement made him shudder. "Ha! Well said. And you wish to be on the winning side in this?"

He looked at her sideways. *Let us say that I know where my own best interest lies.*

"And what is it that you can do for me, cat?" Nina asked, taking her place on her chaise longue again, and curling up in a rather catlike pose herself. "I have servants. In fact, I have more than I need. You do not have hands, you cannot even do what they do."

But I can go where they cannot. His keen hearing had detected something. A familiar footstep, coming slowly, cautiously forward.

Ninette! He very nearly leapt to his feet and ran out of the room then, and it was all he could do to keep himself from calling out Ninette's name. The Troll clearly had no difficulty hearing and understanding his projected thoughts, and he was afraid to warn Ninette lest it should hear. How had she found him? Why was she here? How could he get her to escape? Could she escape?

Say you want to know what your lover is saying about you when you are on stage. I can creep under the seats, or into the private boxes and listen. He began speaking rapidly, hoping to hold the Troll's attention. *I can spy on him, or anyone else, as they sleep. I can find out the secrets of your rivals, I can learn anything you wish to have found out. A cat can go almost anywhere.*

She laughed. "So you say. But I can become a cat too, or better still, a rat or a mouse. You say that a cat can go anywhere, but if I need to learn something all that badly, I can go where even a cat cannot, between the walls where no one would even suspect my existence."

The footsteps had ceased; Thomas could tell that Ninette had stopped just out of sight, at the side of the doorway. Was she listening? Did she understand what she was hearing?

Had she thought to summon help before she came after him?

Oh come now! Thomas reproved. *All these other things you have turned yourself into were quite large. It is one thing to make yourself into something human-sized or larger. But to make yourself into a mouse? I believe you are telling me a tale.*

Nina reddened slightly with anger. "You doubt my abilities?"

Oh, I am sure you can make yourself into the form of a mouse, but it would have to be a mouse the size of a tiger. He licked his paw and rubbed it nonchalantly across his whiskers. *It takes real skill in magic to be able to shrink yourself that way, and I have never actually seen anyone that could do that—outside of a spirit, since they don't have any material body to begin with and can look like whatever they like.*

"You think I don't have the skill?" Nina shouted. She jumped up from the chaise longue. "I will show you, skill, cat! I will show you skill such as you have never seen!"

There came one of those moments in magic when the world seems to turn itself inside out.

This is because, in many ways, it is doing just that.

No human could have done what the Troll did, because no human had control over Earth magic energies and the Element of Earth that the Greater Elementals themselves did. Few humans could travel to any of the Elemental Planes, and fewer still returned to tell their story. And to tell the truth, Thomas had not really expected that the Troll had that level of skill. He had mostly been taunting it, to keep it from noticing Ninette.

The room suddenly seemed simultaneously far too small, and as large as a cathedral. The air thickened, and grew desert-hot. Thomas could not look at the Troll—not because he didn't want to. He literally *could not* look at it. It had become some strange amorphous conglomeration of swirling energy clouds that wrenched at the eyes and felt all wrong, with something vaguely human-shaped in the middle of it. All the senses revolted at what was going on. It was impossible. It should not be. The eyes refused to believe what they were seeing, and then mind shied away from contemplating how the laws of physics were being shattered. The cloud of energies pulsed and vibrated and shuddered.

And the human shape was shrinking.

The more it shrank, the more things felt *wrong*. The air throbbed with power; power that tasted foul and made Thomas's stomach heave. There were no names for the colors in that swirling cloud, no names for the fetid scents that wreathed around him, and above all, no names for what the troll was doing.

Thomas wasn't entirely sure himself.

In theory, what the troll was doing was dividing himself, some of "himself" going back to wherever it was Earth Elementals came from, the rest slowly forming itself into a mouse.

Finally, with a *whuff* of displaced air, the energies dissipated. The air cleared a trifle. And Thomas looked down.

I told you, the mouse said, smugly.

24

NINETTE froze for a moment at the sound of a voice, then moved forward, inch by cautious inch, sliding her feet along the carpet so as not to make any noise at all. She identified the right door, partly from the fact that it was half open, and partly from the voice—

A female voice, oddly without any accent at all, and—speaking only one side of a conversation—

Then she edged a little nearer and suddenly the second "voice" faded into her head.

Thomas.

What was being said still made no sense to her, though:

I must say, I have heard about you Earth Elementals, but I never heard of one as powerful or as clever as you.

"Nor will you, I am unique!"

I can see that. Is it true that you can change shape? I mean, change it to something other than your native form and this one? I had heard that some of the most powerful of Elementals can do that, but I have never seen it. Truly, I was thinking it must be some kind of myth.

"I can take any form I care to, as long as I have absorbed the original. Watch."

Thomas was talking to an Earth Elemental? But what kind? The Brownie couldn't change shape, and what did this have to do with the man who had attacked her?

Surely—surely that man was not somehow connected to the mage that was trying to hurt her and her friends? But his attack had been completely ordinary, the assault on her mind, she was sure, a matter of mere accident. Why suddenly switch from magic to a completely mundane attack?

To throw us off the track? To distract us?

But this Elemental, why was Thomas talking to it?

She felt something, a kind of air-quake, and then there was the sound of completely animalistic growling. She pressed her back flat against the wall, her skin crawling with primitive fear at the sound. Whatever was in there, it was no dog. It said it was changing form—into what?

She lost the next bit of exchange as she fought the urge to turn and run. Thomas was still in there, still frightened, and she could not leave him. She *would* not leave him. Help would be coming soon, she still had her revolver. Jonathon and Nigel could find her by that, for they had handled it, and could track her by it. "Then you have never fallen off a ship in winter," the woman said, when the growls faded and the air quaked a few more times. Ninette blinked. What form had she taken?

The whole conversation had an unreal air to it, the same chaotic, disjointed air of a nightmare.

I will take your word for it. Can you become a bird?

"Of course. But—I do not care to do so for long. There is only so much thinking so little a head can do. So, why is it you have come to me, cat? Have you no loyalty to your mistress?"

Why *was* he talking to her?

For a moment, there was doubt. Then her own good sense told her why. Thomas had thought to spy on this . . . creature. Whatever she was. And she had caught him. He was buying time, trying to find a way out of his predicament by getting her to talk.

I am a cat. When is a cat loyal to anything but his own best interest?

"Ha! Well said. And you wish to be on the winning side in this?"

She *felt* his revulsion. That alone told her that he was trying to bluff his way out.

Let us say that I know where my own best interest lies.

"And what is it that you can do for me, cat? I have servants. In fact, I have more than I need. You do not have hands, you cannot even do what they do."

Ninette frowned. An Earth Elemental? Had servants? That made no sense—Elementals did not have servants. Did they?

But I can go where they cannot.

At that moment she felt a surge of excitement from him, excitement and recognition. He knew she was here!

Say you want to know what your lover is saying about you when you are on stage. I can creep under the seats, or into the private boxes and listen. I can spy on him, or anyone else, as they sleep. I can find out the secrets of your rivals, I can learn anything you wish to have found out. A cat can go almost anywhere.

She laughed. "So you say. But I can become a cat too, or better still, a rat or a mouse. You say that a cat can go anywhere, but if I need to learn something all that badly, I can go where even a cat cannot, between the walls where no one would even suspect my existence."

Oh, come now! Thomas reproved. *All these other things you have turned yourself into were quite large. It is one thing to make yourself into something human-*

sized or larger. But to make yourself into a mouse? I believe you are telling me a tale.

She sensed something from him that she could not read. She concentrated. What was he getting at? And—how could anyone turn into a mouse?

Don't question it, she scolded herself, feeling the air of danger behind the words. *Just listen, and be prepared to act!*

"You doubt my abilities?"

Oh, I am sure you can make yourself into the form of a mouse, but it would have to be a mouse the size of a tiger. It takes real skill in magic to be able to shrink yourself that way, and I have never actually seen anyone that could do that—outside of a spirit, since they don't have any material body to begin with and can look like whatever they like.

"You think I don't have the skill?" The words were shouted, and angry. Thomas was getting her angry, maybe to keep her from thinking. A mouse, a mouse—had she somehow forgotten that he was a cat? "I will show you, skill, cat! I will show you skill such as you have never seen!"

If the magic before had made an air-quake, this made a kind of reality-quake. Ninette closed her eyes, tried to make herself one with the wall behind her, as the world took itself apart and put itself back together again, all in a moment. And then did it all over again. And again.

She was finding it hard to breathe, Whatever was going on in there, it was like nothing she had ever experienced before.

Terror closed in all around her. She went, hot, then cold, and she wanted nothing more to do than to flee in a panic. Death was all around her, and she could feel it breathing down her neck. She had never, in all her life, been so certain that in the next moment, she might very well die.

She fought the terror, and slowly, with infinite care, pulled the gun from her pocket and cocked the trigger. Thomas was counting on her. She could not let him down.

Finally, with a *whuff* of displaced air, it stopped. The air cleared a trifle. Ninette sucked in the first full breath in several minutes.

I told you, a new mental voice said, smugly.

And at that moment, Ninette knew what Thomas had been trying for. Yes, he had wanted the woman to become a mouse, if she could. He had thought he could trick her, then kill her.

But she, even in her anger, had called him "cat."

She had *not* forgotten what he was!

Ninette stifled the warning shriek in her throat and whipped around the corner of the door, shoving it open with her shoulder, revolver at the ready as she had been taught.

She saw Thomas in mid-leap on what seemed to be a helpless mouse.

Except the mouse wasn't so helpless. And whatever it *really* was had been expecting him to do just that.

There was another silent explosion of energies, and Thomas was caught by the neck by something strange, dough-like, smelling of rotting loam.

And Ninette did not even think. As she had been taught, she squeezed off the trigger in quick succession, aiming for the center of—whatever it was.

Six explosions shattered the air in the room. Six bullets, just as she and Ailse had loaded them. *Blessed Lead. Cold Iron. Silver.*

The gun bucked in her hand, but she brought it back to the target each time, each bullet impacting the thing in front of her, a mere eight feet from her, with a force that drove it back a little. Six bullets. *Blessed Lead. Cold Iron. Silver.*

It dropped Thomas, who wheezed as he scrambled out of the way, and then scuttled behind her. And— whatever it was—began to scream and dissolve. She couldn't tell which of her bullets had that effect, but when the gun was empty, she backed up as far as she could, and fumbled more bullets out of her pocket, inserting them into the mechanism without taking her eyes off the thing. The reek of gunpowder filled the room, and a waft of smoke made her eyes water.

It was trying to change shape, only it couldn't settle on one—horribly, the mass was producing an arm, three legs, half a woman's face in one spot, a man's eyes in another. And several mouths, all of them open, all of them *screaming*—

Keep shooting! Thomas shrieked, terror filling him, filling her—as if she wasn't panicked enough on her own! But her hands knew what to do, even if her mind was gibbering in inchoate fear. She got the bullets into the chamber, dropping two. She raised the gun. She took aim and squeezed the trigger, and six more explosions shattered the gurgling screams. *Blessed Lead. Cold Iron. Silver.*

"Where's the head?" she screamed herself, as her hands fumbled more bullets into the hot chambers. *"Where's the heart?"*

There—there! Thomas exclaimed, somehow forcing her to see where he was looking. The spot was between two of the mouths, where the dirt-colored skin seemed thicker and smoother. She took aim. Fired.

Five of the six hit; the sixth went wild as the thing convulsed, and the room somehow rocked without moving at all. A thick wave of fetid air hit her in the chest, and knocked her backwards through the door and into the wall of the hallway, Thomas with her. The thing somehow—

The mind couldn't grasp what it *became*—it was si-

multaneously twenty, thirty, maybe fifty different people and animals, and at the same time, it was a towering
mud-doll that *was* all malice, all malignance, all hatred.
She cried out and brought up her arm to shield her face,
then flung herself sideways, somehow scooping up
Thomas and taking him with her.

The wall where she had been was caved in by the
force of the silent explosion, channeled through the
doorway.

For one moment, it became very, very quiet.

Then—the howling, the mindless, wordless baying
began.

She rolled over, dazed. "What . . ."

Get up! Get up! Thomas shrieked in her mind, his
words like ice-picks jabbed into her brain. *It's not over
yet! Its servants are loose, and without the Troll to control
them, all they want is prey!*

Prey—*and we're the prey!* She struggled to her feet
and lurched down the hall after Thomas.

She stopped at the foot of the stairs as he scrambled
upwards. *But—*

They have us cut off from going down! Up! he urged.
She followed after him, revolver still clutched in her
hand, the other feeling in her pocket for more cartridges. "Will bullets do any good?" she shouted after
him, as from below, she heard the howling come nearer
and felt the staircase shake under the pounding of feet.

They'd better, came the grim reply.

They reached the top floor, where the servants would
have slept—if the servants had been human and needed
sleep. Dust was half an inch thick here, and rose in
clouds as they ran for the farthest room. They darted inside the door. The howling continued from the stairwell.

The bedstead! Thomas shouted. *Make a barricade
across the door!*

Fear gave her strength she hadn't realized that she

had. She slammed the door shut, then dragged the iron bedframe across the tiny room. jamming it in place across the door.

The howling was on their floor now, and the floor itself shook with the pounding of feet.

She reloaded the gun. *Please tell me you sent for help,* Thomas begged.

"I sent for help. I just hope the young man Ailse is seeing is not very fascinating."

Then there was no time. They were at the door.

Without any preamble, they began pounding on it, trying to break it down. The sturdy old oak resisted their efforts for a long time, and Ninette resisted the temptation to either fire through the door, or burst into tears and throw the gun away. Finally, with a splintering sound, a great fist crashed through a door panel.

Ninette began firing, her back to the window.

It's too high, Thomas said in despair behind her. *It's straight down to the street. I can't make a drop like that—*

If he couldn't, neither could she.

She fired and reloaded, fired and reloaded. There seemed no end to the things, or else her bullets were having no effect other than to make them angry. Then her hand closed on the last two bullets.

She swore and loaded them, took careful aim, feeling a helpless despair that made *her* want to howl. This was it; this was—

There was a human shout from the hall, some incomprehensible tangle of syllables.

As Ninette was again knocked off her feet, something *opened* in front of her on the other side of what was left of the door.

It was a good thing that she was on the floor, because otherwise she would have been sucked into the yawning black vortex rimmed with fire that pulled in what was left of the door, pulled in the splintered fragments from the floor, tore the ragged curtains from the window, and created a hurricane in the room as it devoured the very air. Thomas yowled like a common cat, claws gouging the floor as the vortex sucked at him too. She grabbed him before he lost his grip, and rolled over with him tucked into the hollow of her stomach, curled around him, covered her head with her arms and waited for it all to end.

She thought it would *never* end, that she would go mad, or all the air would be sucked out of the world, or that they would both die.

And then . . . it ended.

There was . . . silence.

"Ninette! *Ninette!*" She rolled over in time to see Jonathon vaulting the iron bedstead, running for her.

"I'm—we're—all right—" she said, dazed. She looked around for the gun, but it was gone, gone into the void. "I lost the gun."

Jonathon said something unrepeatable about the gun, and scooped her up, and Thomas with her. "If you *ever* run off like that again," he threatened, Nigel and Alan shoving the bedstead out of the way so he could get through the door, "I will—I will *spank* you! I swear it!"

She began to giggle, first weakly, then hysterically. She hid her head in the folds of his jacket to smother her giggles as he glared down at her.

". . . and so Thomas leapt on the mouse and killed it," she finished. "Only that let loose all of the things that pursued us, though I am not sure how."

Once again, she was tucked up on the chaise longue in Nigel's office, with a blanket around her feet, and a glass of brandy and water in her hand. Once again, they were all gathered around her, listening to her narrative. And once again, now that the terror was drained out of her, so was the energy. All she really wanted to do was to close her eyes.

This is all conjecture on my part—Thomas began, wearily.

"Conjecture away," Nigel replied, as Ninette rubbed her aching head and wished her ears would stop popping.

That creature was an Earth Elemental. A Troll. Now I know for a fact it looked like Nina Tchereslavsky, and it was able to take on the shapes of at least a dozen other people as well. I think that it must have been summoned by—and destroyed—an incompetent Elemental Mage. Once it was loose in the world, it decided that it liked living here. It began killing and absorbing people, and with every new person it absorbed, it got a little smarter.

The others all nodded. "The rest follows from that," Nigel agreed, and swore. "But why we never thought to connect all three 'enemies' and realize they were a single one—"

It had gotten very clever, Nigel, the cat said wearily. *Clever enough that it almost outwitted me. You are hardly to be faulted.*

The men continued to discuss and dissect what had happened, as Ninette leaned her head against the cushions, closed her eyes, and just wished they would leave. Finally they all stopped. She opened her eyes. They were looking at her.

"I just need some rest," she said faintly. They took the hint, awkwardly apologizing, getting up, and scuttling out the door. Jonathon was the last to leave, with a single meaningful look deep into her eyes.

Finally, blessed silence—or as silent as it ever got in a theater—reigned.

She sighed and closed her eyes.

But she was not going to get any peace quite yet.

Why did you tell them that I was the one that killed the Troll? Thomas demanded.

She opened her eyes to see Thomas's yellow ones staring at her with accusation.

She groaned. "Killing that—*thing*—demanded good aim, steady nerves, and a lot of courage. No?" she asked.

True, Thomas agreed. *But—*

"What knight in shining armor likes to turn up to discover the princess has rescued herself and slain the dragon?" she asked.

But we didn't! We only—I mean, I only—I was nearly killed. If you hadn't—

"Nearly does not count," she replied and closed her eyes again. "Besides, it was a good plan. It should have worked. It might just as well have. And I wish Monsieur Jonathon to continue to look at me as if I were La Augustine, and *not* as if I were Jeanne D'Arc. *N'cest pas?*" She yawned. "Therefore . . . I have . . . lost my sword."

For now, she barely heard Thomas say. *For now.*

EPILOGUE

The production of *Escape from the Harem* was an enormous success. Tickets were sold out for the next two months, and it appeared very much as if they would continue to be sold out well into the next season. The little dancer around whom the production had been staged seemed to have a magical way with her audience; even grown men wept at her solo of despair, and were more than half in love with her as she entreated the wicked sorcerer to help her and melted his heart. No one left the theater without a smile.

Therefore it was with extreme disappointment that two of Blackpool's leading lights, the very wealthy financier Bascombe Devons and his—well, she was *not* his wife, but no one was likely to tell his wife that she was with him—*companion* then, discovered that they were to be crowded into a box with three other couples, none of whom they knew, or particularly wanted to know.

"See here!" the man complained to the usher, "What about *that* box? I know for a fact no one is in it! We've been watching the door for a quarter hour now, and not one person has gone into or out of it!"

"Ah, I'm sorry, sir, but that box is taken," the usher said apologetically.

"Nonsense! The nameplate says—"

"Sir!" The usher bent a look of reproach on him. "What *would* you put on it if the party that was taking it didn't want to be known?"

The financier paused for a moment in his bluster, then grew thoughtful. "You don't mean to say—royalty?"

"So to speak . . . I shouldn't say any more." The usher led them past the unopened door, both the man and his lovely "friend" much more content now, with the knowledge that they would be seated a mere partition away from a crown. As to which crown it might be—English? Some visiting prince? It hardly mattered.

Behind that closed door, Thomas the cat pushed the dish of sardines over to his lovely companion, whose white coat gleamed in the dim light from the theater beyond. *Please help yourself, my dear.*

The white cat purred and accepted the token. *I am so glad you invited me here. I have never seen a performance from a proper seat before.*

Thomas smirked. Strangely enough, the Troll had done him a very great favor. It had never occurred to him until that moment that there might be other shape-shifters out there. But once he knew—

A quiet word with the Brownie, a hint to Nigel's Sylphs, a late-night talk with one of the Salamanders when Jonathon was engaged in trying to master the art of flirtation with Ninette—the Elementals were, on the whole, favorably inclined, and a week after the premier of the production, this proud beauty had turned up. She was, she coyly informed him, the offspring of a were-cat and the Afrit who loved her. An injudicious move on her part had locked her into this form.

Or so she said. The Masters at least vouched for her intent, which was benign, and her magics, which were as white as her coat. That was enough for Thomas.

Then I am happy to share this box with you whenever you wish to grace it with your presence, O Orient Pearl, Thomas said, with supreme satisfaction. *And you can rest assured that no one will disturb us here once we have settled in.*

Oh—really? she replied archly, purring with promise.

Oh, yes. Really. Thomas settled himself more comfortably. *Didn't you see the plate on the door?*

I cannot read the writing of your people, O Trollslayer. What does it say?

Thomas smiled. *Why, O Cloud of Whiteness, I believe you must approve. It says, "Reserved for the Cat."*